"Castle delivers a fresh and honest story guaranteed to make you smile, laugh out loud, and even shed a few tears. I can't wait to read more."
—bestselling author Candis Terry

THIS WAS NOT THE TRIUMPHANT RETURN SHE'D HOPED FOR.

Sam froze, unable to do anything but stare at the man looking sheepishly back at her. He was exactly how she remembered him. Except . . . he was nothing like she remembered him. Tall, lean, and broad-shouldered, with dark brown hair that would always be a little spiky no matter how hard he tried to get it to lie down and hazel eyes the color of autumn leaves, Jake Smith had only improved with age. His face was more angular now, and the light growth of stubble on his jaw was a new, undeniably sexy addition. The last time she'd seen him, Sam realized, he'd still been a boy. Now there was no doubt he was a man. And even the torn jeans and flannel shirt couldn't disguise the fact that his body, which had once inspired thoughts her teenage self had been concerned meant she was a complete pervert, had filled out in all the right ways.

His smile was slow, warm, and more than a little incredulous.

He still has the dimples. Shit.

For the Longest Time

The Harvest Cove Series

Kendra Leigh Castle

A SIGNET ECLIPSE BOOK

SIGNET ECLIPSE
Published by the Penguin Group
Penguin Group (USA) LLC, 375 Hudson Street,
New York, New York 10014

USA | Canada | UK | Ireland | Australia | New Zealand | India | South Africa | China
penguin.com
A Penguin Random House Company

First published by Signet Eclipse, an imprint of New American Library,
a division of Penguin Group (USA) LLC

First Printing, July 2014

ISBN 978-0-451-46758-4

Printed in the United States of America
10 9 8 7 6 5 4 3 2 1

PUBLISHER'S NOTE
This is a work of fiction. Names, characters, places, and incidents either are the
product of the author's imagination or are used fictitiously, and any resemblance
to actual persons, living or dead, business establishments, events, or locales is
entirely coincidental.

For the misfits and the dreamers,
and especially for Sara, without whom I would never
have found my voice

Acknowledgments

First and foremost, I'd like to thank Matthew Hamblen, the amazing artist whose work inspired me to write Sam Henry. I'm eternally grateful not only for his beautiful paintings, but for his honesty about the ups and downs of being a working artist. His art inspired mine, and I hope he continues making the world a bit brighter for many years to come. Thanks go, as always, to my amazing agent, Kevan Lyon . . . though this time even more than usual, because she'd encouraged me to try my hand at contemporary romance for years, and without her, I might never have gotten up the courage. Thanks as well to Kerry Donovan, my lovely editor, for taking a chance on me and being a joy to work with. And finally, thanks to my family for continuing to put up with me. I love you more than words can say.

Chapter One

Sam Henry slouched farther down in her seat and took another swig of coffee from the enormous travel mug perched precariously half in and half out of her cup holder. She'd made it this far on what was left of her nerves. She could make it just a little bit farther. Sam kept her eyes fixed on the road in front of her, eyes narrowed behind oversize sunglasses as she passed historic homes that were usually written up as "charming" and "quaint" in travel magazines. Ten years living away, and she was already full of that creeping sense of paranoia that everyone was staring at her. "Everyone" at this point being a jogger, a couple of unsupervised kids whacking the hell out of each other with sticks in somebody's front yard, and an English bulldog that had given her a decidedly judgmental look as she'd rolled by its house.

Loser, that look said. Right about now, she was inclined to agree.

This was not the triumphant return she'd hoped for. But when the combination of intense pressure, dwindling funds, and a roommate who'd decided to bail on the lease to become a high-priced call girl left you with a weeklong crying jag and an empty bottle of antidepressants, it was time to reevaluate what the hell you were doing with your life. Preferably somewhere that included free room and board.

In her case, that was Harvest Cove, Massachusetts.

"Nobody's going to recognize me anyway," she muttered to herself. What color had her hair been last time she'd dragged herself back here for some family function or other—pink? Black? She should be reasonably incognito now that she'd gone just a little lighter than her own naturally pale blond.

And she was kidding herself. This was Harvest Cove. She'd be recognized from a mile away, and by next week there would be a new spate of rumors about the return of the town's prodigal daughter. The best she could hope for was that at least a few would be entertaining.

Anything was more entertaining than the truth.

Sam tapped her fingers restlessly against the steering wheel, the black polish glinting with tiny red flecks in the golden light that had finally broken through the clouds. She made the turn from Hawthorne, which would have led her down into the village proper, onto Crescent Road, which traced the curve of the rocky little Massachusetts cove that her hometown had been nestled into since 1692.

Familiarity washed over her at the sight of the trees, complete with leaves of burning crimson and shades of gold, which arched over the narrow road to create a tunnel that was broken only by the entrances to the long driveways of those who lived here. To her right, the land rolled down to the sea between stately homes that had stood, in some cases for hundreds of years, against wind and salt and storm. The names on the mailboxes out here were still, mainly, ones that had existed in the Cove since its beginnings. Owens. Pritchard. Wentworth.

And, of course, Henry.

Sam blew a stray lock of hair out of her eyes with a shallow puff of air and tightened her grip on the wheel as she turned in at the mailbox that bore her family's name. It was never hard to find, since the vibrant purple kind of stood out. It looked like her mom had recently repainted it. The thought of Andromeda Henry out here with her bucket of obnoxiously cheerful paint was the first thing that had brought a smile to Sam's face in days.

It was a big deal to live on the Crescent . . . unless you were a Henry. In that case, you were just the well-to-do's extremely eccentric and generally embarrassing cross to bear.

With the exception of her sister, Emma, "eccentric and embarrassing" seemed to be genetic. The burning desire to stay put, thankfully, was not. And as soon as she got her feet back under her, Sam thought, she'd be right back down the road and on her way. It had been a long time, but she wasn't stupid enough to think that things had changed here. Nothing *ever* changed here.

Still, as Sam pulled up the long gravel drive, she was unable to stop the overwhelming sense of relief that hit her as she got her first look at the house. It rose tall and stately against the backdrop of the sea and cloudy sky beyond, all arches and sharp angles, with a wide and inviting wraparound porch. The tower room and widow's walk still looked hopelessly romantic, even to a cynic like her, and despite its age and faded white siding, the house managed to be both grand and welcoming. This had been her family's land since the beginning, and somehow, it still managed to look more like home than her tiny apartment ever had.

That was part of the legend of the town, that the original families were bound here, fated to return again and again just like the waves that crashed against the rocky shore. It was one of the reasons she stayed as far away as possible.

Fate, like most things about Harvest Cove, just pissed her off.

Her mom had painted the shutters to match the mailbox. Sam grinned and wondered how often the sight of them made flames shoot out of Emma's ears. Emma, as she liked to remind her wayward sister during their occasional phone calls, was a *respectable businesswoman* now. Sam guessed that meant the stick Emma seemed to have wedged up her ass was not painted this particular shade of purple.

Sam pulled around by the old carriage house that had long ago been converted into a garage, then parked. There was an unfamiliar pickup there alongside her mother's little yellow VW Beetle. She briefly considered wandering down to the water and hanging out until the company took off, then discarded the idea. News of her return would get around soon enough anyway. At least there was no way it was Emma. Whoever owned this truck seemed to enjoy driving through mud.

She killed the engine, sat for a moment, took a deep breath.

This is it, she thought. *I'm back.*

The urge to put the car in reverse and hightail it back out of town was tempered, more than she'd expected, by the thought of heading back to New York to continue beating her head against a seemingly endless series of brick walls.

The mild nausea she felt at even considering it had her opening the car door and planting her scuffed black boots on the gravel. The tiny, high-pitched sound coming from somewhere nearby didn't even register until she'd heard it three or four times.

Mew.

Sam frowned, shoving her sunglasses to the top of her head as she walked toward the sound, every footstep crunching loudly. She paused, waiting.

Mew.

It seemed to be coming from underneath the muddy pickup, and it was definitely feline. A stray, maybe. Her mother hadn't had a pet since Cody, their big golden retriever, had passed away right before Sam had left for college.

She crouched down beside the truck and leaned over to try to get a look at what was underneath. A pair of bright green eyes peered back at her, looking much too large for the tiny black shadow they belonged to.

Whether it was the long trip, the fact that she'd been skirting the edge of a full-on breakdown for weeks, or just the sight of something even more pathetic—not to mention much cuter—than herself, Sam melted.

"Aww," she heard herself coo. "You're just a kitten. Here, kitty. Come here."

She reached under the truck, slowly stretching out her hand toward the crouching shadow and expecting little more than a hiss, and maybe something fun like tetanus for her trouble. Instead, she was surprised when she touched soft, warm fur, the kitten actually moving into her hand so she could draw it out.

It was little more than a ragged bag of bones, Sam realized as she pulled the kitten from beneath the truck. Pitch-black, with ears much too big for its head, it started to purr for all it was worth the instant she cradled it against her chest, interjecting the occasional pitiful *mew* just in case Sam even considered putting it back down.

"Don't worry," Sam told it, staring into bright green eyes she just knew were seeing a flashing SUCKER sign right in the middle of her forehead. She rubbed a finger behind its ear, felt a couple of tiny bumps, and winced.

"Oh, great," she said. "Fleas."

The male voice almost directly behind her startled her so badly she jumped with a muffled yelp, earning her a reproachful sound from the kitten and a warning prick of its claws through her T-shirt. However pathetic it looked, it wasn't completely helpless.

"Hey, Andi! The last one's out here!"

"Yeah, it's also embedded in my skin now. Thanks," Sam said, turning to glare at whoever the genius was who'd thought it was a good idea to sneak up on a woman holding a cat and then shout.

"Shit. I mean, ah, sorry. Wasn't thinking. We were worried that one had crawled off and died. A couple of the others are pretty sick."

Sam froze, unable to do anything but stare at the man looking sheepishly back at her. He was exactly how she remembered him. Except . . . he was nothing like she remembered him. Tall, lean, and broad-shouldered, with dark brown hair that would always be a little spiky no matter how hard he tried to get it to lie down and hazel eyes the color of autumn leaves, Jake Smith had only improved with age. His face was more angular now, and the light growth of stubble on his jaw was a new, undeniably sexy addition. The last time she'd seen him, Sam realized, he'd still been a boy. A beautiful boy, but a boy nonetheless. Now there was no doubt he was a man. And even the torn jeans and flannel shirt couldn't disguise the fact that his body, which had once inspired thoughts her teenage self had been concerned meant she was a complete pervert, had filled out in all the right ways.

His smile was slow, warm, and more than a little incredulous.

He still has the dimples. Shit.

"Sam?"

She arched an eyebrow and, though it took every ounce of effort she had, looked blandly back at him. "Last time I checked." Inwardly, she had to fight back her surprise. After their . . . well, *after*, it seemed like he'd forgotten she even had a name. She'd simply ceased to exist to him. And now he was here calling her mother *Andi*?

"Honey! I didn't know you were here!"

Despite the tension, Sam couldn't help but smile as Andromeda Henry came rushing down the porch steps and across the yard, her broomstick skirt whipping around her legs. Her mother's hair was escaping from the long braid that draped down her back, and her bangle bracelets glinted and chimed as she moved. She was as much a rush of color as she always was, a force of nature dressed like an aging gypsy.

"Hi, Mom" was all Sam managed to get out before she found herself enveloped in her mother's arms, one very unhappy kitten squished between them. Still, she found herself leaning into the embrace, shifting to prevent the wriggling kitten from getting smothered. She hadn't realized until just that moment how hungry she'd been for something as simple as a hug, or how long it had been since she'd been touched with honest affection.

Sad. But then, her life would have to be to have brought her back here with nothing more than an overstuffed hatchback and a couple hundred bucks in her checking account.

Sam was appalled to feel the sting of tears when her mother stroked her hands over her hair and kissed her cheek, then pulled back to look at her with eyes that saw much more than she ever let on. The only thing that helped Sam keep it together was the determination that Jake Smith, of all people, was *never* going to see her cry. She'd done enough of that on his account years ago, not that he probably knew. Or cared. He'd never even kissed her.

But he held your hand. And he told you things he didn't tell anyone else. Because for a little while, you mattered to him. Well, he let you think you did.

She would have wondered why the gods would be so cruel as to shove him directly into her path on her first day back, but lately, the reasons for her lousy luck didn't seem to have any explanation more complicated than "because today is a day of the week ending in 'y.' "

Suck it up, buttercup. Welcome to the rest of your life.

She didn't bother to look at him when her mother said, "You remember Jake, Sammy. He's a vet now, works with Dr. Perry. I called him to see if he could help me get a litter of kittens out from under the porch. I didn't even know they were there until yesterday, and there's no sign of the mother. He's going to take them back to the office and see what he can do for them."

Only then did Sam notice the pet carrier at Jake's feet.

"There are five others," he explained. "Not in great shape. I'm surprised the one you've got was strong enough to get out here. If they'd been much younger, they'd already be dead. I don't think the mother's coming back. Something must have gotten her."

Sam stroked the back of the kitten's neck as it settled more comfortably against her. Jake was still looking at her like he couldn't quite believe what he was seeing, which wasn't a big surprise. Between the scuffed old boots, black leggings, long, rumpled black T-shirt and whatever state her hair was in at this point, she probably looked like she'd just rolled out of the nearest Dumpster.

Well, screw him. If he said anything snide she'd just act like Dumpster chic was the newest thing in New York. What did he know? At least she hadn't been rotting up here collecting flannel shirts.

But when he spoke again, he caught her off guard by being . . . nice. At least, she thought that was what he was trying to be. With him, she didn't really have a good standard for comparison.

"You must have the touch," he said. "It came right to you?"

Sam shrugged, her cheeks flushing despite her best efforts to stop it. "I'm wearing a lot of black. It probably just thought we were related."

He laughed, a lower, warmer sound than she remembered. "I'll have to try that next time. I got a few scratches for my trouble."

She offered him a half smile before returning her attention to the kitten in her arms. He'd said its siblings were sick. Could this one be sick, too? Probably. And then there were the fleas, and who knew what else. She was swamped by a wave of protectiveness that caught her off guard. And there was Jake, former über-jock and King of the World, very helpfully reaching out his hands to take it from her.

Her feelings on that were the first things she'd been dead certain of in quite a long time.

Over my dead body.

"Here. If I didn't manage to embed the cat too deeply in your skin, I'll take it."

Sam took a step back. "I'm keeping it."

He paused, looking startled. "Well. Good. I mean, that's what I like to hear, of course. But it still needs medical care before it's ready to come home on a permanent basis. With luck, the kitten will be ready to travel by the time you're done with your visit—"

"She's not visiting," Andi said, and Sam caught the little smile on her mother's lips. *Damn.* What if her mother didn't want a cat in the house? She hadn't even thought about it. Yet another hazard of moving back home, though this was only going to be temporary. Really temporary. And she'd use that to argue for keeping the little black ball of fluff if it came to it.

"She's home. With company, seems like. It'll be good to have an animal in the house again," her mother said. "I'd thought I might keep one anyway." Sam relaxed a little. One crisis averted, at least.

"Really? You're moving back?" Jake asked. He sounded strangely interested. It was annoying.

"Sort of. For the time being," Sam hedged. If he wanted more concrete information, he could just stick with whatever rumors were sure to come down the pike. It was what he'd done before. Why should that have changed?

"Great," he said, and his easy smile included those damned dimples. She could almost believe he was sincere. That, Sam knew, would be a mistake. Everyone said that people changed, but in her experience, they didn't change that much. And even if Jake had, she had better things to do than find out.

Like mope around her mother's house in her pajamas

eating *queso* out of the jar, for instance. With a spoon. Awesome.

When the silence dragged out, Sam finally realized why Jake was looking at her so expectantly. Sadly, it had nothing to do with wanting extra information about her scintillating life plans.

"You still want the kitten," she said flatly.

Jake scrubbed a hand through his hair and looked almost apologetic. "Uh, well . . . yeah. Provided you'd like it to stay alive, I think this would be a good thing."

Sam sighed heavily, looked down at the green eyes that were full of silent, obvious pleading, and began the arduous process of unhooking its claws from her shirt. It mewed and reattached itself almost immediately. She pursed her lips, looked at the kitten, then up at Jake. She might as well go all in on not caring what he thought.

"A little help?"

In the end it took all three of them to detach what Jake determined, with a quick look, was her brand-new male kitten from her now holey T-shirt. Sam hated seeing him put in the carrier with his siblings, already worried that she wouldn't see him again. His piteous yowling, however, seemed to be a good sign, at least according to Jake.

"You're going to have your hands full," he told her as he loaded the carrier into the passenger seat of his truck. "I can already tell he's not going to give you any peace."

Sam just laughed. "I could use the distraction," she replied before she could think better of it. But even when she did, it hardly mattered. She wasn't a stupid sixteen-year-old anymore. Her life was her own, and she didn't have to share it with anyone but whom she chose. And Jake Smith was long off her list.

Still, the look he gave her was speculative in a way that left her feeling off balance just before he walked away.

"I'll give you a call," he said.

"When you get a better idea of how he's doing?" Sam asked.

"Sure. That, too," Jake said, and flashed his gorgeous, infuriating grin before turning to walk around to the other side of the truck, giving Sam an excellent view of an ass that had lingered in her memory far longer than should have been allowed.

"Let me know how it goes, Jake," her mother called. "I'll pay for whatever they need. I won't have them going in the shelter."

"No, ma'am," Jake called back. "Don't worry. I will."

Sam stepped back as he started the engine and backed out, turned, and headed off down the driveway with the gravel crunching beneath his tires. She stared after him, wondering what the hell had just happened. She'd definitely adopted a scrawny kitten. And she was pretty sure Jake Smith had just threatened to call her for reasons entirely unrelated to said kitten. Which made no sense, since she was still the same girl he'd ignored throughout school, with one notable exception, until he'd graduated and left her, along with her broken heart, in the dust.

Her mother's arm slid around her waist.

"Sorry about that, honey. I'd hoped he'd be gone by the time you got here. I'm sure that's not the first person you wanted to see, but believe it or not, he *is* a good vet."

Sam shrugged, eyes still tracking the truck as it made the turn onto the Crescent. "No big deal. I grew up. I'm not going to go inside, lock myself in my room, and play "Show Me the Meaning of Being Lonely" until your ears bleed. I promise."

That had her mother laughing as she led her back toward the house, giving her a squeeze that allowed Sam to push all of her embarrassment and confusion, old and new, into the back of her mind in favor of simply being grateful for the moment.

"Good, or you'd be in the attic." She paused, and Sam could feel her mother eyeing her. "Though I think you surprised him as much as he surprised you."

Sam smirked to hide her discomfort. Jake was the last thing she wanted to think about. "Yeah, my hair is actually a shade found in nature now. This town will never be the same."

"I liked it when it was purple," her mother admitted.

"I don't know how I feel about matching the mailbox, but I'll keep that in mind. Lavender's in right now, you know."

Andi surprised her by stopping and hugging her tight. This time Sam slipped easily into the embrace, breathing in the light, herbal scent that would always be her mother's.

"I'm so glad you're back, Sammy. I always understood why you needed to go, but this is where you belong. You'll see."

Sam didn't say a word. She just took in the comforting familiarity of the house, the meeting of sea and sky beyond, and tried to make herself believe it.

Chapter Two

Jake propped his boots on the railing of his front porch and took a swig of his beer, enjoying a few minutes' peace while he looked out at the deepening twilight. Tucker, the cattle dog crossed with God-knew-what he'd brought home two years ago, was flopped at his feet, panting happily. Tucker was living proof that there were benefits to bringing your work home with you.

So was the pile of sleeping kittens in his laundry room. Well, until they woke up and started raising hell in there again. For a bunch of malnourished, flea-infested orphans, they'd perked up awfully quickly after a day of attention, medical and otherwise. Still, they were going to be plenty of work for a while yet. Feral kittens always were. And Sam's little buddy didn't like him nearly as well as the kitten liked her. Not that it was hard to understand the attraction.

Samantha Henry. Jake took another drink while he mulled what might have brought her back to the Cove. He hadn't heard a word about it, and considering how many people he saw on a daily basis, he usually heard *everything*. He tried to remember the last time he'd seen Sam, thought it might have been nothing more than a glimpse of purple hair about six years ago when he'd been home on break. Even that brief sighting had piqued his interest with a strength that had surprised him— though it shouldn't have. He'd never really gotten over that first bout of fascination with her. Of course, his younger self hadn't been able to admit that's what it was back then. Not to himself, and certainly not to anyone else.

From the reception he'd gotten earlier, Sam remembered that as well as he did. She sure as hell hadn't forgiven him for it. He tapped a finger against the side of the bottle he held, frustrated by the hold she'd had on his thoughts all afternoon. It had been ten years. Didn't people get to be absolved of their teenage stupidity at some point?

They ought to. Except . . . he remembered her face that day. And he knew that sometimes the answer was a resounding "no," no matter how much time had passed.

Jake flexed his foot to get the rocking chair moving a little as he reached down to give Tucker a scratch behind the ears. The dog leaned into his touch, happy for the attention like he always was. Jake grinned, gave the furry head one last hard rub, and then leaned back into the chair and blew out a long breath.

"She still hates my guts," he said, knowing it was mostly, if not entirely true. Tucker cocked his head, looked keenly interested until he realized that nothing Jake had said involved either a walk or food, and then returned his attention to sniffing the air while keeping watch for squirrels. Which was, Jake thought, a lot more productive than sitting here brooding.

He slid a look at the phone he'd brought out with him, thinking there was an off chance that Sam would call to ask about the kitten. A *really* off chance. Only slightly greater than a snowball's in hell. Maybe.

Jake scrubbed his hand over his face when he realized what he was doing. Seeing Sam hadn't just made him feel like a teenager again. It had turned him into a teenage *girl*.

"Screw it," he muttered, grabbing the phone and punching in Andi's number before he could talk himself out of it. He'd said he would call, so he was calling. In his *professional* capacity. It wasn't a big deal.

"It's not a big deal," he told Tucker, who was so impressed that he decided it was a good time to start cleaning himself. Jake nudged him with his foot.

"You could at least act supportive, jerk."

The phone rang just twice before someone picked up. Luck was with him.

"Hello?" Sam sounded a little breathless, like she'd had to run to get the phone. She also sounded a lot friendlier than she had earlier . . . which told him she just didn't recognize his number. Yet.

"Sam," he said easily, hoping that if he kept it casual and friendly, she would too.

"Jake." The temperature of her voice changed so quickly that he was surprised the phone didn't go cold in his hand. Just another reminder that this wasn't the shy misfit he remembered . . . though there hadn't been much question of that once he'd gotten a good look at her earlier.

"What do you need?"

He closed his eyes. That was, at the moment, a loaded question.

"I thought you might want a kitten update."

"Oh." He could almost hear her switching gears, deciding how to proceed with him. When she spoke again, Sam sounded cautious, cool, but less overtly homicidal. It was progress, Jake told himself. They had to start somewhere.

The question was, where did he want to go?

"Well . . . how are they? Is Loki okay?" she asked.

He paused. "Norse god of mischief?"

"Avengers supervillain. He'll be an adopted orphan, misunderstood because of his fur color, and bent on world domination because he's a cat. I think it fits."

Despite the slightly defiant note in her voice, Jake burst out laughing. "I can't actually argue with that. Loki it is. And he's doing fine."

"Good." He heard surprise, relief . . . and the natural caution that she'd always had with him, with everyone around here, actually. It took him back to the first day he'd really noticed her, sketching in the park beneath the huge old oak they called the Witch Tree. It was early May, the first really warm day they'd had that year, and he'd been out enjoying it on his own, thinking of the upcoming party that night, the impending summer. He'd just turned eighteen, and the world seemed to be waiting for him. Sam had been just shy of seventeen, and she hadn't known what to do with him then, either.

"What are you drawing?"

"Well . . . I . . . um . . . Just things, I guess."

She'd tried to cover up the sketch pad she'd carried with her everywhere, but her hands weren't big enough to hide what had been an incredible rendering of some dark, enchanted dragon, brooding atop a throne of skulls. Jake remembered noticing her chipped black nail polish as she'd hurriedly flipped the book shut. Mostly, he remembered being completely blown away that Sam, who normally only tripped his radar as a black-clad shadow who was teased mercilessly for being a wannabe witch, a freak, and a variety of other unflattering things, was actually talented. What he'd glimpsed had been at least as good as a lot of the comic book art he liked. Maybe better.

Then she'd looked up at him with those big blue-green eyes, and he'd seen her, really seen her, for the very first time.

"Earth to Jake."

Her voice, now that of a woman and not the girl she had been, jerked him back into the present.

"Sorry. Thought I heard the kittens." As an excuse, it worked as well as anything. And it had the added benefit of piquing Sam's interest.

"Oh. Are you still at work?" He could hear the slight frown in her voice, and pictured her standing with the phone against her ear, looking serious and slightly annoyed. It made him smile. In some ways, she looked so much the same it was eerie—the delicate, pointed features, the full lower lip that he remembered her chewing at when she was nervous. But ten years had enhanced what was already there, and banished the awkward teenager. Her smile was more open, the natural grace in the way she moved more obvious. What she wore, while not exactly standard for the Cove, suited her lithe curves rather than looking like baggy armor. And something about that icy blond hair made his mouth water every time he thought about it. Pretty had become beautiful. Sam wasn't hiding anymore.

Well, not from the world, anyway. The jury was still out on whether she'd try to hide from him. That, or just flay him alive with what he already sensed was one very sharp tongue.

"It was my day off. I took them in anyway, since they needed it, but afterward I brought them back home with me," Jake explained. "I've got the room, and they really shouldn't be left alone yet."

"Oh," she said again, and he could tell he'd surprised her. Good. Even if it rankled a little that it meant she still had him mentally filed under Heartless Bastard.

Because it helped him keep her on the phone, Jake slipped smoothly into vet mode, telling her that the kittens looked to be about six weeks old, explaining about the baths they'd had to remove the fleas, how he'd started deworming them, how they were taking the soft food he'd started them on. Sam listened, interjecting the occasional murmur of assent to show she was paying attention. When he ran out of material there, she seemed to be waiting for more. Jake cast around for something else to say. Everything he really wanted to know was none of his business. What had she been doing? Why was she back? All he knew about her for sure at this point was that she was in town, and that he wanted to see her again, preferably as soon as possible. Unfortunately, asking her over for a drink was likely to get him hung up on. Left without options, he decided to just jump into the void.

"So why don't you come by the office tomorrow?"

"Why? He isn't ready to come home yet, is he?" Any warmth he'd heard in her voice vanished instantly, and that old wariness was back full force. Frustration had him gritting his teeth. For a guy who'd never had much trouble attracting women, he was doing a great job keeping this one at arm's length. *Patience,* he told himself.

He was going to have to keep repeating it. Patience had never been one of his strong suits. He was still interested in Sam Henry. Maybe it would burn itself out quickly, maybe not, but he needed to engineer a way to find out.

"No," Jake said calmly, "but Loki and his siblings are feral. I still don't know what possessed him to come to you, because all the kittens are going to need a lot of handling before they're comfortable with people, and he's nowhere near as friendly with me or my staff as he was with you. The good news is that they're still in the age window where they should take easily to human contact. The bad news is that my practice is pretty busy. Between me and Tom, we handle most of the pets in the Cove, so I don't know how much time anyone is going to be able to spend with them on any given day. A foster would be ideal, at least once I'm sure there's nothing pressing, health-wise, but the local cat rescue is swamped. I thought if you had time you might come by and hang out with them for a while tomorrow."

She hesitated. "Just tomorrow?"

"I didn't figure I'd need to ask after that. Kittens are highly addictive."

She laughed, and though it was still more tentative than he would have liked, it at least sounded genuine.

"Yeah, um, sure. I can come in. Is there a good time?"

"Around noon would be perfect," Jake replied, deciding that Sam didn't need to know she was coming in right at the beginning of his lunch hour. No need to complicate things. He'd lure her in with cute, furry things, and then overwhelm her with his charm. Or something.

Right now, it was all he had, so he'd go with it.

"I guess I'll see you around noon, then," Sam said. She still sounded way more cautious about it than he would have liked, as though she was sure he was just waiting to

FOR THE LONGEST TIME 21

spring something unpleasant on her. Still, it was a beginning. He'd see her tomorrow, and they'd go from there.

"See you then," Jake said, and hung up before she
could change her mind.

Sam set the phone on the counter, then turned, shaking
her head, to pour herself another cup of coffee. Caffeine
was probably the last thing she needed this evening, but
then again, it was better than, say, whiskey. Which, considering what she'd just agreed to, was a tempting thought.

If he thought she didn't realize he'd invited her to
come by when he'd be able to hang around and pester
her, he was really dense. Or just male. She could try to
pretend that she was going for Loki—and that was certainly part of it—but the truth was, she was curious.
Twisted but true. Of all the things she expected to happen coming back to Harvest Cove, having Jake Smith
sniffing at her heels was probably last on the list. What
did he *want*?

"Doesn't matter," she muttered, then lifted her mug
to her lips, inhaled the warm, comforting aroma of her
mom's favorite coffee, and took a sip. Sam leaned back
against the counter, crossed one fuzzy purple slipper over
the other, and tried to banish Jake from her thoughts.
She'd deal with it tomorrow. And if he thought he was
getting any closer than arm's length, he was going to be
awfully disappointed.

"Whose demise are you plotting?"

Sam blinked and turned her head to watch her mother
amble into the kitchen from the living room, where she'd
been sitting with her nose in a book when the phone had
rung. Andi looked about as comfortable as it was possible to get in a pair of loose pajama pants covered in little

Eeyores and an oversize T-shirt advertising Merry Meet, a little restaurant downtown. Her long hair was coming loose from its braid, and her reading glasses were perched atop her head. She smiled knowingly as she settled herself on one of the stools situated beneath the edge of the long wooden island, basically a farmhouse table, that occupied much of the middle of the kitchen. Sam stayed where she was, close to the warmth of the massive, white cast-iron AGA. Actually cooking with it remained a mystery to Sam, but she loved the unusual oven nonetheless.

"I'm not plotting anything," Sam protested. "I'm having coffee."

"Uh-huh," Andi replied, blue eyes twinkling. "I gave birth to you, Sam. I know the evil smirk."

Sam shrugged. Her mother had always been an excellent sounding board, but this . . . she wasn't ready to talk about this. Whatever "this" actually was. Leftover hurt and unwanted attraction, she guessed. Hardly worth talking about. So she directed the conversation elsewhere.

"Just planning how I'll take the Cove by storm, starting tomorrow," Sam said. "I'm sure once word gets around I'm back they'll throw me a parade or something."

Andi laughed, but there was a sadness to it that Sam recognized. She knew how miserable it had been for her younger daughter. And she'd never known how to fix it, being a professional misfit herself. The difference was, Andi seemed to relish being different, whereas Sam had just wanted to disappear. Her mother had done the best she could on her own—better than most mothers in much easier circumstances, Sam thought. But there were so many times when she missed her sweet, sensible father, and the balance he had provided, terribly. She'd been ten years old when he got sick, and the cancer hadn't appeared to give a damn that Bill Henry was still very much needed.

Her mother's warm voice pulled her out of memories that would always be bittersweet.

"You'll get your feet under you, honey. You've got everything in the world going for you."

Sam arched an eyebrow. "I'm twenty-seven years old. I have no job, no prospects, and I'm moving back in with my mom. Which part of that bodes well for the future? Because I'm missing it."

Andi gave her a withering look. "Well, your positive attitude should help."

Sam blew out a breath and slouched, looking at her feet. "Sorry," she said. "It's been a long day. I'm at that point in the cycle of self-loathing where I feel sorry for myself, and then feel pathetic for feeling sorry for myself, which makes me feel even sorrier for myself." She looked up through her lashes at her mother, and was surprised to find herself near tears. The emotional exhaustion of the past few weeks, coupled with the warm familiarity of the scene in front of her, threatened to wring out what little feeling she had left. Dismayed, Sam held it together. Barely.

She'd shed enough tears in this kitchen, and she'd come a long way since then. That was her biggest fear— that all the hard-won ground she'd gained would be swept away by coming back here.

"You're looking at this the wrong way," her mother said in a tone that brooked no disagreement. "This is *home*, Sam, not the end of your life. Things get hard. For everybody. So you regroup, start fresh. Wherever you are, that's where you're supposed to be. And I don't give a damn what anyone else thinks—I'm glad my daughter's home."

"Oh. Well," Sam said, and a single traitorous tear managed to escape and roll down her cheek. She snuffled and wiped it away with the back of her hand. Andi sighed, rose from the stool, and came to wrap her arms around her daughter. She didn't say anything. She didn't have to.

That was when Sam finally let the dam break, letting out the rest of the misery that had been following her for months as her carefully built life in New York had fallen apart, piece by piece. But then, things hadn't been right for a while. For all that New York had given her, it hadn't provided Sam with any better sense of where she belonged. It hadn't been her place. She'd known it. She'd fought it.

And she really hadn't wanted to be abruptly kicked out of it before she'd gamed out her other options.

Sam sobbed against her mother's shoulder until the tears slowed, then stopped, leaving her sniffling pitifully but feeling immeasurably better. A little hollowed out, maybe, but better. And in the empty space that was left at the center of her, she could admit that she'd missed this—her mother, the house, the combination of the two things—terribly. It was the rest of this place she wasn't sure about. But centering herself here was a start.

She raised her head, and Andi moved back just a little, tucking a stray lock of pale hair behind Sam's ear and then giving the tip of her nose a playful stroke.

"You're going to be fine. Look, you haven't even been here a day and you've got a cat and an admirer already."

That dried up the lingering tears quickly. Sam wrinkled her nose.

"Mom. Jake isn't an admirer. He's making sure my new cat doesn't die."

"Hmph," was Andi's noncommittal reply, and Sam caught a flash of her mother's own version of the evil smirk before she turned around and went back to her stool. It left Sam feeling vaguely unsettled, even when Andi changed the subject.

"You just missed your sister. Emma's at a conference all this week."

"That's too bad." She hoped she sounded sincere. She was, a little. But though she loved Emma, there were some fundamental differences between them that tended to make things tense. There was also the fact that her older sister, for all her better qualities, was a bossy pain in the ass.

"I can tell your heart is breaking. What are you going to say to her when she offers you a job?" Andi asked.

Sam groaned and shoved her hands into her hair. "I don't want to talk about it."

"That's not going to make it go away. Your sister loves you. She worries."

Sam tilted her head and gave her mother a beleaguered look, taking another sip of her coffee before she responded. "I know. I also know that if she and I work together, we will kill one another. It's a bad idea, Mom."

"You'll hurt her feelings."

She tried to hold back the snort of laughter and was only moderately successful. "Uh, no. No, I won't. Trust me." She was almost positive that Emma would be relieved more than anything that Hurricane Sam wouldn't be hitting her event planning business anytime soon.

And Sam was just as glad that she wouldn't need to be involved with planning things like elaborate children's parties for Harvest Cove's hypercompetitive young professional set. "I'll find something else. This is just temporary, Mom."

"So you keep telling me."

Realizing that her words had stung, though inadvertently, Sam rolled her shoulders and tried to explain instead of just making frustrated declarations.

"It's what I keep telling myself. I have to. This isn't what I wanted. I don't mean you, Mom. I just mean . . . this."

Andi smiled at that. "Don't make me quote The Stones at you, honey."

Sam pursed her lips, ruefully amused. Thanks to her mother's musical taste, she was more familiar than most people her age with classic rock.

"Yeah, yeah. I can't always get what I want, but I might just get what I need. Right?"

"You got it." Andi stood with her coffee mug, stretched a little, and then started back toward the family room. "Well, I've laid enough of my vast wisdom on you for tonight. My book is calling." When she reached the doorway, she turned back with a look Sam knew all too well.

"By the way, Zoe Watson, down at the gallery, wants to meet you. Tomorrow, if you can. She seemed very excited about someone with your experience being in a little place like this." Andi paused. "She's a bit of a newcomer here. You might like her. Gallery opens at ten . . . if you're interested, of course."

Sam could only stare for a moment, too surprised to speak.

"We have a gallery?"

"For the last year or so, we do. Does pretty well, too,

from what I hear. Nothing in there as nice as what you do, but—"

"Mom."

"Well, there isn't," Andi insisted. "But it is nice. Zoe has a good eye. And so do you. You should have a look."

Relief flooded her. And fast on the heels of that was guilt.

"I should have done it myself," she murmured, more to herself than anyone else. When she'd finally decided to come home, it had been the way big decisions usually went with her—sudden, full of emotion, and minus any long-term planning. A job, beyond the fact that she didn't want to work with Emma unless absolutely necessary, was something she needed and had only just begun to contemplate. A gallery job, surrounded by inspiration so that she could maybe, possibly get her own work back on track, would be a godsend.

And it was being handed to her, which hardly seemed right.

Andi didn't appear to agree. She simply watched her youngest child with a mixture of exasperation and affection.

"Samantha Jane Henry. I have no doubt you could have and would have found Zoe yourself. You've spent years trying to do everything on your own, whether or not it was a good idea. But this was something I could smooth the way on, so I did. The job's not yours yet; trust me. Zoe's sweet, but she's a hard-ass where it counts, and that business is her baby." Her voice softened. "You don't have anything to prove here, Sammy. Everyone knows you can make it on your own. But one of these days, I'd love it if you'd figure out that you don't always *have* to."

"I know," Sam said, her shoulders slumping a little. "Thanks, Mom. Really. I mean that."

Andi smiled. "I know you do, Sammy."

She left, and Sam watched her go, feeling all of sixteen again, and just as helpless. The bright spark of interest she'd felt at the mention of the gallery faded, subsumed again by the weariness that had been dogging her all afternoon. She was ready to try to start fresh, like her mother had said. She wasn't afraid of a challenge, and besides, unless she wanted to be some sort of basement-dwelling woman-child with a paper route for the rest of her life, a fresh start was pretty much the only choice. It was just more daunting than most projects she'd undertaken, because Andi had been wrong about one key thing.

Sam had everything to prove. And it was going to take all the energy and luck she could muster to do it right.

Chapter Three

By the time Sam sat across from Zoe Watson at ten thirty the next morning, she was certain of two things: that her mother had seriously understated what a hard-ass the proprietress was, and more importantly, that she really, really wanted this job.

Getting it, however, was very much a work in progress.

"So," Zoe said, her rich, warm voice utterly at odds with the shrewd assessment Sam saw in her storm gray eyes. "What do you think you could bring to Two Roads Gallery?"

Sam fought the urge to fidget. She'd met far more frightening characters in the New York art scene, she reminded herself, and she'd held her own then. And this sleek, intimidating woman, with the South in her voice and steel in her eyes, was hardly the dragon that her former employer had been. She needed to remember that. Sam took a deep breath, collected her thoughts, and answered as clearly as she could.

"I've spent the last three years buying and selling pieces for a small, successful gallery in New York City. I've got an eye for talent, and I'm good with people." She paused, trying to gauge Zoe's reaction, but the woman's expression seemed carved from stone. "I love art. Being around it, being around the people who make it. I think that shows."

"Hmm" was Zoe's noncommittal response. She shifted a little in her chair, and Sam was struck all over again by how different she was from anything she might have been expecting. The unfamiliar name had led Sam to figure that Zoe would be some city-weary yuppie who'd decided to bring culture and taste to small-town America, enlightening the rubes and becoming beloved by all, the star of her own women's fiction novel . . . and who would probably, like most of her ilk, either get disgusted and leave or simply go bankrupt. Instead, Sam had discovered a woman who'd come to Harvest Cove with a very specific, very detailed idea of what she wanted to accomplish—and who was making it happen.

Why she was so determined to make it happen *here* was something Sam couldn't begin to fathom. But what Sam remembered as a little run-down two-story house on Hawthorne, a fixture since the 1700s, looked amazing in its rebirth as a gallery. She'd barely had a chance to browse before Zoe had swept her into the little back room that served as her office, but Sam had been impressed by the pieces Zoe had assembled. There were paintings and glasswork, sculpture and jewelry scattered about the main room of the shop in such a way that one discovery led quickly to another. It was a pleasant surprise to discover that she hadn't been the only artist in the area. Far from it. But then, Sam realized, it had been stupid to think so in the first place. She'd been so young and self-centered that all she'd seen was the surface of things.

What she was seeing *here* gave her a lot of food for

thought. Later, though, when she wasn't in danger of sweating bullets through her simple black jersey dress.

"Your mother tells me you're an artist yourself," Zoe said smoothly. "I was hoping you'd bring your portfolio, if you did decide to come by. I'm very proud that we showcase local artists almost exclusively, and I'm always on the lookout for new clients."

Sam had to fight to keep her voice neutral, though panic welled immediately in her throat. "I'm not interested in getting a showing, Ms. Watson. Just a job."

Zoe's ebony eyebrows shot up. "Call me Zoe, please. And that's a shame. I looked up some of your work, and you're very talented. You've been selling online, right? I checked out the site. Great layout."

Her face felt like it was on fire. Of course Zoe would have looked her up, if only out of sheer curiosity. And she hadn't had the heart to completely shut down her Web site, or her little shop on Etsy, simply leaving up a few images of sold pieces with the notice that she was on hiatus for the time being. It wasn't like she could post the truth—that every ounce of her creativity and passion seemed to have been sucked into a black hole, that she hadn't picked up a brush in months except to throw it across a room . . . or hold it and cry because whatever had once powered it, a light that had once seemed as though it was always fighting for a way to get out, had gone dark.

She could say none of those things. So she went for the simplest explanation possible.

"I was. But I'm not really painting right now. Thanks, though."

"I see," Zoe said, and Sam knew at once that she wasn't going to press her on it . . . though Zoe obviously wanted to. She just had more tact than that. The relief helped calm Sam's now rapidly beating heart. A panic attack in the middle of a job interview would have been a very bad thing in a string of bad things, and she really wanted to break the chain before the only kind of art-related field left available to her was carnival face painting.

"Well, when you decide to get back at it, let me know," Zoe said. Then, to Sam's surprise, Zoe leaned back in her chair, took off the cool, collected facade, and became . . . well, human. A slightly tired, slightly harried, and surprisingly friendly human.

"I'll be straight with you, Samantha, I was ready to hire you the second you set foot in here. It'd be a godsend to have someone I didn't have to teach. And you've got that local connection, which would be . . . helpful."

There was a wealth of meaning behind her words. Sam winced, sympathetic. "It's Sam. Kind of hard to break in, huh?"

Zoe's look said it all. "I've been here a little over a year. People still think my full name is Zoe, That Nice Black Girl from Atlanta. I didn't expect to be a local at this point, but I'd like to stop being a novelty item."

Sam burst out laughing, unable to help herself. Zoe grinned, the smile slowly spreading over her face, and then shook her head.

"I'm sorry," Sam said. "For the Cove, you're pretty exotic." She was beautiful, actually, Sam thought. Zoe's warm mocha skin was a startling contrast to those big gray eyes, and she wore her hair in a way Sam had always envied—hundreds of long, tiny braids, now loosely swept into a bun at the nape of Zoe's neck. She looked like she belonged here about as much as Sam herself did.

Zoe screwed up her mouth and arched an eyebrow.

"I'm not exotic. I'm from Atlanta, not Mars." She sighed. "But yeah. It's been interesting. People are friendly. Business is pretty good. It's just . . ."

"You're still an outsider," Sam finished for her. "It's a small town. Takes a while. Even for locals, sometimes."

"You're telling me. You know Penny Harding? The one who only talks about shoes, how her daddy's the mayor, or that big Christmas party her family throws every year that everyone knows about but only the special people get invited to?"

Sam stared at Zoe in awe. "That's the most accurate description of her I've ever heard. You should win something for creating that."

Zoe gave a rueful smirk. "Well, I sure didn't win an invite to that party. Despite the fact that plenty of the other small business owners did, and that she came in here talking about it at least once a week for two months at the end of last year, and that I helped put on one hell of a classy event for her daddy and his buddies when I'd barely gotten this place opened. No. No 'thank you for bringing your money and class and fine self to the area' invitation." She sighed, rolled her eyes, and shook her head. "Sorry. Thought I'd worked the bitter out on that one."

"Don't worry about it," Sam said. "The Harding party crowd has kind of a small circle of trust. Most of us just get to be rabble. You'll get used to it—I promise."

Zoe smiled, and this time there was plenty of understanding in it. That and determination. "They can have their circle of trust. I just want a night to wear a red dress and eat the Hardings' caviar. I'll get there, though. I love this place."

Sam could only shake her head and laugh, bewildered.

"Why? Seriously, how did you get from Atlanta to Harvest Cove?"

"I drove."

"Ha," Sam replied. "Really, though. We're pretty tucked away. We get tourists, but it's not like, say, Salem."

"That's what I like about it," Zoe replied. "This place is exactly what I pictured, exactly what I wanted. Ever since I was little, believe it or not."

"Oh?"

"Yeah. Anything set in a little New England town, movies or TV, I was glued to it. I had this crazy thing for *Murder, She Wrote* reruns when I was a kid, too. My mom would sit and watch it with me, a lot of times. Love me some Angela Lansbury. I wanted my own Cabot Cove, except with more art and less dead bodies. So I scouted around when I knew I could swing it, and here I am."

Sam burst out laughing. When Zoe looked down, her cheeks flushing, she quickly sought to reassure her before the tentative connection they'd made was broken.

"That's awesome. I mean that. It's the best reason I've ever heard for coming here. I love it."

"Seriously?"

"Seriously."

They regarded each other for a moment. Zoe smiled that slow grin of hers again, and Sam knew immediately that she'd found not only a job, but a friend.

"All right, girl. Be here tomorrow at nine. I'll show you the ropes before we open at ten. I like you, but you're still going to have to prove yourself."

"That's something I'm happy to do," Sam said, nearly dizzy with relief. She hadn't realized just how low her hopes had gotten until right this second. "If you want references . . ."

Zoe waved her hand. "As a matter of fact, I dealt with your former employer once a couple of years back. Mona Richard, right? Andi told me it didn't end well for you there, and trust me, I believe it. What you do here is all the reference you need. If it works, great. If it doesn't, I'll tell you. And besides," she continued with a knowing look, "when you start painting again—not if, *when*—I want your work here. Those dreamscapes you do would make for an amazing show."

Sam nodded, and for once she didn't have the heart to deny that there would be a *when*. Maybe Zoe was right. It was nice to hear that kind of faith, regardless. And nice to hear someone admiring her vision. *Dreamscapes*. Maybe that's why she couldn't paint anymore. Her dreams were buried somewhere beneath the smoking rubble that was her life.

"Okay," was all she said out loud, and when Zoe extended one elegant, long-fingered hand across the desk, Sam took it and shook.

"Two Roads Gallery. The Frost poem," Sam said suddenly. "That's what you named this place after. Two roads diverged in a wood, and I—"

"I took the one less traveled by," Zoe finished for her. "You got it. It made all the difference for me. Hopefully it will for you, too."

"Maybe it will," Sam replied. And was surprised to find that there was a part of her that actually believed it.

By the time she'd stopped by Brewbaker's to grab the biggest vanilla latte they offered and then hopped in her car to make the short drive to Jake's office, Sam felt better than she had in months. Some of it was probably the caffeine, and some of it was doubtless being able to take off those stupid heels to drive in her bare feet, but a lot of it was plain, old-fashioned happiness. She had a job. A gallery job. And she'd be working for someone who, at least right now, didn't seem to be the kind of person who would earn nicknames from her employees like, say, The Evil One. Bitcharella. Or one her personal favorites, Cthulu.

Her good humor over Zoe not being anything like a tentacled demon from another dimension notwithstanding, Sam felt herself beginning to tense up the second she pulled into the small parking lot in front of a building she had no memory of. Harvest Cove Animal Hospital looked like a pretty Cape Cod–style home, pale blue with a low, wide front porch that had ramps on either side of the steps. Big windows gave Sam a good view of a spacious, bright waiting room where a couple of people sat, one with some sort of terrier in her lap.

No Jake. That was probably a good thing, because she needed a minute.

Sam parked, took a couple of deep breaths, and then took a quick look in the rearview mirror to make sure the French twist she'd pulled her hair into wasn't falling out too badly yet. Hating herself a little for caring, she freshened up her lip gloss, then tossed it back into the pit of despair that was her cavernous purse. She would rather have shown up in jeans, or something ripped, just so Jake didn't think she'd made any kind of effort on his account. There just hadn't been time to change, and punctuality was one thing she couldn't quite break herself of.

With a slight wince, she shoved her feet back into the hated heels and slid out of the car, then locked it up and slung her bag over one shoulder, still carrying her giant latte. At least the place didn't seem very busy, she thought. The faces she'd seen in town so far had been friendly, but that luck was bound not to hold. It seemed important that this, her first full day back, was a good day.

Sam tried to look relaxed, to not carry herself so stiffly as she pushed one of the doors open and stepped into the waiting room. Her heels clicked conspicuously against the laminate floor as she headed for the long front desk. Two women sat behind it, both looking up at her approach. Sam didn't recognize the younger of the two, but the other was a face she knew. Cass Tompkins was a good three years older than she was, and so had never bothered with Sam apart from the occasional disinterested "Hello." Still, it was better than it could have been. She knew damn well that most of her tormentors still lived here. And why not? They'd be little fish in a big pond anywhere else.

She preferred the anonymity of the big pond, herself.

"Sam," Cass said, her curiosity evident. "Jake said you'd be by. You'll be taking one of the kittens?"

"Yes," Sam replied with a quick nod, anxious to get past the gatekeepers and get this over with. It was a shame Loki wasn't ready to go home just yet. She could just stuff him down the front of her dress and bolt. He had a good grip. It could work.

"Is he around? Jake, I mean?" Sam asked when Cass continued to watch her with naked curiosity. The younger girl was openly gawking. Sam shifted her weight from one aching foot to the other, wondering whether she'd accidentally applied the lip gloss to her nose or something.

"Yeah, he's here. I'll let him know you're waiting," Cass said, getting to her feet. She stopped on her way out from behind the desk, though, and looked at Sam with a light frown. "You look . . . different. Good, I mean. But I almost didn't recognize you."

"Thanks. It's, ah, probably the hair," Sam replied.

Cass just gave her a puzzled look and headed around the corner, down a short hallway and through a door that gave Sam a quick peek at a wall of cages, a couple of which were occupied, and some equipment. She looked around, trying to focus on anything but the fact that Jake was somewhere in the building, waiting for her. The woman with the terrier on her lap smiled encouragingly, and Sam returned it before trying to look engrossed in a bulletin board covered in fliers for lost pets, pets needing new homes, pet photographers, kennels . . .

"Hey, you're right on time."

She turned, startled at how quietly he'd come up behind her. She didn't have any time to steel herself against him, to stomp her attraction into submission before it could get the better of her. Instead, all she could do was react, which her entire body was more than happy to do. Everything tightened, from her chest to her thighs, and the blood rushed to burn in her cheeks. There were only a couple of feet between them, not far enough that she couldn't smell the subtle, clean scent of his cologne. Not far enough to escape the magnetic pull of the dimples that winked in his cheeks when he smiled with what looked like genuine pleasure.

He hadn't thought she'd show, Sam realized. Which made this a triumph of sorts, even though she felt like disappearing through the floor. She needed to get a handle on how to deal with Jake, and soon. As things stood, his white vet's coat might as well be a bare chest and leather pants.

Mmm. Leather pants.

Oh God, she was a mess.

"Hey," was the only word she could manage at first, and in a breathy sex-kitten voice that she absolutely had not intended to use. It was hard, though, considering taking an adequate breath wasn't going that well.

It was another triumph to see the way Jake's eyes widened as he took a good look at her. "Um. Wow. You look amazing," he said. "There some kind of cocktail party I didn't get invited to?"

"Yeah, no," Sam replied, flexing hands that wanted to start playing with the long strand of Murano glass beads she had around her neck. "I had a thing. I mean"—she blew out a flustered breath and looked heavenward, annoyed with the way she lost the power of coherent speech around him—"an interview. I'm going to be working at Two Roads."

"The gallery? Cool. Congratulations," Jake said easily, and his smile warmed her from head to toe. It was as impossible to resist as it had always been, she realized. What was she *doing* here?

"Thanks," Sam said, and the lingering pleasure from the morning's success burst through in a grin she couldn't manage to hold back. "I'm really excited about it."

"You should be." He hesitated, then said, "You were an amazing artist."

Just for an instant, the years fell away, and she was nothing more than a girl standing in front of him. A girl with her head full of a boy who'd turned out to be little more than fantasy, like most things she'd loved. And in her hand was her heart.

"Jake . . . I . . . can I talk to you for a second? I wanted to show you something."

An incredulous look as his friends began laughing. At her. And she knew she'd made a mistake, finally working up the nerve to talk to him at school. Here, they were supposed to be strangers. Too late, she understood that she'd crossed a line that he never would.

"Uh, thanks, but no thanks. You can keep . . . whatever that is."

Sam's smile vanished, her pleasure crumpling just like that long-ago offering. At least then she'd had the good sense to throw it at him. It was some small comfort that the wadded-up sketch had hit him right in the forehead. She might not be an athlete, but she'd always had good aim.

"So, can I see the kittens?" she asked, crossing her arms as she moved the subject back to neutral territory. He seemed to take note of the change in her, some emotion she couldn't identify tightening his features for just a moment before he relaxed again and nodded.

"Absolutely. Come on back. You can hang out with the monsters in my office while I try to scarf down some lunch."

"Fine," she said, her voice overly bright, and followed when he turned to walk back down the hallway. She could do this, Sam decided. It was ancient history. It was over with. If he wanted to keep it friendly, she was willing. But the girl who'd once looked at him with stars in her eyes was long gone. He needed to remember that. And so did she.

Chapter Four

No matter how weird it was for her that Jake was now both an adult and a guy who merited his own office, Sam could at least be glad that his choice of decor indicated he didn't take himself too seriously.

"Nice bobbleheads," she said, then took a sip of her latte.

He didn't look the least bit sheepish when she turned to watch him shut the door behind her. "Thanks."

"And your Iron Man poster really sets off the diploma next to it."

"Red metal badassery enhances any room, you know," he replied. "Didn't they teach you that at art school?"

"No. I guess I should have taken Decorating with Superheroes 101 for one of my electives."

"I could give you some pointers," he said. "I've been told I'm a natural with the medium."

"Yeah. I'll keep that in mind." Sam smiled despite herself and shook her head, looking away before Jake decided her amusement meant more than it actually did. She had a feeling she was on shaky ground here. It was too easy to fall back into their old, easy banter, even after all this time. The natural advantage still seemed to be his. Jake was as comfortable in his own skin, and with his

considerable appeal, as he'd ever been. And she ...
wasn't. Flustered, and determined not to morph back
into an awkward teenager, Sam let her eyes skim the
room. The space didn't contain much but a cluttered
desk, a filing cabinet, a mini fridge, and a small end table
with a coffeemaker on it. Tucked into one corner was a
large cage full of small, furry creatures making an awful
lot of noise. Relief mingled with delight and made her
smile.

"Kitties!" she said, feeling only a little ridiculous as
she hurried to the cage and crouched down to look at the
little faces smooshed against the door. Jake appeared at
her side almost instantly, too quickly for her to move
away. He plucked her latte from her hand.

"You won't want them knocking this over. Caffeine is
the last thing this crew needs. Go ahead, open it. You can
entertain them while I inhale lunch."

Without another thought, she sat on the floor, took off
her heels, shoved them to one side, and unlatched the
wire door. Six warm little bundles of fur in varying colors
piled out, climbing over one another, big eyes taking in
the wide world of Jake's office as they set out to explore
it. Loki emerged last, and Sam burst into surprised
laughter as he climbed into her lap and right up the front
of her. It was cute enough that she could disregard the
tiny little claws poking through her dress and into her
skin. Mostly.

"Your love is painful, little man. What *is* it with you?"
she asked, looking down into his big green eyes. Since
purring was the only response she got, Sam kept one
hand on Loki to give his precarious position some support and used the other hand to play with his siblings.
They might have been born outside, she thought, but they

seemed to be warming up to humans just fine. Any trepidation she'd felt about being alone with Jake vanished in the face of her amusement at the kittens' antics. In the space of a few minutes, she was too busy laughing, chasing after the unruly brood on her knees while Loki hung on for dear life, and letting her hands get covered in playful scratches to care what the other human in the room was doing. She looked up only when Loki decided that her shoulder might be a better vantage point for him.

"Ouch! Damn it, Loki, let me . . . um . . ."

She paused in the middle of trying to detach him from her dress and had just set him on her shoulder as her eyes locked with Jake's. It suddenly occurred to her that she was crawling around his office on her knees, covered in cat hair, and that he'd been perched on the edge of his desk watching her do that for an extended period of time. Eating a chocolate pudding cup, no less. She blew a lock of hair out of her face. Naturally, she thought, even her hair was working against her.

"What?" It sounded defensive and abrupt, but Sam was caught completely off guard by the look on Jake's face. His mouth was curved up just a little in a bemused smile, and those pretty eyes of his had gone soft and warm. He didn't have any right to look at her like that, she thought as her cheeks went hot. And he didn't have any right to stare at her quietly while she made a complete ass of herself on his floor, which she wouldn't even be doing if he hadn't lured her here with baby animals. Her thigh stung as one of the two tabbies decided it wanted her attention. She shot it an exasperated look even as she sank back onto her butt and helped the kitten into her lap. Loki took the opportunity to try to groom her. That or he was eating her hair.

You're not helping me get it together, here, guys.

Jake dropped his eyes briefly, as though he was as embarrassed to be caught staring as she was to find him doing it. When he raised them again, though, none of the warmth had faded. Her heart did a fluttering, nervous little dance in her chest. Under normal circumstances she might have said to hell with it and bolted, but Jake had planned his little trap well. She was stuck here, covered in fur and kittens and completely at his mercy.

It was diabolical enough that she had to give him some grudging respect . . . even if she still had no idea why he was making the effort. They'd been through this once. She wasn't his type. He'd made it abundantly clear that she wasn't his type. And she, in turn, had tried very, very hard to convince herself that he wasn't hers.

The effort it took to draw in a normal breath was irritating. Sam raised her eyebrows when Jake stayed silent. "Staring while you eat your lunch is rude," she informed him. "And why are you eating a pudding cup anyway? What are you, like, five?"

One side of his mouth curved up. Insulting him was one way to break the tension, she guessed. Though coming off as caustic wasn't necessarily how she'd meant to deal with him. Just another reminder that she had no idea what the hell she was doing.

"Speaking of rude," Jake replied. "Don't judge me for my taste in snack food." He wagged his plastic spoon at her before setting it, and the empty pudding container, aside. She hoped that would be the end of it. He could joke a little; that she could handle. But just as she'd started to relax, his gaze turned speculative again.

"So . . . you settling in okay?"

"For being here all of twenty-four hours, sure," Sam

said, trying to disentangle Loki from her hair. She had an unpleasant suspicion that Jake was going to try to steer the conversation into personal areas, all of which she had decided were off limits to him. He was her cat's vet. She could be cordial. But if he thought they were going to be buddies just because they shared a small, unpleasant slice of history, he had another thing coming.

Of course, that might have been clearer to him if she wasn't sitting on his floor covered in cats.

"Damn it, Loki!"

Jake breathed out a soft, amused exhalation through his nose as he watched her struggle. "Want some help with that?"

"No." Sam gave Loki another tug and managed to get him free from both her shoulder and her hair, though the ripping sound she heard made her wince. The little black kitten mewed angrily and squirmed in her hands before she put him down next to one of his siblings. A quick pounce later, Loki dashed off, his infatuation momentarily forgotten.

"He's easily distracted, at least," Sam said, trying to smooth the hair on that side of her head back into place. It felt like a lost cause, but she had to try.

"My advice would be to invest in a lot of cat toys. And maybe take one of his littermates, too."

"Oh, thanks. Great advice. Not that you have a vested interest there or anything," she replied.

"Of course not. I'm just being helpful. And you definitely shouldn't think about the overcrowded rescue that will have to take the rest. And how they might grow up in a shelter without their own homes. Put that stuff right out of your mind."

Sam pressed her lips together and exhaled loudly. "Is

'guilt' one of the services you offer here? I don't remember seeing that on the sign."

"I consider it a free bonus."

"Uh-huh. What a deal," she replied as he grinned at her in that particular way he had, chin down, eyes sparkling with mischief. Settled on the edge of his desk, he'd stretched out his long legs, his body language completely at ease. He'd always moved with casual grace, and the kind of self-assurance you couldn't fake. She knew. She'd tried. The longer she let her gaze linger on him, the warmer the room seemed to get. Why didn't he find something else to look at? Why did his lab coat have to fit those broad shoulders so well? Why couldn't he have shaved his stubble this morning? And since when did she find stubble sexy anyway?

Heat pooled uncomfortably at the apex of her thighs, and Sam knew she needed to get out of here before she did something stupid. What that might be, she wasn't sure . . . but it didn't matter. Most things she could imagine doing with Jake fell into that category.

We're not friends, she reminded herself. *We never really were. And we're not going to be, because people don't change that much.*

"I should let you get back to work," Sam said, suddenly sure that she ought to be anywhere but here. She had enough crap to deal with right now without this extra, self-inflicted weirdness.

He didn't even bother to look at his watch. "I've got time," he said. Something about the way he said it prickled across her skin and sounded warning bells in the part of her mind dedicated to self-preservation.

"I actually don't," she said, hoping he'd understand it for the all-purpose dismissal that it was. "I've got a bunch of stuff to take care of today. Can't really stay. This is great, though. The kittens and your office and . . . everything." She widened her eyes a little at how idiotic she sounded, gave her head a small shake, and grabbed the two nearest kittens instead of continuing to let words come out of her mouth. She could feel Jake's eyes on her as she scrambled gracelessly to her feet, trying not to think about how high her skirt was hiked up from sitting on the floor. Apparently, the entire purpose of Jake's existence was to help her figure out just how many different shades of red her face could turn in a single sitting. She had a horrible suspicion that right now she was setting some kind of new record.

Then Jake was up and moving, silently helping her gather up the rogue felines and put them in their cage. She tried to move quickly, anxious to put some distance between herself and Jake Smith, Life Ruiner, before she screwed up and was nice to him again. It was easier to just be distant. You'd think she would have figured that out where he was concerned, but apparently all it took was a great pair of shoulders and the right amount of stubble to torpedo her common sense.

Well, and the eyes. He has great eyes.

She yanked her dress back down with one hand after scooping Loki out from beneath the end table and planted a kiss on the kitten's head, feeling guilty about the abbreviated visit as she put him back with his siblings. *Soon,* she told herself. *He'll be home soon, and I can fuss over him without an audience.*

"Bye, sweetie," she whispered as she shut and bolted the cage door.

When she straightened, Jake was only inches from her. She sucked in a startled breath, then tilted her head to try to scan the floor for wherever she'd shoved her shoes. Her stomach twisted itself into a series of intricate knots. He smelled incredible.

I hate my life.

Watching her steadily, Jake lifted one hand. Her heels dangled from his fingertips.

"You really don't have to go," he said when she snatched them and shoved them on her feet, completely annoyed with herself.

"Yes, I do. I really do." Leave it to her to turn a casual nothing of a visit into some kind of major psychosexual drama. It had been a mistake to come. The ground she'd gained since leaving this town had been hard won, and it obviously still needed shoring up before she was ready to engage Jake on any level past walking by him on the street. Retreat sucked, but right now it was better than any alternatives she could come up with.

"Then maybe you'd be interested in dinner. Say, Friday night. I'd like to catch up."

On some level, she'd sensed this coming, even if she didn't get it. At all. But all the parts of her that should have been gloating at the opportunity to finally reject him with a few icy words and a smile seemed to have quit functioning from shock. She was left to scramble with what was left to form a reply.

"I'm pretty busy right now, Jake."

"That's okay. I'm flexible."

Sam bristled at the easy way he brushed off the rejection. Typical for a guy who'd always gotten what he wanted. "I'm not," she said more firmly, grabbing her purse from the corner of his desk. "Look, I appreciate the thought, but I'm not interested."

He was quiet for a moment, which she hoped would

last until she got out the door. She was suddenly desperate for air that didn't smell like Jake's cologne. Or more specifically, air that didn't make her want to bury her face in Jake's neck.

"Just leave me a message when you have a firm date I can bring Loki home," Sam said. "I'll see you around."

"Sam, wait. Just hang on a second."

She paused with her hand on the doorknob, had a quick and furious debate with herself, and then turned back to look at him. He had his hands stuffed into the pockets of his white coat, and something in his expression, so earnest and open, reminded her painfully of the boy she remembered. The memory held her in place like nothing else would have.

"Look, I get it. I was a jerk kid."

She raised her eyebrows, startled by his bluntness. It provoked some of her own. "Yeah," she blurted, "you were. And?" *You were also beautiful, and perfect, and painful. . . .*

His mouth curved into a small, rueful smile. "I did grow up, you know."

"I can see that," Sam replied, hitching her purse onto her shoulder. "Congratulations. Look, I need to—"

"I quit being the jerk kid a while back, Sam. I know you don't have any reason to take my word for it, but I'd like a chance to prove it to you."

She stared at him, completely at a loss. Her common sense commanded her to go. Her feet refused to move. Hadn't she spent an embarrassing amount of time, years ago, imagining scenes just like this? *Let me make it up to you. . . . I was wrong. . . .* She'd even devised really excellent soundtracks to go along with his dramatic apologies, right before he swept her into his arms and things got X-rated.

Reality, as usual, didn't live up to the fantasy at all. If he tried to touch her she was just going to punch him, and the desk she might once have envisioned getting busy on was covered in the remains of Jake's brown-bagged lunch. Her mouth went dry, and she could manage only a one-word response.

"Why?"

He appeared to think that over for a moment before answering her. It wasn't like him to have to search for the right words, she thought. He'd always had them.

"Because the jerk kid screwed up and missed out on getting to know you better when he had the chance." When she said nothing, he took a step toward her, carefully, as though approaching an animal he thought might bolt . . . or bite. "Let me take you to dinner. Just one dinner. If I'm the asshole you remember, you can tell me to go to hell. Publicly, even. No harm, no foul."

A date? He was asking her on a date? It made so little sense that it took her a few drawn-out seconds of silence to formulate a reply. The only thing that finally got her brain to engage was her sudden certainty that she was standing here looking like a complete idiot. And that was something she'd promised she'd never do again. Not in front of him, anyway.

"Jake, we have nothing in common. That hasn't changed."

"You don't know that," he countered. "And hey, if nothing else, I can fill you in on what you've missed around here."

The offer, made innocently enough, was a stark reminder that they'd grown up in two very different universes despite living in the same place. "I already know what I missed," she said flatly. "Nothing. This place never changes."

"You did."

"I *left*," Sam replied, more sharply than she'd intended.

"And now you're back." Jake's gaze was pointed, and Sam felt incredibly exposed, as though he could see all of her failings on full display while she stood there squirming. She wasn't a lovesick, outcast teenager anymore, she reminded herself. She'd been farther and done more than most of the people in this town, Jake included. If anybody ought to be uncomfortable, it was him. He was the jerk.

Which he'd already admitted with basically no shame whatsoever.

Sam crossed her arms over her chest, leveled what she hoped was a cool stare at him, and tried to project a whole lot of confidence that she didn't feel. It was something she'd gotten pretty good at in New York. Hopefully this weird and lingering thing between the two of them hadn't neutralized her skills.

"I'm back *for now*. What if I say yes just so I can tell you off in front of a bunch of people? What if I just decide to stand you up? The chances of that are a lot higher than anything good happening, Jake."

"We were friends once."

"We were *something* once. Briefly. And then we weren't," she snapped. "I don't know why you're pushing this."

He took two more careful steps toward her. "Maybe I have a thing for mysterious blondes who look good covered in kittens."

Sam barked out a humorless laugh. "I'm not mysterious."

He didn't crack a smile. "Sure you are. You always were." She barely had time to digest that before he added, "Anyway, what if we have a good time? That's a possibility, too, you know."

"An infinitesimally small one."

"I'm willing to risk it. I'm the only one with a downside here. Unless you consider maybe enjoying yourself a downside." He arched an eyebrow. "What do you say, Sam?"

She opened her mouth, fully intending to say no. But before the word could cross her lips, the common sense that had deserted her in coming here returned with a vengeance.

If you don't, you'll only look like you're running away. I thought you were done with that. Besides, you've been telling yourself for years that he doesn't matter. So prove it. Otherwise he isn't going to let this go. And neither are you.

"Fine," Sam said, her voice as crisp and cool as a winter morning. "Saturday. Dinner. *Once.* It's not a date. And when we're sitting there with nothing to talk about, remember whose fault that is."

His smile was slow and warm as he leaned in and reached behind her to turn the knob on the door and see her out. "I bet we have more in common than you think." Jake's voice was a low rumble, his breath fanning her face and smelling faintly of chocolate. There were only inches between them, and though she knew she ought to move out of the way and let the door swing open, Sam instead found her body curving into his, pulled by some invisible, irresistible force. She'd never been this close to him before. And though she was no blushing virgin anymore, the charge that sizzled between them was far stronger than anything she'd expected. Her first instinct was to fight it. She had to, for her own sanity. Not to mention her beat-up heart.

"We have one thing in common now, anyway. I don't have any trouble walking away from you."

She didn't know why she said it. Being this close to him was opening old wounds that shut down her common sense. Petty slaps like that wouldn't hurt him. Nothing would, coming from her. But some part of her was still looking for closure, and maybe just a little bit of payback.

And the startled expression that flickered over his face an instant before his eyes hardened and narrowed said that against all odds, she'd left a mark after all.

Rather than pull the door open, Jake went still, bracing himself with his arm and neatly boxing her in. This close, Sam could see the tiny flecks of green in his eyes. His long, dark lashes dropped, and when he sucked his lower lip in to wet it, Sam drew in a single shuddering breath. His body was so close to hers, she could feel it like electricity racing over her skin. This strange chemistry had always been there, crackling between them. But it had changed, intensified.

It had gotten so much worse.

The only sound she could hear was her heart pounding in her ears. She knew she shouldn't . . . but right that second, all Sam wanted was Jake's mouth on hers. He lowered his head, just a little, then flicked his eyes back up to hers as though asking a question. Even now, he wouldn't push it with her. It would be her choice—one she didn't want to make.

Sam swallowed hard, her thoughts in complete disarray. *I want . . . No, I don't . . . No, that's bull. I really want him to . . .*

His nose touched hers. "It wasn't easy," he breathed, his voice a raspy whisper. He lifted his hand to cup her cheek, trailing his thumb along her jaw. "It still isn't."

Words tried to form, then scattered. She lifted her mouth to his, lips parted, ready to melt.

"Dr. Smith?" There was a rapid flurry of knocks along with the sharp voice, and the moment didn't so much break as shatter. Sam jumped a little, then stumbled a few steps backward, out of Jake's reach and away from the pull of whatever alchemy his nearness produced. Jake looked slightly dazed as he watched her move away. Then he took a deep breath, straightened, and pulled the door open.

"Yeah, right here, Angie."

Sam listened with half an ear to a quickly whispered discussion with the receptionist she hadn't recognized, all while the girl shot looks at her as though she might be some sort of enemy spy. That, Sam realized, or an out-of-towner. It would have been funny if she hadn't been standing there shaking, her heart still pounding. He'd done it on purpose, she thought, torn between anger and raw desire. She'd issued a challenge, and he'd picked it right up. Worse, he'd won. Now he knew she still wanted him. And she had no idea how she was going to put her defenses back in place.

She wanted to shout at him for still being such an arrogant ass. When she saw his face, however, Sam knew she'd have to table that. Something was wrong.

"Have them pull around back. I'll be right there," he said to Angie, and when Jake turned back to look at Sam, there was a steeliness in his expression she didn't recognize.

"The Andersens' dog, Shakes, was hit by a car. They're bringing him in now. I've got to go, but I'll call you."

Sam nodded, understanding. He was Dr. Smith now. The change in him had been sudden and complete, shifting him into a man she didn't know at all. Well, almost.

"Saturday," he said, pointing at her and tipping his chin down to give her a look that made it clear the date—or, rather, the not-a-date—was now, as far as he was concerned, set in stone. Then he vanished, and Sam was left wringing the strap of her purse with both hands, wondering what the hell she'd just agreed to. After a moment, she walked to his desk, found a pen, and scrawled her cell number on a sticky note with a brief message.

Let me know what time Saturday. —S

She'd miscalculated somewhere along the line. Jake wasn't supposed to be able to surprise her, which was all he'd done since she'd gotten home. But even if he was right, and a few things *had* changed since she'd been gone, there was one thing that hadn't—and it was going to get her a lot more than almost-kissed if she didn't get a handle on it.

Sam touched her lips lightly with her fingertips, wondering. Then she rolled her eyes to the heavens, muttered a few curses, and walked out the door.

Chapter Five

When one of his days went to hell, which they did on a regular basis, Jake relied on the only surefire method he'd found of clearing his head and salvaging his sanity. He went home, threw on his sneakers, put Tucker's leash on him, and headed out for a run. No matter the season, sun or clouds, rain or snow, there was always someplace he could go to clear the day's debris out of his head. Today, he needed it.

Shakes had hung on all afternoon, but in the end, it had been clear that the kindest thing was to let the sweet old retriever go. He'd done what was needed, been the calm, concerned, competent doctor as he'd administered the injections that would take away Shakes's pain and bring Steve and Ginny Andersen oceans of it. He'd been sympathetic while they'd stroked their four-legged friend's fur and cried. And inside, he'd grappled with the same helpless fury he always did when an animal was lost to a human's cruelty or stupidity. A cable guy who couldn't be bothered to look behind him and see the old dog curled up asleep in the driveway counted as the latter . . . but he'd seen so much of both. It wore on him sometimes, threatening to outweigh the good he knew he did.

So he went home, hugged his mutt, laced up, and found some peace where he could.

Tucker, happy just to be jogging along by his person in the fading light, was always a nice reminder that every day had some good in it if you could manage to be in the moment and get your brain to shut up for a while.

Jake settled into his rhythm, feeling his muscles warm as he headed down his street and hung a right, toward the park. The sky was a vibrant canvas of reds and pinks, striking against the bold hues of the leaves. He breathed deeply, savoring the rich scents of earth and wood smoke that could only be fall, and let his mind empty. Everything fell away as his feet hit the pavement.

His whole Zen running thing lasted all of three minutes before he was back to replaying his meeting with Sam over and over again. Since that was by far the least traumatic part of his day, though, Jake figured it was okay.

He couldn't get past her expression, so soft and unguarded, in the moment when he'd realized that not only was he about to kiss her, but that she wanted him to. Still. Even after all this time. He wondered if she was pissed about it now. Probably, he thought, his mouth curving. That seemed to be her comfort zone with him, though she kept slipping. Like when she'd agreed to dinner.

Not a date, his ass.

His smile faded as doubt tried to creep in. What if she was right and they just sat there staring awkwardly at each other? *It's just a dinner, damn it. She's still beautiful, you're still interested, so now you get to see what happens. You used to talk. So you'll do it again. No big deal.*

But he couldn't remember the longing on her face without thinking that on some level, it was a big deal.

Maybe a really big deal. Part of him had been hoping that time would have made her seem less interesting, that he could ditch the weird combination of guilt and fantasy labeled "Sam Henry" that he'd been lugging around and finally shake her.

No dice. She was the same enigma who'd haunted him off and on for ten years now, except she'd piled on a few layers of some very adult sex appeal in the meantime. It shouldn't have made him nervous. Women didn't make him nervous anymore, damn it.

And he could tell himself that until he was blue in the face, but it wouldn't change the fact that this one did.

"So what are a hick vet and a cultured artist going to talk about at dinner, Tuck? You tell me."

Tucker looked up at him, his tongue lolling out as he panted, brown eyes full of simple joy. That look said it all: I HAVE NO CLUE WHAT YOU'RE TALKING ABOUT HUMAN BUT I LOVE YOU AND I LOVE OUTSIDE AND ISN'T THIS GREAT I LOVE RUNNING YAY I'M A DOG!

"Thanks, man," Jake said. "That's deep."

"Hey, Smith, wait up!"

He slowed, recognizing the voice, as well as the footfalls that sounded more like a Clydesdale was pursuing him than a man. Soon enough, there was a familiar six foot ten inches of solid human next to him. Jake didn't spare Shane Sullivan more than a glance. He wasn't really in the mood for company, but if he couldn't avoid it, Shane was as good as it got.

They'd been friends since the fourth grade, when an attempt to kick each other's asses had resulted in both a stalemate and a joint trip to the principal's office. Shane was bigger, but Jake was faster, and they'd quickly discovered that they were more effective at everything from sports to chasing girls, and later women, as a unit. Their punishments had been fleeting. The friendship had stuck.

"Thought I felt the earth shaking." Jake quickened his pace again, knowing Shane would keep up.

"Nah, that's just your body getting ready to give out because of how much it sucks."

"Huh. I must be confused about which of us is sweating, then." Jake snorted. "So what's up? I haven't seen you out running in a couple of months. Speaking of sucking."

"I thought of you and it motivated me to be a better, more active person. You're my hero, Jake." Shane fluttered his eyelids.

"Jesus. Another groupie."

"Yeah, we're getting T-shirts made. Seriously, though, I heard you were holed up in your office today with some hot blonde. Like, an actual human female. That part sounded suspicious to me, so I had to check it out and make sure you weren't just bringing your blow-up doll to work again."

"Bite me. This is interesting enough for you to chase me down, like, the second you got home?"

Shane shrugged. "I've been home for an hour. There was nothing good on TV."

Jake exhaled loudly and looked at the sky. This was the part about small-town living that was both blessing and curse. "What the hell? I just got home!"

Shane's voice was smug. "Yeah, well, Angie left the office before you did, and you know she and Stump are just about living together. She told him, he called me, and now I need to know where you found a babe like

Angie described in the Cove, because if she has friends and you're holding out, this is not okay. You know I have no life right now."

A quick look at Shane, whose face was now only slightly less red than his short, wavy hair, told Jake that his friend was only half joking. Maybe less than half. And also seriously out of shape, even if his tall, athletic frame wasn't showing it yet. It sure as hell would by the end of football season, after the months of chili dogs and beer they'd all be consuming.

"You want a life, then get one," Jake said. "You're an attorney. If you weren't such an asshole, you'd be a catch around here."

"I like being an asshole," Shane panted. "And I don't want to be caught by anything around here. You know what the Tavern looks like on Friday nights. Same old. Maybe I should have moved to Boston."

Jake shook his head as they rounded a bend in the path, listening to his friend's labored breathing. "Shane, go home. I don't want to be responsible for you having a massive heart attack."

Not that Jake didn't have some sympathy for him. Right now Shane was paying every due Jim Sullivan thought he ought to for the privilege of being his firstborn son and chosen successor, the eventual inheritor of Sullivan Associates. Shane never really complained, but he never seemed very enthusiastic, either. A lot of the happiness seemed to have gone out of him since the days when he'd been the life of every party, and Jake often wondered if maybe Shane really *should* have gone to Boston and gotten away. The Cove could be a haven, if you wanted it. But like any small town, it could also be quicksand.

He knew that was how Sam felt about it. And she'd

made it clear that the move home wouldn't be permanent, if she had any say in the matter. On some level it was hard to blame her. On another, it was irritating that her mind was made up about the Cove before she'd even gotten started.

Shane's deceptively mellow baritone pulled Jake out of his thoughts. "So Angie thought your mystery hookup was local, but that can't be right. Said Cass knew her. From college, maybe?"

"She wasn't a hook-up, and she's very local," Jake replied. "You remember Sam Henry?"

Shane's burst of disbelieving laughter wasn't exactly unexpected, but it put him on the defensive in a way he wasn't used to.

"Sam Henry? Freak show? *No.* No *way.* Wasn't she into animal sacrifice or something? I remember lots of black eyeliner, black lipstick, hair in the face . . . I mean, she was cute if you could get past the weird, I guess, but . . ." He trailed off, frowning as he continued to jog along, then snapped and pointed at Jake, eyes lighting up. "Hey, remember when she had a crush on you? I almost forgot about that. Man, that was sad. You telling me she actually managed to grow up hot?"

Jake flexed his hands, stunned by the flash of temper that nearly overrode his self-control. He had an overwhelming urge to punch the delighted grin off of Shane's face. Why did it figure he'd remember the one day Jake really wanted to forget? Maybe he'd been stupid for not expecting this. Sam had been gone a long time. She was going to be preceded by her reputation, fair or not, until people sized her up again.

It would be fine, he told himself. She didn't need him to defend her.

"She grew up. Aren't we supposed to be past all this shit? It was ten years ago," Jake said. He turned his head to glare incredulously at Shane. "Animal sacrifice? Seriously? She was *artsy*, not a psychopath."

Okay, so she might not need the defense, but he couldn't quite help giving it anyway.

Shane's brows shot up at the snap in his voice. "Jake, granted, I didn't pay a ton of attention to her class—I mean, apart from the hot girls and the guys we played sports with—but Sam kind of stuck out, and not in a good way. Don't get all bent out of shape. You just surprised me. It's not like you were all about her back then. Actually, I have this distinct memory of her pegging you in the head with some crumpled-up paper when you finally told her to take off."

"Yeah. I remember." He said it quietly, his temper subsiding as quickly as it had risen, and his shoulders slumped a little.

After making a noncommittal sound, Shane lapsed into silence, though he kept running alongside Jake as the evening deepened around them. There was no sound but their breathing, the jingle of Tucker's collar, and the pounding of their sneakers on the pavement. Jake knew he wouldn't have to wait long for Shane to lose his patience with the silence.

"So forget high school. Was this just some kind of kinky one-off thing? I thought she lived in New York or something now."

Yep, typical Shane. Jake couldn't keep his lips from curving before he relented and answered.

"She just moved back home from the city. Actually, she was at the office to see the kitten she's adopting. Not kinky, but I did talk her into dinner this Saturday."

"Huh," Shane said, looking vaguely amused by the idea. "Well . . . I'll have to keep an eye out for her. Even if I can't picture her being this blond goddess Angie described, like, at all." Though Shane still looked puzzled, at least he'd pulled back a little from being actively insulting. Jake didn't feel like fighting with him. They hadn't been at odds over anything bigger than what kind of hoagie to get at RJ Grinders in years. Maybe because they had a routine, and they stuck to it. What was to argue about?

The thought gave him pause. There was a fine line between being comfortable and being in a rut. He'd been walking the line for a while now, and he knew it. Life was good, mostly. The job was fulfilling. But his house was still kind of big and fairly empty, and he hadn't dated anyone interesting in at least a year — despite his friends' constant and increasingly annoying efforts to set him up.

Well, no one in their right mind would have set him and Sam up. That alone made it promising.

"Hey," Shane said, a little breathless now from the exertion but brightening at once. "Max said he was going to call you about movie night this Saturday. You're supposed to bring beer." He frowned. "Oh. You've got the big date with the, ah, Sam." Jake heard the hesitation before her name, and he knew Shane had been about to call her something other than her name. An ugly memory surfaced, of Thea Hanover's narrowed eyes in her eighteen-year-old face as she watched Sam hurrying across the cafeteria, head down.

"Look at that freak. I don't even know why she bothers to come to school. It's not like she has any friends."

The disdain had been reflexive back then. Hell, he'd been guilty of it too, before he'd noticed that the shadow with the sketchbook was an actual human being. Not that the revelation had changed things, in the end. He'd still been embarrassed to be seen with her.

I can make up for that, at least.

Why did it figure that Sam would be the movie cliché that never seemed to happen in real life, the odd duck who returned as a swan? She'd gone from shy alt-girl to edgy Nordic goddess. Though he had to admit that even if she'd shown up with pink hair and facial piercings, he'd still be chasing her around. The woman pushed all of his damned buttons. All of them at once.

"If dinner goes well, maybe I'll bring Sam with me. We don't usually get the movie in before nine anyway."

Shane gave him a strange look. "Yeah, sure," he said with a soft, incredulous laugh. "That won't be awkward."

Jake arched an eyebrow. "It won't be if you don't *make* it awkward."

"Jake, I'm not going to make it anything. But movie nights are kind of our *thing*, you know? It works. Toss in artsy awkward loner girl who nobody liked and it's just going to mess up the night. I mean, what are we supposed to talk to her about? The good old days? Impressionism versus modernism?"

"Well, you know, there's always talking to her like she's a human being you just don't know very well. I think you'd be surprised," Jake said, his annoyance returning.

"By the way she looks? Yeah, sounds like maybe. But no matter what she looks like now, she was *weird*. That shit doesn't change. The Henrys are all wired that way to begin with. And let's face it, Jake . . . you're pretty normal. We all are."

And there it was. *"We."* He'd been a member of their

circle for so long, he'd almost forgotten what it was like to be outside of it. Sam's words echoed ominously in his ears: *"Nothing ever changes here."* He found himself stubbornly determined to prove her wrong.

"You have your head up your ass, as usual. Emma's not weird," Jake pointed out. "And Andi is a sweetheart."

Shane rolled his eyes. "Oh, come on. Emma's trying so hard to buck genetics that she's gone too far the other way. Having actual fun would probably make her snap. And Andi's a complete hippie. Sure, she's nice. Pot makes everybody nice. That doesn't mean painting your shutters a different shade of the rainbow every week just to piss off your neighbors is normal."

"She's not a pothead!"

"You don't know that," Shane insisted. "Who knows what goes on at that house? They've got a ton of land. It's not like anyone goes sniffing around out there. They're scared of being caught and tie-dyed."

Jake slowed to take a good look at Shane. He hoped he'd find some hint that his friend was joking, but there was none. They never talked about the Henrys—never any reason to—but Shane's family lived out on the Crescent. The small-town snobbery Jake often forgot was there was showing, and he didn't much care for it.

"Way to be open-minded," he said flatly. Shane was unfazed.

"I'm not pretending to be. Not even telling you what to do. But the Cove isn't *Mr. Rogers' Neighborhood*. And you can bet Thea hasn't forgotten that Sam gave her a black eye right before she left for college."

"I— What?" Jake nearly tripped over his own shoes.

Shane's expression was smug, and Jake took some small satisfaction in the fact that his friend was now huff-ing and puffing to keep up. "Yeah, maybe you should ask Sam about that. It's dinner conversation, anyway."

"Maybe I will." Sam had *punched* Thea? How the hell had he missed that? Even more surprising was that Thea had never said a word about it to him.

"Uh-huh. And while you're at it, keep in mind that Cici's back in town, and probably coming Saturday night."

Another surprise. Maybe it was good Shane had hauled ass out here after all. Forewarned was forearmed, and Cecilia Ferris definitely merited some warning.

"What, did someone light the Bat-signal for everyone to come back to the Cove? I haven't seen Cici since the Christmas before last. She was with that guy she married. Hedge fund manager guy," he said.

"You mean douche. The guy was a douche, Jake," Shane said, so serious that Jake started laughing. "I guess they split. I don't know what happened. But she's back in town. If she looks half as good as she did last time I saw her, you're going to want to be as single as possible."

"We've been through that. Didn't work the first time. Wouldn't work now."

"Why not?" Shane asked. "Be like old times."

Jake shot Shane a beleaguered look. "No. Cici split right about the time she figured out I was serious about expressing canine anal glands for a living. We ended it friendly, but it definitely ended. It's going to stay that way."

"So . . . you don't care if I hit on her, then?"

They looked at each other, and all of Jake's irritation evaporated as Shane waggled his eyebrows at him. Especially because he knew that Shane was dead serious. He was, for better or worse, basically a twelve-year-old with a law degree.

"Have at it," Jake said.

Shane gave an exaggerated fist pump, hissing out a dramatic "Yesssss." Then threw his head back, groaned, and announced, "Okay, enough exertion for me. I'm going home to my couch and a pile of paperwork. You have fun running in the dark. Watch it, though. You'll probably attract the Cove's lone mugger."

"Tucker would eat him." At the sound of his name, Tucker looked up at Jake happily, tongue lolling as he trotted along.

"Yeah, or something," Shane said. "I'll catch up with you later this week."

"You got it." He watched as Shane lifted his hand for a single wave and jogged off, slowing considerably once he could set his own pace. Jake was just glad for the quiet. Shane made it sound like he was bringing a social outcast to the cool kids' table, not having dinner with an interesting woman. Hopefully that wasn't a sign of things to come. Especially because he had a feeling that reactions like Shane's were exactly what Sam would expect.

He didn't want her to hate it here. That was, for whatever reason, important to him. He wanted her to enjoy their dinner. And he really wanted to know about Thea's long-ago black eye. Simple enough requests, he thought. Even if nothing about all this seemed very simple anymore. The woman herself in particular.

The sky was a beautiful, deepening red now, and the lights atop the old-fashioned lampposts dotting the route glowed. Jake's breathing was rhythmic, his movements fluid. The scenery, both familiar and comforting, helped him find some balance again. Sam had thrown him off — in good ways, mostly, though he guessed the jury was still out on what the end result would be. But things would smooth out again quickly enough, he told himself.

They always did.

With the memory of Sam's big blue-green eyes dancing through his head, Jake gave himself over to the run and found, after a while, a little peace.

Chapter Six

Sam got up early Tuesday morning, dressing carefully in skinny black pants, spindly heels, and a long, loose black sweater with a little shimmer in the thread. A little mascara and gloss, a simple pair of silver hoop earrings, and a quiet argument with her hair later, she clicked downstairs for her coffee. A quick look at her phone revealed a text message that couldn't be from anyone but Jake.

> Burgers? Sushi? Help me out here. I have planning issues.

The time stamp on the message was six a.m., an hour ago. Had he been thinking about her when he got up? The thought had her stomach doing a strange little dance. It wasn't helping with the nerves she already had going on this morning. She considered ignoring the text until later, but that lasted all of about thirty seconds. She took a sip of her coffee, tapped a finger on the counter, then wrote back.

> We can figure it out on Saturday. It's not a big deal.

She pushed SEND, then wondered how the man could be up in arms about a dinner days away at this hour of the morning. She could barely think about food until lunchtime, at which point she'd be inhaling whatever she could find. Eating a granola bar was about all she could manage before then. But thinking about sushi before breakfast? Ew.

The buzz as the phone vibrated on the counter surprised her. She frowned at the lit screen where his return message waited. The butterflies in her stomach were joined by reinforcements. He'd been waiting for her to answer him. She was talking to Jake over her morning coffee. Somewhere deep inside, her sixteen-year-old self was making the sort of high-pitched sounds that could shatter glass.

Nope, no good. Need a plan.

Sam exhaled loudly through her nose, amused despite herself. She remembered this secret type-A side of his. It had surprised her then. Now, it was a useful way to twist his tail a little. She smirked to herself and texted back.

Then make a plan. I eat. That should be enough to go on.

This time her phone was silent for a couple of minutes, so she thought he might have given up. There was a pang of disappointment when the screen stayed dark, which she tried to shame herself out of. Then, just as she was getting up to make cup number two, there was another buzz. This time, she dashed back across the kitchen to grab it. What the hell, no one was looking. She couldn't stop the burst of laughter when she realized he'd sent a picture of Loki's face, along with the message:

Don't make me play the "I have your kitten" card.

Sam sighed, and rubbed at her forehead. She remembered this, the good-natured teasing, his sense of humor. It had always been so easy to fall into conversation with him, even though he'd been talking to someone who was basically forbidden to him because of his social status, and she'd been overwhelmed that he was interested enough to risk the ridicule. Well, for a while, anyway.

It shouldn't be this easy to fall back into their old pattern. She needed to stay wary, proceed with caution. And she would. But . . .

Sam narrowed her eyes, considered for a moment, then texted him back. He wasn't the only one who could tease.

You just did. Vengeance will be mine.
After burgers.

She sent the message, only realizing afterward that she was grinning like an idiot. Not that she could really stop it. Sam stirred a little sugar into her coffee and scrolled through the morning news, just starting to get interested in an article when what seemed to be Jake's final word on the subject popped up.

I never said I was above blackmail.
Burgers it is. Good luck at work today.
P.S. The cat was in on it.

Sam smiled, even if her heart seemed to be beating too fast and she felt oddly light-headed. Wishing it was just nerves didn't change the truth. Jake was funny, and charming, and handsome as sin. Just like he'd always been. And she'd be willing to bet that he also ran with the same people and went the same places as he always had. That made it hard not to think that whatever his interest in her was, it couldn't be deep enough to overcome the fact that he was woven into the fabric of the Cove in a way she never had been, and never would be.

Still, the thought behind the messages was sweet. It was . . . well, it was something, anyway.

And she had a busy day ahead, Sam decided, picking up her mug and heading for the granola bars in the pantry. She'd figure all of this out later. After. Hopefully. But for now, the safest thing to do was to put Jake and his messages out of her mind.

Still, she found herself picking up the phone to respond one last time.

Thanks. You, too.
P.S. You only think the cat works for you.
Start sleeping with your eyes open.

Sam smiled to herself, satisfied, and went to rinse out her mug. Ready or not, it was time to start the day.

Zoe was lying in wait when she arrived at nine, and from then on out, Sam no longer had space in her head for anything but art. After the last few months, that was a state she was relieved to find herself in.

"We rotate the work monthly," Zoe was saying, "to offer fresh perspective and showcase new pieces. We also participate in First Fridays—I'll e-mail you the schedule—with a different theme each month."

Sam looked up from tracing the fluid lines on a wooden rocker with her fingers.

"The Cove does First Fridays? Since when?" she asked.

"Since about four years now, from what I understand," Zoe replied, looking bemused. "When you said you didn't get home much, I guess I should have believed you. I like to pick a theme for the evening, then have some of the artists come in and hang out with the public. We have hors d'oeuvres and things, and Grace Levrett—that's her work there, the nature photos— usually handles the music. It's been really successful. Makes the work much more accessible, and it always thrills people when they realize someone they know has a real gift."

"Oh," Sam said, liking the idea, even if it meant she might have to mingle. She could be social when she had to. Even here. It was probably a good thing she'd have the outlet, really, since she had complete confidence in her inability to cultivate a whirlwind social life here.

"October's is coming up this Friday, as a matter of fact. It'll be a nice chance for you to meet our artists. You'll like Zeke," Zoe said, inclining her head toward the rocking chair. "He's a retired salesman who just happens to be a master woodworker. Mouth like a sailor and looks like one of those doomsday preppers, but as nice as they come underneath it all. And his work . . . well, you can see the quality."

Sam nodded. Some people might look and see just a pretty, unique chair. She saw hours of work and finesse, an eye for simple grace with just a touch of whimsy, and a clear respect for the wood itself. It gleamed in the filtered light, cherry and rosewood. She ran her hand over the curved back and could almost feel the love that had been poured into this.

Deep inside, she felt something that was almost inspiration, though it quickly twisted itself into despair. *I'll never feel what this artist felt again. It's gone.* Wallowing was counterproductive, though, so she pushed it aside.

"It's amazing," she said, forcing her hand away from the silken wood.

She knew she'd sounded stiff, because Zoe tilted her head at her, speculation in her storm gray eyes. Sam found herself relieved when Zoe simply kept on with the tour.

"Here, let me show you some of our newest pieces. The sculptures over here are by an emerging artist named Aaron Maclean. He's getting some very nice attention, and so are we for having him here."

Sam followed, enjoying herself as Zoe's voice, rich as warm cream, washed over her. After Gallerie Mona, which had exhibited only established artists—and only work that conformed to Mona's rather specific taste—seeing so much variety was a treat. She was walked through the work of artists who specialized in oil, in acrylic, in glass. There were two incredible photographers with very different interests, a silversmith, three potters and a jeweler who worked with natural stone and hand-crafted polymer beads. In all, according to Zoe, there were twenty-five artists whose work was on offer at present, with several others on a wait list for when space opened up.

"We have a boilerplate contract, and a separate one-time contract for the artists who are only doing a show. That's more unusual, given that we're still getting established and we're not exactly in the middle of everything, but I've been happy with the few we've done. We'll go over the terms of each contract so you're familiar with the specifics, but there isn't anything out of the ordinary. Standard fifty percent commission. Two Roads is also available for small events for no more than fifty people. Cocktail parties and things. It's been a good source of some extra income."

"Nice," Sam said. It was a beautiful space. She imagined it would lend itself well to small gatherings. Zoe had pursed her lips and looked like she was remembering something unpleasant.

"It is nice. Unless Al Piche is on the invite list. I didn't used to bother checking on specific people, but I finally had to make an exception. He's not welcome back unless someone promises to tie him to something."

Sam winced. "Oh God. Big Al." She wasn't surprised he was still around. She was afraid to consider what he might have decided on for a career, though. Not that he probably needed it. The family had money to burn. "Did he get naked?"

"No. He kept his fancy T-shirt—you know, one of those shirts that's supposed to look like a tux, with the bow tie?—on. Why, is getting naked on the list of things he does?"

"There aren't really a lot of things *not* on the list of things Big Al does," Sam said. "He's like a Cove legend. If it's stupid and survivable, he's probably done it. Usually with an audience and someone holding his beer."

"I guess we got off lucky with a few broken pieces of pottery, then. And a YouTube video of him doing the Pants Dance that I don't ever want to see again." Zoe closed her eyes and shook her head. "Anyway, with the tourism built in here, we get a lot of traffic and interest that we wouldn't otherwise," Zoe said. "It's one of the reasons I picked this place." Then she took a deep breath, looked around, and nodded approvingly. "There've been bumps, and I haven't made Harvest Cove the art mecca of New England yet, but so far we're making out."

Sam's eyebrows lifted. "Just making out? I do know how to use the Internet, you know. Six months ago you had a great write-up in *The Boston Globe*. Not to mention that this place looks amazing." It did, too, Sam thought. Zoe had managed to open the old house up and give it a more modern feel without sacrificing its original character.

Zoe lifted her shoulders, tipping her head from side to side in what seemed to be partial agreement. "Okay, the *Globe* thing was pretty incredible. One of their "Arts" writers has family here, and I guess we impressed him when he was visiting. I just always feel like I could be doing better. This place is my baby."

"It's a pretty baby," Sam said, and meant it. Two Roads wouldn't be competing with the opulent gleam of larger city galleries, but it pretty obviously wasn't meant to. There was a warmth to this place, and for all her mixed feelings about the Cove, she had to admit that Zoe had done an amazing job of evoking the best of her hometown. Everywhere she looked there was something that sparked a memory, and to her surprise, none of those memories were bad. A midwinter scene of a snow-covered field, oil on canvas, brought back images of her father pulling her and Emma in their old sled and singing a ridiculous song while they laughed. A glass sphere filled with undulating ribbons of color took her back to summers that had seemed endless—ice cream and fireworks and pinwheels, bursts of flavor and color that were as pure as the days in which she'd first experienced them. Even the scent of the gallery, one Zoe had no doubt chosen with care, triggered a cascade of images that startled Sam with their clarity. She breathed in apples and cinnamon, and all she could think of was her mother pulling a pie from the oven at the holidays, all the warmth of home she'd convinced herself she didn't need.

The wave of crushing sadness that crashed through her said otherwise.

Dismayed at the sting of tears, Sam blinked rapidly and cleared her throat.

"What about the upstairs?" she asked, forcing herself to focus on more important things than the messy, happy kid she'd once been. That was then, this was now, and having some kind of weird emotional breakdown in the middle of her new place of employment was not going to fix the fact that it was no longer acceptable for her to make mud pies and wear overalls. "You own the whole building, right?"

Zoe nodded. "Mmm. You want to know if I have studio space."

Way to start off your job by giving sage advice to the boss. But she'd already blundered on in like a hippo in a tutu and there was nothing to be done for it, so she pressed on. "Well, from the outside it looks like you might have the space, but you didn't mention that you offered any and it doesn't look like you want people up there right now, so I just . . . wondered," Sam said, glancing at the velvet rope hung between the posts at the bottom of the stairs.

Zoe didn't look the least bit perturbed by the question. Instead, she studied the stairs. "That rope won't be up much longer. Apart from a little finish work, the studios are almost ready to go. It took some doing, though. Before I got the contractors in here, I didn't even like to set foot upstairs. I kept expecting to walk into a room and find the girl from *The Ring*. Or one of those things that looks like a person but has stretchy arms and legs and walks on all fours. And eats people's souls."

Sam winced. She'd never been able to sit through horror movies. Her sleep was broken enough as it was. "Great. Um, maybe I'll wait until they're all finished before I have a look."

"Chicken." Zoe's mouth curved into a smile. Then she laughed. "Not that I blame you. It's going to be great, though. Six shiny new studios, and I've decided to keep the largest one handy for on-site classes. We've held some off-site that have been very popular." There was a quirk of her eyebrow, a mischievous grin. "Maybe you'll decide you want one of those studios for yourself. I'll even give you first dibs."

Sam's smile felt pasted on, and she instinctively started scrambling for some lame noncommittal response. "Well—"

Zoe waved a hand, neatly cutting her off. "I know, I know. I can see it all over your face. But a girl can dream, all right? Don't crush my dreams on your first day. Not before I've had my second cup of tea."

She relaxed almost instantly. It was such a welcome change to be working for someone who acted like a real human being. Mona had been able to pull off a professional veneer most of the time, but all of the gallery employees were well aware that there were claws and teeth underneath it.

"Tea?" Somehow, this was not a surprise. She eyed

Zoe, who was apparently one of those women born to make jeans look good. Today she wore them with a long, fitted gray sweater, a forest green scarf, and a pair of brown leather riding boots. Her hair was back in a low ponytail, the braids cascading down her back, and diamonds glinted at her ears. She looked every inch the Lady of the Manor at leisure. Tea should have been a foregone conclusion.

Zoe pointed one long red fingernail at her. "Oh, I'm serious about my tea. You just wait. I'll have you converted in no time."

"Sorry. Coffee and I are in a relationship."

Zoe settled her hands on her hips and arched a single imperious brow. Sam thought she now looked like a very disgruntled aristocrat. The silvery ring of the bell above the door sounded behind her.

"Then I will guarantee you're going to be unfaithful with my Monkey Picked Oolong," Zoe said, a determined glint in her eye that Sam suspected boded ill for her lifelong tea avoidance. Amused and more comfortable than she could ever have expected in Zoe's company, she opened her mouth to say something obnoxious. But she caught Zoe's sudden expression, widened eyes, a flash of real irritation directed at the front door. Curious, Sam turned and saw a familiar face.

"Jason, if there is mud on your boots *again*, I will kill you."

Jason Evans, who Sam remembered being tall, thin, and minus any facial hair, clomped into the gallery in boots that were anything but clean and offered Zoe a half smile that was far more defiance than manners. "You can't kill me," he said, his voice gruff. "I'm a cop."

"You're a *forest ranger*. This isn't a forest, and all the outside you carry around on your clothes and your shoes doesn't belong inside my gallery."

"Whatever. I'm here to spend money. You'll live." He finally seemed to notice Sam as he walked farther in. His eyebrows lifted. "Hey, Henry. Heard you were back in town."

"Hey, Jason." It was exactly the same greeting he'd used on her during her entire childhood. Same through elementary school, then through high school. He'd never tormented her, Sam thought. He hadn't talked much either, but she'd been happy just to be left alone. Of course, if he'd looked like this back then she might have reconsidered. He'd done some filling out. Okay, a lot of filling out. And going by the stubble on his face, the facial hair thing was no longer a problem.

"Don't you have some squirrels to chase or something?" Zoe's voice was strained with temper, and it was easy to see why. Jason's path into the gallery was clearly marked with twigs, leaves, and clumps of dirt. She watched him shrug as he made his way to the rocking chair Sam had been admiring.

"I'm off today."

Zoe's gaze lingered on the trail of debris before she squared her shoulders, took a deep breath, and strode over to where Jason was examining the chair. Sam hung back, fairly sure that the tension now crackling through the air meant her interference wouldn't be welcome. Besides, it was actually pretty entertaining to watch stylish, put-together Zoe go toe-to-toe with a giant in ripped jeans, an old T-shirt, and a worn jacket that did a hell of a job showing off just how broad his shoulders were. He was

Jake's cousin, as moody as Jake was outgoing, but the two of them had always seemed to get along well enough.

Unlike Jason and Zoe, apparently.

"I'll take it," Jason said, straightening to tower over her.

"Oh, you will, will you? You're finally going to buy this chair?" Her eyes were narrowed as she glared up at him.

"Yep."

"Does this mean that you're going to stop dragging your dirty, woodsy self in here every few days?"

"Probably not," Jason replied, and Sam would swear she saw the corner of his mouth twitch. "I like some of those," he continued, jerking his head toward the area where some of Grace Levrett's photography was displayed. "Gotta think about it, though."

"Of course you do." Zoe's voice had gone flat. She looked at Sam. "Could you take care of him? That one's forty-five hundred. I'm going to get the vacuum cleaner." She stalked off into the back before Sam could do more than nod. After a long, silent moment, she turned her attention back to Jason. He was staring in the direction Zoe had gone, his expression unreadable. It felt weirdly intrusive to speak, but whatever issues Zoe and Jason had, they weren't hers. And besides, she really wanted to complete her first sale. Starting off with a pricey piece of furniture seemed like a good omen to her.

"I can take care of you at the register, Jason, if you're ready."

He started a little before turning a pair of very intense brown eyes on her. It was as though he'd forgotten she was there. "Yeah, sure," he grumbled, then followed her to the rough-hewn maple cabinet that served as a counter. It was a relief to find the register setup familiar, and Sam had no trouble taking the payment when Jason handed over his credit card. He was silent for most of the process, though his deep voice rumbled to life again as he was signing the slip.

"Surprised to see you back here," he said, scribbling something that sort of resembled his name and handing the slip to her. "City didn't work out?"

"Not really," Sam replied, surprised when he looked interested.

"I could have told you it was a bad idea. Too many damn people." Then he smiled, a lazy, lopsided grin that changed the entire look of his face. It made him look boyish again—and made Sam realize exactly how much he'd grown up since. That was disconcerting, but at least he was friendly.

"You're right. That was at least part of the problem," she said. "I'm not up for living in the woods, though, so here I am again."

Jason snorted softly. "There's a lot to be said for staying in the woods—trust me. Nice and quiet." His mouth twisted into a wry smirk. "Plus you can track dirt wherever you want to."

"I'm going to go out on a limb here and guess you do that last part regardless." When all she got was another smile, Sam just shook her head. Looked like Jason was still an odd one, but knowing he was a regular customer was strangely comforting. Not that Zoe would probably agree. "Are you going to want this delivered?" she asked.

"Nope. I brought blankets for it in the truck. I'm right out front, but I could use a hand with the door," he said.

Sam obliged, watching Jason lift the rocker as though

it weighed nothing and carry it past her. She assumed the mud-spattered SUV was his, and was proved right when he headed for it. "Thanks, Henry," he called over his shoulder. "See you around. I'll be back in before long to look at those pictures."

"Maybe with cleaner shoes next time?"

She heard his low chuckle as he headed around to open the back of the truck. "That wouldn't be half as fun."

She shook her head, hearing the vacuum cleaner roar to life behind her. She had a suspicion Zoe had been waiting for Jason to leave before she reappeared, and wondered what the story there was. That level of irritation could mean any number of things. Maybe at some point Zoe would tell her. It might be nice to have a girlfriend to complain about men with again. Especially considering her old roommate's main issue with the opposite sex was their method of payment. Those conversations had gotten awkward really fast.

Sam raised her hand as Jason drove off, then paused in the open doorway, savoring the scent of October air. The trees lining the sidewalk were ablaze with color, their leaves littering the sidewalk. To her right, Hawthorne Street rolled gently down toward the harbor. Lunchtime traffic had begun to pick up as cars made their way toward the restaurants downtown, and she could hear the faint sound of music playing somewhere nearby.

It took her a good minute to recognize what held her in place, but finally, it came to her—or really, more like landed on her like a ton of bricks.

For the first time in months, she'd relaxed. What she was feeling was peace.

Sam struggled with it for a moment, but it didn't last. After everything she'd been through lately, it seemed stupid to *want* to be unhappy somewhere. Maybe the impossible had happened. Maybe she'd stayed away from the Cove long enough that things really were different, that the old rules she'd chafed at so badly no longer applied. She thought of Jake, and dinner, and decided she was going to find out soon enough. The thought was enough to take her little moment of Zen and shred it into tiny pieces.

Zoe's voice rose above the din of the vacuum. "Sam? Come here. You need to see this. Somehow, that man dragged half a tree in here on his feet. I'm not kidding! He doesn't look like Pig-Pen, so how does he carry a damn field around with him? I swear on all that is holy, if this machine breaks because it tried to suck up a log . . ."

As the complaints lapsed into frustrated muttering, Sam laughed softly, all her worry vanishing as quickly as it had emerged. For today, at least, reality was a lot more interesting than anything she could come up with to worry about.

"Coming," Sam called out as she went back inside.

Chapter Seven

Sam had expected to be nervous by the time the gallery closed on Friday, giving them an hour to set up before reopening at six as the First Friday activities got under way on the square. Instead, she found herself surprisingly calm. Maybe it was because, out of everything she'd done in the last few weeks, this was the first thing that had felt normal. Or maybe it was the mouthful of liquid antacid she'd chugged just in case. Either way, as the artists began to trickle in to help out, she felt like she was among friends.

She was setting out plates of hors d'oeuvres on a foldout buffet table draped in white linen when a hand snaked around her and snatched a handful of crackers before she could do so much as blink. Sam whipped her head around.

"What the—"

"You didn't see anything," the thief informed her.

"Sorry. I can't understand you around the chewing," she said.

He put up a finger to indicate that she should wait, finished chewing, and swallowed. "Mmm. Did you make the stuff on the crackers?"

"The ones you didn't eat, you mean?" Sam asked, unable to help her smile when the lean, handsome interloper gave her a cheeky grin. His long, slim figure was clothed in a pair of skinny jeans, a crisp white button-down shirt, and a trim pin-striped vest, and his spiky shock of blond hair had a bright blue streak in the front. The blue in his hair matched his eyes, which gleamed with the sort of mischief Sam had always admired in a person. She wasn't much of a troublemaker by nature, but this one was plenty of trouble, and completely adorable.

"Hey, I can hear the accusation in your voice," he said, pretending to be wounded. "Look, I'll even help you rearrange the plate so there isn't a hole. Well, not quite as big a hole."

Sam laughed softly. "What's your name? Trouble?"

"Trouble is my *middle* name, thank you very much." He fussed with the crackers, camouflaging the damage he'd caused with ease, and then gave her a look of triumph. "There! Good as new."

"Thanks. I think," Sam said, then settled her hands on her hips, stepped back, and looked over the spread meant to draw people in. There were crudités, chips and dip, the crackers, platters of cheese, and chocolate dipped fruit. There were also glossy postcards advertising the gallery and its work, with the dates of upcoming shows on the back. Though this month would be quiet, owing to the need to finish the work on the studios, things were going to pick up in November. Sam felt a flutter of excitement in the pit of her stomach at the thought, then another at the fact that she could feel that way about work again. Not her own work . . . but a start.

"You must be Sam," the man said, drawing her attention back to him. "Zoe was just all about you on the phone yesterday." He stuck out a hand. "I'm Aaron."

She immediately made the connection between the name and a sculpture of wings that she'd been drooling over since her first day. His grip was firm, and though his fingers were long and elegant, she could feel the calluses. "Aaron Maclean, the sculptor. Your work is amazing," Sam said, and meant it. He looked to be around her age, and she wondered if they'd gone to school together and she'd simply missed him. It would be just one more regret if she had.

"Thanks," Aaron said, his grin flashing, bright blue eyes crinkling at the corners. "Yours is pretty awesome, too. Zoe mentioned it," he said quickly before she could ask. "I'm really nosy. Just for future reference."

Sam snorted. "You must be from around here, then."

"Nope. I'm from a little town in upstate New York where my genius was unappreciated."

"So you came . . . here," Sam said slowly, trying to find the sense in it. Aaron chuckled, seeming to understand.

"I followed a cute firefighter. Don't judge."

Sam widened her eyes dramatically and leaned in close. "I would *never*."

That prompted a musical laugh. "Oh, hang around me a little more and you definitely will."

Sam decided she was willing to see if that was true—Aaron seemed like fun, and she could use more of that in her life. Of course, he also seemed like the kind of friend who might occasionally require bail money, but it seemed like a risk worth taking if she could start laughing regularly again. She missed having artist friends . . . even if she wasn't sure she was really an artist anymore.

They'd just settled into conversation when Zoe appeared at Aaron's side. She barely came up to his shoulder, but her presence was twice her actual size. One hand settled on her hip. The other tugged at his sleeve.

"Sorry to take you away from *eating all of my food*, Aaron, but I need you to do more than stand around looking pretty for a minute."

He looked down at her, amused. "Stepladder not high enough for you again?"

Zoe's gray eyes glittered in the light, one eyebrow arching dangerously. "You know, no one's going to buy your beautiful sculptures if I shove them all where I'm thinking of shoving them."

"Ouch."

"You know I love you, Aaron," Zoe said, lips curving even as her expression said he'd better get his butt in gear. Sam stifled a laugh. Aaron sighed loudly.

"Your love is a painful and frightening thing. But since I'm a gentleman, I'll go reach things for you." He inclined his head. "Nice meeting you, Sam. Let me know when you're in the mood, and we'll go out and make a spectacle of ourselves."

"Definitely," she replied, and Zoe flattened her hands on his back to guide him away, shaking her head no at Sam with a mixture of horror and amusement.

She turned back to straightening the table, then moved to start lighting the candles. It was only when her cheeks began to ache that she realized she was still smiling. As Friday nights in the Cove went, she decided as jazz music began to drift softly through the air, mingling with the chatter of the Two Roads artists, it didn't get better than this. And for once, she didn't mind the feeling at all.

Jake threw his head back and laughed, his warm breath rising like fog in the night air. He was glad he'd let himself be dragged out for dinner at Merry Meet, which was running specials because of First Friday. It had been a tough week, and he hadn't been able to find his footing to weather it the way he usually did. Tonight, though, his world finally felt right again.

Shane gave Max a good-natured shove as they wandered in a laughing, constantly shifting mass down the sidewalk. Thea and Kallie had their heads together, and he heard the word "Cancun." Probably already hashing out the spring vacation, which they all chipped in on and took, with very few exceptions, every year. Not last year, though . . . he'd begged off. Work, he'd told them, unable to articulate the actual reason. All he'd known was, the thought of participating in the creation of another album full of pictures of all of them drinking and dancing on or around a beach somewhere had made him want to go on a vacation in the opposite direction. By himself. To a place where he might actually be able to meet women without his entourage scaring them off.

Jake shoved the thought away, feeling his mood hovering somewhere just above his head like a black cloud and threatening to descend again. What the hell was wrong with him? He had good friends here, and a spare bedroom full of unruly fur balls back at home, with Tucker keeping watch by the door. It was a beautiful early October night. Life was just fine. It was normal. It was—

"Did you guys want to turn around? All that's left up here is the tea shop and the gallery," Thea said, looking around as though she hadn't realized how far they'd gone. Max had an arm slung around her, the way he had since high school. It had always struck Jake as more than a little possessive, but Thea seemed to like it. As slim and dark haired as Max was burly and blond, Thea should have looked like an odd match for her husband. Instead, Jake had a hard time imagining one without the other. They were the glue, he thought, that held the rest of them together.

Or maybe just the people who make sure the bubble around them stays intact and impossible to get into . . . or out of.

Jake blinked. *Shit.* He hadn't quite shaken that mood off after all.

Jake turned to look in the direction they'd come from, seeing the soft glow of the lamplights around the square. A band called the Shoes played classic rock on a make-shift stage near the Cove's famous Witch Tree in the square, and he could hear a decent rendition of "Layla" being played. The street was lined with cars, and despite the deepening chill it seemed like most of the Cove was out milling around, sampling food and drink, shopping the displays on the sidewalk. Even up here, near the edge of the celebration, there were plenty of people. And as Jake turned, he could see why.

Sometime over the course of the past year, Two Roads had become a draw.

"The gallery's pretty cool," Kallie said, shivering a lit-tle in the thin jacket she'd worn. She slid a quick look at Ryan, who was as oblivious as usual. That torch had to be getting heavy after carrying it all these years, Jake thought.

"Why don't we check it out?" Ryan said, stuffing his hands deeper in his jacket pockets and pointedly ignor-ing Kallie's looks. He raised his eyebrows at Jake. "They have food and heat, and I'm freezing my ass off. This is the coldest night we've had so far."

He could hear the soft sound of live jazz from inside as the front door opened and shut, warm chatter drifting out to them. He wondered, not for the first time, if Sam was working tonight. Maybe not, but probably. And wanting to find out hadn't quite overridden his concern that if he saw her before their date she'd find a way to back out of it, the occasional funny text message notwithstanding.

Still, the thought that she was only feet away was impossible to ignore.

When he turned his attention back to his friends, though, Jake could see he was in the minority.

"I don't feel like looking at art," Thea said stiffly, and in an instant, Jake knew she'd already heard who was working there. His visions of some sort of pleasant reconciliation, vague though they were, started crumbling around him. In the empty place they'd left behind, annoyance bloomed.

"I didn't feel like looking at ceramic pumpkins with weird faces on them," Jake replied. "You didn't hear me complaining. Come on. I haven't been in here before."

There was a flicker of temper across Thea's face, gone almost as quickly as it had appeared. She could be a sweetheart, Jake thought, but he'd seen the flip side of that, too. He just ignored it when it wasn't directed at him . . . which was almost always. It bothered him even less than he might have imagined to take some heat now. She'd get over it.

"Fine," Thea said stiffly. "Just for a few minutes, though. They've got drink specials at the Tavern, and I'd rather be having a half-price beer than staring at some cut-rate artist's abstract painting of boobs. This isn't New York City."

The sharp edge to her words startled him into speech before he could think too much about it. "Jesus, Thea. If you're that excited about parking it at the amazing Harvest Cove Tavern—*again*—go for it. I'm about done for the night anyway."

She blinked, as though his words didn't quite compute. "What?"

Max puffed up and glared at him, which was the usual progression of things. "What crawled up your ass and died, Jake? She's tired of walking around. I think we all are. You don't have to be a dick about it."

On a normal night, he would have shrugged it off, made some stupid joke, and they would have gone on with their plans at the Tavern. But on a normal night he wouldn't have made an issue of going into Two Roads in the first place. This was a just-for-fun night. He was happy as long as he was occupied and in good company.

He was now tired of being occupied, and the company was quickly headed south. Now he remembered why he'd begged off last month's First Friday and watched a movie with Fitz, the only member of their usual crew who was missing tonight. Fitz had gotten awfully good at going missing when he felt like it . . . which was increasingly often.

Since that never seemed to elicit more than grumbling from one or two people, Jake thought, maybe he should ask for pointers.

"If my wanting to do something different upsets you, go for it," Jake said, putting up his hands as he took a couple of steps back and then turned around. "I'll be in here getting warm. See you guys later."

There was a weight off his chest the second he turned around, so sudden it surprised him. It shouldn't have been a big deal. He was ditching a night at the bar for an art gallery, which sounded a lot nobler before you factored in Sam. Still, the fact that he didn't feel much but relief was a warning sign he couldn't ignore. He'd always been easygoing off the field—and these days, out of the office—unless it was something he felt strongly about. But that didn't equal pushover. Never had.

He guessed it was time for a reminder.

Jake walked away, turning onto the walk up to the gallery's front door without bothering to look back. He could feel their eyes on him, and their surprise. He heard a muttered, "Screw this. I'm freezing," then rapid footfalls, and Ryan fell into step beside him. Jake half expected to see Kallie too, but it was quickly apparent that she'd chosen Thea this time around. Another old, hard-to-break pattern. Tonight, he was grateful for it.

Ryan shot a look at him. "You in a bad mood?" he asked.

"Nope," Jake replied. "Just want to see something beautiful."

There was a soft chuckle. "I guess I heard something about that."

Jake turned his head to look at his friend curiously. "So are you really that cold or do you actually want to look at art?" he asked. Ryan was a former baseball player who taught history and coached at the high school now. He wasn't necessarily someone you'd expect to discover in a gallery, but then again, Jake thought, still mulling the ugly reactions of the friends now walking away from them, it was possible to discover new things about people you'd known for years. Or at least, it was possible to find things you'd willfully overlooked.

Ryan shrugged. "Both, I guess. I've been in here once or twice. It's pretty cool."

Jake didn't have much time to mull that before pushing open the door and being hit with a welcome blast of warmth from inside. They stepped in, letting the door shut behind them. He looked around, taking in the surprise that was all around him as his senses filled with the sounds of conversation and music, the scent of cinnamon and spice, and the mix of color and shape and form that manifested in dozens of different ways all around him, drawing his eyes from painting to sculpture, photograph to carving. He took another step in, slightly overwhelmed, but in a pleasant way.

This sort of thing wasn't at all his area, but he found it welcoming and interesting just the same. Even more because his first thought was that this was Sam's world. He wanted to know who and what else inhabited it.

"Ryan! I was hoping we'd see you!"

He turned his head to watch Zoe Watson, whom he'd never officially met, approaching them. Her eyes were as warm as her smile, the gray striking against her skin. Jake took a moment to appreciate the curves showcased by the belted tunic sweater she wore over black leggings. He'd only ever seen her from a distance. She was much prettier—not to mention shorter—than he'd realized.

Struck by a sudden suspicion, he glanced at Ryan, wondering if maybe this was the reason for his interest. But while his friend was returning her smile, there was nothing out of the ordinary about it. Actually, he looked a little uncomfortable. Probably, Jake thought, because Zoe Watson had just made a liar out of him. A greeting like that said he'd been in here more than just a couple of times.

Why it would bother Ryan to have him know that was something he'd consider later. Right now, he was more interested in finding a certain artsy blonde.

"Hey, Zoe," Ryan said. "How's it going?"

"Good," she said, stopping as she reached them. "We've had a really nice crowd tonight. Think I drummed up some business, too." Even in her tall, heeled boots, she barely came up to Jake's shoulder. He looked down at her curiously. She seemed to sense his attention and met his gaze with a frankly curious one of her own.

"I don't think we've met," she said, and extended a hand. "Zoe Watson. This is my gallery."

Jake smiled and shook, enveloping her small, warm hand in his own. "Jake Smith. I'm one of the vets at the animal hospital here."

"That explains why I haven't met you." Her smile was slow and genuine. "I've been so busy with this place I can't even keep houseplants alive. A pet is probably a year or two away."

"That's a level of self-awareness more people ought to have. Believe me," he said.

"Well, I'm also self-aware enough to know I'll probably get the kind of dog you hate to see coming. Small, yappy, bites ankles, adorable when not trying to harm other animals or humans. You know."

Jake groaned. "I do know. Only too well." He let his eyes sweep the room as she laughed. It didn't stop her from noticing.

"Looking for someone?" Zoe asked.

"Yeah, actually. Is Sam Henry working tonight?" That piqued her interest so quickly he could almost see her ears prick up.

"You're in luck. Sam's back there, by the really bright

canvas just to the left," she continued, indicating the direction with a nod of her head. She didn't bother to disguise the interest and speculation now clearly visible in her stormy eyes.

"Thanks," Jake said. And along with his flush came what felt like a completely ridiculous grin. He felt like he'd just told a fellow five-year-old that he liked a girl. And unlike the people he'd walked here with, Zoe actually seemed to enjoy hearing about it.

"No problem. And welcome to Two Roads. It's nice to see new faces in here . . . whatever the reason," she added, with a knowing look at Jake.

He turned to go, then paused when she continued talking to Ryan. "You know, the sculptor of the piece you've had your eye on is with her. I'm sure he'd be happy to tell you a little more about it, if you're interested. If not, he'll talk your ear off anyway. Fair warning."

Jake turned his head and only just caught a glimpse of the oddest look he'd ever seen on Ryan's face before it relaxed into his usual affable expression. "That's great, thanks."

He brushed the odd moment off quickly enough once he caught sight of ice blond hair glinting in the light. With a final wave to Zoe, Jake made a beeline to where Sam stood in the midst of a group of people he didn't know, holding court in a way he wouldn't have expected from her. He slowed as he got closer, as captivated by her as her audience appeared to be. In all the chatter, he couldn't quite make out her words, but he saw every nuance of her expressive face, every gesture, the way her smile widened as someone said something that amused her.

As he watched, she lifted a hand to tuck her hair behind her ear, shifting her attention from a wild-looking bearded man in a string tie and a checkered shirt to a tall, whip-thin guy with a blue streak in his hair. There were others in their little group, too, but they faded into the background for him. All Jake saw were the long waves of hair, the open, beautiful face, and the way her short, shapeless little dress that rippled with her every movement somehow managed to make his mouth water more than any bikini ever could.

"Holy shit," Ryan muttered beside him. "No wonder you told Thea to shove it."

As he started forward again, she threw back her head and laughed, a loud, sensual roll of sound that was an echo of something he'd heard long ago, and then only a handful of times. She'd been too nervous, or too serious, always watching and cautious about reacting. But a few times, she'd laughed like that. The confident, beautiful woman in front of him had been only a glimmer then. He'd seen it, though.

And then he'd walked away.

The guilt hit him like a punch in the gut. It was as though Sam could feel it—her eyes met his right at that instant, and he could see her hesitate, falter.

No. Don't you disappear on me.

He closed the distance between them, feeling the curious eyes of her friends on him. None of it mattered. The only one he wanted to see was her.

"Hey," he said, hoping he seemed as casual as he wanted to.

"Hey, yourself," she replied as people shifted to make room for him. Whatever she'd done to her eyes tonight made them look lit from within. He'd seen those unusual eyes in his dreams for years—deep, burning blue lightening to bursts of green around each pupil. They were wary as she watched him now, but not as bad as that day he'd asked her out. Progress was progress.

"Who's this?" blue streak asked. "Boyfriend?"

The awkward question, so smoothly delivered, was worth fielding just to see Sam's face. She looked like she might choke on her own tongue. "Um, n—"

"Old friend," Jake interjected. "We're just getting re-acquainted."

Blue streak's lips curved into a suggestive smile as he looked between the two of them. "*That* sounds fun."

Jake bit back a laugh. Sam gave her friend a solid smack on the arm.

"Rude," blue streak informed her, then introduced himself. "I'm Aaron Maclean, God of Art."

"Cool. I'm Jake Smith, Beastmaster. This is my buddy Ryan Weston, God of B—"

Okay, God of Balls is not going to be taken the right way. Don't say it.

"Baseball," Ryan finished for him, seeming to sense that Jake's foot in his own mouth was imminent. They all shook, including Sam as she was reintroduced to Ryan. She didn't seem especially bothered by seeing him. He tried to take that as promising, though Ryan had never been much of a standout in the jerk department. He also seemed pretty preoccupied, which had to make it easier.

"I've been looking at some of your work," Ryan was saying to Aaron. "Especially the one called *Unfurl*. It's . . . it's really something."

It was such an un-Ryan-like comment that Jake opened his mouth to tease him about it. Sam caught his eye at the last second, though, and something he saw there made him hold his tongue. Her eyebrow arched, ever so slightly, and there was a barely perceptible shake of her head. Aaron was looking with interest at Ryan, his head slightly tilted.

"Oh?"

Ryan shifted uncomfortably and seemed to be trying to disappear into his jacket. "Yeah."

"Well, thank you. It's one of my favorites too, actually."

Jake watched a smile of genuine pleasure bloom across Ryan's boyish face. And just like that, something clicked deep in the recesses of Jake's brain. His eyes widened as they darted between the artist and his buddy. His old school buddy, whom he'd known for-freaking-ever. And who, he now realized, hadn't had a steady girlfriend that anyone had actually *seen* in all the years he'd known him.

Because . . .

Sam had sucked her lower lip into her mouth and seemed to be trying very hard to contain her amusement at his expense, which meant he looked like he'd just been hit by a ton of bricks. He quickly schooled his expression back into pleasant interest, though he couldn't keep from darting another look at Sam's mouth. That full bottom lip looked tasty as hell. He'd like to try it himself. Nibbling . . . sucking.

He dragged his eyes away and shifted uncomfortably. He needed to get his mind out of the gutter before everyone, Aaron Maclean included, got a good look at just what kind of reacquainting he was thinking about doing this evening.

Aaron, at least, seemed too distracted to notice. "Would you like to go have a look at it?" he asked Ryan. "I can answer any questions you've got better than anyone. If you're really interested, that is."

"I am," Ryan said quickly, then laughed and rubbed a hand across the back of his neck. "I mean, yeah. I'm definitely interested. Let's have a look."

The two of them walked away, and when Aaron turned his head, Jake could tell he exchanged some sort of look with Sam. She flashed a devastating grin that made his breath catch. Then it was just the two of them, the rest of her little group having moved on to talk with other people. Jake stepped closer. For just a few minutes, he wanted her to himself. And he planned to enjoy it. He'd wrap his mind around the whole Ryan thing later. It wasn't a bad surprise, but it still just about knocked him on his ass.

He tried to imagine Ryan announcing his plus one for the Cancun vacation was a guy. The girls would be fine with it, though Kallie was going to take this hard when it came out. The guys ... he wasn't sure. He wanted to think it would be okay.

Of course, he wanted to think they'd be okay with Sam, too, and that was seeming like more and more of a long shot right now. But she wasn't one of their own. Ryan had that advantage.

"Huh," Sam said, looking in the direction Aaron and Ryan had gone. "Didn't see that one coming."

That made two of them. Sam seemed to have relaxed, at least. And the humor glittering in her eyes was good to see, even though he knew he was the one who'd caused most of it. She returned her attention to him, a faint frown marring her brow, and said, "I thought he would have come out long before now."

He inhaled so quickly that he started coughing, which startled Sam before sending her into fresh peals of laughter. It took him a minute, but once he'd started breathing normally again, he shook his head balefully.

"You did *not* know about this."

"I have two eyes and a brain, so, *yes*, I knew about this," she replied. "I take it this is complete news to you, though."

Jake tried to articulate his shock. "I think . . . I think Ryan was actually *blushing*."

Sam widened her eyes indulgently and nodded. "Uh-huh."

"I didn't." He blinked a few times, then looked at Sam beseechingly. "But . . ."

She gave his back a tentative, sympathetic pat. The warmth of her touch, light though it was, went a long way toward helping him find his footing again.

"It's okay, Jake. Ryan is following in the footsteps of giants. Mr. Sulu. Gandalf. Dumbledore. Totally, awesomely gay. This is not a world-ending event."

He shook his head slowly, trying to put his thoughts into words. "I know it's not. I just don't know how I missed this. Seriously."

She shrugged. "Probably because he's not comfortable telling you yet. Seriously. I doubt he even knows how obvious he is." Then she grinned. "Our friends like each other. It's so cute. We can pass notes for them in class."

He winced. "Uh. I'm pretty sure Ryan can handle himself." His eyes closed. "I said that wrong. You know what? Never mind. How's the night going?"

Sam sighed softly and looked up at him. "Just don't flake out on him if and when he actually tells you, okay? I've known too many people who had to go through that."

She was cute when she was lecturing him, he thought, torn between bemusement and irritation. *She doesn't know you anymore,* he reminded himself. Still, it wasn't flattering that she thought there was even a possibility he would abandon his friend just because he was into guys.

Because obviously he'd never abandoned anyone for an even stupider reason before.

"Sam. Ryan is one of my oldest friends. It's different, but not a big deal," he said.

Her look of relief banished the irritation completely. She wanted everyone to be accepted, he thought. Even former jocks who wouldn't have given her the time of day. That said a lot about the kind of heart she had.

Which brought him right back around to feeling like a jerk. At least *that* was familiar.

"Well, good," Sam said with a small nod. "And to answer your question, tonight's been great. Lots of people, lots of artists I can finally put a face to. And the food, which I've been too busy to eat. Which reminds me . . ." She trailed off and rose up on her tiptoes, craning her neck to see the buffet table. Then she cursed softly.

"I need to replenish everything. That table looks like it's been visited by locusts."

"Need help?" he asked. For a moment he thought she was going to accept, that she'd lay down her arms without any more bother and let herself fall back into the easy rhythm they'd once had with each other. They could—he knew it, had already sensed it in the moments she'd let her guard down. They could start getting to know each other again tonight, instead of tomorrow. But nothing about Sam had ever been easy, and when she looked between him and the table, the line of her mouth hardening with determination, he knew this would be no exception.

She hadn't decided what to make of him yet.

The "yet" kept him from pushing. He'd see her tomorrow. They had time.

"I'm good," Sam said. "I can handle it myself." She paused, considering him with a look he couldn't read. "Thanks, though."

"Anytime," Jake replied. She studied him, then nodded and offered him a small smile.

"Ryan's going to be upset you're dragging him away."

"He can stay. I'll let him know I'm out of here, though, before I go," he said. "He might want to catch up with the others."

"Ah," she said, her eyes going shaded. "Big plans tonight, then."

"Not for me," Jake replied. "My plans involve my couch, my dog, and the TV. And making sure the current crop of fur balls doesn't wreck what's left of my spare bedroom." When she looked surprised, he leaned in close so she could hear him better—and so he could breathe in her perfume just a little bit more. There was something she needed to understand, something he'd keep repeating until Sam accepted it as the truth . . . because it was.

"I told you, Sam. I grew up. You're going to find that out."

"Maybe," she replied quietly. "I'll see you tomorrow, Jake." Her voice was firm, but her eyes lingered on him, questioning, before she walked away.

Chapter Eight

As much as she wanted time to just slow down so she could either prepare for or indefinitely delay it, Saturday arrived in a blaze of mild nausea and at least ten outfit changes. By the time there was a series of rapid-fire knocks at her bedroom door, it was five thirty and Sam was standing helplessly in the middle of the room in her underwear and a retro Depeche Mode T-shirt, her hair piled on top of her head in a makeshift bun. And panicking. Quietly.

"I'm fine, Mom! I don't want the herbal tea. I mean it. I'll be fine," she said in response to the knocks, hoping she sounded more together than she was. Her mother had been trying to force chamomile tea on her all afternoon, insisting it would help her relax. Just to be contrary, Sam had drunk several cups of coffee instead.

The fact that her entire body now seemed to be vibrating told her she hadn't really thought that one through very well.

The door opened partway, and a dark head poked around the side. A pair of big blue eyes gave her a quick, dispassionate once-over. There was a sigh, a shake of the head.

"You need help."

"Nice to see you too, Em," Sam said, then stuck her tongue out at her older sister as she walked in and shut the door behind her. As usual, Emma looked practically perfect in every way, Mary Poppins minus the whimsy. She was classically beautiful, ivory-skinned, with delicate features and big blue eyes. Her trim little pin-striped suit jacket coordinated with everything from her jeans and her kitten heels to her pearls. All she needed was an umbrella and a carpetbag.

"Jackie O called. She wants her wardrobe back," Sam grumbled as Emma began digging through the clothes on the bed. Emma didn't even look up.

"Better Jackie O than Lady Gaga. You can't go out in your underwear." Emma sighed again, a sound that set Sam's teeth on edge. "Where are you going to eat?"

"Someplace with burgers," Sam replied. It shouldn't be this big a deal. She'd seen him last night and nothing catastrophic had happened, right? But that had been a relatively brief meeting in a crowd of people. Tonight, it was just *them*. And if he showed up looking half as good as he had at the gallery, she ran a much higher risk of things like awkward staring and dropping food on herself. She wasn't sure whether the feeling mixed with the panic right now was actual excitement or just impending doom.

"Burgers?" Emma looked at her strangely. "Really?"

"It's not a date." It sounded stupid and defensive even to her, but she was sticking to it.

"Well . . ." Emma hesitated, then seemed to decide it wasn't worth getting into. "Okay. But you should still look like you put in some effort." She looked over the pile of clothes on Sam's bed and poked it tentatively. "What's . . . ? No. You can't wear *that*."

Sam crossed her hands over her chest and watched as her sister sorted through her wardrobe with all the efficiency of a well-trained soldier. Resistance, she knew, was futile. On the upside, no matter how long it had been since they'd seen each other, it was always as though no time had passed. Of course, that was also the downside.

"I thought you were still out of town bossing other people around," Sam said.

"I was. That got boring, so I came back to boss you around. Having fun yet?"

"No."

"Excellent," Emma replied. "And for the record, I hate that you wear so much black. You look like an undertaker." In rapid succession she tossed onto the bed a pair of dark jeans, a plain black V-neck tee, and a red infinity scarf. She turned her triumphant gaze to Sam. "There. Heels. No necklace, big earrings. Oh, and that leather jacket I saw wadded up on the bench downstairs. You'll look like you, but not quite so much like . . . you. Any questions?"

"Yes," Sam replied, looking at the bed. "Were you adopted?"

"No, you were. Because the aliens left you here." Emma looked at her for a long moment, and finally her lips curved into a small but genuine smile. Sam returned it, feeling an odd tug at her heart, bittersweet and strong. Maybe she'd actually missed some things about Harvest Cove after all. Or maybe she was getting very close to having a complete nervous breakdown.

Yeah, probably that.

Still, Sam gave in to the mushiness and threw her arms around her sister, giving her a bear hug. Emma stiffened right up—she always did—but Sam was used to it. She simply hung on until Emma relaxed and hugged her back. Sam breathed in her sister's scent, something with blackberries and musk. She'd always smelled good, even when they were kids.

"It's good to see you," Sam said.

"You too," Emma replied, sounding both sincere and like she was resigned to the display of sisterly affection. She hadn't always been so uptight. Sometimes, like now, she even let the shields down a little. But when their father had died, a little piece of her sister had gone with him . . . and Sam knew that at this point, it probably wasn't coming back.

"Isn't he supposed to be here in half an hour?" Emma finally asked.

"More like twenty minutes now, but yeah."

"You're stalling."

"Maybe."

Emma pulled back, and Sam was dismayed to see what she thought of as her sister's "disapproving schoolmarm" face. The moment between them, such as it was, had passed. At least it had helped her remember that Emma wasn't *always* impossible. That she even genuinely missed her. Sometimes.

"Do you want my opinion?" Emma asked.

"No."

"I thought you came home to get your head on straight," Emma said, ignoring her. "You just got back. I don't think this is going to help."

Sam looked at her sister strangely, feeling her temper flicker to life. Yeah, this was back to normal, all right. "I didn't need to get my head on straight. I needed a job. A roof over my head. *Funds.* My head's on just fine, though, thanks."

The eye roll she got in return put her back up even further.

"Sam, being an artist who doesn't actually make art is *not* having your head on straight," Emma said.

Sam bristled. "I paint."

"No, you don't," Emma shot back. "You haven't put anything new on your site in months, and I know you. When something is wrong, you hide."

The news that her sister had actually been keeping up with her work was both thrilling and infuriating. She hadn't thought Emma paid any attention. And now she had to wonder whether it was out of genuine interest or simply another part of her need to control everything in her universe.

"I am not *hiding*." She glared at Emma, who was now standing with her hands on her hips looking imperious. It was a look her sister had perfected over many years, but having seen it a thousand times didn't make it any more palatable. "Don't you listen? No, never mind. I already know the answer to that."

Sam grabbed the jeans from her bed and pulled them on with a series of angry little jerks. She wished it wasn't always like this with the two of them. Things started off fine, then went to hell in a handbasket within ten minutes or so every single time. It wasn't that she thought Emma didn't care. It's that she was always so amazingly, obnoxiously condescending about it.

"You didn't even tell me you were coming back!" Emma said, her cool facade already cracking. The ability to do that had long been one of Sam's great triumphs in life. "The last time we talked you were talking about finding a different place, looking for a different roommate—"

"Things came to a head kind of . . . abruptly," she replied. "Michelle didn't feel like waiting for me to sort out my living situation, things at work had totally dead-ended, and I just . . ." She trailed off, searching for words that wouldn't come. Finally, she just sighed and spread her hands. "What else could I do, Em?"

It was, as she suspected, the one thing Emma didn't have an answer for. And that was a relief, because she didn't really have room in her evening for a blowout with her sister. Her anger had already gone, replaced by the weariness she felt anytime she thought too deeply about what had brought her back. She didn't want to think about it anymore. She'd spent what felt like ages thinking about it. All she really wanted to do was move forward, if she could figure out how.

"Well," Emma finally said, "I wish you would have at least called. You didn't even ask me about a job before you went looking."

Sam arched an eyebrow. "Seriously? You don't want me working for you any more than I want to be working for you. You don't get to be offended about that. The gallery suits me. Event planning? We both know how good I'd be at that."

She saw she'd hit her mark when Emma pursed her lips, considered, then sighed. "Fine. But I still think—"

"No. No more about how I should start over and maybe get a business degree and join the damn Garden Club. I can handle my own life, Em," Sam said firmly, cutting her off. She didn't want to fight. She wanted to dwell on her impending train wreck of a date. Leave it to Emma, who was forever lecturing her on poor planning, to screw up the few plans she actually had.

Emma tucked a lock of hair behind her ear and tilted her head. "Really. Because you don't *look* like you're handling it. You're living with Mom. I don't even *know* what some of these clothes are," she said, wrinkling her nose as she prodded a pair of leather pants, "and you're going to dinner with Jake Smith. Jake the Life Ruiner."

She'd been waiting for that. At least Emma was loyal; she'd say that for her. That awful day she'd pegged Jake in the head with the picture she'd done, she'd gone home and called the only friend she had, imperfect though the relationship was—her sister, away at college but always willing to listen. There had been no lecture that day, only sympathy. And as far as she knew, Emma had never forgiven Jake for being the source of Sam's misery.

A closer look at Emma's worried frown confirmed that. Guilt twisted like a knife in her gut.

Sam pulled on her shirt. "It's just dinner," she muttered, looking away.

"Hmm."

"Don't *hmm* me, Em. I'm not in the mood. It's dinner. End of story."

Emma fell silent, but she didn't seem inclined to leave, so Sam decided that ignoring her was the best option. She took her hair down, letting it fall in the loose waves that the bun had created, and raked her fingers through it. Then she looped the scarf around her neck, trying to remember if she'd ever even worn it before. She had only a vague recollection of buying it. It was so . . . red.

When she finally glanced back at Emma, she found her sister lost in thought, her eyes far away. In that moment, Sam was startled to see an expression that she'd often seen on their mother's face, especially the year their father had died. Emma looked like the weight of the world was on her shoulders. She looked . . . tired. Sam frowned, jarred by the sight. What did Emma have to worry about? She actually *had* her shit together. Enough that she was probably qualified to give annoying lectures to other people about it, even. Just not her.

"What?" Sam asked, glad when it seemed to jolt Emma out of her own thoughts, her lovely face settling into more familiar lines.

"Nothing," Emma said, her posture returning to its usual rigid lines. "Just remember what you came back for. Eyes on the prize. That's all."

Emma was actually worried about her. It was both touching and weird, so Sam sought to dispel that as quickly as possible.

"Do you think it would help if I came down the stairs blaring "Eye of the Tiger" when Jake gets here? That would send a message."

Emma closed her eyes briefly, looked like she was praying for patience, and then turned away "Whatever. I'm going down to see Mom. Do what you want." She hesitated, then glanced back at her, her voice gentling slightly. "You look good. Not as much like a vampire. A little color goes a long way, you know. You ought to try it more often."

Sam blinked. "Oh. Thanks." She'd been annoyed enough that she hadn't remembered to argue about the clothes Emma had picked, even if they did look good together. That seemed like kind of a big oversight on her part. She made a mental note not to forget again.

"You're welcome," Emma replied.

Sam distinctly heard her sister mutter an additional *"Idiot,"* as she shut the door. And with that, they were back on familiar footing. She shook her head and headed to the dresser to dig in her makeup bag. The evening at least required some lipstick. And her hoop earrings, which she'd been planning to wear regardless. Emma didn't know *everything*. When she found the tube of lipstick she wanted, Sam straightened in front of the mirror. The sight of her own reflection startled her enough that she simply stood there for a moment, staring.

"Huh," she finally said. The scarf should have been a small thing. Instead, it changed the entire outfit, accentuating her unusual eyes, the color of her skin. The effect was ... different. Maybe Emma was onto something.

"Or maybe even a stopped clock is right twice a day," she said to herself, frowning. She was perfectly comfortable with the way she looked now, a huge change from the last time she'd lived in this house. And she *liked* wearing black. She started to pull off the scarf, frustrated. Black suited her. Why mess with what worked? Her hands stilled as some part of her immediately arrived at an answer.

Maybe because it's good for style to evolve, genius. Style and everything else. Isn't one of the reasons you left New York because you were tired of feeling like you were standing still?

Sam let the soft fabric drop back against her chest. Arguing with Emma was one thing, but it wouldn't do much good to argue with herself. She sighed, then put on her lipstick. Red, like the scarf. She was about done with change for the time being, but a little thing like this—a little splash of color where there had been none before—couldn't hurt.

She hoped.

It had been a while since he'd felt like an awkward teenager, but standing on the Henrys' front porch shuffling his feet certainly did the trick.

Jake heard muffled voices inside once he rang the bell, a laugh he recognized as Andi's, and an irritated retort from—hell, was that Emma? Of course it was. This didn't feel anything like a garden variety date. It was more like being thrown into some kind of weird time vortex. He was eighteen again, except this time he'd finally gotten the balls to get over himself and go apologize. He saw a slim figure in dark clothes descend the stairs, distorted by the glass. Any second now Sam would open the door, and he could almost believe it would be her seventeen-year-old self looking back at him. She would still have been furious with him, he thought. But it would have been easier to make it right. It would have been—

Damn.

"Hey." Sam stepped out the front door, shutting it quickly behind her. Jake drank her in, momentarily at a loss about what to say. At some point he was going to have to get used to the way she looked now. Soon, hopefully, since the sight of her kept knocking him on his ass.

Jake let his gaze drift over her from head to toe. Last night, and even the day at his office, she'd been the sexy professional. Tonight, she was just Sam, and that was even better. She wore black again—that seemed to be a theme with her. Still, he couldn't complain. Everything she wore showcased her figure perfectly, skimming over the lithe curves she'd once hidden. Even her leather jacket left him inordinately preoccupied with how her waist nipped in. Then there was her hair, a mass of pale blond waves that made him wonder how it would feel in his hands. Or how it might look spread beneath her on his bed.

"Nice scarf," he said, his voice sounding strained. It

was a nice scarf, he thought. Too bad his attention had been everywhere but. He could pretend, though. The color, at least, had registered.

She wrinkled her nose at the compliment before giving him a quiet "Thanks." He didn't know what that was about and hoped that, for once, it wasn't him. They stood there on the porch, staring awkwardly at each other while pretending to be perfectly relaxed in the chill evening air. Sam had been easier to read, once. Now all he saw was cool and collected.

He wished he'd brought Loki along. "Cool and collected" seemed to go out the window when there was a kitten on her head. Or when he got close enough to kiss her.

"So," he said, feeling like a complete idiot.

"So," she echoed, but with a tiny curve of her mouth and a slight arching of one brow, as if to say, *"Yes, you are a complete idiot."* Somehow, feeling like they agreed on something helped him to relax a little.

"You look beautiful," he said. He could see the compliment startled her, but at least it didn't seem unwelcome. Uncomfortable, maybe, but not unwelcome.

"Oh. Thanks." Her gaze turned more direct then, her composure slipping a little. "You look good, too. Very, ah . . . your coat. It's nice." Sam closed her eyes and smiled as if to acknowledge the complete absurdity of the situation. When Jake couldn't suppress a chuckle, she laughed too, a soft, breathy, slightly embarrassed sound.

"Well," Jake said, "I am pretty stylish."

Sam opened her eyes again, and they were far warmer than when she'd stepped out the door just a few minutes ago. "I can see that. Wore the formal high-tops and everything."

He looked down at his feet, and at the newish Chuck Taylors that had only recently replaced the ones with the holes in them. They seemed okay. No mud. He looked up, and was treated to a slow, broad smile that lit up her entire face and made her eyes gleam He remembered that smile. And his reaction, a punch of heat that rushed through his system like wildfire, was just the same.

"That's a low blow," he informed her, determined to stay calm, casual. "I wore my fancy shoes just for you."

"I bet." She shoved her hands into her jacket pockets. "So, I'm sure my mother and sister are in there trying to listen to us. Can we go before this turns into a makeover show? I'll never hear the end of it."

"Absolutely," Jake replied. "If we keep it up you're going to notice the hole in my jeans." He held out his hand, wondering if she'd take it. "Come on. Your chariot awaits."

Sam studied his hand, her expression guarded, before leaning to the side to look past him. "Why does my chariot look like a muddy pickup truck?"

"It's camouflaged so it doesn't get stolen. If you see any dog hair in there, that's camouflage, too. Just so you know."

This time she laughed, and Jake didn't bother hiding his grin. For a moment, all the tension and baggage between them had vanished, and they were just two people heading out on a date.

"See?" he said. "Told you we'd find things to talk about."

Sam widened her eyes, but the smile didn't leave her face as she headed for the truck. "Yes, you did. And I'm a little afraid to find out what's next."

"That's not fear. That's breathless anticipation. I get that a lot, you know."

He worried for a split second that she'd hear arrogance instead of a joke, but Sam's soft laugh said he didn't need to.

"I bet," she said. "Running away will definitely make you short of breath."

"Ouch."

"You take hostage pictures of my cat, this is what you get," she replied.

They walked through the grass together to the driveway, not quite close enough to touch. He could smell her perfume, light and sensual, winding through the autumn air. Jake got the door for her, noting the look she slid him before getting in. Some of what he saw was pure curiosity—she still didn't understand what they were doing here. Neither did he, really, so that didn't bother him. But the rest of what he caught in those striking eyes of hers threatened to make him hot in ways that were going to wind up really embarrassing if he let his mind wander too much.

Don't screw up, he told himself as he headed around to the driver's side. Sam didn't trust him, but she was still stuck with him for the next few hours. Not ideal, but not nothing, either. And he was good at working with what he had.

The problem was, he didn't know what exactly he *did* have here.

He just hoped he had enough time to figure it out before Sam decided it wasn't enough and walked away, out of his life. This time for good.

Chapter Nine

He took her to a place she'd never heard of, Beltane Blues, which was housed in a building with weathered clapboard siding down on Lammas Street, a block from where the rocky cove gave way to a stretch of sandy beach.

"Wasn't this Geno's?" she asked, frowning as she looked around. It smelled fantastic, but nothing like pizza. Jake came around the side of the truck, and she had to take a moment to remind herself that, yes, she was actually here with him. For all her teasing about his sneakers, he couldn't have looked more mouthwatering tonight if he'd tried. The wind ruffled his dark hair, and with his collar turned up by the breeze there was something darkly romantic about his looks. She'd always thought so, despite his all-American boy existence. Which made her glad all over again that he had no idea how many pictures she'd once drawn of him doing various darkly romantic things.

She felt the heat trying to creep into her cheeks. Some of the work had been pretty good, at least for her age. But even thinking about it made her feel like more of a Napoleon Dynamite than a Vincent Van Gogh.

He was a veterinarian, not a dark prince. And that

was fine, Sam thought. But ... the way he turned his head to look at her in the fading light, the last of the sun glittering in his eyes and turning them to gold, made any regrets she'd had about drawing him so many times with swords and armor — or just breeches — vanish. He'd been a perfect subject for a young girl's fantasy.

And though she'd grown past that, long ago realizing that abstract landscapes were really more her thing, she had to pat herself on the back for her taste. The man had great bone structure.

"Yeah, it used to be Geno's," Jake said, looking up at the building himself. It was nothing fancy, but Sam knew from long experience that the best places usually weren't. "Trey Abernathy bought it about three years ago, kicked the roaches out of the kitchen, and turned it into something pretty cool."

"Huh," Sam said. Apart from the touristy things in the Cove, like the historic little downtown and, of course, the Witch Tree, "cool" wasn't a word she would really have applied to anything here. She was skeptical, but she liked the old-fashioned neon sign, cursive letters lit electric blue. There was also the fact that her stomach was now growling piteously.

She turned her head to find Jake watching her intently. "I see I managed to surprise you already. Score one for me."

She didn't really have an answer for that, so she just gave him a disgruntled look and headed for the door. He was beside her in an instant, and every brush of his arm against hers sent tiny shocks sparking through her. Her entire body felt tense, alert in ways it hadn't been in longer than she cared to remember. It was good to feel awake this way again. She just knew she was going to have to watch it, or she'd wind up climbing Jake like a tree. Of course, he might like that. . . .

Not even going there. Friendly dinner, Sam. Friendly, fully clothed, not at all sexual dinner!

Jake opened the door for her, and they stepped inside the dimly lit restaurant.

"Oh," Sam said before she could stop herself. Nothing about the outside had prepared her for the interior. She'd been thinking something New England-y, like everything else around here—kitschy and cute, with some lighthouses or boat gear. Instead, she saw dark, gleaming wood floors, brick walls, a scatter of square and round tables with intriguingly mismatched chairs, and an eye-catching assortment of instruments and art hung on the walls. A long bar occupied most of one wall, and there was a raised platform at the far end of the room. The barstools had leopard print seats, and there were ornate candlesticks with burning candles scattered about the room. The soft, bluesy wail of a guitar wound through the comfortable din of conversation.

"Sam. Your mouth is open."

She snapped it shut, immediately embarrassed. Jake seemed amused, at least.

"Well?" he asked.

"I feel like I just walked into an alternate universe ruled by Aerosmith," she said. "But . . . it kind of works for me." She looked around again. "I hate to say this, but you've actually brought me someplace cool."

"Told you. Wait until you hear the band," Jake replied. He was looking awfully pleased with himself. "Believe it or not, this is an honest-to-God blues bar on weekends."

"Huh," Sam said again. What else could she say? Putting a blues bar in the Cove wasn't something that would ever have crossed her mind. And if someone had told her there was a need for that sort of thing here, she would have laughed. Yet here they were, and the place was bustling.

A hostess got them seated with a couple of menus and hurried off, leaving them comfortably ensconced at a corner table. Sam quietly perused the menu until their server had taken their drink orders. She was no longer just hungry; she was starving . . . and if the food on the menu was even half as good as it sounded, this place was a gem.

"So what do you think?" Jake asked. Sam arched an eyebrow.

"What do I think of what? The place? I told you, so far I like it. Pretty sure I've gained five pounds just looking at the menu."

"If you order a salad I may actually hold your cat hostage. Just so you know. This is like a temple of fried food. Eating healthy things here would be sacrilege."

Sam arched an eyebrow. "If you must know, I would probably eat cardboard if it was breaded and fried, so you don't need to worry. None of the grease gods will be angered in the ordering of my dinner."

Jake chuckled. "Just making sure, since I want to do the bacon cheesy fries for an appetizer and I'd rather not have a heart attack on the way home from eating them all myself."

Her mouth watered, partly from the description and partly from the way the corners of his eyes crinkled up when he grinned. It was a sorry fact that she had little willpower against either. Sam sighed and tossed her menu on the table in front of her.

"Sold. And just so you know, I'm going to hold this

against you when I get on the scale tomorrow." Especially since the burger she'd decided on was covered in even more bacon and barbecue sauce. "They even have fried pickles here. And hush puppies," she groaned, "I'm in so much trouble."

"They do lunch and takeout," Jake replied. "So, yes, you are. Maybe you should come running with me. It helps with the guilt."

"Running," Sam repeated. Did she look like she did that sort of thing? She wasn't usually mistaken for an athlete—her preferred footwear wasn't built for speed.

"Sure," Jake replied, so relaxed he might have been talking about the weather instead of pressing her to spend more time with him. *Already.* Her heart skipped along unevenly in her chest, and she was in serious danger of simply blurting out something stupid like, *"Okay!"* That would have been bad on a number of levels, the greatest of which was probably that she didn't run. Or in fact do much of anything aerobic if she could help it.

Their server arrived at that moment, sparing Sam from having to answer immediately. They ordered the appetizer and their burgers, and then Jake surprised her by adding on both fried pickles and a basket of hush puppies to the order. She stared at him in fascinated horror as the server walked away.

"We're never going to eat all that!"

He shrugged. "That's what take-home boxes are for."

"Well . . ." This was the part of Jake she'd forgotten about, mainly because she hadn't dealt with much of it personally. He was as stubborn as a mule. It was one of the things that had made him an excellent lacrosse player. It was also, she realized, what had gotten her here tonight. She exhaled loudly through her nose.

"I'm paying for half of this," she said.

"Nope."

Just like that, her wishes were dismissed. Sam fought the urge to bare her teeth at him. "Don't argue with me, Jake. I told you this wasn't a date, and I'm not treating it like one."

It wiped the smile off his face, but none of the stubbornness from his eyes. "I'm not arguing with you. I invited you. I'm paying. It's not a big deal, Sam."

She bristled, glaring at him helplessly. That was the root of the problem, she supposed, right there. To him, this was all no big deal. Everything was so easy for him. Getting her into his office, getting her here, buying dinner. Life. Some part of her knew the amount of anger she felt was outsize, but she didn't feel like fighting it. It wasn't just him. It was everything she didn't seem to have any control over. Which was . . . well, everything.

"Fine," Sam said flatly. "Whatever."

Jake looked at her for a moment. Then he said, "Is that something they teach you in New York?"

"What?"

"The amount of 'fuck you' implied in the word 'whatever.' Because that's seriously impressive."

Sam took a deep breath, licked her lips, and then braced her hands on the table. "Okay," she said. "Look, let's just forget this. It was a bad idea." She felt the blood rushing to her cheeks and wished she'd driven herself. Stupid mistake on her part. She started to rise, but Jake rose with her and caught her hand in his. The shock of contact, his warm skin against hers, stopped her long enough to listen.

"No, Jesus. I'm sorry, Sam. Just . . . sit, okay? If you want to split the bill we can. Whatever you're comfortable with. I was just trying to be a gentleman. Especially since I pushed you into coming. I figured it was the least I could do. Just . . . stay. Please."

Sam looked at him, those pretty eyes of his big and earnest, and felt like an ass for being so prickly. It was a reaction she had a hard time turning off with him, even though he hadn't done anything to deserve it. Yet. She just kept expecting him to. She sighed and sank back into her seat. Jake's hand lingered a moment longer before he pulled it away. Her skin tingled where it had been.

"Sorry," she muttered, shoving a hand through her hair. "For the implied 'fuck you,' I mean. I know you were trying to be polite. I just—"

"You expect me to be a jerk. I get it." Their server appeared to deliver their drinks, and Jake took a sip of his beer. Sam slid a finger down the side of hers, tracing a path through the condensation and avoiding his gaze. She'd expected the elephant in the room to be an issue at some point. She just hadn't expected it to wander over and sit on the table quite so soon.

"That's part of it," she admitted.

"If you hate me that much," he finally said, "why did you come?"

She looked up at him, startled by the bluntness of the question. She was even more startled by the hurt in his eyes. "I don't hate you," she said. This was the second time she'd felt like she'd actually landed a blow. She guessed she ought to feel triumphant, but she couldn't muster anything beyond guilt. It provoked an answer she might not have been inclined to give him otherwise.

"Honestly? I don't know what to make of you, Jake. A week ago, I wasn't thinking about doing anything but getting out of the city and leaving that mess behind. I figured I would see you, but I didn't think it would be anything more than a few seconds of embarrassment every now and then." She shifted uncomfortably.

"I hurt you," he said. So direct, just as he'd been in his office the other day. It was still unexpected. Though that wasn't saying much, since she'd expected nothing.

"Yes, you hurt me," Sam replied, her voice taking on the edge it always did when she was pushed into dealing with something she would rather have ignored. "We were kids. It was forever ago."

"And it left a hell of a mark. We might as well get this out in the open, Sam, because I'd really like to see you again, and you being pissed off at me on a permanent basis makes that a lot less likely to happen."

"I'm not—"

"Yeah, you are. So how do I turn that off? You tell me." He interrupted her smoothly. They stared at each other while their server cheerfully slid their appetizers onto the table, unaware that she'd wandered into the middle of a discussion that was more like a minefield. Once she'd gone, Sam grabbed a fried pickle chip, dipped it in the dressing that had come in a cup on the side, and popped it in her mouth. It was delicious, and afforded her a few seconds to figure out what she wanted to say.

"Okay," she finally said. *You can do this. After all this time, you might as well. And it makes more sense than dumping the fries over his head and storming out, since he's at least trying, for once.* "Here's the thing. Despite whatever you may think, I don't hate you. I would rather hate you, but I don't. In fact, I came tonight because you've been annoyingly likable every time I've seen you since I came home. I don't really know what to do with that."

Jake swirled a hush puppy in the honey it had arrived with. "Well, you could just accept that you like me and go with it."

He made it sound so easy. Like she shouldn't worry at all about her heart being reduced to a pile of smoking rubble. *Again.* "Sure. I could do that. And then you can pretend you don't know me when we run into your buddies. You can even tell them I'm still a . . . what did you tell them that day? That I was just some creepy little stalker? Pretty sure those are the words I heard when I was walking away. It would be just like old times."

He winced, but this time she didn't feel any guilt at all. Maybe he didn't remember that day very well. Why should he? She'd been little more than a blip on his radar, one of a lot of girls who'd adored him. Not having been an athlete or a cheerleader had made her interesting to him at the time, briefly, but not enough to subvert the pecking order. She should never have let him in . . . but that was one thing she could forgive her younger self for. He'd seemed so genuinely fascinated by her work, by the one thing that kept her sane in that school. And then he'd just seemed fascinated by *her.* She hadn't stood a chance.

"I'm so sorry, Sam. You don't have to believe that, but I wish you would, because I mean it."

She tried one of the fries, unable to keep her eyes locked with his. He looked so miserable. Enough that she wanted to believe he was sincere. And maybe he was. They were both adults now. But this place had left scars, and though not all of them had been caused by him, she'd associated him with hurt for so long that she wasn't sure trusting him would be possible. She kept her expression neutral, trying to move calmly and deliberately as she picked at the food.

"I can accept the apology," she said. "I can even appreciate it. But that doesn't mean I'm all that sure about what you'd do if your friends—and I'm willing to bet most of them are still here—got on your case for dating me." Sam couldn't help a small smirk. "With the exception of Ryan, that is. He seems to have developed some taste."

"I don't care what they think," Jake said, frowning. "Give me some credit, Sam. I'm not eighteen anymore."

"I know that," she said, sensing, as she had during the brief month of flirtatious semi-friendship they'd had all those years ago, the gulf between their experiences. "I also know how this place works. I'm a Henry, remember? We don't deserve to be on the Crescent. My dad should have married up instead of that hippie who is now mooching off the family legacy. When Dad died, a bunch of the kids said it was because he was cursed. Not that we'd ever heard of a Henry curse, but hey, one of the original settlers of the town, accused of being a witch, was a Henry, right? So, cursed, obviously."

Jake watched her closely, his attention completely focused on her. He looked sympathetic. She just wasn't sure she wanted his sympathy. Hell, she didn't know *what* she wanted. She waved her hand and shook her head, as though she could simply banish all of this baggage she'd been lugging around with her.

"I don't know, Jake. I know we're not kids anymore. But I don't know who you are. I barely knew who you were back then. You're right. I do keep expecting you to be a jerk. That's probably not fair, but not much is."

She scooped up a bunch of fries and shoved them in her mouth, hoping that would prevent her from saying anything more. Jake wasn't going to want to hear about all of this. Her problems were her own.

"I didn't know that," he finally said. "About your dad."

She shrugged. "Kids are mean. I think we've already established that."

"They are," he said. "But I was never a target, so my knowing it is a little different from my having lived it. I had the opposite problem, actually. I was supposed to be perfect."

Sam snorted. "You *were* perfect. That doesn't sound like a problem to me."

Jake looked away, shifted in his chair, and sighed before returning his gaze to her. "Just because it's something different from what you dealt with doesn't mean it was awesome, you know."

It wasn't a hard jab, but it hit its mark. "Okay," she said. "So . . . you didn't like being a popular jock?"

That earned her a small, self-deprecating smile. "No. I liked it fine. I just wasn't big on being pushed to stay in that box. *My* father did a lot of living vicariously through me. He coached all my teams right up until high school. Don't you remember? Maybe you wouldn't."

Sam shook her head. "I remember you had issues with him. You mentioned it enough times that I knew he pushed you too hard. Sports weren't ever my thing, though."

"Yeah, well, they were his. I loved to play, but there was always pressure. I had to be good enough to keep people from complaining that I was only getting the play time for being the coach's kid, and I had to deal with the fact that I never got to leave any game on the field. It all came home. I was supposed to be the best. According to my father, I was also supposed to go to a Division I school on a full scholarship and continue to be the best."

"Did you play?" she asked, curious. "You'd said you

weren't going to." It was something he'd told no one else, and it had surprised her at the time. It had made her hope he would break out, too, like she planned to. That maybe they'd leave this place in the dust, find each other somewhere else . . .

God, she'd been young.

Jake ate another hush puppy. "Nope," he said. "I wasn't good enough. Good, sure, but good enough for that, no. I knew it. He didn't. It caused some friction for a while. I wasn't trying hard enough, he said. The pre-vet stuff was beyond uninteresting to him." He considered for a moment while he chewed. "Actually, my job is still pretty uninteresting to him. He's keeping busy, though. I grew up, so he decided that *he's* a teenager now. Dyed his hair, bought a sports car, got a girlfriend younger than me and moved to Boston."

Sam's eyes widened. "I'm sorry. I didn't know."

She barely noticed when her burger was placed in front of her, despite the fact that it smelled heavenly. Somehow, she'd convinced herself that she was the only one here who'd had real problems. It was more of a shock than it should have been to discover that Jake's life wasn't cardboard-cutout perfect, either. Jake looked uncomfortable, his cheeks flushing faintly.

"Well, thanks, but I'm not telling you that to make you feel bad. I mean, it's not ideal to have your father be kind of a dick, but it was a few years ago and Mom is with a great guy now. She's happier. I'm used to the way things are. And it sure as hell doesn't excuse me for what I did to you. I'm just . . ." He tapped his fingers on the table, looking down at them and frowning. "You're right. We don't really know each other. I'd like to change that. Without all the teenage bullshit this time."

Sam looked at him, turning over what he'd said. She didn't remember Jake's father very well, but he sounded like a complete creep. That couldn't have been fun. She'd never considered what might have been going on behind the scenes back then. He'd told her things, things that in retrospect were indicators of bigger problems. But to her, even his issues had seemed like the sorts of things that only the perfect, lucky people dealt with. That was part of the age, she guessed—everything revolved around you, and everyone else must be exactly as they seemed. Heroes or villains in black and white, never any shades of gray.

But she was older now. And she ought to know better. That realization, more than anything, enabled her to finally relax her death grip on the grudge she carried and let just a little of it go. At least where Jake was concerned.

Sam nodded. "Okay," she said.

Jake stared at her while she picked up her burger and sank her teeth in. It was, as promised, fantastic. She felt lighter, somehow. Though the food was probably going to take care of that before long.

"Can you elaborate?" he asked. "I'm a doctor, not a mind reader."

Her lips curved up as she finished chewing. "You forgot the 'damn it, Jim' before that last part."

He laughed, and she knew it was going to be okay. For now, at least.

"If you're into Bones impressions, I can try to work them in more often. Seriously, though. What are you thinking? I meant it when I told you that you were always kind of a mystery to me, Sam. I never realized how much of the talking back then was from me. You're not an easy read."

"I'm thinking this burger is amazing," she replied, amused when he heaved an exasperated sigh. "And I think you're right. We should give getting to know one another a chance. You're obviously a little different now. And so am I. So . . . why not?"

Common sense immediately came up with dozens of reasons why not, but the delight on Jake's face knocked the wind out of her. He was still, hands down, the most beautiful man she'd ever laid eyes on. And for some crazy reason, he was interested in her. Despite all the warning bells going off in the back of her mind, she knew she'd never forgive herself if she didn't at least take a few baby steps in this direction to see what he was all about. Still, she needed to remember the mistake she'd made before, caring far too much far too soon. That couldn't happen again.

"So if I ask you out again, you're not going to pour my beer over my head and storm out?"

"No," she replied. "Probably not."

"Probably not?"

"I have to maintain my air of mystery," Sam said. "Mystery with a hint of danger. Will I accept, or will I hurl the ketchup at you and make a scene? You'll have to ask to find out."

His hazel eyes were warm as he laughed softly and shook his head. "You're still different from everybody else, Sam. I like it."

She took another bite, feeling her cheeks flushing. She hated that blush reflex. How Jake continued to think she was a puzzle when she had the tendency to turn volcanic red around him was a mystery all in itself, but she certainly wasn't going to argue with him about it. Once she was finished chewing, she said, "Just remember you said that the next time I decide to wear my leather pants out in town."

He paused with a French fry halfway to his mouth. "You . . . have leather pants?"

"Yes. We wear such things in that magical far-off land called the City. Especially when dealing with hipper-than-thou clientele."

"If you're trying to run me off, you should know this is having the opposite effect."

Sam nodded. "You're a leather-loving perv. Noted."

Rather than acting embarrassed, Jake simply grinned. "Guilty."

Then they laughed together, and the tension between them vanished like so much smoke. Left behind was an entirely different feeling, one Sam remembered from the day Jake had first approached her, sketching beneath the Witch Tree. At the time, she'd hardly understood it. Now, she knew it was the low and pleasant thrum of desire, though far more intense than it had been. Maybe because now she was well aware of what the end result would be . . . if she chose to let things go that far.

That was still a big "if" as far as she was concerned. She'd never been good at detaching her body from her heart. But a few dates, indulging her curiosity . . . that she could do. That couldn't hurt.

This time, she wouldn't let it.

Chapter Ten

If there was a non-creepy way to invite a woman back to your house on the first date, he didn't know of it. Still, he felt like he should make the offer, if only because of the small furry creatures currently making a mess out of his spare bedroom.

Not that the prospect of being completely alone with Sam wasn't enticing. But he could tell she'd stretched her limits where he was concerned about as far as they were going to go tonight, and pushing further wasn't going to get him much but a door shut in his face. And maybe, if Shane hadn't been completely full of shit, a punch in the eye.

God, he wanted to hear that story.

"So, do you want to visit your cat for a few, or should I just take you home?" he asked as they walked out of Beltane Blues. They'd stuck around to listen to the band for a little while, but conversation had quickly devolved into yelling into each other's ears. Being close enough to Sam to smell her neck was the only plus, but he couldn't just linger there and breathe.

She turned her head to look at him curiously. A chill breeze ruffled her hair, and she pushed it out of her face. Jake flexed his fingers. It was all he could do not to brush her hair back for her. With someone else, he might have just gone for it. Most of the women he dated would have found it sweet, or sexy. The normal rules didn't seem to apply here, though. It was part of what intrigued him about her.

She might have agreed to give him a chance, but he was under no illusions about her trusting him. Tonight he'd seen just how much ground he had to make up with her. And telling her how long she'd haunted him wouldn't make a bit of difference.

She wouldn't believe him. And since he didn't even know what it meant, if anything, he'd just keep that to himself.

"Loki's still at your place?"

"Him and his siblings, yeah. That's what happens. You take them home once, and suddenly they're yours." He shrugged. "They're not the first creatures to mess up that bedroom. Won't be the last, either."

She smirked. "Sucker."

"I'm not the one keeping one of them, am I?"

She rolled her eyes, shifted her weight from foot to foot, and seemed genuinely torn about whether to let the date go any longer. The gravel crunched beneath her feet. Finally, she blew out a breath, and the night was cold enough that he could see the steam when it hit the air.

"Yeah, let's go. If you have a pit in your basement, though, I don't want to see it."

"It puts the lotion on its skin," he told her, earning him a swift punch in the arm. "Ow," he said, laughing as he rubbed it. She was stronger than she looked. "Did you really . . ." He stopped himself before he could finish the question, but she seemed to know what he was talking about. He wished he hadn't brought it up, because her expression went from open to forbidding in less than a second.

"How about this?" she asked. "If we're really starting from the beginning here, then all of that? Including the thing you're trying not to ask me about? That's off limits for now."

He walked with her to the truck, opening the door for her before she could get it herself. She gave him a look, but he silently patted himself on the back. If he couldn't pay for her dinner, he could at least open the door for her. No matter how little she wanted to be charmed.

He lingered while she buckled her seat belt. "Well, wait. . . . So which things are off-limits? We can't have rules if I don't know about them."

"Okay. I don't have a bunch of funny, nostalgic stories about high school. What happened with Thea isn't something I really want to talk about. It isn't going to go anywhere good, and it doesn't matter anyway." She paused, eyes searching his face. "Just out of curiosity, who told you about that?"

"Shane Sullivan. But I didn't get details, just the gist. There was a black eye. Beyond that, I'm in the dark."

He wished he'd never brought it up. She chewed her lip briefly, looked away, then said quietly, "So . . . Shane is still around."

"Yes."

"And Thea is still around, I guess."

"Yes."

"Has your social circle changed at *all* in the last ten years?"

The flat way she asked it made it clear that she already knew the answer. "Well . . . not really."

Sam nodded, speaking softly to herself. "Not really. Okay. That's . . . good to know."

He was quite sure she thought it was anything but. "Sam, it's—"

"Different now. I know what you're going to say. Great. Well, then, this should be interesting, anyway."

He wanted to contradict her, but Jake realized that he wasn't entirely sure he ought to. Shane's laughter was still too fresh in his mind. He couldn't imagine it would be that big a deal when word got around, though he was a little less certain of that than he had been. Regardless, it rankled that she thought so little of his life. Of the things he'd chosen, the people he'd kept. He kept things simple; he kept things familiar and comfortable. And he was happy, damn it. Or content. Mostly.

"The Cove is more than you remember, Sam," he said. "Just try to keep an open mind about it, okay? I'm going to make you see the good things about this place. Show you a few new ones, too. You'll be glad you came back."

He shut the door and headed around to the driver's side. Sam was waiting, her mouth twisted with skepticism. "Uh-huh," she said. "Well, you get points for tonight, but if you think you're going to make me fall in love with Harvest Cove, you're going to end up disappointed. Tolerance is about all I can muster."

"A challenge, huh? I accept." He started the truck and headed out of the lot, turning onto the street. The sky above had gone to inky blackness dotted with stars, cold and clear. When he glanced at Sam, she was looking up at it from her window, eyes raised. For just an instant, she seemed very young and impossibly innocent. The year between them in school had prevented him from knowing her when she had been. Maybe things would have been different.

But probably not. He hadn't been a hero.

"Do you think you'll stay?" he asked, pushing the uncomfortable truth from his mind. Sam shrugged.

"I hope not. But right now it's not like I have so many options. On the upside, my job is awesome."

"Seemed like it last night. I hadn't met Zoe before. She seems nice."

"She's great," Sam replied. "So focused, really savvy about the business, and very supportive of the artists she shows. Plus she's just fun. Zoe takes everything seriously but herself. I love working with her."

The change in her when she talked about Zoe was profound. She went from wistful to enthusiastic in the blink of an eye.

"Sounds like you found *one* thing you like in the Cove, then."

Sam shot him a look. "Three. Zoe, Two Roads, and the food tonight. Oh, and my cat. So that's four."

"I'm not on the list yet?"

"You're still in consideration," she said. "If you make it on the list you'll be notified by mail within six to eight weeks."

"You're tough," he told her, turning onto his street. "So are you going to be showing your work at the gallery? I'd love to see it." Actually, he *had* seen it, but she didn't need to know that. Curiosity had driven him to her Web site more than once, and while her talent hadn't surprised him, her vision had. Sam's paintings were devoid of people but full of color, whimsical and sometimes foreboding, but always beautiful. Often she focused on something solitary, like a tree, and turned it into a glorious representative of whatever otherworld she pulled her inspiration from. He'd spent more time than he would ever admit looking at her work, fascinated by the way they beckoned to even a non–art lover like him. It had been a while since he'd checked on her site, mainly because he'd actually been tempted to buy one of her paintings and wasn't sure how weird that would be.

Still, he was impressed by her depictions of what he thought of as beautiful escapes, the kind that even a guy like him would want to dive into. And now that she was here, he hoped to see more of her work in person. Even if he still wasn't sure how weird it would be for him to buy one. He'd never set foot in Zoe's place before last night, and up until a week ago, he hadn't had any interest in doing so. Art was a foreign country to him. Kind of like Sam.

It took him a few beats of complete silence to realize that Sam had stiffened up again. He bit back a frustrated comment. Was this on the list of things they couldn't talk about, too? He wanted to know about her life, not interfere with it. Or maybe she thought he was too boring and small town to understand the artistic process.

The hurt and anger that accompanied that thought startled Jake enough to allow him to lock them down before they came out of his mouth. They were just starting to feel each other out. He had to give this time, or there was going to be a hell of a lot of walking off in a huff.

Sam finally rolled her shoulders and said, "I'm taking a break from painting right now. Until things settle down." His initial reaction evaporated in the face of curiosity. Whatever her stiffness was about, it wasn't him.

Her answer felt rehearsed, with a nugget of information and a lot of nothing otherwise. All he knew for sure was that right now, Sam was only selling art, not making it. And that seemed like a damn shame.

If things had gotten bad enough for her to stop, then no wonder she'd come back. But he couldn't ask. She wouldn't tell him, not now. He would have to be patient . . . and that had never been a particular virtue of his.

"Oh," he said, keeping his voice even. "Well, hopefully once you get settled in."

"Mmm," was the noncommittal sound from her side of the car.

They pulled into his driveway. He'd left some of the lights on for Tucker, and he could already hear the excited barking from inside the house. He looked quickly at Sam to try to gauge her reaction—did she even like dogs? That seemed kind of important. He was relieved to find that she looked interested.

"I guess you did mention you had a dog," she said.

"Tucker," Jake replied, turning off the engine. "Hopefully he'll keep all four paws on the floor, but he gets excited, so . . . I apologize in advance."

Sam just laughed. "Trust me—I can take it. Dogs are way easier than people."

They got out and headed onto the porch, where Jake fiddled with the key. The sensation he felt was so alien to him that it took him a minute to identify it. His stomach felt . . . odd. God, was he actually sweating? Silently, he berated himself for the sudden attack of nerves. He'd been fine before dinner.

But they hadn't been alone in his house at dinner. And at the restaurant there had been no possibility of stumbling across his underwear on the floor. Or finding his dog chewing on his underwear in the middle of the floor.

Not dating much this past year had been good for his sanity, but it hadn't exactly made him a meticulous housekeeper.

Jake could hear Tucker's nails clicking on the floor as the dog did his Dance of Joy.

"You might want to hang back for a sec," he said, then turned the knob. "Hey, b— *Oof!*"

Tucker hurled himself at his owner in a fit of ecstasy, barreling into Jake like a spring-loaded bag of bricks. Jake took a couple of quick steps back to brace himself, then set about trying to calm Tucker down as he said hello.

"Hey, boy! Who's a good boy? Who's my good boy?" He scrubbed his hands quickly over the dog's sides, grinning as Tucker wagged every bit of himself that he could, panting through his big doggy smile. He briefly forgot Sam was right behind him, his only excuse for letting his voice go several octaves higher while he greeted his buddy. Then her voice sounded right beside him.

"Oh, he's really cute!"

He watched Tucker's attention shift in a split second. Jake barely had time to get out a warning before the dog turned all his energy and affection on Sam. Time seemed to slow to a crawl in the instant he saw Sam's eyes widen and Tucker's expression turn to one that could only be described as "YAY!" The next thing he knew, Sam was sitting on the floor being lavished with sloppy kisses as she halfheartedly defended herself with her arms and giggled helplessly.

"Damn it, Tucker!" Jake grabbed him by the collar

and hauled him back far enough for Sam to right herself. Tucker, completely devoid of shame, had the audacity to give him a wounded look. How dare he deprive him of fun? "Sorry. Are you okay?"

She was adorably rumpled as she picked herself up, and the fact that she was smiling seemed to be a good sign.

"You're lucky I like dogs," she informed Tucker. Then she looked at Jake, her cheeks flushed and her eyes seeming to glow, blue into green, in the light. "He's a hot mess, isn't he?"

"That's putting it mildly," Jake replied. "He was one of a litter of puppies we had dumped on our doorstep a couple of years ago, back when I first started with Dr. Perry. I didn't plan to take one, but Tucker here attached himself to me. He saw the word "sucker" written on my forehead, I guess. I couldn't let him go. So here we are."

"Was he always this . . . excited?" Sam asked, watching as Tucker tried to wriggle away from him.

"This is actually an improvement. You're looking at one of the only dogs to flunk out of Furry Friends Obedience School. Also, when he was about eight months old, he ate my couch. That's not an exaggeration."

"I can believe it," Sam laughed. She reached out to rub behind Tucker's ears. "So this is mellow."

"No, he'll calm down in a few. Calm being relative. He does know some commands, depending on whether or not I have food in my hand. And he's a good running partner," Jake said. At the sound of the F-word, Tucker went completely still, cocked his head, and looked up at him. "Crap."

"Go ahead, I know what you have to do. My dog growing up was the same. Where are the kittens?" she asked.

"Upstairs, first bedroom on the left," he said. "Just watch it when you open the door. They're escape artists."

"Got it." She gave him a small salute and turned away. Jake watched her go, then looked down at his dog. "Honest to God, Tucker. Way to make an impression. Come on. Treat time."

Tucker burst into action, galloping down the hall toward the kitchen and leaving Jake to walk after him. He heard the door upstairs open, heard Sam's delighted coo, and smiled. There was nothing like being slobbered on by a big mutt to make you comfortable someplace, he guessed. He liked seeing her here, seeing her with his ridiculous dog. Under all the stylish black clothes Sam was still as earthy and real as he remembered.

Which was good, because if he was going to sell her on sticking around the Cove for any length of time, she was going to need to be okay with a certain amount of earthiness. He was having a hard time imagining her covered in dirt, though.

The light on his answering machine was flashing, which surprised him. Mostly people just called his cell, though because of his job he tried to have more than one method of contact available. He pulled the cell out of his pocket, frowning at it, and saw he had a missed call. Must be he hadn't felt the vibration.

Shit. All he could do was hope that it wasn't urgent, and that if it was, someone had gotten ahold of Dr. Perry. There was a twenty-four-hour emergency vet down in Salem, but sometimes, there wasn't time to get there.

He hit PLAY on the machine and immediately wished he hadn't. It wasn't an emergency. It was a dispatch from movie night. He could hear laughter in the background as Shane's voice piped up on the speaker.

"Hey, man, are you coming over? You've still got time before we fire up the movie! Don't just sit there with your dog, you asshole. I know you're probably just standing there listening to this."

In the background, there was an amused, feminine chorus of "Jake, we miss you!" He recognized Cici's voice among them, bright and crystal clear. The idea of seeing her again, of her being back in town, didn't bother him much . . . though her absence last night had been a relief, considering. He had a feeling that putting Sam and Cici in the same space might not go very well. Even if she didn't want him anymore, Cici had been territorial as hell. And Sam, well, he didn't remember her being a fighter. Would that dynamic hold? He wasn't really sure he wanted to find out. Not anytime soon, anyway, while he and Sam were in the early part of . . . whatever this was going to be. He dug in the cupboard and fished out a jerky treat for Tucker while the message finished.

"Anyway, come over," Shane said, and then another voice piped up in the background.

"Don't bring the freak!"

Cici.

There was a burst of laughter, a click, and the message ended. Jake blew out a breath and leaned against the counter. Well, that wasn't promising. He'd figure out a way to deal with it somehow, though. Because blowing this for a second time wasn't an option. If he walked away this time, it would be for the right reasons. Not this crap.

But he needed time to show Sam some of the good he'd promised her before he even attempted to navigate this brewing issue with his friends. It pissed him off that they would even make it an issue. Were they really that insular? He'd just looked at it as having a close group of old friends. It bothered him to think that from the outside, it might look like something a lot more intimidating. And that his easy acceptance of the way things were might not have helped.

Unsettled, Jake headed upstairs to where he could hear Sam crooning softly to the kittens. She had a nice voice—another surprise. Sweet and low and soothing. And she was singing, of all things, "Don't Stop Believin'." Jake turned the knob and slipped quickly in before any of the furry crew could make a break for it. Sam was perched on the edge of the bed, Loki gathered up beneath her chin in what looked like a state of complete bliss. The kitten's eyes were half closed, and when Sam abruptly stopped her song Jake could hear the faint purring.

The other kittens played or groomed themselves or nibbled on the food in the dish. One of them looked to have made a mess with the water. Again. Sam looked up at him, charmingly embarrassed.

"Um. I like my cat."

"I noticed. Journey isn't something you sing to just anybody." She laughed, and he decided that Sam and her matching kitten were the most fetching things he'd ever laid eyes on. Her pale hair tumbled over her shoulders, and her eyes were luminous against her fair skin. She watched him steadily, wary but far more open than she had been, and he wondered if he'd been quite right about her not being a fighter. She'd given Thea a black eye all those years ago, supposedly. And though he'd seen a range of emotions from her so far, fear wasn't among them.

He wanted to know about her time in New York. He wanted to know what had happened to her, wanted to know everything. The thought was sudden and fierce, and Jake pushed it back, completely unnerved. This was a first date, not a damned engagement. They had time to figure each other out and whether they clicked.

He didn't know why he couldn't just enjoy himself. That was usually something he was good at.

Jake settled himself on the floor and joined Sam in fussing over the kittens, trying to simply be in the moment for once.

"So . . . you missing out on something? I could hear Shane's voice all the way up here," she said. His heart clenched for an instant, but she didn't appear to have heard the parting shot.

"No, just a stupid movie thing," he said. "We do it a lot. I know what I'm missing, and it isn't much."

"*We* meaning . . ."

"Max, Thea, Shane, Fitz, Kallie, Ryan." Cici's name was on the tip of his tongue, but something held him back. He was wary of spoiling the night when they finally seemed to have achieved a little bit of comfort with each other. The month he'd quietly hung around Sam had been during one of his breaks from Cici—breaks that had, at that point, been increasing in frequency. It had taken another couple of years for it to end completely, mostly because they'd been physically compatible longer than they'd worked in any other sense.

He knew Sam would remember the first part. He didn't feel like getting into the second.

"Wow. The roster really *hasn't* changed at all."

"Yeah, well, we're all still here. It kind of made sense," he said.

"Do you get out of town much?" she asked. "I mean, what do you *do*?"

It seemed to be an honest question, not a dig, so he didn't mind answering. "I don't know. I work. I watch movies in Max's basement. We go to the Tavern sometimes. Cookouts in the summer. Fitz has a sailboat."

The corner of Sam's mouth curved. "Oh God. You're a complete townie now, aren't you?"

He frowned, feigning hurt. "Hey. I go to Salem sometimes."

"Sometimes."

"Once in a while," he said, unable to quite remember the last time he'd gone. It had been a while. Maybe quite a while.

Shit, I am a townie.

"Maybe I'm not the only one who needs an education on some things," Sam said. "I'm going to need to think about this."

"That sounds ominous," Jake replied. "I'm afraid."

"Yeah, well, you should be. I'll curse you with my Henry weirdness. Next thing you know you'll be coloring your hair blue and wearing leather pants of your own."

"That's . . . terrifying, actually."

They laughed, and something in Sam's smile pulled at him in a way he was completely unused to. It wasn't just desire—though there was plenty of that. She was simply so different from anyone he knew. Their eyes met, and Jake wished he could remove all the kittens from the equation for just a minute so he could kiss her. He saw the flush in her cheeks, and knew she understood exactly what he was thinking. Sam cleared her throat and looked away, breaking the moment.

"Well. This has been great, but I really should get back."

"Big plans for the rest of the night?"

"Yeah," she said, "pajamas. Cocoa. Possibly scarfing some of the oatmeal raisin cookies my mother baked earlier. A real walk on the wild side. You know." She looked down at Loki. "Are you sure I can't have him yet?"

"One week. He still needs his littermates. They come to work with me, get socialized, and this week they'll get their first round of vaccinations. They're all pretty consistent with the litter box, at least, even if they're a mess about everything else. But I'd like him to be eight weeks before he heads out into the world. It would be a huge help if you know anybody who might take some of the others."

She pursed her lips. "I know all of three people well enough to ask, and two of them are my family. Don't think that's going to be much help."

He tipped his chin down to look at her. "Where there's a will, there's a way. Artists like cats, right? You now work with a bunch of artists. So, that's perfect. I can also strap you to a chair and make you watch depressing animal rescue ads until you agree to help."

She gave him a beleaguered look. "I'll see what I can do." Then she looked around at all the kittens and sighed. "I'm not really much of a joiner, so I never got into rescue or anything, but . . . I really will ask around. In my sad and limited capacity. Okay?"

"Good enough."

Jake put the kittens he'd been playing with in the round pet bed he'd tucked into the corner, then stood. Sam reluctantly detached Loki from her scarf and put the mewing kitten with the others. The two of them slipped quickly out the door and headed down the stairs. Tucker looked up from where he'd flopped in the foyer, and his tail began to thump against the floor.

"Don't even think about it," Jake told him. Still, the

dog scrambled to his feet and greeted them all over again, though minus the jumping this time. They headed back out into the night, stepping onto his porch. The air had the crisp bite that he loved about October, and he watched Sam pull her jacket a little tighter around herself while he locked up again.

"You sure you're not interested in sticking around? We could watch a movie or something," he said, knowing she wouldn't accept even as he wished she would.

"No. You have your own movie to go to, and my pajamas are calling. I'm not a late-night girl anymore."

"I'm just going to come back here and hang out on the couch with Tuck," Jake replied, enjoying the surprise on her face. She didn't seem to think she was enough entertainment for an evening. What she didn't realize was that anything after this would pale in comparison.

They stood there on his porch, under the single light above the door, and the tension that always thrummed between them quickly intensified. He could smell her perfume again . . . hell, he could almost taste her. He wanted to. The only thing holding him back was how still Sam had gone, like a deer scenting a predator. Her eyes never left his face, and she seemed to be waiting . . . though he wasn't sure for what. He'd just have to make a guess. Or engage in some wishful thinking.

Or just go for it.

Jake stepped closer and was relieved to see he'd guessed correctly. She tipped her chin up to look at him, taking the final step to finish closing the space between them. He managed a smile as he lowered his head to hers. "Sam," he murmured.

"Mmm?" she asked. But her eyes were already closing, her mouth lifting to his.

He savored the brief, final moment of anticipation, and then sank into the kiss he'd waited years for. Her lips were petal soft, and parted at his touch. There was a teasing brush of her tongue, and Jake met it with a languid stroke of his own, sliding his arms around her.

She fit so perfectly to him, every curve and hollow. Jake felt her slide her hands over his shoulders, then higher as one hand curved around the nape of his neck. She pressed against him, and he let her set the pace as she angled her head, toying with his lips, his tongue, and then plunging with a speed that took his breath away.

Sam's confidence caught him off-guard. Maybe it shouldn't have—she was a beautiful woman. Anyone could see that. Still, the speed with which she took control of the kiss nearly brought him to his knees. She rose to her toes, fitting herself against the length of him, against where he was already hard and hot. Sam sighed against his lips, the pleasure in that sound reverberating through him. The sweetness in that first touch of their lips vanished, burned up in the flames that quickly caught between them.

Jake's hands skimmed over her back, through her hair, his breathing growing ragged as Sam's body shifted gently in time to each thrust of his tongue. Every light pulse of her hips arrowed straight to his core, shattering every rational thought until there was nothing left but the way she felt in his arms. When he reached down to grip her hips, pulling her hard against him, she gave a soft, breathless moan and fisted her hands in the fabric of his coat.

He couldn't get enough of her. The kiss turned wild, feral, as the night dissolved into red-hot nips and licks, the rake of her nails through his hair, the restless movements as they chafed against the clothes that separated skin from skin. He'd had no idea it would be like this. That she could possibly want him as much as he wanted her.

That this much want was even possible.

The blast of a car horn crashed through his haze, blowing a hole in the warm cocoon they'd wrapped themselves in. Still, it took a few seconds for his brain to reengage, even when Sam stilled and gasped, pulling her mouth from his to turn her head when a voice shouted at them.

"Get a room!"

There was raucous laughter as a beat-up old car sailed by, full of what looked like teenagers. Jake wasn't sure whether to laugh or throw rocks. He looked down into Sam's face, and felt a purely male satisfaction at the sight of her swollen lips, her cheeks reddened from rubbing against his five-o'clock shadow. She looked up at him with an embarrassed little smile, one eyebrow arched.

"Oops."

"They're just jealous," Jake said. He hesitated, then said, "I don't suppose you'd want to come back inside." He didn't want to sound desperate, but his heart was still thundering in his chest, his mind full of heated images that refused to let him be.

"Sure I would," Sam said, but before he could celebrate, she added, "But what I want to do and what I'm going to do are two different things tonight. I need to go home, Jake."

She was still pressed against him, warm and soft and incredibly feminine. The taste of her was still on his lips, and when he looked at her, he could see that the sexual haze hadn't entirely dissipated for her, either. But he didn't miss the determined look in her eyes, and Jake knew she'd made up her mind.

Just like that, his fantasy for the night was ground to dust beneath her stylish black heel. He sighed and tried not to sound too pathetic about it. There would be other nights, he told himself. Soon, if he had anything to do with it.

"Okay," he said. "Come on. I'll drive you home."

Chapter Eleven

Sam had Thursday off, and she lucked into a bright, crisp day that was the best of what a Harvest Cove autumn had to offer. She rolled out of bed around eight with no plans, enjoying the fact that for once, she didn't have anything pressing to worry about. There was no rent to be paid, no evil boss to fear, no roommate who left seriously inappropriate "work related" items in strange places around the apartment to get angry at. There was just the big, quiet house, the soft rush of the heat kicking on, and the lingering memories of Jake's mouth on hers.

It seemed silly that a single kiss could color her entire week, or that the random texts Jake sent her every day could lift the clouds that had been following her around for some time. It was dangerous, she told herself, to let him back in so quickly. She was older and wiser and ought to know better.

But there had been so much ugly in her life lately ... was it really so wrong to take some enjoyment where she could? Maybe it was a weak justification, but it was what she had. That, and something that felt perilously close to happiness.

She wrapped up in a sweater and had her morning

coffee in one of the Adirondack chairs out back, looking out over the gentle slope of the rolling lawn to the sea. She sat that way for some time, eyes picking out the blues and grays of the sky and water, the still-vibrant green of the lawn, and of course, the trees. She tried to imagine herself with her palette, canvas in front of her, paint on her fingers. And slowly, she could envision it. Her free hand twitched while she visualized the long brush strokes she would use for the sky, the short, quicker strokes when she did the leaves . . . she could *see* it.

She was so engrossed in her daydream that she jumped at the creak of the chair next to her.

"Morning, honey. Still waking up?" Andi asked, settling in with her own coffee.

"Yeah, I guess I'm not quite there yet," Sam replied. Her little fantasy vanished, but it left behind a lingering warmth that Sam wanted to hang on to. It made her hope. It made her want to try again. Maybe soon, she thought. *Maybe.* It was what she'd told herself for months. But this was the closest she'd come to acting on it. She wasn't sure she was ready to stand in front of that canvas again, brush in hand, and feel nothing.

It was worse than fear, worse than anger. Those things could fuel art. But the only thing that came from nothing was just that. Nothing.

The two of them sat in companionable silence for quite a while. A light breeze toyed with the pieces of hair that had come loose from Sam's braid as she tried to turn her brain off and just be in the moment for a little bit. When she breathed in, the air smelled of earth and sea. Good smells. The smells of her childhood. Sam found she savored them as much as the taste of the coffee.

"You're looking better, Sammy," Andi said, and Sam turned her head to find her mother watching her with a soft smile. "It's good to see."

"It's all the cookies you've been feeding me," Sam replied. "You're obviously equating 'better' with 'fatter.'"

Andi chuckled. "That must be it." She looked out over the water and sighed. "Hard to believe Halloween is just a little over a week away. The leaves are all coming down, too. Won't be long before the trees are bare again and we'll have snow."

It *was* hard to believe, Sam thought, startled when she realized it was the sixteenth already. "I guess I'll have to buy some decent boots. It never snows that much in the city."

"If you're nice I'll knit you a scarf and hat."

She grinned. "Purple? I want to match the house."

"You know it, kiddo." Andi chuckled, then sighed contentedly before taking a sip of coffee. "It'll be good to have you here for Christmas. I've missed having both my girls for the holidays."

Sam felt a pang of regret at the wistfulness in her mother's voice. She'd tried to make it home for at least one holiday a year, but sometimes . . . especially the last couple of years . . . it just hadn't worked out. Her solution had been to lure her mother and sister to the city, which should have been the best of both worlds.

Unfortunately, no place that had only one bathroom could ever be the best of both worlds. Especially when you had a sister who always, by some dark magic, managed to get in there first.

"You didn't like the Rockettes? Or Rockefeller Center? I loved it when you and Emma came to New York," Sam said.

"Oh, we had a ball, Sammy. But it isn't the same as having you here. This is home. We had lots of good Christmases here. Lots of wonderful holidays."

"Mmm. Some of which I dyed my hair to match," Sam said.

Andi frowned a little as she thought about that. "Wasn't it brown with orange streaks for Thanksgiving one year?"

"More than one year," Sam replied, amused at the memory. "I looked like an anime character."

"You looked beautiful. You always did, even if you refused to listen to my opinion about that," Andi said.

"You're my mom. You made me. Your opinion doesn't count."

"Does so."

"Hmph." Sam took another sip of coffee. Her knees were tucked into her chest, and her fuzzy slippers were keeping her feet warm. The thought of being here for all of the holidays this year was strange. Not bad, just ... different. It had been a very long time since she'd watched the leaves turn and fall, and eventually come back again. She would see that this year, she thought. *With Jake?* She buried the thought before it could take root. They were taking it slow. *Slow* slow. And not even thinking about the future, thank you very much.

Now if she just repeated that ten times a day, maybe she could make herself believe it.

Andi's voice was a welcome distraction.

"I thought I'd take a drive into town a little later. You interested? I've got some books to take to Jasper at the used book store—I want to pick up a few more, too— and if you're with me, I've got an excuse to have lunch out. Thought I'd swing by the animal hospital, too."

"What? Why?"

"Well, I've been thinking. I know you're going to hog that kitten, and this house has been too empty for too long. So I'm picking one of my own. Jake brings them to work, right?" Andi asked.

"Usually." Sam tried not to feel just a little giddy at the prospect of seeing Jake and failed miserably. She knew it had been a crazy week at work for him and hadn't expected to set eyes—okay, maybe not just her eyes—on him until this weekend. Even just a quick hello would be nice. It was just touching base, she told herself firmly. It was just a friendly, brief, not at all important visit—

Oh, screw it. If I'm going to be this pathetic, I might as well own it.

"Great," Andi said, interrupting her thoughts with a knowing little smile. Sam bit back a groan. Was she that obvious? *Probably.*

"So what do you think? Mother-daughter day out?"

"It's a date," Sam replied, and rose to go rinse out her mug.

Wandering downtown wasn't something she'd done in a long time, so Sam was curious about whether much had changed. At first blush, things were much the same, though some of the shops she remembered had been replaced with others.

Andi parked her car in front of Petite Treats, a cute little bakery that was one of the newer—at least to Sam—additions on the small, historic square that sat just above the harbor. Sam got out and breathed in air that smelled like spun sugar as she looked around. This time of year, Harvest Cove was at its best. The buildings on the square, the original town center, were all incredibly old and meticulously maintained as historic buildings. Made of wood and stone, together they held more than a hint of fairy tale. Many had seasonal displays in the windows, or outside the doors—Indian corn, pumpkins and gourds, scarecrows and lanterns. And of course, there were plenty of nods to the town's history, with pointy black hats and witch's broomsticks, painted black cats and cauldrons full of everything from glitter to mysterious purple mist that rose lazily into the air. The trees here were big, many very old, and though they were still full and ablaze with color, the sidewalks and cobblestone streets were littered with leaves. Sam crunched through them, quietly delighting in the sound they made beneath her feet.

It had been a long time since she'd done this. Longer since she'd seen Harvest Cove in its prime season. The weekends would bring a lot of tourists this time of year, but today, things were fairly quiet apart from the occasional tour bus that would rumble through, full of people looking to snap pictures of an authentic New England town.

"Can we see the tree?" Sam asked on a whim.

"Sure. It's still there, same as it ever was," Andi said, carrying a handled paper bag that she'd loaded with worn paperbacks. "Why don't we head into Jasper's first, since it's right here, and then you can go say hello."

Sam snorted softly. "I want to see it, not have a conversation with it." Still, seeing it meant more to her than she wanted to say. The Witch Tree was sort of the town mascot, emblazoned on the little flags that hung from the wrought-iron lampposts, on posters for town functions, worked into several of the stores' logos, and had been photographed in all its glory for a number of national magazines. More importantly, it had been a refuge for her, an old and silent friend when she'd needed one most.

Of all the things in Harvest Cove, that was one piece that truly felt like hers.

They headed a few doors down into Jasper's Used Books, where Andi dropped off what she'd read before engaging in an animated discussion with Jasper Reed about a mystery series they'd both been enjoying. Sam found a couple of books for evening reading: an urban fantasy and a British mystery Jasper had recommended.

"This one," he said, putting it into her hands with a knowing gleam in his friendly brown eyes, "is best read with a blanket and a cup of tea. You'll love it." His own British accent had been tempered by the many years he'd been in the States, but it was still recognizable, and lovely to Sam's ears. He was in his early sixties, lanky, with hawkish features and thinning gray hair that he always wore in a small ponytail at the nape of his neck. A small diamond glittered in one ear. He'd aged since the last time she'd seen him, Sam realized, dismayed at the obvious passage of time etched on his face. Still, there was a roguish charm about him that was the same as ever.

When they finally strolled out, Sam was laughing. "I need to introduce him to Zoe, if she hasn't met him yet. They can compare notes on tea. Maybe then she'll stop harassing me about it."

"More likely they'll gang up on you," Andi said. "You have to watch out for the tea people. They'll push it on you until you crack, and all of a sudden you're down to your last five bucks with a cupboard full of exotic leaves and a nasty scone habit on the side."

She flashed a wicked grin and gently swung the handled bag, now full of a completely different set of books, as she walked. She looked good today, Sam thought, in one of her long skirts and a thick sweater that negated the need for a jacket. Her ubiquitous braid was rolled into a knot at the crown of her head, and her cheeks were pink with good humor and the chill air.

Happy, Sam thought. Her mother really was happy in the Cove. For a long time, Sam had assumed that Andi stayed only because of the house, and because it was where she'd lost a husband and raised her children. That wasn't the case, though. Andi had found things to love here.

"Mom? Why do you like it here so much?" she asked. It was out of the blue enough that Andi looked surprised by the question.

"What's not to like?" Andi asked. "Take a look around. If you're into history, you couldn't ask for a more perfect place."

It was a fair point, Sam thought, looking around again. This time of year, the Cove looked like Halloween incarnate. But looks, as she well knew, weren't everything.

"Okay," Sam said. "I'll give you that, but you know that people . . . say things. About us. About you."

Andi only shrugged. "Honey, *some* people. People with nothing better to do. And that's nowhere near everyone in this town. Now, I'm never going be a part of the moneyed social set here, even though I have more money than most of them put together and the best piece of land on the Crescent. I knew that almost from the beginning. Your dad was supposed to marry local, preferably a local with the right pedigree. Instead, he went to Vermont and found me working at the ski resort where he was staying. He knocked my socks off." She winked. "Among other things."

Sam groaned. "*Mom*. My ears. I need brain bleach. Come *on*."

"Oh, you're no fun. How do you think you got here? Anyway, he told me what to expect."

"And you came anyway?" She wrinkled her nose. "That's love, I guess."

"Definitely love," Andi laughed. "But that's not what got me comfortable here. The biggest thing in any new place is to find yourself a few allies. Doesn't need to be many. Two or three, or even just one will do. But people who have staying power. People who'll be there to laugh with, cry with, occasionally drink too much with. They're not always easy to find, but when you do, it can make a place home." She gave a little shrug and a smile. "Worked for me, anyway. When I found Clare and Joanne, the Cove got a whole lot brighter. And one margarita night with them is worth a thousand of those stupid Christmas parties at Mary and Bob Harding's." She gave Sam a meaningful look. "When your father was alive, we went every damned year. The invitations stopping is about the only silver lining I can think of in his passing. Those Nordic-looking Christmas sweaters with the reindeer on them still give me the creeps."

Sam filed away the visual to share with Zoe when she got passed over for an invitation again this year.

"So you think that's what I need to do here," she said. "Find some friends and get happy."

"Oh, I don't know. I just want you to *be* happy, Sammy," Andi said, throwing an arm around her daughter and giving her a squeeze. "How you go about it is entirely up to you. But in the meantime, you can be semi-miserable as long as you keep your room clean and cook something once in a while."

"Doable," Sam said.

They made several other stops while Sam mulled over what her mother had said. She made it sound so easy. But then, Andi had been here for over thirty years. She was as local as it got by now, though there were some people who would never look at her that way. Andi had never seemed to care much, going about her merry way. Sam smiled as they walked along, remembering Andi's announcement, about a year after her husband's death, that she was going to find something to do during the day while the girls were at school or she was going to go insane. She'd taught preschool for years, wearing glitter-covered sweaters that had delighted the kids and singing them everything from "Pop! Goes the Weasel" to Pink Floyd. A couple of years ago, she'd decided it was time for something different, "something different" being to work at her buddy Joanne's yarn shop part-time. She taught knitting classes and fussed with yarn and, Sam was pretty sure, spent a lot of time gossiping with Joanne. It kept them busy, though not necessarily out of trouble.

Andi was content, Sam thought affectionately, and she deserved every bit of it. Maybe she'd get there herself someday. Or maybe she'd have to one day be removed from her hovel via forklift, having grown enormous on a diet of ice cream and tears.

For today, at least, just listening to her mother's warm voice gave her a little more hope for the former.

The two of them browsed through a trinket shop that Sam didn't remember, and where she bought a cute little black cat key chain. They poked around in the jeweler's, read a couple of menus, and smelled just about everything in a store that crafted soaps and lotions. By the time they emerged from there, both of them were hungry, but Sam didn't want to leave without walking into the small park at the center of the square.

"You go on ahead," Andi said, settling herself on a bench beside one of the lampposts. "I'll dig into one of these books while you have a look."

"You're not coming?"

Andi was already pulling her reading glasses out of her purse. "Honey, I live here all the time. I love the tree, but I know it's special to you. You take a minute. I'll be right here."

Sam knew there would be no budging her, so she walked to the corner, took the crosswalk and walked through the open gates of the four-foot black wrought-iron fence that surrounded Oak Shadow Park, and her tree. The Witch Tree.

Sam had to stop for a few seconds, just to take it in. It was an oak, one of the oldest in the country, and its gnarled branches had become a huge canopy that cast shade in a wide radius around the thick trunk. It was hundreds of years old and looked it, an unchanging fixture that anchored the Cove to its past. The founding witches, supposedly a Henry, an Owens, and a Nightingale, were said to have planted the seed and, like any witches worth their salt, cast a spell on it. As long as the tree grew strong, so would the town, went the tale. The heart of the tree was the heart of the town.

It was a charming story, fun to pass down and great for local advertising. But even if it hadn't had a story behind it, Sam knew she would have loved the tree.

The leaves, a vibrant orange, were everywhere on the ground, but there still seemed to be an endless supply in the branches above. Sam walked toward the tree, smelling the rich scent of decaying leaves, of earth and grass and wood. Even now, the world seemed to be hushed beneath the branches. When she'd been very young, she'd been convinced that there must be a secret door in the trunk that led to a magical place. The older version of her still couldn't quite let go of the fantasy, or the fact that for a long time she'd misunderstood "witch" as "wish," and made a lot of requests to whatever sylvan spirits abided here accordingly.

Sam reached out and touched the trunk she'd leaned against and lain beside countless times. Just her and her sketch pad and the dreams she took out and turned over in her head like a smooth stone. The bark was rough beneath her fingers, but she still could imagine the life thrumming through it.

Hey, she thought, feeling vaguely silly even as it felt like the right thing to do. *I'm back. And I did a lot of the things I used to say I was going to do. But none of it made me happy. So if you've got any ideas, a push in the right direction would be great.*

She closed her eyes, just for a moment, and waited just like she had as a child for some acknowledgment that magic was about to happen. And though, as always, nothing happened, Sam opened her eyes feeling as though something small but important had shifted today. She didn't know what—only that she felt better today than she had in a long time. She never would have expected to have that happen here, since the town was so much like she remembered, but . . . right this second, that wasn't necessarily a bad thing. And if you didn't want to get too technical, Sam supposed that could be considered a magical happening of some sort.

Find some allies. Kick some ass. Get happy. Then she thought of Jake. *You could also get— No, you know what? Three things on the list are enough for today. It's not much to go on, really. But it's a start.*

Sam gave the trunk an affectionate pat, then turned and walked away.

Late that night, when the house had gone quiet, Sam tossed and turned until it was more an effort to stay in bed than get out of it. Finally, she shoved off the covers and swung her legs over the edge of her old bed, the white wrought iron seeming almost to glow in the near dark. *Why can't I just go to sleep?* It had been a good day. Watching her mother pick a kitten from their big cage in the back of the animal hospital had almost made up for the lack of Jake's presence. Apparently, he sometimes made house calls to the couple of farms outside of town.

The thought of Jake mucking around under a cow had only contributed to her good day, not that she thought he would appreciate that if he knew.

In any case, she and Andi had come home tired, happy, and full of Merry Meet's excellent shepherd's pie. Loki would be coming home this weekend with one of his sisters, a pretty little dilute tortie whose fur was a blend of creams and peaches and grays, and who was very sweet when not taking down her siblings with a well-placed paw to the head. It was going to be interesting.

And it still didn't explain why she couldn't sleep. Insomnia had rarely been an issue of hers. She was only ever up all night when she was sick. Or when a project had captured her completely and she needed, not just wanted, but *needed* to paint.

She sat there a moment, dangling her legs and grappling with what she wanted to do.

I'm just going to screw up a perfectly good canvas and end up junking it. That's all that ever happens anymore. This felt different, though. For months, her only attempts at painting had been forced. This was more a compulsion. This was new. Or maybe it had just been gone so long that it was new again.

"All right," she said softly. She stood, slid her feet into her slippers, and padded silently out the door and down the hall to the attic stairs.

The attic had long been one of her favorite places. Open and airy, with the roof peaking high above and dormer windows to let the light in, it had never been a scary place to her. She and Emma had spent hours up here, playing dolls or hide-and-seek or whatever weird game Sam could con her sister into. And when Emma had started to balk at playing, she'd treated the attic as an escape. One of the last things her father had done for her was to fashion a small "studio" for her under the eaves, by one of the windows where the light was best. Even at ten, she'd treasured the gift.

She hadn't actually worked up here in years, but her mother had left things just as they were: an easel, a stool, a small table, and some shelves for her paints and brushes. It was simple, but she liked simple.

Her boxes of paints and supplies sat unopened beside the stool, and the two blank canvases she'd brought, remnants of a time when purchasing such things had been fun, were here as well. She'd just brought them up and left them leaning against the wall, but the positioning had changed a bit.

Sam smiled when she saw that Andi had placed one

on the easel. It looked as though it was waiting. She supposed it was.

She walked slowly to the boxes, crouched down and pulled the flaps open to reveal tubes and jars of paint, her brushes and cups, her palettes. There was only a moment of hesitation . . . and then she was pawing through the colors, plucking out what she needed, her fingers moving with the kind of purpose she'd almost forgotten. Reds and oranges, browns and greens — the image in her mind hovered over her as she chose.

And there it stayed when, twenty minutes later, brush touched canvas. Sam drew in a breath in the silence of the attic, waiting for the need to wither and die again. But this time, as her hand began to move and guide the brush, she instead felt something begin to unfurl.

Like the petals of a flower beginning to bloom.

Chapter Twelve

Jake was sitting at his desk, hands stuffed in his hair, staring at nothing in particular when Angie poked her head in.

"Sam Henry's here to see you. Are you busy?"

Sam? Here?

"Yeah, send her back," Jake said, rousing himself out of his near stupor. He ran through a quick mental checklist, mostly involving what he might smell like and what sorts of things might have left marks on his lab coat. When he decided she probably wouldn't run screaming, he scrubbed his hands through his hair, pretty sure he looked like he'd recently suffered an electric shock. At this point, he'd expected that the highlight of his day would be going home and falling onto his couch, eventually passing out in front of the television with his dog. It was possible a can of something with pasta in it would find its way into his mouth at some point before he lost consciousness.

He looked at his watch. Almost six. So close to freedom. And Sam was here. So maybe the end of his Friday wouldn't be quite as pathetic as it had been looking up until now.

There was the sound of footsteps, and after a few seconds, Sam appeared in his doorway clutching a Ziploc bag. She looked almost as surprised to find herself there as he was to see her, but whatever had prompted the visit, Jake had no interest in questioning it.

She was by far the best thing he'd seen all day.

"Hey," she said.

"Hey," Jake said, smiling. "Everything okay? Your mom decide to take the whole litter instead of just one more?"

Sam laughed, a low and sultry sound. "No. I think she's out at Pet Palace buying more stuff, though. We still on for the big handoff tomorrow evening?"

"We'd better be. I need less housemates. Marin's taking them home tonight. I think we've convinced her she needs another cat, so this should seal the deal. Anyway, I need a night off from the wrecking crew. Pretty sure Tucker thinks there're a bunch of demons living in the spare bedroom."

Her eyebrows lifted. "Tucker's afraid of cats?"

"We're manly men. We prefer the word 'cautious.'"

"I'll try and remember that." Sam flashed a smile, then began to fidget, digging one toe into the linoleum. "Are you okay? I can take off. It's no big deal. I just wanted to drop these—"

"No, no," he interrupted her quickly. "Stay. They'll be locking the doors in a minute, and we've cleared almost everybody out. Finally. I just finished up, and Tom's with the last patient now. I'm just . . . it's been a really long week. I've been up to my ears in . . . never mind." He looked again at the bag in her hand. "Oh my God. You brought me cookies?" He looked more closely. "Are those your mom's oatmeal raisin cookies? Oh my God. You just made my entire day."

Actually, the smile she gave him made his entire day. He'd tried to be cool this week, messaging her but keeping his distance. This was new. She wasn't sold on it yet, and he didn't think clambering all over her like an over-stimulated puppy was going to do anything but send her back into hiding—no matter how much he wanted to after he'd finally gotten his hands on her. But as Sam finally stepped over the threshold, he decided a week was way too long to wait, and he wouldn't be doing it again.

He drank her in from head to toe. She'd pulled her hair back into a loose bun, and pale tendrils had escaped to frame her face. She wore a dress that looked more like a long sweater, with a cowl neck that fell into a hood at her back. Then there were the gray leggings and the black knee-high boots. Stylish, a little edgy, a lot out of place. That was Sam. She looked a little like a beautiful angel of death. The kind who would have no trouble making her monthly soul quotas.

She was certainly hot as hell.

"Here, then," she said, depositing the bag directly in front of him. "You look like you could use these."

Even sealed in a bag they smelled like heaven. Jake hesitated, looking up at Sam from where he sat. But when she just looked back expectantly, he threw caution to the wind, opened the bag, and stuffed an entire cookie in his mouth. His eyes rolled back in his head. He made some sort of sound. It was hard to hear with all the pleasure centers of his brain lighting up at once.

"Bad day?" she asked, her voice laced with amusement.

"Ungnmm," he replied, then finished chewing and swallowing. "Sorry. Yes. This week has been crazy. It al-

ways happens like this, though. When it rains, it pours. And this week, it's definitely pouring."

"*Hmm,*" Sam replied, and he could feel her eyes on him as he stuffed another cookie in his mouth. He avoided eye contact, since he was concerned she might see just how close he was to shoving his face in the bag. And then he might fall asleep in the bag, and it was a plastic bag, so . . . yeah, maybe he needed to slow down a little.

"Are you sure you're okay?" she asked.

"Just wiped out," he said. "I'll make it. Do I really look that bad?"

She pulled her bottom lip into her mouth and considered him. He could tell she was trying to find a way to be diplomatic without flat-out lying.

"Well, 'bad' isn't the—"

"Jake, I just let the Prices out. Doors are locked, and we're good to—hi, I don't think we've met."

Jake watched, resigned, as Tom Perry caught sight of Sam and lit up like a Roman candle. He walked the rest of the way into the office and extended a hand. Sam shook it, smiling.

"No, I think I moved away right about the time you took over from Dr. Mullins. I'm Sam Henry. Nice to meet you."

It was odd to see Sam being polite, mostly because it wasn't something she'd felt the need to be with him. At least he could enjoy the sight of Tom, who Jake was pretty sure had been hit on by every single—and sometimes not so single—woman with a pet in the county, trying like hell to keep his tongue in his mouth. Not that he was worried about Tom trying to poach. He was a genuinely good guy, even if the Clooney comparisons he was constantly overhearing sometimes had Jake on the verge of stabbing himself or others with the nearest pointy object.

"Nice to meet you, too. I'm Tom Perry. You're one of Andi's daughters." His smile broadened.

"That's me," Sam replied, and Jake could see her wariness almost immediately. It bothered him to see how defensive she was about her family. It bothered him more to know he'd contributed to that. Once she got to know Tom at all, though, he was sure she'd figure out that the defensiveness wasn't necessary. The transplants who stayed here because they loved the Cove, Tom among them, didn't tend to pick up much of the long-standing crap that the locals refused to let die, and that was a good thing.

"We love Andi around here," Tom was saying. "Her donations have done a lot of good. Did I hear you're keeping a couple of the kittens your mom found?"

Her obvious surprise made Jake smile. She needed to get used to people being nice around here. He wanted her to expect it.

"Yes! Yes, I am," Sam said, her smile returning, shoulders relaxing. "I mean, we are. Mom decided yesterday to take one of the torties. The little black one is mine."

"I'm glad you're taking him. People are strange, you know. The black cats are still the hardest ones to adopt out." He looked at Jake. "I'm heading out. Pete and Marin are cleaning up. Go get some sleep so I can kick you around again on Monday, okay? And think of me tomorrow when you're on your butt eating Doritos and I'm here trying to figure out how to look at Shmoo Martin's teeth without losing fingers."

"The Shmoo is nothing. Last Saturday when *I* was on

my own, someone brought in a pissed off chicken. No sympathy," Jake said.

Tom looked at Sam. "You actually dating this guy? I could tell you stories, you know."

Jake groaned. "No."

"Stories, huh?" Sam asked, sounding interested. "What kind of stories?"

Tom smirked, shooting a look at him. Jake drew a finger slowly across his throat.

"The fact that he's threatening me with violence should tell you what kind of stories."

Sam laughed, and to Jake's ears it sounded just a little evil. It was sexy, even if he was a little preoccupied with Tom's probably not very idle threat.

"I know where you live, Tom," Jake said, narrowing his eyes. "Remember that."

The other vet sighed dramatically. "I don't want to be checking all my locks and windows for the next few years, so I'm going to have to leave you guessing. I could tell you where his hands have been today, though. That's an interesting story, too."

"I'm going to have to take a pass on that one," Sam said, looking between them and clearly amused. "I haven't eaten yet, and I was kind of looking forward to that. It was nice meeting you, though."

"Probably a wise choice. Nice meeting you, too," Tom replied. "I'm sure I'll see you around. Welcome back." He flashed a grin at her, then looked at Jake. "I mean it. Get some sleep. And maybe eat something besides ramen and a pudding cup. You look like shit." Then he vanished, leaving the two of them alone again. Sam looked at the space where he'd just been.

"I like him," she said.

"You would." He started to get up, noting that his body now felt like it weighed about a thousand pounds. When he was finally on his feet, he braced his hands at the small of his back and stretched. "Ugh."

Sam just looked at him and shook her head. "He was kidding about the pudding and ramen, right?"

He tried to remember the last time he'd gone grocery shopping, and what was left in his pantry. "Maybe."

"Do you even *have* food at your house? Like, real food?" she asked, beginning to frown.

"By some kind of loose definition, sure."

He loved the look she gave him, the chin down, arched brow, *God you're an idiot* look. It was very cute, despite what it said about her assessment of his life skills. And despite his weariness, and the fact that they'd planned to get together tomorrow for the transfer of the kittens and maybe a movie, he suddenly very much wanted her to stick around.

"Listen, are you busy tonight?" he asked. "I need to go home and let Tucker out . . . the dog walker gets him at lunch, but he's going to need some running-around time. I can grab some fast food on the way, though, if you want to join me for some . . . tacos? Fried something or other? What do you like?"

Her nose wrinkled, and for a few seconds he thought it was a reaction to his question. The pang he felt was quick, sharp, unfamiliar. She was going to say no.

Except she didn't.

"Yes, on the dinner. No on the grease. Give me fifteen minutes. I'll be over. And if you fall asleep before I get there, I will hurt you." Not all the wariness was gone, but she still surprised him. Something about her seemed different today. He just couldn't quite put his finger on what.

"You're going to . . . cook?" The sweetness of it caught him completely off guard. He'd found Sam fascinating, frustrating, and completely desirable. But not sweet. This was new. He watched her, fascinated.

"You look exhausted," she said, tucking a piece of hair behind her ear. "I can cook. Sort of. It's not a big deal."

"For my pots and pans it is—believe me. I think they're still there. Hopefully." He stared at her while she looked uncomfortable, a little irritated, and—in the case of her cheeks—bright pink. It was a good color on her. "You really want to come over and cook for me?"

Sam rolled her eyes. "You're a mess, Jake. Go home. I'll be there in a few. It's not like I had so many other exciting things planned anyway."

The bluster was transparent, maybe because he was getting used to it. She actually cared that he was sort of a wreck today. Maybe it was because he was so damned tired, but the realization affected him more than he might have expected. Jake had a sudden, overwhelming urge to grab her and kiss her senseless. He took a step toward her with that in mind, but Sam had apparently reached her current limits for outward affection.

"Uh-uh," she said, backing up with a knowing look in her eye. "Home."

"You sound like my mother," he grumbled.

"Just for that, I'm burning your food," Sam said. "Let's go."

Painting deep into the night had injected Sam with a dose of confidence that she'd cruised on all day. It had sent her to work with that bag of cookies, it had brought her a couple of big sales, and now it was going to take her all the way to Jake's by way of the grocery store.

It's finally happened. I've gone completely insane.

As she watched Jake get into his truck, she had to wonder whether she'd been given a much-needed boost to her bruised ego, or a good reason to lock herself in a room for twenty-four hours the next time she painted something that didn't make her want to put her head through the canvas.

Either way, she was in for it now. She'd seen the look on his face, the flash of heat in his eyes once he'd realized she was serious. And the tight, heavy feeling low in her belly was giving her fair warning about being alone with him. She could tell herself all she wanted that she just felt sorry for him, that if she didn't do something he was just going to slither home, eat a can of pasta rings better suited for a ten-year-old's lunch, and pass out in his clothes. And for all his friends, the man really did seem to need a keeper.

But that wasn't the whole story—or even most of it—and she knew it.

Take it slow, right? Like you ever could where he was concerned.

Sam got into her car and watched Jake climb into his truck, his hair impossibly mussed and his eyes sleepy. She tapped her fingers restlessly on the steering wheel, turned on the stereo, and pulled out behind him, returning the wave he gave her.

Act natural. Act natural. Not a big deal. Jesus, Samantha, you'll be lucky if he's still awake when you get there. Except that was bull. He'd be awake, and he'd be waiting.

She called her mother on the way to the grocery store to let her know she'd be back late, then headed to Fresh Pride and hurried in to grab what she needed. It had to be a quick meal to assemble, so pasta seemed the most likely option. She was no gourmet chef, but she'd cooked often enough in the little apartment in New York, cramped though that sorry excuse for a kitchen had been. She had some ideas.

Ten minutes later, Sam emerged with the seven ingredients she needed and hopped back in the car. She made the quick drive to his house, then parked in the driveway and headed up the steps, hearing Tucker's excited barking from the moment she got out of the car. It seemed like a good idea to tighten her grip on the bag before she rang the doorbell, just in case. There was a bunch of thumping, a grumbled, "Damn it, Tucker, *sit*," and then the door was opening.

She felt her heart clench as he smiled at her, his pretty eyes reddish and a little puffy, like he'd been rubbing them. *Trying to stay awake,* she thought, and melted just a little.

"You were serious," he said, looking at the grocery bag and running a hand through hair that was already standing on end. On him, it was ridiculously appealing. So were the plaid pajama pants he was wearing with an old T-shirt. Everything hung just right on his tall, lean frame. It was enough to make a girl want to start removing those things with her teeth.

Sam shifted her weight from foot to foot, trying to stay focused on something other than Jake's pants. "Yes, well, don't get all excited. This is basically glorified mac and cheese."

"I can't help it. Real food *is* very exciting." He stepped aside. "Come on in. Tucker's pretending he has manners."

She stepped inside and looked at the dog, who was only barely in what could be called a sitting position. His entire body was wiggling, and he looked like the restraint that being in one place required was just about killing him.

"You have a treat in your hand, don't you?" she asked as she walked by.

"If there's another thing that would make him sit, I'm not aware of it."

She eyed Tucker, whose attention was completely fixated on Jake's fisted hand. "Just give me a minute to get this stuff on the counter, okay? A running start."

"I can do that, but you'd better hurry," Jake said. "He's approaching critical mass." Tucker was indeed starting to bounce his weight back and forth between his front paws, eyes now darting between Jake's hand and Sam.

"Crap," Sam said, then dashed away on a hysterical giggle.

She flew down the hall and hung a left into the kitchen, getting the bag onto the counter just in time to hear Jake's "Good boy, Tucker!" Then there was the frantic clicking of nails on the wood floor racing in her direction, so she did the only thing she could think of. She put her back against the counter, crouched down, and braced herself.

"Incoming!" Jake called.

She managed a laugh before the impact sent her sprawling, and then she gave in, filling her hands with Tucker's soft fur and unsure whether it was the dog or Jake's throaty laugh that had taken her breath away.

Chapter Thirteen

Twenty minutes later, Tucker panted happily by Sam's feet while she finished up the sauce for the cooked penne pasta. Jake had vanished without much fuss after she'd kicked him out of the kitchen. He looked like he needed to sit somewhere, and she needed to concentrate on what she was doing so that nothing, including herself, caught on fire.

That was less likely while he was being babysat by the sports channel and she didn't have to wonder whether he was looking at her butt.

The quiet, with nothing but the sounds of Tucker's breathing and the drone of the TV from the other room to break it, gave her some time to decompress. This was one of her favorite go-to recipes—just a little basil, a little garlic powder and black pepper, some heavy cream, half a cup of sun-dried tomatoes (several of which she may or may not have eaten while cooking), and a bag of shredded four cheese blend, and voilà! Sun-dried tomato cream sauce!

She poured it over the pasta in another pot, stirred it up, and then set it down on the stove so she could hunt up plates. After a few minutes of searching, she found them. They were old, probably hand-me-downs from his mom, and dated, but they would work. Two plates went on the table, along with forks and a pair of mismatched glasses. She didn't even bother looking for napkins, instead just folding a couple of paper towels into something workable.

Some part of her had imagined him as perfect. This was actually sort of refreshing. He was such a *guy*.

"I smell food. Real food. How can this be?"

Her mouth curved up when she turned her head to look at him, standing in the doorway. "Magic. And the use of a couple of pots that I had to clean the dust out of. Sit."

He obediently wandered over to the table and sat down. Sam grabbed the pot, along with the large spoon she'd found sitting all by its lonesome in a drawer, then walked over to put some of the pasta on each of their plates. By the time she sat back down, Jake just about had his nose in it. He hadn't picked up his fork, though.

"Aren't you going to eat?" she asked.

He raised his eyes to hers, honey gold in the light. Striking eyes, with lashes so dark that he could almost have been wearing mascara. She wondered fleetingly how he would look in guyliner and immediately had to stop thinking about it. He'd look like a pirate. A very bad pirate.

The kitchen suddenly felt much too warm.

Tucker flopped onto his side in front of the stove, gave a heavy sigh, and closed his eyes.

"The one thing he doesn't do is beg? Your dog is weird, Jake. Not that I'm complaining."

"Me, either. Not begging is the first thing he and I worked on. He's really good about it, I just wish it hadn't taken up all the available space in that thick head of his."

He forked up a bite, popped it in his mouth, and chewed slowly.

"Mmm," he said, closing his eyes.

Sam watched him with wide eyes for a few seconds, then forced her gaze onto her own plate. This is what she got, she thought. This is what she got for not having sex for the last nine months. Okay, ten months. Barely. All Jake had to do was make something like an O face at his food, and her ovaries started the final countdown to explosion.

Maybe eating would fix that. Or maybe she would just stop being hungry and continue wanting to crawl across the table. That was more likely.

"This is awesome," he said. "Thanks, Sam. This is at least a thousand times better than anything I would have come up with."

She looked around. "You probably have a cupboard full of canned dinners and junk food, right?"

He smiled. "Maybe."

"Tucker probably eats better than you do." She forked up another bite, then looked around curiously. It was a nice kitchen, really. Maple cabinets, granite countertops. This was an older house, so someone had redone it in the not too distant past. But if it had been Jake, he hadn't gone to a lot of trouble setting it up afterward.

It just felt kind of empty.

"What's the deal with this place, anyway?" she asked.

"What do you mean?"

"Well, you have this nice big house close to downtown. Some recent remodeling. Actually really clean, especially for a guy. But there doesn't seem to be a lot in it. I mean, apart from the couch, the ugly recliner, and that huge TV. I definitely noticed the huge TV."

"It's a man thing," Jake said, his face completely serious. "We measure our masculinity by the size of our electronics. Didn't you know that?"

"It's something I've long suspected." She stabbed several pieces of penne with her fork. "Masculine anthropology is a hobby of mine, you know."

That made him laugh while she enjoyed the food. She'd done well, she decided. It wasn't gourmet, but it was good.

"I don't know," he finally said. "It's just me and Tucker here. I liked the place. Figured I'd fill it up eventually. I just haven't had the time yet."

"How long have you been in it?"

"Little over a year," he replied, then arched an eyebrow at her look. "What? I work a lot."

"I just hope you're not sleeping on a mattress on the floor. People who have dusty pots and one serving spoon do things like that," she said. "And if you have one of those tie-dye blankets hanging on the wall for decoration anywhere in this house, I don't want to see. Ever."

"Hey, I let my roommate keep that after college. And for your information, I have a perfectly good bed," Jake said.

Her thoughts spiraled immediately back down into the gutter. *No. It's too soon, and you promised yourself you'd give this some time. Tying him to the bed doesn't fall into that category. Not even a little.*

"Well," she said out loud, "that's something, at least."

They sat in silence for a few minutes, until Sam started to worry that her thoughts were written all over her face. Especially the impure ones, since they were legion.

"What about you?" he finally said. "You're the one

who had a place in New York. So what was that like? I'm going to assume it was furnished better."

She stiffened despite his smile. That stupid apartment . . . it made her stomach turn just thinking about it. It wasn't terrible, just tiny. But it had gotten to feel like a cage by the end. Okay, maybe it had actually been like living in one of the outer circles of hell.

"It wasn't that interesting, really."

Jake looked skeptical. "Oh, come on. I'm the boring one. Small Town Vet Guy. I know everyone and don't go anywhere, remember? So tell me some stories. Or just brag about your furniture. I don't care. I want to hear about it."

"I never said you were boring." She'd implied his life was, though, and she knew it. That had mattered substantially less before she'd fallen back into the habit of liking him. The speed with which that had happened was really unnerving. Still, New York was a subject she didn't really want to canvass. Possibly ever.

"You've been in the city since college, right?" His voice softened a little. "You, ah . . . you were really determined to go. I remember. I know you went to NYU."

"Who told you that? My mom?" she asked with a soft laugh. It had to be her mother. One thing Andi Henry was not shy about was bragging about her girls. It was a surprise when Jake dropped his gaze and shrugged.

"I might have had a look at your Web site once or twice."

That floored her. All this time, she'd assumed he'd walked away and forgotten about her. Knowing he hadn't was . . . nice. And strange. And sweet.

And it hurt, though not with a sharp pain. This was

more of a dull ache that spoke to an old wound and the passage of a great deal of time.

"Oh," was all she said. Then she fell silent, poking at her food while she turned this new bit of information over. He'd seen her work, she realized. Like Emma, he'd been watching from afar without her even being aware of it. Watching and, she thought, maybe even silently supporting. There was a strange sort of comfort in that, even if she didn't know quite what to say about it.

"So," he finally said, breaking the silence. "New York. What is it like, living there? I've always wondered."

Somewhere deep inside, she felt a part of herself she'd locked up tight begin to crack and crumble away. There were a bunch of things she didn't like to remember behind that barrier, but before she could shore it up, a little of the truth escaped.

"It was big. And noisy. And really amazing," she said. "There's always someplace to go, something to do. When you live right in the city, like I did, it's easy to forget that anything exists outside of it. There's just so *much*, you know? It feels like the center of the universe." She remembered how she'd felt at first, like everything she'd ever wanted was right there, just waiting for her to grab it. The city had pulsed with life, and she was a part of it. Finally a part of something bigger than herself.

It might have been an illusion, but it had been nice while it lasted.

Jake was nodding. "I've been to New York a couple of times. Loved visiting, but I have to be honest: I don't think I could live there. Times Square was nuts."

Sam tried to smile, though it felt brittle. "Yeah, it's nuts because that's where the tourists go. It's a huge city, but I wouldn't call Times Square normal. You do have to be okay with living basically on top of thousands of other people, but . . . it can still be pretty lonely."

"Seriously? How can it be lonely when you can't hear yourself think?" he asked.

"Oh, you'd be surprised. After I was there a while, I figured out that crowds are some of the loneliest places you can be."

"Is that why you stopped painting?" he asked. There wasn't even a hint of mockery in his words. Still, this was the last thing she wanted to discuss with him, or with anyone. Not even now, when she finally had a little bit of hope that she hadn't lost everything. *Especially* not now. Last night, she'd tapped into some part of herself she'd thought had vanished. Whether she could do it again was completely up in the air. And though she knew it was silly, she couldn't help but be afraid that she would jinx it just by acknowledging it.

The cool light of morning had shown her a partially finished painting that might just be good. Really good. But until it was done—until she was sure—it was only for her.

"I don't want to talk about it," she said. The words were quick, automatic. To her they seemed innocuous enough. But she caught the flash of irritation on Jake's face before he looked away. Her hand tightened on her fork. It was so frustrating. How could she explain her issues to him when she didn't really understand all of them herself? She took a breath and tried again.

"Look, it's just a hard thing to talk about. I can't paint right now."

"Can't?"

She wet her lips. "I have no idea what you want me to say. I can't. I don't. I don't because I can't. Does it really matter?" It didn't to her. The block mattered. So did finding the mental dynamite to fix it. Not just a little, but all the way.

Jake heaved a sigh, and it rippled right through her. "Sure, it matters. I'm trying to get to know you, Sam. You're not making it easy."

"That's not true." Sam wrinkled her nose. "We've talked plenty. What am I making difficult?"

Jake's plate was clean, and he carefully set his fork down beside it. "You joke around with me, and you listen to me. Actually, I never realized how much listening to me you did back then. But I try to get beneath the surface and you put the brakes on. It's like everything before you came back is off limits."

"Because it's not important," she replied, forcing herself to keep her eyes locked with his. Maybe—maybe—he had a valid point. Joking and listening were comfortable. Talking about herself? Not so much. But poking at her wasn't going to get him what he wanted.

Jake stared at her, aghast. "How is it not important? Where you worked, people you knew, things you did, why you even came back . . . you're putting a huge part of yourself out of reach from the get-go. I don't even know what I'm allowed to ask you about. The weather?"

"Why are you so nosy?"

"Why are you so prickly?" he shot back.

Sam's voice rose. "Why can't you just be happy I'm here?"

Jake's rose accordingly. "Why can't you be happy I'm interested?"

She threw up her hands and let out a furious growl. "Stop pushing me! God! Were you always like this? You didn't give a damn what I thought about before, so why do you now?"

"That's bullshit," Jake said flatly. "The difference is that before, I didn't have to ask. I might have done a lot of the talking, but you told me things. About how you wanted out, how much your art meant to you, how you were never going to try as hard as Emma had to fit in. You didn't understand your mom. You missed your dad."

Sam stared at him, momentarily startled into silence. "I ..."

"You thought I wasn't paying attention," Jake said. "I might have been a typical self-absorbed teenager, but I heard every word you said, Sam. So don't tell me that I don't get to hear the rest of the story."

"I thought we were starting over," she said, knowing how defensive she sounded. She didn't know what to do with the intensity she saw looking back at her. The real Jake was turning out to be much different from the one she'd been constructing in her mind all this time. The hurt had colored her memories until she had forgotten how much he really *had* listened. Not only that, but he'd remembered.

"We *are* starting over," Jake said. "I just want to know where you're starting from."

She could tell him to piss off and walk away, she knew. But all that was going to do was add to her pile of regrets. She had to learn to deal with all this baggage before it spilled all over everything here and made it impossible to dig out. But sitting here with Jake was a start, she thought. It could be a start, if she let it. Especially when he was looking at her like he didn't know whether to kiss her or shout at her. She took a deep breath. Sighed. And spoke.

"I'm starting from square one. I worked in a really up-scale gallery in New York. Gallerie Mona. She seemed interested in my work at first, but she ended up indifferent, then actively hostile. It wasn't all bad. I mean, I worked my ass off, learned that side of the business, made contacts. I had a good eye for what would sell, and to who. Clients liked me, enough that quite a few of them started to ask for me. When you work for a complete narcissist, that tends to be a problem." She tucked the back of her hand beneath her chin and played with her fork.

"This year, I finally saw the writing on the wall. I'd been selling work independently, and that was okay. You saw my Web site. I did have buyers, and the extra money was nice to have, even if I couldn't have lived on it. A big show was something Mona had been dangling in front of me since she'd hired me, and she's influential enough that I didn't want to piss her off by trying to get a look from other galleries. When she fired my friend Zack, though, I knew I was next in line. He was the one ally I had left in that place, and even better at his job than I was. So, I did what I should have from the beginning. And it worked. I was offered a show at another gallery, smaller, but well thought of and known for really increasing the visibility of the emerging artists they showcase." She shook her head, remembering how naive she'd been in her excitement. "I thought . . . I was finally going to catch a break. When I wasn't at work, I was painting. And not like I'd completely lost my enthusiasm for it, but I had my heart in it again."

"What happened?" Jake asked. She'd been so focused on telling the story that she hadn't realized, until right then, just how engrossed Jake seemed. She wasn't used to having anyone hanging on her every word. She straightened in her chair, tucking some of the strands of her hair back behind her ears.

"Mona Richard happened," Sam said, keeping her tone matter-of-fact. Pity, especially Jake's pity, wasn't something she wanted. "She was in her glory. I think she'd been waiting a long time for me to screw up so she could really let me have it. My looking elsewhere for exposure was taken as a personal affront. I was ungrateful, worthless. I should have been working my ass off to impress *her*, not sneaking around trying to, you know, be an artist. My work was amateurish. I wasn't up to contemporary standards. The only reason anyone would show my work was because I was taking advantage of the connections she'd helped me make, and those people felt sorry for me. Also, I was a backstabbing bitch." She considered. "I may have missed a few things, but that was the gist. It wasn't a great conversation. I think people in the next building overheard it."

Jake didn't look like he pitied her, at least, so that was something. Instead he looked awed. "Jesus. She sounds like a psycho."

Sam gave a soft, humorless laugh. "Yeah, a psycho with a stupid amount of money who knows everyone. My show was canceled, no reason given. I got a flurry of rejections from other places I'd submitted work. Oh, and after enough time had passed that Mona could enjoy my misery firsthand, I got fired. That was almost three weeks ago. And so . . . here I am."

"Here you are." Jake's eyes were huge. "Wow."

"Uh-huh," Sam replied. "Oh, and this was right about the time my roommate decided to bail on the lease, since one of her clients was putting her up in a penthouse somewhere."

"Client . . ."

Sam shrugged. "You know, client, john, whatever."

"Your roommate was a *hooker*?"

"High-priced escort," Sam corrected him. "It was kind of a newer venture for her. Apparently it pays better than being a barista."

"Wow," he said again.

"Yeah, pretty much." She felt drained after throwing all that out there in one go. Apart from her mother, Jake was the only person she'd dumped this on. He couldn't say he hadn't asked for it, though.

"You did say you wanted to know," Sam said. "So there it is. I waved the white flag, threw all my stuff in the car, and came running home. Epic fail. The end." When he said nothing, she finally looked at his face. His expression was impossible to read. Maybe he thought she hadn't tried hard enough. Maybe he thought she was nuts. Both of those were questions she grappled with often enough. But Jake surprised her by reaching across the table and covering her hand with his, stroking his thumb over her skin so lightly that she was surprised into a shiver.

"That wasn't completely terrible, was it?" he asked with a half smile. The question surprised her enough that she returned the smile.

"Living it? Yes. Telling you?" She gave a little shrug. "No. It wasn't." In fact, she felt like a little of the weight she'd been dragging around had vanished. It hadn't disappeared, but neither had Jake. And that counted for something.

"Okay," he said. Just a single simple word.

"Okay?"

"Okay, I'm glad you told me. I'm sorry all that happened. I really want to know how you ended up with a hooker for a roommate." Another light caress of the thumb, one that rippled all the way to her core. "And I'm really glad you're home. I don't think that's a fail. Actually, that's the best part of the story so far."

"Oh." She tried not to feel all warm and melty inside, but it was impossible. So she gave in and enjoyed it instead. "Thanks."

After a moment, she pulled her hand away, though it tingled where it had touched his. Her heart kicked into an uneven rhythm, and she was suddenly very much aware of how alone they were. Sam picked up her plate. She felt ridiculously awkward with those steady, dark golden eyes on her.

"I'm just going to, ah, clean this off." She stood, silently praying to every deity she could think of that she didn't stumble and land on her face. Somehow, she made it to the sink.

"No, here, let me do it."

She heard the warm rumble of Jake's voice behind her, but she already had the plate beneath the warm stream of water. She could actually feel him standing there, so close that if she took a step back she'd be plastered against him. Just as she felt his hesitation, Sam knew she wouldn't even need to use words to ask for what she wanted. It was just a single step. But some part of her refused to give any more than she already had. She'd come this far. . . . He could close the distance.

When Jake's hands slid over her hips, Sam let out a shaking breath she wasn't even aware she'd been holding. He stepped against her, chest to back, and pressed his face into her hair. His movements were smooth, deliberate, but she could feel the pounding of his heart against her back. When he breathed in, inhaling the scent of her hair, Sam's own breaths grew shallow.

This connection had always been there, crackling beneath the surface. She'd never forgotten it, and never felt it the same way with anyone else. That had always been the problem. How did you stay away from something—someone—you were drawn to like this?

She forced herself to set the dish in the sink, shut off the water. Then she put her hands on his, spreading her fingers. She leaned against his chest, warm and solid. His fingers began to lightly knead at her hips, rhythmic pressure that focused all of her thoughts entirely below the waistline. Her muscles tensed, and her breasts felt heavy and full as the nipples tightened to buds beneath the thin fabric of her dress. Heat coiled pleasurably between her legs, radiating outward to warm her body, making the core of her slick and tight. She could barely breathe.

Oddly, that no longer seemed like a pressing concern.

"I thought about this all week," he murmured against her hair. "God, you feel good."

Her thoughts felt shrouded in haze. "So do you." It wasn't much, but at least it was coherent.

His hands slid upward to her waist, pulling a little of her dress up with it. She had a brief vision, a hot flicker of a thought involving being bent over the sink, Jake pumping into her from behind. The muscles between her legs pulsed and jumped, and she drank in a soft little gasp of air. It didn't seem to have escaped Jake, who moved his head to speak directly into her ear, mouth brushing the sensitive lobe.

"This counts as helping with the dishes, right?"

She smiled, then sighed as he began to kiss her ear, gentle presses of his lips interspersed with the gentle scrape of his teeth. She tilted her head to allow him better access, arching a little as she tried to maneuver him closer. Jake moved from her ear to the sensitive skin below it, then to the side of her neck.

Sam closed her fingers around the edges of his hands and pulled them upward, over breasts that were now so sensitized that the friction made her moan. Jake gave a harsh gasp against her neck, and he squeezed lightly at the same time his hips moved against her. He was rock hard, the clothing between them a thin barrier that did nothing to disguise it.

This, she thought, *is definitely one of the perks of growing up and starting over.* At sixteen, she'd wanted him without fully understanding what the benefits of catching him might be. Now she had both the knowledge and the boldness she'd once lacked.

She turned in his arms, catching a flash of Jake's eyes before his mouth was on hers. Their last kiss had started sweet, but this one was explosive from the start. His mouth was hard on hers, demanding, urging her to keep up as they wound together in a hot tangle of lips and tongues and teeth. He pressed her back against the edge of the counter, the length of him rigid against her lower belly. Sam let her hands roam over him, over the hard planes of his chest, the jut of his hips, then back up over broad shoulders and into the soft brush of his hair.

This is happening, she thought, though she couldn't quite convince herself. She'd wanted him for so long that this seemed like it could be just another fevered fantasy . . . though it left all other fantasies in the dust.

She felt a light tug at the back of her head, heard the soft clatter of metal in the sink, and then her hair came down, tumbling over her shoulders as Jake filled his hands with it. Sam laughed breathlessly against his mouth, impressed.

"You're a little too good at that."

"You like to wear it up. I've been thinking about how to get it down all week. I had a strategy." His breath was warm as he punctuated his words with hungry little kisses that Sam met eagerly.

"You're scary," she informed him, even as she slipped her hands up beneath his thin cotton shirt to explore the expanse of smooth, wiry muscle. Jake's laugh ended on a groan.

"You have no idea."

She loved the feel of him, fingers cruising over flesh that jumped and tensed at her touch. It was good to know that she wasn't the only one who needed this. Every ragged breath Jake took stoked her own need, until she found herself clinging to him, nails digging into his hips, one leg hooked around his to take advantage of the delicious friction as he kept her pinned against the sink.

"Come upstairs with me," he breathed against her lips.

"Upstairs . . ."

"Or the couch. Or the floor. The edge of the counter's going to leave a mark. . . . I mean, unless you like that sort of thing. Totally not judging."

That he could make her laugh even when she was about to burst into flames was one of the things that made him almost impossible to resist. And she didn't want to resist this. Not really. Still, some tiny sliver of cold rationality managed to find a path through her deepening sexual haze.

If you do this, there's no going—

"Bed," Sam said, ruthlessly shutting down the internal debate. She was sick to death of rationality. For once, she just wanted to have what she wanted when she wanted it. She'd spent so much time worrying what might happen. Just for tonight, she was going to concentrate on what was actually happening.

And considering that Jake having his hands all over her was happening, it didn't seem right that she should divert her attention elsewhere.

He didn't say another word, only grabbed her hand with his and headed out of the kitchen, down the hall and toward the stairs. Sam tried to catch her breath, but her heart was threatening to burst out of her chest and go skittering off across the room somewhere. Jake moved quickly, and the thin flannel pants he wore made it pretty clear why. Sam couldn't help the self-satisfied smile from curving the corners of her mouth.

Tucker, who had apparently gotten disgusted with the scene in the kitchen and left, looked at them from where he'd flopped and thumped his tail a couple of times before sighing and closing his eyes again.

Sam followed quickly up the stairs, surprised at how easy it was to keep the doubt from creeping in. Maybe it was because there wasn't any. Or maybe it was just that impending sex with Jake canceled everything else out. Whatever it was, she'd take it, because all she felt was a wild kind of excitement that reverberated all the way down to her toes.

The light was on in his bedroom, and she was glad to see that Jake did not, in fact, sleep on a mattress on the floor. There was a real bed, and furniture. In fact, she decided as she looked around, it was probably the most inviting room in the house. The walls were painted the color of milk chocolate. There were even curtains.

"Is this the only room you live in?" she asked.

"I like to sleep," Jake replied. "And I read in here."

That would explain the glasses on the nightstand, she thought. Sam then tried to picture Jake in his glasses, reading in bed. Shirtless. As though he could read her mind, Jake pulled his shirt over his head.

Her thoughts scattered to the four winds.

However good the man looked in clothes, he looked even better out of them. Sam let her eyes roam over his bare chest, which was lightly muscled without being bulky. His broad shoulders tapered down to a narrow waist, below which a dusting of dark hair vanished beneath the waistband of his pants.

"Wow," Sam murmured. "Shit, did I say that out loud?"

He smirked and pulled her toward him. "Mmmhmm."

She skimmed her hands down his chest. *All mine,* she thought. It definitely left her giddy with power, though she thought that right now, a maniacal laugh might kill the mood. Instead, she reached down to grip the hem of her dress, but Jake surprised her by taking her hands.

"Can I?" he asked.

Surprised, she nodded and let go. There was something incredibly sensual about the way he slowly dragged the fabric up over her thighs, the backs of his fingers brushing over her hips, her waist, the sides of her breasts as she lifted her arms to allow him to take it all the way off. As he watched, she unhooked her bra and tossed it where her dress lay crumpled on the floor. All that was left were her boots and leggings.

It had been a long time since she'd felt so exposed in front of someone, unclothed or otherwise. Her nerves, absent until now, reemerged in a flurry of self-doubt. It was impossible to tell what Jake was thinking as he looked at her.

"I look like a topless superhero," Sam said with a half

laugh, beginning to play with her fingers. Jake blinked rapidly, as though she'd woken him from a stupor, and then smiled as he shook his head.

"Sam," he said, stepping closer. "You. Are. Beautiful. And please remember, I'm a guy, so . . . topless superheroes are really okay with me."

He snagged her waistband with his finger and tugged. She went to him without resistance, unable to help the soft sigh when the bare skin of her breasts connected with his chest. Then he was teasing her again with his tongue, his clever mouth, making her forget her embarrassment and stoking her desire until she was moving restlessly against him, silently asking for more.

Jake steered her backward, around the edge of his bed while he kissed her senseless, until the backs of her knees hit the edge of the mattress. Sam pulled back and slid down to sit, then pushed herself backward. Jake pulled the drawstring on his pants and slid them off slim, muscular hips. Sam's breath caught as his single remaining piece of clothing vanished onto the floor, revealing the contours of his thighs, the sculpted muscles of his abdomen . . . and the rigid thrust of his cock.

She hadn't realized it at the time, but Jake would have made an even better nude model than a clothed one. Shame she hadn't asked. Then again, some things were worth waiting for.

He crawled onto the bed after her, pausing to remove first one of her boots, then the other, and finally pulling off her leggings and panties in one quick sweep. When he'd thrown those somewhere on the floor, he gave her a slow, thorough perusal that made her feel as though she was blushing everywhere.

"Wow is an understatement," he finally said, his voice

a low and sensual growl she'd never heard from him before. Jake gently pushed her legs apart while she watched
him, propped up on her elbows, back arched. What remained of her self-consciousness vanished at his obvious
appreciation. They both liked what they saw—and what
they felt. It would be stupid not to revel in it.

His beautiful hazel eyes were more wolfish than human tonight, and he kept them fixed on her as he
pressed his mouth to the inside of her knee. His lips on
her skin tickled a little, and she smiled, her laugh a soft
puff of air. Then he moved up a little farther, giving the
skin low on her inner thigh a teasing lick. This time,
there was no laugh, only a soft moan as the small frisson
of pleasure rippled up her leg. He slowly worked his
way up, giving each side ample attention until Sam had
dropped full onto her back, unable to do much but respond to each brush of his mouth and tongue. When he
finally parted the slick folds of her sex with his fingers
and pressed a lingering kiss on the throbbing bud between them, she arched her back, mouth opening on a
near-silent gasp.

Her hands fisted in the comforter as Jake began his
sweet torment in earnest, teasing her with light strokes
of his tongue, then interspersing them with hard presses
that had her winding tighter and tighter, until the only
breaths she took were shallow sips of air timed perfectly
with every stroke. Her hips moved of their own accord,
lifting into his mouth over and over. She could feel herself rushing toward climax, pulled along by a current she
couldn't control.

Sam opened her eyes, looking down to see Jake's dark
head between her thighs. It was enough to give her a final push as his tongue flickered over her swollen sex. She

cried out, body bowing upward as every muscle in her body clenched tight, then released on a wave of crushing pleasure.

She felt him move, showering her lower belly with kisses as she rode each ebbing wave. Sam watched him, her vision hazy. Her body was so sensitized that when he rose above her and his heated skin met hers, she quivered, giving a breathless moan while she twisted beneath him. He hardly looked real to her, his skin flushed, eyes alight. It was a fantasy made flesh—only so much better.

"Jake," she murmured, lifting hands that felt weighted and boneless to stroke down his chest. His heart beat rapidly beneath her fingertips.

His breathing was ragged. "So beautiful," was all he said. He pulled back, and she heard the drawer of his nightstand open, the crinkle of a wrapper. She waited, lids heavy, knowing he wouldn't be long. A few shallow breaths and he was against her again, sinking into her with a groan, filling her so that she stretched tight around him. Sam lifted into him, her head falling back as she skimmed her hands down to his hips. She could feel every pulse of him, and she lifted up, urging him even deeper. He began to move, slowly at first, sinking into her, stoking her desire until it was thrumming through her once again.

Sam gripped him more tightly, and Jake's thrusts grew faster, harder, until the bed shook with the force of them. His soft, guttural moans were driving her wild, pushing her back toward the edge of her control. Everywhere their bodies touched set off shock waves of pleasure, until she found herself ready to fall once again. Jake pulled back enough to look in her eyes, his hair wild from her fingers in it, his skin glistening. And she felt something inside her, in the dark and hurt places she kept hidden, finally begin to warm. To heal.

Jake touched his forehead to hers, and she could feel him shaking, waiting at the edge himself. For her.

She pressed a kiss to his lips, different from the ones that had come before. Then, with only a hint of pressure from her hands, she asked him to take her over. Jake began to move in her again, his eyes closing as his head fell back. She could feel his muscles straining, and she clung to him, giving herself over to the moment. To him.

He thrust into her hard, a single word on his lips. Her name.

"Sam."

And this time, they leaped off the edge together, wrapped around each other as the world narrowed to a tiny point of light, then burst into stars.

Chapter Fourteen

Jake had never been a huge fan of mornings, but as he drifted slowly up out of sleep, one of his first coherent thoughts was that he could learn to enjoy them. As much as he loved Tucker, he was glad that for once, the other body in the bed wasn't covered in fur.

He breathed in deeply as his body gradually woke up, just enjoying the fact that the person curved into an "s" so he could fit her perfectly against him, tucking his knees behind hers and nuzzling her hair, was Sam. She smelled like a wonderful combination of her own light perfume and his cologne.

She smelled like *his*. And though he prided himself on his brains and breaking the dumb jock stereotype, he was just enough of a caveman to enjoy it.

"Mmm," she said, a soft sound in her sleep. His hand rested on her hip, and he took pains not to move too much and wake her. He carefully lifted up just enough to be able to see her, eyes closed, dark blond lashes twined together, full lips slightly parted, and cheeks still a little pink from being abraded by his own. He guessed he'd have to start shaving a little more regularly. And maybe learn to cook something other than canned spaghetti for the next time she came over.

No way he was letting her be the only cook in the relationship.

Relationship. He turned the word over in his mind. If they hadn't been there before, they certainly were now. And that was fine with him. Sam might take a little more convincing, but she'd had a rough go of it. After what she'd told him last night, it was no wonder she didn't have much faith in people.

So he'd just show her she didn't have anything to worry about anymore.

Jake leaned over and buried his face in her hair, breathing deeply and pulling her closer. She stirred against him, stretching languidly and yawning. Her wiggling woke him up the rest of the way.

"Morning," he said, moving his mouth against the back of her shoulder. It was the first time he'd noticed her tattoo, a small black Halloween cat arching its back, almost tribal in its design and simplicity. It was a hidden surprise, and ridiculously sexy, he thought. It was also apt, and in more ways than one. Sam was cuddly when she wanted to be, but she definitely had claws.

"Morning," she replied, turning her head enough that he could see her sleepy expression. Her lips curved in an inviting smile. He planned to take full advantage. Jake leaned in to nibble on her earlobe when Tucker started barking downstairs. An instant later, the bell rang. He frowned. Then he remembered.

Shane. Fitz. The boat.

"Shit."

Sam's brow arched, and she twisted around to look at him as he fumbled out of the bed. He'd never been sorrier to leave a woman in bed in his life. Her mass of pale hair was a sexy mess, tumbling over her shoulders. She didn't bother to cover her breasts, small and perfectly sized for his hands, instead letting the comforter tangle around her slim little waist. She looked like a satisfied nymph. And if he stared at her any longer, he was going to end up back in the bed while his friends went and found the spare key.

Some serious awkwardness would ensue. Not that that was really avoidable at this point.

"Problem?" Sam asked, shoving her hair out of her face and yawning again. She frowned and looked around as he yanked on his pajama pants. "Morning . . . morning . . ." Her eyes cleared all at once. "Oh my God, it really is morning."

"Yep."

"What time is it?"

"Um." He grabbed his watch from the top of his dresser to have a look. "Eight thirty."

Sam let out a guttural growl and threw off the covers. The sight of her creamy skin and long limbs in the morning light—*in his bed*—had him cursing the gods, his friends, and his own stupidity. Why had he agreed to this again?

Only because they threatened to tie you up and throw you on the boat if you said no.

He'd been accused of being preoccupied and unavailable lately. He couldn't imagine why.

"Shit," she said. Jake couldn't help but laugh. And the disgruntled glare she gave him didn't give him much incentive to stop. She threw a pillow at him with a surprisingly good arm.

"You jerk. I have to get home and change before work. I can't go in like this."

"I like it," Jake said as the doorbell rang again and

Tucker went into an ecstasy of barking. "I vote you stay this way all the time."

Her look was withering as he headed out of the room, though he turned to watch her for just a few seconds more as she tried to find her clothes, scattered on the floor from last night. Some part of him still couldn't quite believe she was in his room. Naked. After having been thoroughly and repeatedly ravished by him.

Then he had to leave the room, before he said to hell with it and had her back on the bed beneath him.

Jake hurried down the stairs to where Tucker was dancing excitedly in front of the door. Shane's face was pressed to one of the side lights, deliberately grotesque as he let the glass push up his nose. Fitz was leaning against the other one. He unlocked the door and let Tucker greet them, thrilled as always to see friends. Especially these friends, since both Shane and Fitz had been known to sneak people food to the dog whenever they spent any time with him.

"One of these times I'm going to make you clean the glass," Jake said.

Shane took one look at him and threw back his head with a groan. "Seriously? Did you just roll out of bed?"

Fitz, as always, was more understated as he rubbed Tucker behind the ears. "We'll watch TV. Just hurry it up. It's a perfect day to be on the water."

They started to shove their way through the door, both looking startled when Jake moved to block their entrance.

"Why don't you guys just wait outs—"

He didn't get a chance to finish. The look of astonishment on his friends' faces was too comical, and they muscled their way past him before he had a chance to finish speaking.

Jake turned his head, following their gazes to the top of the stairs, and saw what he expected to—Sam, self-consciously tucking one long lock of hair behind her ear as she made her way toward him. Even slightly rumpled and barely awake she was striking. She looked between Fitz and Shane before fixing her gaze back on Jake.

"I've, ah, got to get going," she said. "Work."

"Okay." He caught her hand as she tried to slip by him at the bottom of the stairs. "Sam, I don't know if you remember these two idiots. Shane Sullivan and Henry Fitzroy?"

"It's just Fitz," Fitz said, putting out his hand. Sam shook it, wearing an uncertain smile that wasn't much like the bright, open one Jake enjoyed seeing so much. Still, it was something. He tried to remember any particular interactions between Sam and Fitz, but he couldn't. Hopefully that was a good thing.

"I remember seeing you around. Soccer, right?" she said.

Fitz flashed a grin. "Yeah, better at kicking than catching."

Shane was studying her so intently that Jake had no idea what was going through his friend's mind. Sam seemed to sense it, avoiding looking at him until he spoke to her directly.

"How've you been, Sam?" Shane asked. He made no move to offer his hand, and neither did she. Jake could feel the sudden rise in tension, and wondered what it was about.

"Good. I'm . . . fine. Hey, this has been great, but I really do need to go." She looked at Jake, and he was surprised to see that she was close to panic. "I'll see you later?"

"Seven sharp," he said. "I'll bring the kittens and order pizza."

That, at least, got a smile out of her. "Sounds good. Have fun doing, ah . . ."

"We're going out on Fitz's boat. I kind of forgot." For some excellent reasons, which he would repeat in a heartbeat if given the opportunity. He gave her hand a squeeze to try to reassure her, but she was already pulling away.

"Well, have fun anyway," was all she said with a fleeting smile as she headed for the door. "Nice seeing you guys."

Then she was gone, vanished in a flash of black and gray and blond. Jake watched the door shut, then looked directly at Shane. "What the hell was that about?" he asked.

Shane shrugged, though it wasn't exactly an "I don't know" shrug. More like he just didn't want to talk about it.

"Nothing," he said. "I told you it would be awkward."

Jake had no intention of letting this go. Not after the look on Sam's face. "*What* would be awkward? What am I missing?"

Shane shifted uncomfortably, looking like an overgrown kid in that moment. Then he sighed. "I gave her a rough time after we figured out she had a thing for you. It was stupid, nothing major."

"Define 'nothing major.' "

Shane hunched his shoulders. "Standard taunting. You remember what my mouth was like at that point. You figure it out. I'd kind of forgotten about it until you brought her up a couple of weeks ago, but I guess she didn't."

"You think?" Jake rubbed his face with his hand. "Great. Fitz? You, too?"

"Nope. Too busy trying to get into Hayley McEnroe's pants."

"Awesome." He glared at Shane. "You could have mentioned this."

Shane gave him a long-suffering look. "Why? You should always assume I was a dick in whatever situation we're talking about. I've told you that for years, and you ignore it."

"Because you're not always a dick," Jake snapped, utterly frustrated. "Why don't you just—"

"No."

Jake stared at him. "I want to introduce her to everybody, Shane. An apology would probably go a long way."

"Dude, it was *forever* ago. What do you want us all to do, line up and tell her we're sorry for treating her like shit back when she was weird and we were snotty teenagers? It was no big deal," Shane growled.

"To you."

"It shouldn't be to her, either. It was nothing. You weren't exactly polite to her, and it doesn't look like you're having a problem."

"Because we *talked* about it," Jake shot back, exasperated.

"Well, I'm not going to," Shane said flatly, and the edge in his voice was a clear indication that he wasn't budging. Jake had known him a long time. When Shane dug his heels in, that was it. "Aren't you the one who was telling me we should be past all this high school crap? So let's be past it. Let it go, Jake. It's not like anybody's going to egg her house or anything."

"That's easy for you to say," Jake said. "You aren't the one who ended up with the scars."

Shane snorted. "We scarred her. Yeah, I can tell she's just barely handling life now. Okay. Whatever."

"What do you *think* making somebody a target for years does to them?" Jake snapped. He hated this. He hated seeing this side of his friend, and he hated himself a little for having known it was there all this time and ignoring it. Because it had been easy. He was never in the line of fire. Even now he was just on the periphery.

Shane's laugh was sharp and humorless. "Jesus, Jake. This girl shows back up and you go from zero to champion in, like, the space of a couple of weeks just because she's hot and puts out?"

Something on Jake's face must have clued Shane into the fact that he'd crossed the line. He stepped back quickly and put his hands up, even as Jake was balling his hands into fists.

"Okay, look, maybe that was a little—"

"No, it was a *lot* over the line," Jake said, his voice now deadly calm. Inside, he'd filled with a rage so potent it seemed bottomless, all the more because his own guilt was mingled with it. He wondered whether Shane had any idea how close he was to knocking his ass out onto the sidewalk. From his expression, he understood enough to stay out of range.

"Sam and I were friends back then," Jake growled, noting the surprise on his friends' faces. "For a little while, anyway, until I screwed it up. I'm not screwing it up this time. And if you can't deal with her being around, then we've got a problem."

"Wow. Nothing like throwing down the gauntlet." It had been a while since he'd seen Shane look remotely guilty about anything. It made him wonder what else he didn't know about. And how he'd managed to be so oblivious back then, though that wasn't as hard to figure out. Not long after he'd embarrassed Sam, Cici had shown up at his window one night full of apologies and minus a lot of clothes, and he'd fallen back into their old pattern. Even then, he'd had to suppress the nagging feeling that being with her was more about habit and the comfort of the familiar than actual want. But their breakup had strained friendships and was promising to mess up his summer social activities, and he'd wanted things calm.

He'd wanted things easy.

That wasn't going to cut it this time.

"I'm dead serious."

"I can see that." Shane hunched his shoulders a little, looking at him like he might a dog with its teeth bared. "Fine, I'll be nice, if it matters that much. I'm not getting into all that high school crap, Jake. I'm not. But I'll be nice. Does that work for you, or are you going to take a swing at me?"

They stared at each other, and it didn't bother Jake to take a minute to think about it. Ultimately, though, what decided him wasn't what Shane had said—which was only slightly better than noncommittal—but the way he'd said it. It took a lot to get Shane to back down. But on this, he was giving ground. And having been friends with him for as long as he had, Jake understood that for Shane, that was a bigger deal than it might appear to the casual observer.

"Are we going?" Fitz asked. "I could leave and go myself if you two want to fist fight, but it's kind of a waste of all the stuff I put in the cooler."

Jake turned to look at Fitz, who didn't seem particularly intimidated, only curious, and who'd cut through the bullshit in a way that only Fitz could. He still nearly said no. But he was up, and Sam was gone. He and Tucker could use some fresh air. He had a life vest for the dog, and Fitz was always happy to have him on board.

It was a way to fill time between now and tonight, when he'd get to watch Sam and her Velcro kitten be reunited for good. The thought eased his mind a little.

"Yeah, we're going," Jake said. The flicker of relief across Shane's otherwise impassive face told him the subject of his choice in girlfriends was closed, at least for now. That was probably a good thing. Even if he knew this wouldn't be the end of it.

Jake hurried up the stairs, catching the faint scent of Sam lingering in the room. And because Tucker would never tell, he pressed his face in the pillows to find it there as well, breathing in the ghost of her. She was a breath of fresh air in so many ways. And she made him wonder what else he might have been missing all this time.

He shook his head and put the thoughts aside for now. The only thing he was sure of was that he'd miss even more if he didn't jump in the shower and get some clothes on.

Ready or not, it was time to start the day.

Chapter Fifteen

"All right, spill it."

Sam jumped a little at the sound of Zoe's voice, then turned to find her only a couple of feet away and wearing a look that would have given an invading army pause. Fortunately, Sam was comfortable enough with her to know that Zoe's stern face was not currently covering up anything but nosiness.

"Spill *what*?" Sam asked, amused by the way Zoe's eyes widened.

"You've been walking around all morning looking like you're about to burst into song, Disney princess style. It's about time you let me in on the secret. Especially if it involves who I think it does." One hand drifted to rest on her hip, and she tapped a finger restlessly as she waited for an answer.

Sam slowly put down the pen she'd been using and folded her hands in front of her.

"Why does it have to be because of a guy?" she asked. "Maybe I bought new shoes or something."

Zoe leveled a bland stare at her. "Uh-huh."

Sam sighed, shuffled a few papers around, rolled her eyes, and finally returned her gaze to Zoe. She hadn't moved, except to cross her arms over her chest. She looked more like a cop about to begin an interrogation than an art dealer. And Sam already felt herself cracking under the pressure—though it was probably just because she hadn't had anyone to actually share this with. Not that she was entirely sure what "this" was yet. Last night had . . . well, last night had been . . .

"See, this is what I mean. You're gazing off into space with that little smile on your face. Again." She shook her head. "I'm going to have to bow to your skills. A year and a half here and my hottest date was probably sitting at home with a bottle of wine and *Thor* on the TV— paused on Idris Elba's face. It was a nice view, but the only thing satisfying about it was the cheese plate I ate all by myself."

"I eat like that even when I'm not pretending I'm on a date with movie stars," Sam said. When Zoe looked like she might start growling, she relented. "Okay. It's Jake Smith. I guess we're . . . dating."

Or having hot monkey sex. Take your pick.

She flushed at the memory as she watched Zoe revel in her triumph. "I knew it! And you tried to tell me he was just some old friend, like I didn't see you two drooling all over each other. He's hot. Speaking of pretty gold eyes." She nodded approvingly. "Nice. So you saw him last night, right? And maybe this morning, too. That's what the smile says."

"No comment." But there wasn't a thing she could do about the huge grin that was as guilty an expression as she could think of. Zoe burst out laughing.

"All right now, you know I want details. Let me live vicariously a little."

"Zoe," Sam said, "please don't tell me you haven't been on a single date since you've been here."

She lifted her chin and arched her brow imperiously. "Nobody here is up to my exacting standards. Besides," she continued, "you know I'm right here most of the time. The only man I see regularly is Treebeard, and rolling around in some pine needles is not my idea of sexy."

"Treebeard. You mean Jason?" When Zoe nodded, Sam burst out laughing. She'd never thought of him that way, and he was a lot better looking than one of Tolkien's tree people, but still, there was something very apt about the description. She was going to have an awful time not laughing the next time he showed up in here.

"This is what I get for the whole Cabot Cove influence. My life has turned into a G-rated television series," Zoe said. "Which is why, Miss Samantha, you need to share some of your story with me. Not the kinky parts," she added, "just the setup. I don't even remember what a night out looks like."

Sam started to answer, but the bell above the door jingled and a pair of women's voices drifted in.

". . . can't believe they're finally getting some decent places to shop around here. Not that this is anything like Charlotte. You should *see* the shopping in SouthPark— anything you could want. Of course, I suppose I won't need to worry as much about competition when I decide to throw a party here. Just not throwing it at the fire hall would be a big deal."

"You'll have to help me with the Christmas party this year, Cici! We still make a big event out of it, and I don't want people to think it's getting stale. . . ."

Zoe leaned in close and muttered, "Oh look, Petunia Fussybottoms found a friend. This should be fun."

Sam only barely managed to swallow her laugh. Petunia Fussybottoms? She didn't even need to look to know

that was Penny Harding, who had graduated with her
but had always prided herself on being tight with a few
of the girls a grade ahead of them. A glance told her that
Penny didn't look much different—her face was small
and pinched, though her tiny stature had long qualified
her as "cute." She'd always looked like she had just
smelled something bad. That hadn't changed. And neither had her fixation on that stupid party, apparently, just
as Zoe had warned her.

Penny was annoying, but she could handle it. The
sight of Penny's companion, though, had Sam's stomach
in knots in an instant. After seeing Shane Sullivan this
morning, another unwanted reunion hardly seemed fair.

"Feel free to have a look around," Zoe said, her voice
like melted butter. "The oil paintings on the far wall
there are new this week, by a wonderful artist we're featuring named Tegan March. He has a really striking
style."

Penny and Cici murmured their assent, though Sam
could see right away they had no real interest. She caught
a word of Cici's whisper to her friend—"pedestrian"—
and began to flex her fists. If that idiot thought Tegan,
whose kaleidoscopic abstract paintings had already drawn
in quite a few passersby, was devoid of talent, then she
hadn't changed a bit from the snotty bitch she remembered.

And considering what had happened the last time—
in fact, the only time—they'd had something resembling
a conversation, to say her memories of Cici were not
good would be a serious understatement.

Sam watched them wander, hoping against hope that
they wouldn't see her, or that if they did, they'd simply
be cordial and move along. Their eyes were restless,

though, and it didn't seem like either one of them was very interested in the art. They were looking for something else. And when Cici's cool eyes fixed on her, Sam knew immediately what it was. They'd come in looking for her.

What did you expect? Word gets around. At least Cici was married now, Sam thought. Or at least, she'd heard that somewhere. Probably from Emma, who had always agreed with her on one very important point: Cici Ferris was an evil beast from the deepest pits of hell.

"I know you," Cici said, her lips curving into a small smile. "Samantha Henry. I heard you were back home. Living with your mama, right?"

She'd affected some kind of weird semi-Southern accent, Sam noticed, which blended oddly with the New England accent she remembered. She was still gorgeous to look at, though. Cici had the build of a natural athlete, long and lean, and a mane of rich brown hair streaked with gold. Perfect body, perfect features, perfect everything. She wished that Jake's ex-high-school sweetheart had really let herself go, but no. Of course, she also wished that Cici had stayed in Charlotte. Hopefully she wouldn't be in town long.

"For the time being," Sam said, feeling Zoe's eyes on her. The tension in the air was close to suffocating.

Stand up straight, don't look away, pretend you have millions of dollars in the bank, she told herself. None of those quite did the trick. *Remember who was in Jake's bed last night,* she thought. Sam smiled, and it was genuine. That seemed to unsettle Cici. Something unpleasant flickered across her fine features before they schooled themselves back into polite interest.

"Isn't that funny?" Cici said lightly. "I'm back, too,

though I bought a house. After the divorce I couldn't stand staying anywhere near my ex-husband. Coming home made sense. I was hoping for something out on the Crescent, but you know how rarely something comes available, so I bought one of those beautiful old Victorians over on Emmett Street. My parents are long gone to Florida, so I've been imposing on poor Penny in the meantime."

"Oh, stop. I love having you, Cici," Penny said. "It's just like old times."

Sam put on what she hoped was a pleasant expression and hoped they went away soon. It figured that Cici would be back permanently. Just her luck. And it more than explained the interest, she thought with a sick feeling starting in the pit of her stomach. Cici was sizing up the competition. She didn't want that to be true ... but her instincts told her it was.

She'd made it very clear, long ago, that intrusions on her territory weren't welcome. Especially not from ugly little freak shows like Sam Henry. The days when Sam could be cornered and intimidated into slinking away were long past—if nothing else, working for Mona had seen to that. Still, the old feelings, long dormant, were hard to swallow back ... the racing pulse, the urge to get as far away from the source of her trouble as possible. She'd been surprised into giving in to those instincts this morning when she'd caught sight of Shane Sullivan. Sam refused to do that now. But Cici was still trouble, and ignoring that would be at her peril.

"Well, I hope the move goes well. Is there something in particular you're looking for today? Thinking about decorating?" Sam asked, determined to turn the conversation away from anything personal and make it as businesslike as possible. Cici's eyes were sharp as they looked her over, missing nothing. Sam felt oddly bare, exposed in a way she'd almost forgotten. It took her back, and not in a good way. All of this did.

She would wonder what Jake had seen in someone like this, but the reasons were obvious, and only skin deep.

Cici's smile was more like a baring of teeth. "Maybe I'll have a look at some of *your* work. You left to be an artist, right? You must have some things in here. Or lying around. Somewhere."

The hair at the back of her neck actually stood on end at the pure, feminine malice behind that simple question. No, Cici hadn't changed a bit. And Sam doubted she'd forgotten all their brief interludes in the school hallways over the years. *"Nice trash bag, Henry. You're supposed to put garbage in that, not make a dress out of—oh, wait . . . ."* She remembered the giggles that had followed, and trying to pull herself even farther into the loose black dress she'd worn.

"Sam is actually putting together some pieces for a show right now," Zoe said. "Kind of her big reintroduction to the Cove. We're keeping everything under wraps because I don't want to spoil it, but it's something really special."

If it wouldn't have totally given it away, Sam would have thrown her arms around Zoe and given her an enormous hug. As it was, all she could do was try to play it cool and hope her gratitude didn't show. She was relieved at how calm she sounded when she quirked an eyebrow and spoke.

"I can keep you posted on that. Actually, we have a list for e-mail updates if you'd like to sign up."

Cici didn't bother to hide her displeasure behind a smile as Penny shifted uneasily beside her. "No, I get enough spam. I'm sure I'll hear about it." She looked at Penny. "Let's head to lunch. I'm starving, and I want to get down to the docks to see the boys when they get off the boat."

She might as well have stuck a stiletto in her chest, Sam thought. Those words caused the same amount of pain. Doubt landed on her like a ton of bricks. *The boys. Her* boys, she meant. Were they talking? Had Jake seen her yet? A little voice played in her head, dredging up from the place she'd tried to lock it away: *No sad little Goth slut is going to screw up my summer. You can stay away from him, or I can make sure your life is even more hellish than it already is.*

Considering that the very next day was the day Jake had voluntarily removed himself from the picture, maybe she should have just heeded the warning instead of picking that particular hill to die on.

It was so stupid. She'd dated good-looking men, had an actual social life, worked in a respected gallery. She'd sold her paintings all over the world. Parts of it had sucked, but at least she'd felt like a real person, no more reviled or special than anyone else. But being here made her feel . . . less, somehow.

Then she felt it, a light, bolstering touch on her back from Zoe, silent support. She remembered what her mother had said about finding allies, and realized that she had one right here. It mattered more than she might have imagined . . . and it gave her courage she might not have found otherwise.

"If you see Jake, could you tell him I think I left one of my rings on his dresser this morning?" Sam called sweetly after them as the women hurried out of the gallery. Penny turned her head to give her a wide-eyed look, but Cici didn't bother. Then they were gone, vanishing into the cloudy, blustery day. Sam watched the door swing shut and felt something between terror and triumph.

She'd just done the equivalent of shouting, "Come at me, bro!" Why, she had no idea, except that some part of her needed to let Cici know that the playing field had changed. Just how much remained to be seen, but it wasn't the same. And neither was she.

Sam took a deep breath, exhaled, and tried to force her shoulders to relax. It felt like steel rods had replaced her bones, and she knew she'd end up with a headache if she didn't watch it. The sense that she'd won her first skirmish with the ghosts of her past wouldn't replace her need for medication and a dark room if that happened, even if the rush was nice.

Zoe gave her back a quick pat before removing her hand.

"Look at you, making new friends."

Sam turned her head to look at Zoe and managed a weak laugh. As the triumph faded, she felt a little like throwing up. There was no way Cici wouldn't find a way to hit back at her. None. And she had a bad feeling that the leverage was all with Harvest Cove's queen bee. After all, she and her courtiers were all Jake's friends. This wasn't exactly starting out on the right foot.

"That was Cici. She hates my guts."

"I got that. Her reason is . . ."

"A mystery?" Sam pulled the hair of her low ponytail over her shoulder to toy with. "You just met one of the reasons I was so anxious to get out of here. I, um, didn't have a great time in school. Most of the people who facilitated that didn't leave, so I did. Not like there was anything for me here anyway." She rolled her eyes, flustered. "It shouldn't matter."

"Of course it matters. People's roots run deep in a place like this. There are certain patterns, and if you stay, you're expected to fall into them. If you don't, there's usually trouble." Zoe's smile was full of understanding. "You're trouble. It's one of the reasons I liked you right away."

Sam's smile felt as though it covered her entire face. "I like you, too. What does that make you?"

"Also trouble. Birds of a feather and all that."

Sam thought it was entirely possible that she'd never liked anyone quite as much as she liked Zoe in that moment. "Thanks for covering for me," she said. "They're going to figure out it was crap eventually, but I'll just deal with that when I have to."

Zoe only shook her head. "You can't let those two get under your skin. I don't know the one who has a hate-on for you, but Petunia—"

"I swear to God, Zoe, if you keep calling her that I'm going to screw up and do it in public."

"I certainly hope so. Anyway, Petunia and her friends aren't everybody around here. They're not even most of everybody. Just because they're an outsize pain in the butt doesn't mean you should write off Harvest Cove. I'm not going to fold up and leave just because I'll probably never get an invite to that damn party. Which is a shame, since I'm nosy *and* I like to dress up."

"Yeah." Sam tapped her fingers on the table beside her. "That's Jake's ex-girlfriend. And Petunia and her friends are also his. That's my issue."

"I guessed that after your parting shot. Which was really well done, by the way. I think you scored a direct hit." Zoe considered her, looking inordinately interested. "So how did trouble hook up with one of the town princes? I feel like there's an older story under the new one here."

Sam tipped her head from side to side. "I guess."

Zoe crossed her arms over her chest. "You going to make me pry it out of you?"

Sam thought about it. "I don't know. You really want to hear about all that? It's not very interesting."

"Maybe not to you." She heaved an exaggerated sigh. "All right. I was holding off on this because you didn't seem like you needed one more thing to deal with, but you leave me no choice. You can get your butt over to my place this weekend. There will be tea—*maybe* coffee if you're lucky—and you are going to lay it on me about you and this place. After that, it will be my turn to dump some of my problems on you. When these things are done, you and I will officially be in this together, no going back, point of no return, abandon all hope, ye who enter here. And may God have mercy on your soul, because I am not the easiest woman in the world to have as a friend, but Lord knows we both need one."

Sam stared at her in awe. She had known very few people like Zoe. They were forces of nature, capable of wielding great power and apt to get very pissy if what they saw as the natural order of things was upset. She tended not to get that close, being prone to a certain amount of chaos herself. But this time, her chaos and Zoe's order seemed to work together just fine.

Maybe because, just as Zoe had said, they were both trouble.

"I thought we were already friends," Sam said.

"We were. I'm just moving it to a higher level."

She couldn't stop the smile, though she did manage to stifle the laugh that wanted to ripple out of her throat. "I'm getting a cat tonight. How's tomorrow?" Gallery hours were shorter on Sundays, and she'd have most of the afternoon to herself. Spending some of that with Zoe sounded like an excellent use of the time.

Zoe gave a curt nod. "Good. I'll buy the chocolate." She studied her. "For what it's worth, she's got nothing on you. If the hot vet doesn't see that, then I will personally send Treebeard to his house to dump a forest on his floor."

"It's probably already happened. They're cousins."

Zoe groaned. "Everyone here is related. I'm going to need you to make me some kind of flowchart. In the meantime, let's sell some more of our horrible pedestrian artwork to the masses and make enough money to throw our own obnoxious I'm-better-than-you party."

"You heard the pedestrian comment?"

"I have five older brothers. I hear *everything*." The bell above the door rang again as a couple of regular browsers wandered in. Sam returned their friendly waves, and Zoe followed suit before continuing.

"Get them to buy the March they've been drooling over. I've got a couple calls to deal with, and then I'll go grab us some lunch." Then, her orders given, she flashed a quick smile, turned, and strode off toward her office in the back. Sam had the strangest urge to salute.

"Next level friends still doesn't mean I'm drinking tea," she informed Zoe's retreating back.

"Oh, yes, it does."

Once she was gone, Sam quickly got back to work,

losing herself in the usual bustle of a Saturday afternoon. The March went home with the Blackmons, several pieces of pottery sold to a nice older woman she remembered working at Henderson's Store when she was a kid, and a group of mothers openly ecstatic about getting an afternoon out treated themselves with jewelry. It was hours before Sam found herself in the quiet again, standing in front of Tegan March's grouping of paintings. They pulsed with life, vivid and bright. If she had the money, she'd want one for herself. As it was, she was just glad she got to admire them on a daily basis.

That was when she felt it again, the snap of the spark that had propelled her into the attic two nights ago. She thought of the half-finished painting. She thought of what needed to be added, and more, realized there was another idea lurking in the wings asking for attention. Everything she'd felt today asked to be let out, poured onto a canvas, bursting with color.

It was a better method of expression, and catharsis, than heading down to the docks to toss Cici Ferris into the water, even if the latter might be just a tiny bit more entertaining in the short term. Still, as the ugliness of the meeting faded, Sam found herself looking forward to the evening. Jake would bring her Loki. She would paint. And all would be right with the world for just a little while. The thought gave her one more burst of courage that carried her back into Zoe's office.

"So I was thinking," she said as Zoe's curious gray eyes met hers, "about the studios upstairs."

Chapter Sixteen

S he'd expected to hear from Jake by six.

When that came and went, Sam thought it might be more like seven. At seven thirty, with both texts and a phone call she'd sent unanswered, she stalked upstairs, threw on her pajamas, then returned to the kitchen to get herself a glass of wine. Apparently, seeing both Shane and Cici in one day had been an omen she should have paid attention to.

She wanted her kitten. She was increasingly furious with Jake. She had no interest in listening to her mother assure her that something must have happened to keep him without letting them know. And since that left no one to take her ire out on, she headed to the attic to inflict her mood on a fresh canvas. The colors were violent. Her technique was loose, but effective. And by the time Andi's voice sounded behind her, the beginnings of a scene had unfolded on the canvas in front of her.

"Honey? Are you up here? Jake just called and he—"

Sam jumped, then whirled around to find her mother staring openmouthed at what she'd been up to. "Oh, Sammy. You're painting again? That's . . . This is . . . Sammy, that's beautiful!"

She wasn't quite sure what to do with her mother's

obvious joy. Joy was about the last thing she felt capable of dealing with right now. But some part of her thrilled at it just the same. She had also, Sam realized, calmed down enough to be able to tell Jake exactly where to go calmly enough that he would hear actual words instead of incoherent high-pitched rage noises.

"Thanks, Mom," she said. "Don't tell anybody, okay? I'm not really ready for that yet."

"I won't." But she still threw her arms around Sam and gave her a huge hug, which forced a half smile out of her despite her best efforts. "I'm just glad you're painting again. Even if that piece looks like everything is on fire," she said when she pulled back.

"Everything *is* on fire. I was about to start painting the bodies in it. It's a new direction for me."

Andi winced. "I don't think that'll really—"

"I'm kidding. Mostly. What did Jake want?" she asked.

"He's been at the hospital with his mom. He would have called sooner, but his phone disappeared. And of course, he was a little upset. Hadn't realized what time it was."

She immediately felt like the world's biggest jerk. Sam didn't think she'd ever managed to get un-angry so quickly.

"Oh my God. Is she okay?" she asked.

"They think so. It was a mini-stroke, probably blood pressure related. More scary than anything. She seems fine now, and they're doing some tests. He sounded tired. . . . Sammy, are you okay?"

Robbed of her anger, Sam felt oddly deflated. The emotions that flooded in to fill the void were just as unpleasant, but all directed inward. Worry. Regret. A high level of self-loathing. She gently set down her brush. The painting was good, she decided. But she would finish it later, with a cooler head and minus the flaming bodies. The anger in it was already there, and it worked for the picture, even if she was embarrassed about where it had come from.

"I'm fine," she finally said. "I just, you know."

"Uh-huh. You have to stop expecting the worst of people, Sammy. Not everybody's out to hurt you."

"I don't expect the worst of everybody."

Andi sighed. "Then where are your New York friends? You haven't mentioned a one."

"I had friends," she insisted, though she hated the defensiveness she heard in her own voice. "Just not really close ones! It's not like I sat around by myself all the time, Mom. I worked. I did things. It was hard to get too close with anyone at the gallery because we were all in danger of being fired, and the one good friend I did make moved to Philly once Mona cut him loose. We text sometimes, but he's busy." She paused, frowning. "Don't look at me like that."

Andi tilted her head. "I'm your mother. I can still look at you any way I want to. And I know how you are. You let people get just so close before you back off. It wasn't always like that, but the older you got, the more I noticed. I wish I'd known what was happening sooner. Maybe I could have fixed it."

"No," Sam replied with a soft, humorless laugh. "No. You couldn't have. And me being, well, me didn't help."

Her mother looked so sad that Sam wished she could erase all of it, all the years of worry and not knowing what to do for her misfit daughter. "You were just expressing yourself."

"Yes, well, the nastier the kids got, the more creatively I expressed myself." Sam shrugged, trying to downplay it. She remembered thinking of her increasingly interesting hair and clothing choices like costumes, like armor. It was easier to deal with school if she was playing a part, rather than running the risk of being vilified for who she actually was. "Look at it this way, Mom. It probably helped my art."

"Oh, bullshit. You would have been an artist whether you were unhappy or not. All school did was make you hightail it out of here for the better part of ten years."

"That, too."

Her mother looked again at the work in progress, and at the partially finished work from a couple of nights ago that she'd set aside. Then she looked at Sam again, and the pride in her mother's eyes was so fierce that it stunned her.

"You keep going with these, Sammy. They're beautiful. Just promise me you're going to show them to Zoe at some point."

"I'm going to," Sam replied. "I'm moving most of this stuff into one of her studios on Monday." Even though the thought of it brought on the sort of nerves she hadn't felt over showing off her work in a long time. That was what the months off had done . . . they'd sent her back to the beginning, in more than one way. But Zoe had been ecstatic. And her mother looked ready to burst with pride. Those things counted. They mattered.

"Good," Andi said. "Your dad would have loved that you were painting up here again, you know. Especially now."

Sam looked around, and though he'd faded in her memory like a well-loved and worn photograph, she could still see him up here, the grin on his face as he threw his arms wide.

"Ta-da! What do you think, kiddo? Today the attic, to-morrow, the art world!"

"I think so, too." She felt herself getting a little misty and cleared her throat. "So, um, am I supposed to call Jake? Or, but you said his phone was gone."

That was an unfortunate coincidence, and Sam couldn't quite believe it *was* a coincidence after she'd basically announced to Cici that she was sleeping with him. But maybe Andi was right and she should start from giving her the benefit of the doubt.

After all, Cici could be a complete bitch without being a *sabotaging* complete bitch. It was possible. Not likely, but possible.

"He said he'd be by in the morning. I told him you work ten to two, so I think it'll be early."

"Okay," Sam said, then kissed Andi's soft cheek to say good night. She was grateful that her mother had been there to pick up the phone, grateful that she hadn't managed to light into him before he could explain that he was actually dealing with an emergency. And along with that, she was scared as hell. Because the anger and pain she'd felt before she knew the truth were so strong that it meant she was doing a terrible job of taking her time.

Falling for Jake—really falling for him—was a risk she wasn't ready to take. Nothing she'd been through had broken her yet, but putting herself on the line one more time and having him walk away? That would do it, and she wasn't sure just how she'd get the pieces back together again afterward.

"Sammy? You might want to give Jake a chance not to hurt you, either."

Andi had paused at the top of the stairs, and Sam just

smirked and shook her head. "Don't worry about it, Mom. It's fine."

"*Hmm.* I'm taking my book to bed. If you finally feel like eating, the leftover pizza's in the fridge."

"Got it." She watched her mother head down the stairs and realized that she might actually be hungry, now that she could think straight again. Cold pizza in pajamas was always a good idea. And then she thought she might do some work on the piece she'd started two nights ago. She really loved what she had, and it wouldn't take much to finish it. There was something missing, though. Maybe it was because she'd been expecting Jake, or maybe it was just the comedown after allowing her head to almost explode, but it would have been nice to have some company.

Frowning, she went and picked up her cell phone off of the stack of boxes she'd set it on. It was almost ten. Too late to call Zoe, since she wasn't sure what sort of hours Zoe kept yet. There was, however, one other person who might be available. And when in doubt, it was always best to pester someone who really had no choice but to put up with you.

She scrolled through her contacts and touched the right name, then put the phone to her ear. When an irritated female voice answered, Sam grinned.

Jackpot.

"Yes, I know what time it is. No, nobody died."

She listened a moment, then rolled her eyes. "I have cold pizza and a stack of superhero movies and nobody to share them with. Come over, Em. I know you have about as much of a life as I do." Sam moved to start collecting her brushes to clean, and then laughed at her sister's grudging agreement.

"Yeah, I know I'm lucky you love me. Just come over. It can be a slumber party. Like when we were kids, except with wine. Okay. Bye."

Sam hung up, finally feeling as though she'd done something right. Emma had been a grump like always, but she'd also sounded surprised. And she'd agreed pretty quickly. They would probably bicker, because that's just what they *did*, but Sam couldn't shake what her mother had said about not letting people get too close. She had a bad feeling Emma was on that list, at least in her mother's opinion.

Maybe, maybe not. The distance between them over the last few years had grown, and that was on both of them. Still, Sam decided, as long as she was here she could try to own the part that was hers and do what she could to repair it.

They were sisters. If they couldn't get rid of each other, they could stare at eye candy together and try to make it work. *Allies,* she thought. She didn't need many, just a couple of good ones. And if she couldn't count on her big sister, then she might as well hang it up and start saving for a personality transplant. Emma could be a butt, but she wasn't unfair. She also needed to lighten up, but that's what the wine was for.

There was just one more thing she needed to do before she could get comfortable and settle in for the night. She had to look up Jake's home number—she hadn't needed it before. At least it was easy to find. She lectured herself while the phone began to ring.

You're seeing him. You seem to be sleeping with him. So it makes sense that you would leave a message. This is like, not love.

Even if just the thought of the l-word made her feel

all weird and fluttery and remember the way he'd looked at her last night when he'd been deep inside her. Like she was beautiful. Like she was everything.

No, damn it. Think of something else. Like pie.

"This is Jake, leave me a message and I'll get back to you."

Sam laughed quietly at the furious barking in the background, then started to talk. "Hey, this is Sam. I hope your mom's doing okay. I wanted to ask if you could do me a favor tomorrow." She made her request, even said good-bye. But something, some awful sneaky part of her that refused to think about pie was fixating on things better left alone, had a simple addition to make that fell from her lips before she could stop herself.

"I missed you tonight," she said, and it didn't sound like her. It sounded too vulnerable. Too honest.

Too much like the girl who'd offered him that damn picture all those years ago.

"Okay, bye," she said quickly, and hung up. *Smooth, Sam.* Her cheeks flushed, and her thoughts were agitated, jumbled. Maybe it was the paint fumes. Or maybe she'd just tell herself that and go watch Captain America save the world with only his shield and the power of extreme hotness.

She started to pick up the brushes again, and almost managed to convince herself that nothing had changed since last night. Not really. And she almost managed it.

Almost.

Much later, in the darkest part of the night, Sam lay curled beside her sister and dreamed. Some part of her knew, as she leaned back against the worn bark of the Witch Tree and began to sketch, that she'd done all this before. But as she focused on the drawing, on the warm breeze and the soft background sounds of birds and passing cars and bits of conversation, the knowing slipped away.

She was sixteen again.

"Sam?"

She knew that voice. It was one she homed in on instinctively whenever she heard it, no matter how many times she told herself just how pathetic that was. Guys like Jake Smith didn't talk to girls like her. And it was just as well, because if he did, she doubted she'd like what he had to say.

Except she was pretty sure he'd just said her name.

"What are you drawing?"

Her eyes widened. It sounded like he was right beside her. Which meant he could see—

"Well . . . I . . . um . . . just, things, I guess." She splayed her fingers over the sketch she'd been working on, an attempted copy of some fantasy art she'd seen at the comic shop. The dragon was coming along pretty well, she thought. But there was no way Jake would see it as anything but weird. And not in a good way.

She flipped the book shut as quickly as she could, took a deep breath, and made herself look up into a face she knew as well as her own. He was never this close, or this completely focused on her. It was as though one of her stupid daydreams had bled over into real life. And it made it almost impossible to speak over her pounding heart.

He probably just came over to say something stupid. His friends are probably close by, laughing. Instinctively, Sam curled her knees into herself, a physical defense against the expected verbal attack. But Jake just kept watching her with those bright gold eyes, a look on his face she'd never seen before. It was something like ... awe.

"Did you seriously draw that?" he asked. His voice was soft and warm, the kind of voice you'd use to try to coax a wild animal into letting you near it. She was no wild animal, but she supposed she might look like a strange creature to him.

"Yeah," Sam said, nervously tucking her hair behind her ear. She had no idea what he wanted, or what she was supposed to say. Part of her wished he would just leave. The rest desperately wanted him to stay.

"That's amazing. I mean ... that looks, like, professional." He laughed softly, incredulously, shaking his head. "I didn't know you could do that."

Big surprise. "Well, I can," Sam replied, knowing she sounded defensive. Of course she could draw. She'd always been able to. He might know if he'd ever bothered to look. She thought the snap in her voice might send him off, but instead she found herself watching in shock as he sank slowly down beside her.

"Um ... can I see it again? Do you have any more stuff like that?"

She arched an eyebrow, completely at a loss as to how to deal with this. Where was the punch line, here? Was it her?

"I, ah ... Why do you want to see?"

Her frown didn't seem to deter him, but then she'd watched him enough to know he was stubbornly good-natured everywhere but on the lacrosse field.

"Do you like comics?" he asked. "Because that looked so much like something I saw down at Four Eyes Comics. It was—"

"On the wall. Yeah," Sam said, "I was trying to draw it from memory." She could hardly believe he'd recognized it. Or that he spent much time in Four Eyes. But his expression, almost painfully earnest, said he did.

"I didn't know you could do that," he said. "I've never known anybody who could do that. Seriously, can I see what else you have in there?"

She didn't know why. But something about the way he asked told her that this time, just this once, it was safe to come out of her defensive crouch and share. Sam swallowed hard, enveloped by the light scent of the cologne that all the guys wore but that smelled so singular on him. She tried to keep her hand steady when she moved to open her sketchbook to the first page.

"Um . . . well . . . okay."

"Cool," he said, settling in so close that his leg brushed hers, eyes alight with interest. And that was when she knew that Jake Smith was different. He was as special as she'd imagined he might be. And he wouldn't hurt her. He wouldn't . . .

Sam's eyes flew open in the darkened room, and she sucked in a breath. It took a few seconds to wake up enough that she knew where—and when—she was. Then reality sank in, along with a deep sense of relief. She'd forgotten just how starry-eyed she'd been, all those years ago. The memory, fresh now, was bittersweet. She couldn't forget what had come after.

Sam shifted around, turning over to see Emma's pretty face relaxed in sleep, her dark lashes entwined, lips parted. As Sam watched, she started to snore softly. That made her smile, made her remember just how far away all of that wonder and pain at sixteen was.

She'd thought she'd seen the beginning and the end of

anything she might ever have to do with Jake. But here she was, and everything was different.

Everything except the feeling, all that fear and excitement and longing tumbled together at the very thought of him. That had remained. And it threatened to become a great deal more.

Her smile faded, and Sam snuggled down into her pillow, closing her eyes. For one night, she didn't want to wonder whether the past was simply repeating itself. She didn't want to remember the past at all.

She just wanted some peace, and some sleep. And though peace eluded her, after about an hour, Sam slipped gratefully into dreamless darkness for the rest of the night.

Chapter Seventeen

Emma was still passed out in a pile of blankets when Sam fumbled her way downstairs the next morning, nursing a mild headache from the bottle of wine she and Em had shared and feeling like her mouth had been used as a truck stop during the night. She'd piled her hair on top of her head in an extremely sloppy bun before coming down, just to avoid drinking her hair along with her coffee, and had thrown her enormous old cardigan on over her tank and pajama pants. The AGA kept the kitchen warm, but the rest of the house could get drafty, and there was a breeze that moaned around the rafters this morning, looking for ways in.

Andi was up and moving, though not in much better shape than her daughter. They grunted good mornings at each other as they worked around each other for their daily infusion of caffeine. Sam perched on a stool and stuck her face in her mug while Andi found a spot across the island and started to scroll through the morning news on her tablet.

The kitchen was blissfully quiet. Not completely clean, considering the empty pizza box she and Emma had left out beside the wineglasses, the empty bottle, and a bowl that had nothing left in it but a scatter of popcorn kernels. But quiet.

She was on her second cup and just beginning to think about finding clothes when there was a soft knock at the door. Suddenly, she was wide awake. Her eyes darted to the microwave clock. Seven thirty.

"Oh God." She looked at her mother, who seemed like she was trying very hard not to smirk as she kept her eyes fixed on the tablet. Somehow, Sam doubted it was the news story she found funny. "Mom, did you know he was coming this early? Mom? *Mother?*"

"I'm old," Andi said lightly. "I forget things." She then primly picked up the tablet and walked out of the kitchen. "I'm going to get dressed. Could you get that, honey?"

"You're not old. You're fifty-four. If you're really that senile I'm putting you in the home." There was no response but an amused chuckle.

Gritting her teeth, Sam picked up her mug and shuffled toward the front door. After their talk last night, Sam supposed this could be intended as some sort of lesson. Like, "He cares about you, and you will see this when he sticks around even after he finds out you look like you dug your way up from hell instead of rolling out of bed like everyone else first thing in the morning." More likely, though, it was just her mother's twisted sense of humor.

Her irritation evaporated when she saw the shadow of him through the wavy glass of the sidelight. Everything she'd felt yesterday morning, when she opened her eyes and discovered that she'd spent the entire night with him wrapped around her, blew right through her like a hurricane. She'd been telling the truth in that message last night. She really had missed him.

Her dream said she'd been missing him for a lot longer than that.

Nerves tangled in her stomach, an unpleasant echo of what she'd relived in the night. Could he possibly know what all of this was doing to her? He had to have heard it in her cheesy message last night, in her nervous little "Okay, bye" at the end. Would he have been weirded out by that? Had she sounded weird? Could she be any more ridiculous right now?

Hoping the answer to all of the above was no, she started to reach up to smooth her hair, decided she didn't want to know exactly how much of a lost cause it was, then unlocked and opened the door.

Jake looked up, and the smile he gave her nearly melted her on the spot, banishing everything but the pleasant buzz of having him here, right now, with her. He looked better than anyone had a right to at this hour in faded jeans and a tee and flannel shirt, both layered beneath a battered jacket that had seen better days. His hair was adorably mussed, his hazel eyes more green than gold today against the faded olive of his jacket. She couldn't miss the smudges beneath his eyes, or the weariness in them. But because it was Jake, he tried to cover his exhaustion with a tease.

"Excuse me," he said, "but do you have a moment to talk about the saving power of kittens?"

He made her laugh. Even at seven thirty in the morning. It didn't do much for her multiple theories on how she was maintaining boundaries that were appropriate for a new relationship, and how she was still very much in the safe zone. Because she was basically evil before eight unless you were on her short—very short—list of special people. Even then it could be iffy. And yet here she was, grinning like an idiot as he slid his arms around her and pressed a kiss to her forehead.

"You look cute," he said. "You have Rainbow Buddies on your pants."

That gave her pause. She'd forgotten what she was wearing. "Emma bought these for my birthday last year." Which was not an excuse for actually wearing them. Like, a lot. She looked down at the fat little multicolored unicorns gamboling all over her pajama bottoms and tried to come up with a better explanation for them.

It was early. She wasn't finished with her coffee. There was no explanation.

"I didn't even know they made those for adults," Jake said.

"Well," Sam said, "now that I know you like them so much, I'll get you a pair."

He nuzzled her behind the ear, which he seemed to have figured out was one of those places that caused her brain to stop working properly. "As long as you take them off me, I can deal with that."

She giggled, realized that she had emitted a sound that could only be described as a giggle, and then shoved at him so that she would stop making silly girly noises. "How are you so awake? And how's your mom? Is she doing okay?" Then she looked down at the hard-sided pet carrier sitting by his feet. "Oh, the kitties! Here, just come in. Do you want coffee?"

He chuckled, his brows knitting together in mild disbelief as he shook his head. "I guess now I know how to wake you up. Which part of that am I supposed to answer first?"

His solution seemed to be not to answer any right away. Instead, he picked up the carrier and brought it in. She led him back to the kitchen, which was still deserted. Despite the lure of the new kittens, Sam expected that her mother would take her sweet time coming back. At some point while she'd been gone, Andi had come around to liking Jake. Not that Andi was particularly inclined to dislike many people, but she knew very well that he'd hurt her daughter. Now that she thought about it, Sam realized that would have meant Jake had a much higher bar to clear before getting into her mother's good graces. It said something for him.

"It smells good in here," Jake said, setting the carrier on the island. "I think I'll take you up on the coffee."

"Sure thing. Just one second," Sam said. She opened the mewing carrier, quickly extracted Loki, and barely managed to shut the door before there were several escapees. "Hey, baby!"

He'd gotten bigger again, a sleek, well-fed kitten with big green eyes and an even louder voice than she remembered. She kissed his nose, rubbed her face against his cheeks, and cradled him while rubbing his oversize ears and furry neck. Loki bore it admirably while she fussed over him, purring loudly and giving her a slow, sleepy "I love you" blink as she cooed nonsense at him. Finally, though, he began to wiggle, so she stuck him on her shoulder where he sniffed her hair and then gave her cheek a kiss with his sandpaper tongue.

"There," Sam said, smirking at Jake. "Now I can get your coffee."

He rubbed a hand through his hair and laughed. "If there really were Henry witches," he said, "you must have inherited some kind of black cat whisperer gene from them. Even when he's nice with other people, he's not *that* nice."

"See? Being a Harvest Cove Henry has benefits. People don't know what they're talking about."

She grabbed a mug from the cupboard as there was a flurry of loud thumps coming down the stairs. Sam looked up just in time to see Emma, her hair doing a full-on Einstein, stop halfway down the back stairs. She looked at Jake, eyes widening.

"Nope," she said, then turned and hurried back from whence she'd come.

"Your sister's here?" Jake asked. "I thought she had her own place in town."

"We had a sleepover," Sam said, setting a steaming mug of coffee in front of him and then bringing the cream and sugar. "I wanted company."

"That explains the pizza carnage," Jake replied. "I'm sorry I didn't call earlier, Sam. The time got away from me. I didn't know what was going on. Greg—that's mom's boyfriend—was really upset, and my damn phone fell into a black hole somewhere. I can't think where it went. I'm going to have to replace it if nobody finds it by tomorrow."

"Your mom's going to be all right, though?"

"We think so. It was a TIA, like a mini-stroke. Greg said her speech got kind of garbled and then she just went completely unresponsive, just sitting there without actually being there. Scared him. Me, too. At least we were off the boat by then so I could haul ass to the hospital. I'm going back up this morning after I leave here. They think she'll be discharged today."

"I'm glad."

"Me, too." He doctored his coffee, then took a sip,

closed his eyes, and swallowed. "This is so much better than what I have at my house."

"Now that I've been in your kitchen, that doesn't surprise me."

He uttered a soft "Hmph" before taking another sip.

She didn't want to ask. She couldn't give a damn about Shane Sullivan and his big mouth, though Fitz seemed nice enough. But Cici's visit had been playing on a more or less permanent loop in the back of her mind since yesterday, and between throwing down the gauntlet with her and the disappearance of the phone, Sam finally gave up and just asked the question.

"So . . . how was boating?" by which she meant, *Did you see Cici and did she slobber all over you?* But she was trying to retain a little nuance. And she could swear he looked just a little uneasy before he answered.

"Fine. We had fun. Tucker played ship dog. We had some beers and talked football. After that I took Tucker home and we all went and sat at the Tavern. Pretty lazy afternoon."

We all. Yeah, Cici had found him. Irritated, Sam pressed him, and more bluntly than she might have otherwise. "Just the three of you?"

He dropped his eyes again, just for a second. But it was incriminating enough.

"No, well, pretty much everyone showed up. I was accused of being a hermit. Thea took stupid pictures that she'll put online somewhere. In other words, exactly like every other time I've gone to the Tavern, which is why I don't always go."

No, he wasn't going to tell her that Cici had been there. She didn't understand why, apart from maybe a desire to keep her from feeling the way she was feeling right now anyway. He didn't want it to be a big deal. Maybe it wasn't to him.

And there was no earthly way she could bring it up without ruining the morning, since any sentence that began with, "Hey, I saw Cici Ferris yesterday," was not going to end with anything good. Jake likely didn't know about the long-ago discussion that Cici had decided to have with her, but he couldn't have missed the animosity before and after.

She didn't think Shane had ever told him either, which was interesting. He'd definitely been there. Not actively participating, but there. He still looked at her more like she was a bizarre, slightly distasteful insect than a human. She'd never figured out why. He'd grown up right down the road. They'd even ridden bikes together a couple of times until his parents had put a stop to it.

Her mother had said for years that the Sullivans were kings and queens among assholes. Jake must see something in him, but she couldn't imagine what.

With Cici, it wasn't as hard to figure out.

"So," Sam said, forcing herself to change the subject. "I see you brought all the available fur balls."

"As promised," Jake said, and he seemed to relax again. "Marin kept one of the other girls. The solid gray one. You sure you can con Emma into this? She's always seemed like kind of a tough customer. I know grown men who are terrified of her."

"They're wise, then. But remember, as a younger sister, I know all the weaknesses. I think she's in hiding now that she knows you're here, so we'll wait for my mother and then I'll go work my magic."

Jake breathed out a laugh. "Almost makes me wish I wasn't an only child. Almost."

She remembered him musing about that before, a very long time ago. Back then, she'd thought he sounded lonely. Well, maybe not exactly lonely, but finding and retaining a circle of people who functioned as surrogate siblings had sounded like it required more work than she would have wanted to expend. Friends could walk away. It was a little harder with blood.

Which meant she was going to have to try to get along with . . . *them*. That was the next big hurdle, and she knew it. The thought of being with the entire group of them at once had her heart rate picking up instantly, but it was going to be the price of trying to date Jake. Stomping her foot and demanding that he choose between her and his friends was a bad cliché, and not her style anyway. They were all adults now. How bad could it be?

She recalled Cici's venomous stare, and decided that she didn't really want to think about that, either.

"Work today?" he asked.

Sam nodded, grateful for the distraction. "Short day on Sundays, and Mondays we're normally closed."

"Still like it?"

"Definitely. Zoe didn't mention she was looking for more of a right-hand woman than an employee, but it's good. It's everything I enjoyed about the gallery in New York minus the ugliness in the work environment. I'm pushing her to start taking a day off too, but she says she wouldn't know what to do with herself."

"I bet she'd love to get you painting again."

It was said innocently enough, but when he spoke something in her hardened, cocooning protectively around her secret. The art she created was one of the most personal things she could share, and so far, what she'd done here was raw emotion. Maybe that was to be expected, a cathartic release after months of nothing. But the fact was that Jake, and her feelings about him, were all wrapped up in what she was creating. She couldn't bare that to him. Not yet. Not when she still worried that he might look between her and someone who fit more cleanly into the life he'd built here, and walk away.

She'd removed much of the armor she'd worn. But not all. Not yet. And the fact that he was hedging about yesterday told her that it wasn't safe to cast off the rest just yet. There was enough of her exposed as it was.

"She would," Sam said. "I just told her what I told you. I'm not painting right now. Maybe someday. We'll see."

She reached up to stroke Loki's head and scratch absently behind his ears, enjoying his ridiculously loud purr. "Anyway . . ."

"There they are! Good morning, Jake," said Andi as she hurried toward the carrier. She'd braided her hair again and wrapped it into a bun, though wavy pieces of hair were already escaping. Her long, bright blue sweater matched her eyes. She looked damn good for her age, Sam thought as she watched her, whether she was in full-on hippie mode or going for relatively normal, like today. Her mom still had curves in the right places without having collected any in the wrong ones. All she could do was hope she'd inherited those genes. It was weird that she never dated. Then again, maybe she did and was sneaky about it. Then *again*, this was Harvest Cove. Sam tried to imagine who her mother might hook up with, shuddered at the possibilities, and put it out of her mind.

"Hey," Andi said, giving Jake a look as she extracted her kitten from the cage. "I said one, not *all*. I would, Jake, but I think two is enough. Loki and Peaches will keep us busy."

"No, Mom, I—Peaches?" Sam wrinkled her nose. "You're naming her Peaches? Like the song? Billions of peaches, peaches for me . . ."

"Like the color she has in her fur," her mother replied, happily stroking her kitten. "You named yours after a supervillain in a stupid hat. It's not like you can talk."

Sam narrowed her eyes, but Jake stepped in. "Actually, I brought them because Sam has some nefarious plan involving your other daughter. I didn't get the details." He smirked. "Plausible deniability."

Andi's eyebrows shot up. "Do I want to know?"

"Probably not," Sam said, picking up the carrier. She tried to lift Loki from her shoulder, but he hung on stubbornly and meowed. Bemused, she left him there, feeling a little like some sort of twisted pirate. She lugged the carrier to the bottom of the stairs, then turned to look back at Jake and her mother. For just a moment, she was struck by how right they looked there, just sitting in her mother's kitchen enjoying coffee, waiting for her. Because they were hers.

She pushed it aside quickly. Getting attached to the idea of some cozy little vignette of life with Jake was a bad idea. It was too soon. But even as she forced her mind back to the present, she couldn't shake the warmth the picture had left her with. Or the feeling that even now, she was in way too deep.

"If you hear shouting, just ignore it," she told them, putting away her fears for now. Then she grinned and headed up the stairs.

Chapter Eighteen

He had no idea how she managed it, but by the time he left, he was down another kitten. It was especially mysterious because the one thing he very clearly heard from upstairs was Emma's desolate wail of "No!"

Still, when Sam had waltzed back down the stairs with Loki draped over her shoulder like an eccentric accessory, the carrier was just a little lighter, and her grin was mercenary.

"What did you do to your sister, Samantha Jane Henry?" Andi had asked, and it had taken all the willpower he had to keep from laughing. Especially considering the disgruntled look Sam had given her. With her hair piled on top of her head that way and the silly pajama pants, she looked messy and adorable, much as she had when she'd rolled out of his bed yesterday morning. But this was more than just sex appeal. There was a sweetness and a playfulness to Sam that she tended not to let the outside world see.

Here, though, she was in her element. This was as relaxed as he'd seen her. In pajamas with her family and sporting a kitten seemed to be her ideal state, a far cry from the edgy, black-clad artist she played outside the confines of this house. This part of her was one he'd only had glimpses of years ago. Now it was the one he wished she'd let everyone see. Whether she did or not, though, he had no interest in hiding away the fact that they were together.

If yesterday was any indication, he had some work to do before some of his friends even acknowledged that he was dating anyone. Until she was right in front of them, Sam was just an idea. But he wanted to make her a part of his reality. All of it.

As he walked to the door, Jake could feel his stress levels rising back to where they'd been when he'd woken up. At least he'd had a break for a little while. It surprised him how easy it was, fitting into the rhythm of the Henrys' big house, drinking coffee in the huge but surprisingly cozy kitchen and watching Sam and Andi's affectionate verbal fencing. He hated to go, but Sam had work, and he needed to drop the last two kittens at home and let Tucker out for a bit before heading back to the hospital. It was a comfort knowing Greg was right there by his mom's side, but he needed to be there, too. She'd always been the anchor, the rock, in his family. The thought that anything could hurt her was an ugly shock to the system.

Emma emerged from the far reaches of the house just as he was getting ready to go. This time, she was dressed, long brown hair back in a ponytail. She was in jeans and a sweatshirt, and her feet were bare. It was more casual than he'd ever seen her around town, and she didn't look particularly pleased about the fact that he was seeing her now.

It seemed like both she and Sam wore their own sorts of armor in public. This was their territory, though. And from the look on Emma's face, he was an invader. The only thing soft-looking about her was the little brown tabby in her arms. She'd picked the only medium-haired kitten of the bunch, a lazy little bundle of fur that already liked belly rubs ... unlike Loki, who seemed to regard a hand anywhere near that part of his body as a declaration of war.

"This is all your fault," she said by way of greeting.

"Nice to see you too, Emma," he replied. "It wasn't my idea. I was just transportation."

"I don't need a cat," she replied, rubbing little circles on the kitten's back while he lolled in her arms. "I'm busy."

Jake shrugged. "Then I can take him back. The tech who took one of the others has a friend who's interested. I think they'll all have homes by next week."

Emma pressed her lips together and glared at him. Her eyes were very big, and a brilliant blue. He'd never actually noticed before. She was usually moving too fast to get a look, and he'd always considered her slightly terrifying besides. He knew she'd built Occasions by Emma into quite an operation, but she seemed like the sort of person who had an unhealthy attachment to spreadsheets. He never knew what to do with people like that.

Since Emma had ignored him for years, that had never really been an issue until now.

"Yeah, give the kitty back, Em," Sam teased her, prodding her sister with her foot. "Go ahead. Hand him back. Say good-bye."

Emma turned her glare on her sister, though he noticed it wasn't quite as harsh as the look she'd given him. "You suck," she said. "This wasn't part of the deal. I came for popcorn and movies, not to get a bunch of kittens dumped on my head first thing in the morning."

"You were already awake," Sam replied. "And your house needs something fun in it."

"Even if I agreed with you—which I don't—there are lots of things that fit into that category that aren't *alive*."

Sam raised her eyebrows. "So give him back. Even though he climbed right under the covers with you. And would love to warm your cold, cold bed."

Emma made a disgusted noise, then returned her gaze to Jake. "When do I bring him in for more whatever-he-needs?"

"A couple of weeks," Jake said, biting back his grin.

"Fine."

"You're going to want to watch him. He's a little food fixated, and he's the biggest in the litter anyway."

"Maybe I'll take him to the gym. I hear they have a new trainer," Emma said, her voice deceptively light. It was a solid punch in the gut, though. And those pretty blue eyes were as cold as ice. Sam may have forgiven him for what had gone on years ago—at least, he hoped she was heading in that direction—but Emma, it seemed, hadn't. That was a warning shot. She knew about Cici, who'd been excitedly chattering about her new job at the gym yesterday. And Sam, who merely rolled her eyes, obviously didn't. But he bet she would after he left.

Shit. Why hadn't he just told her?

Because he didn't want her to worry. Because he didn't want the fallout.

Because he didn't know what the hell to say that would make Sam feel any better about it. For better or worse, Cici was part of his old circle of friends. She'd come back and picked up where she'd left off. Avoiding her would be impossible.

And, yeah, it might have been better if he'd just said

that instead of ducking the issue, but all he'd wanted this morning was a respite from yesterday's stress. So much for that.

"Just some toys would work," he finally said.

"Uh-huh. I'm sure I'll manage. We'll see you." Her smile was cool as she turned away, bumping her sister's hip on the way by as she tossed Sam an insult that was a lot more affectionate than the good-bye he'd just been given.

"Butthead," Emma said.

"Takes one to know one," Sam replied. Then she turned her attention to Jake as Emma headed back into the recesses of the house along with Andi, who offered a friendly smile and wave. Then it was just the two of them at the door. Well, three. He wasn't sure Loki was ever going to get down.

"So," he said.

"So," she replied, and he was reminded of the first night he'd picked her up here. Most of the awkwardness had gone, but he still couldn't shake the impression that she was holding him at a distance. The barriers between them had vanished in bed, but here and now, he could see that a few had gone back up. They were smaller, maybe, and fewer in number, but he could feel her tension. Alone, she still didn't know quite what to do with him.

Lucky for her he had plenty of ideas. Enough for them both.

"Did you want to get together later?" he asked. "After work, I mean."

"I promised Zoe I'd go over to her place for a while," Sam replied. "Something about chocolate and tea. And bonding. She was pretty adamant." When she smiled, he could see it in her eyes. She was settling in here, he realized. But in her own way. One that didn't, so far, appear to include many of the things and people who had lived here when she was growing up in the Cove.

They'd existed in very different worlds back then. It was going to happen again, he suddenly realized, if he didn't start trying to bridge the gap.

"I can come by afterward," Sam said, looking at him closely. He must have had an odd expression on his face. It wouldn't surprise him. The thought had been fleeting, but powerful—that instead of coming together again, the two of them would find that their lives didn't mesh and drift apart. He would see her around town occasionally, a flash of black, maybe a smile. But not often. She would still be walking a path outside of his comfort zone, here but not in a way he could touch.

At its heart, it would be just like before.

"Are you okay?" she asked, frowning.

"Yeah, just tired. Sorry," Jake replied. He reached up to tuck a stray lock of hair behind her ear, silk through his fingers. "After would be great." Loki swatted at his hand as he traced his fingers down her cheek, and she laughed.

"Bad kitty."

"Hey, I got you here," he informed the kitten, who glared back at him. This one was always going to be a one person cat, probably either disdainful of or ornery toward everyone else. He'd picked his person, and Jake could go pound salt.

"I'll leave him home," Sam said. "Promise."

"Good, because I'd really like to touch you without bleeding out."

She laughed, and it pushed him to ask her something

he'd tabled for a few days, hoping for the right time. It was a strange twist of fate, that now he'd be the one concerned that Sam would refuse to go somewhere with him, but he supposed it was karmic justice.

"There's a Halloween party next weekend. Just the usual costume thing at the Tavern, but everybody goes. I wanted to ask if maybe you'd want to come with me."

He saw the hesitation immediately, and knew this was exactly the kind of situation she'd had no intention of putting herself in when she'd come back to Harvest Cove. Silently, he willed her to say yes.

"I don't know, Jake. I don't have a costume or anything. . . ."

"Sam, you could probably throw together something amazing in about five minutes. It's going to be all pirate hookers and guys dressed as pregnant nuns anyway."

"You're going to be a pregnant nun?" she asked, eyeing him.

"Not if you come with me," he replied. "I really want you to meet everybody, Sam."

"We've met."

"Not the right way. It's fun, Sam. I think you might be surprised." He moved closer, keeping a wary eye on the kitten and his suddenly twitchy tail. "Please?"

He saw her struggle with it, and he saw the moment she relented. He released a breath he hadn't even been aware he was holding. It mattered that she'd give this a shot for him. And he'd do everything he could to make sure she enjoyed herself, replacing ugly memories with good ones.

"I guess. All right." She took a deep breath, exhaled, and then nodded. "I'll figure out some kind of costume. Just . . . what you heard about me punching Thea? That was true. And I haven't actually seen her since then, so don't expect too much, Jake."

Hell, he'd forgotten about that. "Are you ever going to tell me what happened?" he asked.

Sam pressed her lips together, looked into the distance while she thought. Finally, she said, "It was about you. Well, me and you. Beyond that it doesn't much matter. I know I was quiet and weird, but even I had my limits, and she crossed them that day. Not that punching someone in the face is ever a very good answer, but I wasn't great at snappy comebacks."

"You weren't weird."

She tilted her chin down and lifted her eyebrows. "Are you kidding? Don't insult me, Jake. I purposely cultivated the weird."

"Well," he replied, "you were beautiful under the weird."

"Hmm," was all she said, and he saw the flicker of hurt in her expression. It was an old hurt, and one that apparently ran deep. She was never going to forget that he'd thrown her stubborn individuality in her face when he'd walked away. So he would just have to keep showing her that he hadn't meant it. That it was one of the most attractive things about her.

On impulse, Jake braved Loki's claws and leaned down to press his mouth to Sam's—a gentle brush of lips, then a longer, lingering kiss, melting into each other. His hand came up to cup her jaw, angling her head so that he could tease her, taste her. He could feel her body rise, and felt his heart quickening in response. They had this, he thought. This need for each other. That it had remained so long, after ten years apart, had to mean something.

And so did the fact that already, the thought of being without her was accompanied by a vague but increasing sense of panic. Maybe because before, women had come and gone, and he'd never had to worry about how one fit into his life. Usually, they worked until they didn't, and it hadn't bothered him. He hadn't been looking for more.

Sam was a puzzle piece with edges that would give the most dedicated puzzle hobbyist fits. He thought some perverse part of her might even like it that way. She seemed to be managing to wedge herself into a spot anyway, but would she stay? He had no idea.

He didn't know what it was like not to fit. All he knew was that she seemed to fit with him.

Jake pulled back, stroking her cheek and enjoying the pink flush, the hazy look in her eyes.

"Give me a ring at the house when you're coming," he said. "I'll have food. Real food. Okay?"

Sam nodded. Then she surprised him by lifting up on her tiptoes and pressing another, fleeting kiss to his lips. There was a look in her eyes he couldn't decipher, a flash of determination or desperation or something in between. He didn't know why. All he could do was appreciate that whatever her thoughts were, he seemed to be heavily involved.

He thought again of yesterday, and of how it seemed like all the old patterns were trying to reassert themselves. Cici had stuck to his side without invitation, and the others acted as though it was a given that the two of them would function as a pair. Darts? He hadn't even had a chance to pick a partner. Seating? Thea had cleared out so that Cici could assume the spot beside him. The worst of it was, he'd hardly noticed at first. She was the same old Cici, flirty and chatty and as beautiful as ever, and it had felt perfectly familiar that she was there. But after an hour or so, he'd begun to notice the little things—her hand on his shoulder felt off, the way she leaned in close to talk to him that had him pulling back. The approving smirks between the others.

It was strange to realize that after so many years enjoying the safety and familiarity of his life in the Cove that he didn't want more of the same. It was almost as though nothing had changed yesterday with his friends. Except everything had. Cici's touch was the wrong one; her voice wasn't the one he wanted in his ear. She wasn't his anymore. Just an old friend, part of his past.

He wasn't interested in the past. Not when the present looked so fetching with an ornery kitten on her shoulder and had just agreed to see him tonight.

And not when she let him know he'd been standing there staring too long by blushing and prodding him with her toe. "Go. You're supposed to be gone when I do my maniacal laugh because I've just been using you for your veterinary abilities."

"I'm going," he laughed. "Except . . . are you saying you only like me because I can play doctor? I think I might be okay with that."

Sam made a disgusted noise and rolled her eyes, but she was smiling when she shut the door on him. And so was he as he headed out into the morning, eager to get started so that he could find her again at the end of the day.

Chapter Nineteen

Zoe lived in a cute little saltbox not far from the gallery. It wasn't at all what Sam had pictured. She'd imagined something bigger, something with a little more drama. Instead, it was a simple house painted brick red, with a low, white picket fence and a pair of oak trees shading the front yard on either side of the walk to the front door. There was a small detached garage around back, accessible by a narrow street that mainly functioned as an alley, though there were several tiny one-story homes lining it.

Sam parked out front while Zoe went around back, and they met at the front door. As much as she'd teased Zoe about her "next level" friendship comment, meeting outside of work did feel significant in a way Sam hadn't expected. Here, there were no calls to make, no art to sell, no forms to look over. Here, they were just friends.

It felt . . . nice.

"Excuse anything I forgot to put away," Zoe said, unlocking the door. "I'm not a slob, but I get busy sometimes and leave things lying around. I'd get all type A about it, but I really don't have the energy or the time."

Sam thought back to her roommate in New York and

chuckled. "Honestly, it takes a lot to get me to bat an eye. Don't worry."

"I'll take your word for it." The door opened. "Come on in."

Sam stepped in behind Zoe and immediately smiled. It was all so very New England, and because it was Zoe, done impeccably. The floors were wide plank, gleaming dark wood, while the paneled walls were painted the pale yellow of buttercream. To their left was the dining room, with a big, rustic farm table and white colonial chairs, and to the right was a parlor that had been styled as more of a library. One wall had been converted to bookshelves, with a cozy love seat and wingback chair for reading comfortably. Sam followed Zoe farther in, dumping her big, slouchy purse on a parson's bench in the hall at her friend's instruction. The back of the house was one large room, with a country kitchen featuring a big stone fireplace at one end and a living area at the other. The colors were light, the fabrics rich prints, and the wood of the various pieces antiqued.

It was just shy of fussy, and absolutely perfect.

"Pick a spot," Zoe said. "I made brownies. They're from a mix, so don't get too excited, but they're good."

"I love your house," Sam said, settling into a chair at the round kitchen table. "Just saying."

Zoe turned her head and smiled as she opened one of the cupboards and got out a pair of dessert plates. "Thank you," she said. "I'm picky about my things. You may or may not have noticed."

"I noticed."

She pulled back the foil on a glass pan that sat on her counter, and Sam caught a whiff of chocolate as Zoe started cutting. Her mouth watered.

"Here we go," Zoe said, placing a big square brownie onto each plate. Napkins appeared from a different cupboard, and then she was sliding the plates onto the table. "Fork?"

"Only if you really insist on manners."

Zoe laughed. "At this point, I think I'd worry about you if you *did* want a fork, Sam. Go for it. I'm going to put the tea on. Now, I'm not going to force you. But if you haven't tried it, there's nothing like a cup of tea at the end of the day. Helps me relax. I've got a great blend here. Wait until you smell it brewing."

Sam sighed. "One cup. Mostly because I love drinking out of teacups and I never have any reason to."

"Success!" Zoe clapped her hands excitedly, then walked back over to fill her teapot and dig her tea ball out of a drawer. When she opened a tall cupboard beside the stove Sam caught a glimpse of a terrifyingly organized collection of tins.

Sam looked around while Zoe busied herself, picking out the pieces of art Zoe had chosen to fill the room. Everything was subtle, no one piece jumping out but everything together drawing her interest. Different from what she would have done, but she enjoyed the way Zoe had pulled things together for the space.

Ten minutes later, they sat at the table together, sipping cups of steaming tea from china cups and working on the pan of brownies. Sam was trying to keep her nose close to the cup without being obvious about it—the steam that curled upward smelled of spice: cinnamon and ginger and a couple of other things she couldn't identify.

Zoe looked smug as she sipped from her own cup. "You like it, don't you?"

Sam took another bite of brownie. "I have no idea what you're talking about."

"Of course you don't. Just watch it. You're going to face-plant in the cup if you're not careful." She sighed happily, holding her teacup with both hands, her elbows propped on the table. "In case you were curious about the tea you don't like, it's a rooibos chai. It's colder today, and this always warms me up. Plus it makes the house smell good." She tapped a finger against the china. "If you went into SereniTea downtown, they could hook you up. Theoretically speaking, of course. I can tell you're completely nauseous."

"Hmm?" Sam asked, eyes heavy-lidded as she took another sip. She would have to hide this tea thing from her mother. She wasn't sure she could deal with Andi's gloating. It might be endless. Maybe if she got a small stash, she could hide it somewhere. . . .

"Exactly," Zoe said. She watched her for a moment over the edge of her cup, her striking gray eyes curious. "So. Now that I have you alone, Miss Samantha, you really do need to tell me the story of you and this place. People know you but don't really know you. You've got a hot boyfriend whose ex just got back and doesn't seem to want to stay ex. You took off running ten years ago, you live in a huge house that you really need to let me inside, and best of all, you're painting again."

"I'm still getting it together in that area," Sam said quickly. "Nothing's done yet."

Zoe sipped primly, watching her over the rim of her cup. "Lots of almost-done, though. I peeked."

"Zoe." She wasn't surprised. And Zoe wasn't contrite.

"Lots of amazing, too. A show? You know I have to ask."

She thought of her paintings hanging on the walls of Two Roads. Then she thought of Cici and Penny. "Yeah," she said, nodding slowly. "I'd like to make that happen. I'm just not sure when. I'd stopped for quite a while, so this just feels new right now. I hope it lasts."

"It will," Zoe said, and Sam couldn't help but smile over her confidence. "Now. Tell me the story of you and this place. Because I feel like there's a lot to tell."

Sam wrinkled her nose. "You sure?"

"I made brownies. I'm sure."

Sam looked around and considered. She had hot tea, brownies, a warm kitchen ... and most importantly, a sympathetic ear. Whatever she'd expected to find in Harvest Cove, a friend hadn't been on the list. But she'd been wrong about quite a few things.

"Okay," Sam said after taking a deep breath. "So here's the thing."

Three hours, half a tray of brownies, two pots of tea and two glasses of wine later, Sam was flopped on Zoe's couch, laughing as Zoe told another story about her brothers and the trouble they'd gotten into growing up.

"I don't know," Zoe was saying, shaking her head. "To this day, they will not tell me how they caught that damn possum. I'm just glad it wasn't rabid, considering. They just about had to pull my mother off the ceiling, and I cried for a week."

"But it bit you!"

"Yes, it did. There were also scratches, and a trip to the doctor just to make sure I wasn't infected with who-knew-what. But I loved Mr. Chompy. It took them forever to convince me that he wasn't just a really ugly cat."

"Mr. Chompy," Sam repeated, then lapsed into laughter again.

"They gave him that name," Zoe said stoically, keeping a straight face and tipping her chin up. "Marcus told me he was named that because he liked to give love nibbles. And that he slept a lot."

"You really believed that?"

"I was *five*. When you are a five-year-old who wants a pet, and one of your brothers hands you one, you don't ask questions. Until he regained consciousness, Mr. Chompy was a wonderful pet." Then she started laughing. "I'm still not a hundred percent sure that one was Marcus's idea, but he deserved what he got anyway. He didn't even get in trouble at all half the time. Oldest children are sneaky."

"Emma isn't," Sam said. "She was always very in-your-face about whatever she was doing. And no matter what, she always tattled first. It was a point of honor with her." She thought about it. "I think it still is, actually."

Zoe huffed out a laugh. "She should meet Marcus. They could run the world together."

"That or have an epic battle for supremacy," Sam said. "I don't think Emma would share." She rolled onto her stomach and crossed her ankles. "I bet they all miss you. You're pretty far away."

"Oh, they do," Zoe said. "I miss them, too. But it's not like there are so many jobs in Madison, Georgia. We all left. Marcus went to Charleston, Jeff is in Virginia Beach, the twins were in Atlanta with me, and Theo went all the way to Paris. At least it gives me an excuse to visit and a nice place to stay. Makes up for some of his continuing obnoxiousness. Mama and Daddy are very loud about wanting everyone to move home, but to do what?

They've got a beautiful house in a pretty little town, but in this economy . . ." She trailed off, shrugged. "We were raised to work hard and follow our dreams, so that's what we did. I'm grateful, even though I'm pretty sure they feel like it worked a little too well. I'd like to get them all up here for the holidays, but I'll probably end up flying home again for Christmas, at least. I'm not sure you could pry them out of that house with a crowbar. I keep trying anyway."

"I hope it works sometime," said Sam. "I'd love to meet all of them."

"We are a loud family," she replied. "So be careful what you wish for." Then Zoe sighed, stretching out in the wide chair she'd draped herself over. "I'm glad you came over. I haven't had this much fun in I don't know how long. Nice to get a girls' night. Well, afternoon."

"Same," Sam agreed. "Unlike next weekend. Which is going to be a failure of epic proportions."

"That's a winning attitude," Zoe said. "Maybe some things are better. You haven't seen most of these people in ten years, right?"

Sam arched one brow. "One I punched in the eye for telling me that Jake and Cici were back together, and that I didn't need to worry about getting good-looking guys like him anyway because ugly little freak girls were all lousy lays and guys knew it."

Zoe winced. "Ouch."

"Shane hates me for reasons unknown, and Cici is going to be in my face and all over Jake just because I don't think she can help herself. Fitz seemed nice."

Zoe waited a beat. "That's it? He seemed nice?"

"Yeah. Nothing objectionable. He's cute, has a boat. I don't remember seeing him much. I think he kind of drifted around the edges of that group. He just ended up staying here, so I guess that's why they brought him into the circle of trust or whatever."

"Well, that's a positive, right? One non-jerk."

"You'd have to know how the others were. I'm not optimistic."

Zoe groaned and threw her head back. "Sam, you have to try and think positive about this! Even if they're still horrible people making bad decisions, they comprise like a handful of this town. If everybody was like that, I would have left immediately."

"I know," Sam groaned, rolling onto her back and pressing her hands to her forehead. "God help me, I'm even finding things to like about this place. Not just you and the gallery. Things I'd forgotten, like the Witch Tree, or new things like Beltane Blues. I guess I just worry because these are his people, you know? His friends. His awful, miserable friends. Since forever."

"You liked one. You'll probably like some of the others," Zoe pointed out.

"I forgot about Ryan," Sam said. "Maybe he'll bring Aaron. That would make him likable."

"Aaron is a handful. Again, be careful what you wish for." Zoe laughed. "I got the impression they're still dancing around each other, though. I got an earful when he called yesterday." She shook her head. "You all are making me grateful to be single, honestly. Working with artists is enough drama for me."

"I'd like to avoid drama," Sam said. "I just don't think it's possible with these people. The weird thing is, Jake is really sweet and down-to-earth. I don't know what he sees in them."

"Shared history is a powerful thing," Zoe said. "It's

not that easy to cut people loose when you live nearby and you've grown up together. I had a couple like that. I know."

"I thought of that," Sam said. "That's why I'm giving it a shot. Also because he said please."

"That word is hard to resist coming from the right mouth," Zoe agreed. "I'd come with you, but that party has so many wheels I don't know which extra one I'd be."

"You would?" Sam asked, zeroing in on that part of her statement like a laser beam.

Zoe seemed to realize what she'd said. "Um, no. No, that's not what I meant. . . ."

"You should come," Sam said. "Moral support. Come on."

"Sam, I'm not really all that excited about going to a bar in costume and standing around *by myself* for hours."

"You can hang out with us. The Harvest Cove cool kids. If I have to deal with all of them, they can handle it if I bring a friend. Anyway, didn't you say you wanted an in to Penny's stupid Christmas party? Here's your foot in the door."

Zoe stared at her, considering. "I really kind of doubt that."

"You won't know unless you try."

"Mmmhmm." Zoe pursed her lips. "I know I'm being suckered here. Tell you what: I'll think about it. If I can find someone else who's going, you'll see me there, okay?"

"Deal. And thanks. For everything. I really needed this." Sam sat up and stretched. Her stomach was full, she'd talked so much that her jaw was actually tired, and she found herself completely content. It was an unusual state for her, but one she meant to enjoy.

"You and me both," said Zoe. "I meant it when I told you I loved this place, but it gets lonely sometimes. I do miss home. I miss having people I'm used to and comfortable with. I'm not the easiest person on earth to live with, and I know that. It takes me a while to warm up, and not everyone wants to wait that long. You, though . . . you're stuck with me."

Sam grinned as she rose. "Same goes. Tell you what: We'll do this at my house next week. I'll see if I can extract my sister from her busy life of paperwork and planning to come by, too. She's wound kind of tight. I think she could use a break once in a while."

That had been driven home to her last night, when they'd actually managed to have fun—especially once she'd plied her sister with some wine. She still didn't have a good read on what, exactly, Emma's social life consisted of outside of work. She had a sneaking suspicion it wasn't all that exciting. Dragging her sister kicking and screaming into enjoyable social interaction might be entertaining all in itself.

"This is Occasions by Emma, right?"

"That's her. The party girl who hates to party."

Zoe's eyes widened. "Ooh. This could be good. I'd really like to partner with someone for the events we do. Offer packages and things for people who want to hold parties at the gallery. I never seem to run into her, and I just hadn't gotten around to making an appointment. She does good work."

Sam wrinkled her nose. "That sounds like a conversation I might let you two have on your own. But sure. She basically does nothing but work, so that would probably thrill her. I'll hook you two up."

Zoe clapped her hands. "That makes my day even

better. Now I'm going to finish it off by getting into my yoga pants and finishing off a couple more brownies while I watch trash TV. I'd invite you to stay, but if I had the choice I'd probably head for the hot vet too."

"He's . . . definitely hard to stay away from," Sam conceded. The instant she let herself think of his hands on her, she could feel herself flush with heat. It wasn't just that, either. He genuinely seemed to want her to be a part of his life. Not just hidden away, a secret indulgence that he would jettison at the first hint of friction from everyone else. It was a big change, and a welcome one. It was also a scary one, because no matter what he said, all she could think was that if things didn't go well, he'd end up backing off. It wouldn't be as abrupt, but it would be just as painful.

She didn't want to care about fitting in anymore. But the impending party brought back the kind of anxiety she hadn't felt in years. New York had been different. It was easy to deal with people she had no history with, no matter how miserable they were. They took her at face value. She had remade herself in New York, maybe not perfectly, but into someone who blended into the world she'd chosen.

Of course, she still hadn't been happy. And it hadn't been right. But she hadn't felt like this.

"Look at that blush," Zoe said, pulling Sam out of her thoughts. "No gloating about your sex life in my house. I'm about two cats and a handful of doilies away from collecting dust permanently."

"I'm not gloating," Sam said, though she knew she sounded unconvincing. Because it had been good. Better than good. And she suspected that was only the beginning.

"I'm about two seconds away from throwing this pillow at your head."

"Yeah, yeah, I'm going. You need to stop it, though. I
bet Jason would be happy to save you from celibacy."
She started laughing when Zoe's mouth dropped open.

"What is this thing you have about me and Treebeard? I'd end up with pine needles in delicate places.
The man is dirty!"

She wiggled her eyebrows. "I bet."

Zoe had excellent aim. The pillow connected so well
that it nearly knocked Sam off her feet. "Get. I need to
sit here and recover from the images you just put in my
head. Honestly." But she was laughing, and as Sam bid
her good-bye and headed to get her purse, she reveled in
how good it felt to just hang out and tease and be herself.
That it was happening here, in the Cove, seemed like a
minor miracle, but she couldn't deny it.

Maybe it was an illusion. Maybe she was fooling herself. But after all this time, and all these years, Harvest
Cove was starting to feel like home.

Chapter Twenty

She was most of the way to Jake's by the time she realized she'd forgotten to call him, but considering the time, Sam figured he'd be there anyway. She'd already called home to check on the kittens, who were apparently passed out after chasing each other over, under and around every available surface, and her mother had been adamant that she stay gone for a while longer—probably so she could read in peace. Sam sang along with the radio happily, knowing she was slightly off-key but making up for it, she thought, with sheer volume. She just felt good. Really good.

And she had every intention of letting Jake benefit from that as soon as she walked in his door.

She cruised on her mood right up until she saw the unfamiliar car parked in his driveway. It was a white Mercedes. That alone would have pinged her radar, because the Cove just wasn't the kind of place you saw a lot of those, even on the Crescent. It was the North Carolina plates, though, that took a sledgehammer to all her good feelings.

Cici. Great.

She tried to be rational, even as her heart started to pound. She knew Jake wouldn't have invited his ex-girlfriend over at the same time as his current—well, she *was* his girlfriend, right? Not that he'd referred to her that way. Not that she should suddenly be freaking out about that. But regardless, Cici was here, the two of them were alone, and Sam wasn't sure which of them she was angrier at. Yes, Cici was a bitch, but she was overt about it. Jake couldn't even be honest about the fact that he'd seen her yesterday, or that she was in town at all.

Her first instinct, a very old and well-honed one, was to turn her car around and flee. But there was a newer, harder part of her, surprising in its sudden appearance and strength, that refused to let that happen. She pulled up in front of the house, killed the engine, and got out. It was a little like having an out-of-body experience. She felt light-headed as she focused on the door, the lights inside. A thousand awful scenarios unspooled at once inside her head. She would answer the door. No one would answer the door. They would be obviously rumpled and *both* answer the door.

Her hand was shaking when she pressed the bell and Tucker came flying around the corner to bark ecstatically. She could hear him, but Sam refused to so much as peek through the sidelight. She wanted to see. She didn't want to see. She—

"Sam!"

Jake opened the door, barefoot in a pair of ragged jeans and an old T-shirt, looking good enough to take a bite out of. His eyes looked like molten gold in the light, and his smile seemed full of genuine pleasure. There was something more, though, Sam thought. Something just a little different in the speed with which he pulled her inside. Relief? That was probably too much to hope for. Still . . .

"I wondered why I hadn't heard from you yet," he said.

"I forgot," Sam replied, struggling to keep her voice even as she let him usher her inside and shut the door. "You have company?"

He looked more than a little stricken. "Yeah, ah, you remember how I lost my phone yesterday. Cici found it, so she decided to drop it off."

"Oh," Sam said. She put every shred of her anger into that one, lightly spoken word.

Jake's voice dropped to a whisper. "Sam, I—"

"Who's that, Jake? Did Shane decide to . . . Oh." Cici rounded the corner from the family room, tall and lean and perfectly made-up, as comfortable as if she lived in the house herself. Sam had the fleeting, awful thought that she looked like she belonged here, far more than Sam ever would. Then she banished it to the dark recesses of her mind.

That's bullshit. I belong here, too. It would be nice, though, if she could make herself believe it.

"Cici, Sam's here. I told you she was coming over. You two probably remember each other . . . right?"

He sounded like he wanted to sink through the floor, and Sam watched him scrub one hand through his hair until it stood on end. Right now, she had absolutely no sympathy.

"Sure. We ran into one another just the other day," Sam said, and took a nasty sort of pleasure in the brief shock that passed over Jake's face. *Yeah, I was going to be nice about that. Now, not so much.*

"Yes, we did," Cici said, giving her a cool smile. "How's the show coming along?"

"Great," Sam replied. "How's the moving in?"

"Oh, fine. I'm lucky I still have all these men here to drag things around for me." She walked up to stand by Jake and gave his arm a squeeze. "That's what I love about the Cove. I can come back and it's like no time has passed."

Sam tried not to give her the satisfaction of fixating on the way her hand lingered on Jake's arm.

"Oh, I don't know," Sam said. "It's not quite the same as I remember. You're right, though. . . . Some things really don't change."

Cici smiled sweetly as Jake discreetly pulled away. That, at least, was gratifying. But Sam couldn't stop her fury at him for allowing this in the first place. Did he really think that she and Cici would be buddies? That things would just fall into place without any resistance?

"Well, I'll let you two get at your dinner. Jake never could cook worth a damn, though. Do you remember —"

"Yeah, no stories, Cici. My current skills are embarrassing enough." He looked flushed, and a little angry. That made two of them, Sam thought. Only Cici seemed completely unaffected as she moved to get her purse and coat, then slid her arms around Jake for a quick hug good-bye. Her eyes, though, were on Sam, and there was an ugly triumph in them.

"Let's try and get together this week," she said. "I've missed you, and we need to talk about costumes for the party. Thea had this idea that the four of us could coordinate."

It was like she wasn't even here, Sam thought, slightly amazed. Like her presence just completely didn't matter. Of course, it never had, so why should it now? Her mouth opened, and she heard herself saying in a firm, clear voice, "Actually, I'm coming with Jake, so it would be a little weird if he were dressed to match someone else. Sorry."

Sorry meaning "up yours," that is.

Cici lifted her brows, her smile sugary. "Oh. Sorry. Nobody told me you were coming." It was a dismissal, though Sam was at least glad to hear the hint of annoyance in it. It was better than just being ignored.

"I thought everyone would expect it, considering you all know Sam and I are seeing each other," Jake said, and the irritation in his voice cooled her anger a little. At him, anyway. She even felt a little — very little — bit sorry for him. He was staring at Cici like she was visiting from an alien, and not very benevolent, planet, and he had no idea what to do with her.

Sam had a couple of ideas, but they were felonies.

Cici seemed completely unaffected by Jake's rebuke. "Don't be mad. I just *forgot*." She opened the door and headed out, giving Jake a half wave and not sparing Sam another glance. "Let's try to do lunch this week. It was so busy yesterday I didn't get to tell you even half of everything."

"I'm busy, Cici. You can tell me the other half at the party."

She turned her head just enough for Sam to see her roll her eyes. "Okay. Just thought you might want to come out of hiding and eat real food for once. I know how you get when you're working too much."

She was good, Sam thought. Wounded sincerity, a nod to their shared past . . . she was throwing it all out there. A glance at Jake told her he wasn't completely unaffected . . . but that it hadn't affected him nearly as much as intended, either.

"I'm not working too much. I have other plans," he

said. "I also have a girlfriend you're trying like hell not to notice. Things did change while you were gone, you know."

Cici's eyes narrowed ever so slightly, though her voice remained mild. "Nice. I didn't think friendships counting for something changed, whether or not you had a *girl-friend*, but I guess I stand corrected. Have lunch with whoever you want, Jake. Don't let me cramp your style."

Sam didn't pay much attention to Jake's angry parting shot as Cici flounced off in a huff. She was too busy fighting off the bloodred haze that descended over her vision and threatened to make things come out of her mouth that she wouldn't be able to take back. She would have taken off immediately, but there was no way in hell Cici was going to see her leave. She had a feeling that this was the sort of fight Jake's ex had won before, probably more than once. Still, standing in Jake's house, despite all her excitement earlier, was the very last place she wanted to be right now.

It wasn't so much about what he had or hadn't said. It was that he'd let tonight happen at all. Maybe he wanted to be Switzerland where his friends were concerned, but sometimes you had to pick a side. Even if it meant walking away from a viper like Cici Ferris.

The door shut. Jake looked at her. "Shit. Sam—"

"Don't." She held up her hand. "I honestly don't think I can hear this right now."

He looked stricken, even as Tucker danced happily around his feet. "It isn't what you think."

She curled her lip. "How do you even know what I think?"

"I can guess," he said. "I know I should have told you she was back. I just didn't want you to worry."

"Oh, well, that worked out well. Especially since she'd already been to see me anyway. You *know* how this town works, damn it!"

He heaved a soft, humorless laugh as he scrubbed at his hair again. He was starting to look like a very cute victim of electroshock therapy. "There's nothing between me and Cici anymore. Not for a very long time. I want *you*. God, the look on your face right now ... This isn't high school, Sam. This is now. She and I were finished years ago. We stayed friends, but that's it. I swear, I didn't even know she was coming over. Look, you heard what I said to her. I'm not exactly hiding the fact that you and I are together!"

"Whether you hid it or not, I'd say somebody doesn't consider that much of a problem." She stepped away. If he touched her right now, she might lose her resolve, and this was a stand she needed to take. "If this is how it's going to be, Jake, I can't. I can't watch her find excuses to show up here, or conveniently forget I exist, not to mention paw at you while you pretend it's no big deal."

"I didn't say it wasn't a big deal, Sam. And I wouldn't let her paw at me!"

"You're not very good at stopping her, from what I just saw. She might as well have peed on you."

He blinked, then looked torn between amusement and worry. *"Sam."* Her name was a plea, but she couldn't respond to it. "Listen to me, damn it. *I don't want her.* If I did, I'd be with her. It's not like I can't figure it out!"

"It wouldn't be the first time," Sam snapped, then immediately regretted it. They hadn't been a couple back then. They'd been ... something more than friends, but less than a couple. And she'd been as confused about it as he had, though for different reasons. She shook her head, trying to ignore the anger and hurt that flashed across his face. "Forget it," she said. "I'm going home. If I stay, I'll end up taking another cheap shot like that and both of us will regret it. I need some space."

Jake threw up his hands. "Fine. Jesus, Sam, it's like you want to believe the worst of me. I never get the benefit of the doubt, right? You just jump right to the bad place."

"Maybe I wouldn't if you were honest with me," she said. "I knew you were with her yesterday. She told me where she was headed."

"Why didn't you say something?"

"Why should I have to?" She'd clenched her jaw so tight that it ached. "I'm not the one who walked away the last time."

Jake closed his eyes and breathed deeply. "I just didn't think it should matter. And I didn't want to upset you. That's on me."

"Yes," Sam said, "it is."

"But you need to stop thinking I don't want to be here, Sam," he continued, opening his eyes to pin her with his gaze. "We're not kids anymore. I'm not playing at this."

Her stomach tightened, and a shiver ran over her skin. She wanted that to be true. She wanted it far too much. But every time she started to believe it, she'd think of a thousand reasons why it couldn't possibly last. That, she knew, was her own fault. Her own problem. She was falling, far too fast, and she didn't know how to make it stop.

If she gave in and let go, she might just fly apart.

His hands were on her then, gentle as his voice, and this time she didn't pull away. She stiffened, trying not to give in.

"I'm sorry," he said. "I screwed up. I know how close

you are to bolting on me, Sam. I can feel it all the time. So I put this off, and naturally, it's worse." He sighed. "I'm better at navigating a lacrosse field, or the digestive system of your average canine, or . . . pretty much anything."

She felt herself relenting. It was easier to stay angry, but she was finding it impossible. Mostly because she knew he meant it. She was new for him. It was making him stretch, just like he was doing the same to her. She just wished she knew where it would end up, and how far they could both go.

"I wish you would have some faith in me," he said, and the weariness in his voice tugged at her, deep in her chest.

"I'm trying," Sam replied softly. "But if I'm going to do that, then I need you to step outside your weird little circle and try to see things from my perspective. I can handle a lot, but most of the things in Cici's arsenal are way past my limits for tolerance. You know what she wants, Jake. Ignoring it isn't going to change her mind. So if she shows up at your door again, quit thinking you can friendzone her into submission and maybe just pretend not to be home instead. It's not a lot to ask. But it's what I need."

He nodded. "I can do that. In fact, I would *rather* do that." Then he surprised her by sliding his arms around her. "I didn't want to think she was serious, Sam. I hope you believe that. Cici and I broke up for the last time years ago. Revisiting all that just seems . . . really uninspired. I didn't think that would be her style." He sounded so genuinely surprised that she was prompted to give him a bit of truth.

"There's nothing boring about you, Jake. Not ten years ago *or* now." She tucked her head beneath his chin, lifting her arms to encircle his back, and rested her head against his chest. She heard his soft sigh, and the steady beat of his heart. Sam closed her eyes, warmth flooding her. She could feel the last of her defenses giving way, crumbling until she had nothing left but the way she felt about him. The way she'd always felt about him.

They said you never forgot your first love. She hadn't expected to forget him, but she'd never realized that there was a part of her that had never managed to fall out of love with Jake. Not until now, when she couldn't muster any more justifications and rationalizations to hide behind.

The boy she'd loved was right here in her arms. And no amount of anger or past hurt could change that everything that had drawn her to him remained.

Jake pressed a kiss to the top of her head as she clung to him, eyes wide as the realization hit her with all the force of a speeding train.

She loved him. Still. Again. *More.*

And it terrified her.

Sam felt the subtle shift as he pulled her even closer, as he freed her hair from its simple chignon with a few gentle tugs, then slid his hands into it.

"I love your hair," he murmured into it. "Please don't go."

She ought to go. She knew it. But how could she? It was all she could do not to sink to her knees. This wasn't the way it was supposed to go. She was supposed to be able to walk away if she needed to. Instead, the feel of him, the scent of his cologne, even the steady sound of his breath held her in place. She turned her face to press it into his chest, the soft cotton of his shirt brushing her nose, her forehead, and breathed in. The feeling was so overwhelming that there was no hiding from it.

There was nowhere else on earth she'd rather be.

Sam exhaled and closed her eyes. Her hands closed, loosely fisted in the fabric at his back. His fingers slid through her hair, circling lightly over her sensitive scalp, making her skin tingle. She leaned into his touch, breath quickening as comfort slowly bloomed into desire. She was so tired of struggling against this.

Sam lifted her face and found that Jake had been waiting for her. She caught only a flash of hot golden green before his mouth was on hers, hot, demanding. There was nothing sweet in the kiss—this was all raw need. Sam sank into his hot, openmouthed kisses, drinking in every breath. He backed her against the door, and his hands slid down to grasp her hips and pull her hard against him. Sam gasped, then writhed as he ground against her, letting her feel how badly he wanted her. Desire swept away every fear, every other thought, and Sam welcomed it. All she wanted was to lose herself in him, just for a while.

She heard his breath, ragged and catching, and a hand moved to cup one of her breasts through her shirt. She leaned into it, making a soft sound of pleasure when he squeezed, then dragged his hand down to unbutton her jeans. He slid his hand inside her panties, stroking where she was already slick with need. Sam pressed her hips into him, beginning to move rhythmically to his strokes. She nipped at his lower lip, dragging it through her teeth, reveling in his hiss of pleasure. He took his free hand and grasped one of hers, pressing it between his legs where he was rigid and throbbing.

"This is what you do to me," he groaned. "Every time, Sam."

The power of his simple statement was heady. She stroked him hard with the heel of her palm, keeping time with his clever fingers while the pulse between her legs quickened. She felt the muscles in his lower belly tighten, and his brows drew together, eyes dropping to half-mast as his pleasure intensified. The only sounds were shaking breaths and soft moans, the rustle of clothes as they moved against each other.

Jake's fingers were sweet torment. He rubbed and stroked, slipping one finger inside and thrusting gently before returning to tease the throbbing nub of her sex. Sam began to quiver as the world narrowed to a single bright point, pressure building until it was unsustainable.

"Come for me," he breathed, pulling his mouth from hers. His eyes locked with hers. Sam leaned hard against the door, breath coming in short pants. "Let me see you, Sam."

He pressed a finger hard against her, and the world burst. She cried out, and the world flickered out like a candle as she surged against him, her head rocking back. Every pulse was a shock wave, and she was helpless to do anything but ride them until finally, they had ebbed enough for her to grasp a few strands of thought.

She still cupped him through his jeans, rock hard. "You," she murmured. "Now you."

He moved like lightning, stooping to scoop her up. She draped her arms around his neck, laughing softly as he carried her up the stairs.

"This is very cinematic," she said. "I feel like I should be wearing an evening gown."

"In a minute you're not going to be wearing anything," he growled. Jake carried her quickly to his room and shut the door on an unhappy Tucker, who couldn't seem to understand why he wasn't invited to the fun. Sam heard the dog sigh and flop down against the door on the other side.

Jake set her on the bed and stripped quickly out of his clothes. Sam did the same, forcing her languid limbs to cooperate. She already wanted him again. She wasn't sure it was possible to stop wanting him. Her eyes roamed over his taut, muscular body as she discarded the last of her clothes. Then, meeting his eyes, she deliberately rolled onto her stomach, up onto her knees, and then looked over her shoulder, presenting him with her backside and quirking one eyebrow.

"Like this?" she asked.

He made some soft, strangled sound, and an instant later the bed creaked beneath his weight as he positioned himself behind her. Jake entered her quickly, completely, a single thrust that buried him all the way to the hilt. Sam bucked against him with a gasp, loving the way he filled her. His hands gripped her hips, hard, as he began to ride her. There was nothing gentle about the way he moved—hard, quick thrusts that rocked her forward. Sam fisted her hands in the covers and began to rock back into his thrusts, tightening around him as she rushed toward another climax, this one as hard and fast as the way he pumped into her.

His moans mingled with hers, and she could feel his movements begin to hitch as he neared his own climax, losing the rhythm as the pleasure took him. She was close, so close ... and then Jake reached between her legs to flick his finger over her. She clenched, then shattered, whipping her head back as she arched into her climax. He drove deep into her once, twice, and then gave a hoarse cry as he came, shuddering while she still pulsed around him.

Sam sank to her stomach slowly, no longer able to hold herself up. She felt lovely, weightless. Any thought that formed skittered merrily away the instant she tried to catch it, so she didn't bother, instead just curled up against Jake when he slipped out of her and flopped down beside her.

They were quiet for long moments, the only sound was that of their deepening breathing. Sam drifted pleasantly, eyes half shut, Jake's warm, heavy arm draped over her. She'd almost thought he'd gone to sleep, until she heard the deep rumble of his voice beside her.

"Wow."

She grinned, her eyes slipping shut. "Yes. Wow."

"Mmm," was his response, almost a purr. She felt him move away, just for a few seconds, as the covers were tugged and shifted around beneath her. Then the comforter was tossed over her as Jake resituated himself behind her and buried his face in her hair. He had a real thing about her hair, Sam thought with a lazy smile. And she had a real thing about all of him. Picking a favorite part would be impossible. Though trying to decide . . . she could spend hours doing that.

Hours, days, years . . .

Her smile faded as she snuggled against him. One thing life had taught her was that you never knew what was coming next, and that nothing was forever. So she needed to try to enjoy this now, whatever happened.

She needed to make now be enough.

In case now was all she got.

Chapter Twenty-One

Something was different. He just couldn't put his finger on what.

Jake walked out of the animal hospital at one on Wednesday, hungry and in need of some fresh air. Wednesdays were surgery days for him, and by the time he got a break, he normally needed one. It didn't take much to recharge his batteries. Sometimes he just took a quick walk while he ate a sandwich. Today, though, what he really wanted was company. He wasn't sure if Sam would be busy, but it was worth a shot to go see. Especially since he'd come up with such an awesome plan this morning in the shower.

Well, he thought it was awesome. His shower ideas seemed to stay unappreciated outside the confines of his bathroom, but he hoped this one would fly.

Jake checked the small cooler he'd put on the backseat, then made the short drive to Two Roads. Sam's little car was out front, still in dire need of a bath, alongside Zoe's shiny little MINI. Those two were like *The Odd Couple*. Somehow, it worked.... Sam invariably lit up whenever she talked about her friend. It was good, he thought, that she was finding people. Just so long as he stayed one of them.

Something seemed to have shifted between them since Sunday night. He wanted her trust, badly, and her conditions were ones he was more than willing to meet. The episode with Cici had been eye-opening. Not in a good way, but in a necessary way. His old "friend" had made her intentions clear enough that he couldn't keep ignoring them. Ignoring her had never worked in the past . . . so that mistake was on him. And so was the hurt he'd caused Sam by trying.

Owning that responsibility had helped clear the air in a way they hadn't managed before. But there was more, a new sort of tension between him and Sam. He didn't know what it was. All he knew was that it pulled his thoughts to her countless times a day, and that he had begun to crave the low and pleasant thrum of whatever that force was until his world didn't seem quite right unless she was in it.

He thought he'd been through it all when it came to relationships—the years-long roller coaster with Cici should have seen to that. But being with Sam was an entirely different animal, turning him into a blundering kid trying to find his way in the dark with nothing but an unreliable flashlight.

It was scary as hell. But after a lot of years of skimming along the surface of things, it was also exactly what he'd needed to wake up again.

Jake pulled in beside the MINI, then hopped out of his truck and headed in.

The bell above the door jingled, echoing a little in the open, wood-floored space. He hadn't been in since First Friday, and looked around curiously now that there was no crowd blocking his view. The place looked decidedly bigger when it wasn't stuffed with people. He could also get a better look at the groupings of art, which were all eye-catching, even if he didn't know what the hell he was looking at. A floorboard creaked beneath his foot as he walked slowly toward the sculptures that Ryan was apparently so interested in.

Well, sculptures, or artist, or both . . . the jury was still out on that, and Ryan wasn't talking. Jake was starting to wish he would, actually, even if the whole "I like guys" thing wasn't really his area. It bothered him to think that there might be such an important part of himself that Ryan had been afraid to share, whatever the reasons. They were all supposed to be better friends than that.

Of course, Jake was starting to think they'd all quit sharing the *really* important things a long time ago. All that was left seemed to be history with a coat of gloss on it.

The thought made him sad, and he shook it off as soon as he heard footsteps approaching. He shifted his gaze to see Zoe heading toward him.

"Jake," she said, surprised but welcoming. "What can I do for you?"

"Is Sam around?" he asked. "It's my break, and I thought maybe you'd let me steal her for a few minutes if things are quiet."

She hesitated, very briefly, before answering. For a split second he thought he'd misjudged and overstepped, but then she smiled. "No, of course I don't have a problem with it. Slow day. She should be down in just a few minutes. . . . She was just cleaning something up for me in one of the studios."

"Oh yeah, I saw you had renovations going on here," Jake said, remembering the various trucks that had been parked here over the summer. "Studios. For artists to work in, right?"

"Yes, I'll be renting most of them and offering classes in at least one other. It's definitely a good thing." Her eyes flicked toward the stairs. It stirred his suspicions, though he couldn't quite figure out what she—and possibly Sam—might be up to. He was immediately determined to find out.

"Cool. Mind if I have a look? I'll grab Sam while I'm up there."

He was already at the foot of the stairs by the time Zoe answered. "Ah . . . you know, why don't I just go get her? I've still got a little cleaning to do, and I don't—"

"Don't worry about it," Jake interjected smoothly. "I'm a vet, remember? I fear no dust bunny."

"Um . . ."

She looked more than a little worried, but he was bounding up the stairs before she could come up with another reason to have him wait. Curiosity pulled him quickly past a series of small, clean rooms set up to accommodate artists at work. He could hear low, soft singing, the way people did when they were listening to music on their earphones. Jake smiled when he recognized the tune: some punk-pop that had been in heavy rotation on the alternative station.

He stopped, poked his head around the side of the doorway to say hello. But when he got a look at what Sam was doing, he was left with his mouth hanging open in silence. This wasn't just a studio she was cleaning up. It was *her* studio.

She was painting again.

The sting of the fact that she'd kept it from him mingled with a surprisingly fierce burst of pride in what he saw. There were three paintings in progress that he could see, each full of the warmth and color and imagination even he could recognize as entirely Sam's. They were beautiful, full of life. Like her. There were built-in shelves loaded with paint, along with a semi-organized bunch of tools he wouldn't have a clue what to do with, but that looked both cared for and well used.

The woman herself was wiping up some water by the sink. It looked as though she'd just cleaned her brushes, and she grooved quietly to the song in her earbuds. She'd spent her lunch break painting, he guessed. And he'd never seen her look so in her element as she did now, her hands still dotted with color, her hair back in a ponytail, and a ratty old paint-stained sweatshirt thrown on over the decidedly dressier pants that were part of her work outfit. The sweater that went with them was folded neatly over the back of a chair.

Jake leaned against the door frame and watched her, an odd and aching pull deep in his chest. This, he thought, was the woman he'd seen in the girl all those years ago. And she was still real to him in a way that he didn't think anyone else ever could be.

She executed a little turn, caught sight of him, and yelped.

"Jake!" she grabbed her chest, eyes wide, and yanked out the earbuds. "Oh my God, how long have you been standing there?"

"Just a minute or so," he said, and then gave in to the thing he couldn't help but do whenever she was near him. He closed the distance between them, slid his arms around her, and gave her the kind of kiss that made him forget where he was. He could feel her uncertainty when he touched her, just as he felt it melt away as their lips met. By the time he pulled back, Sam's eyes were hazy, a little smile curving her mouth.

"What's all this about?" she asked. "Not that I'm complaining."

He shrugged, savoring the warmth of her against him. "I was thinking about you."

"Oh." She studied him, and he could feel that odd tension wrap itself around them again. What was she thinking? He wished he knew. "You might want to re-think the hugging," she finally said. "I'm kind of . . . paint-y."

"I can see that," he said, though he didn't release her. If he got paint blobs on him, so be it. "When did all this happen?"

Her cheeks flushed. "Not long after I got back, actu-ally. I mean, at first I was pretty sure it was going to be another bust, and I'm definitely a little slower than I was, but as of right now I think maybe . . . maybe I'm back. At least a little."

Jake looked around at the small and colorful kingdom she seemed to be constructing and nodded. "Not just a little. I don't know art or anything, but these look great."

"I was going to tell you." She rushed out the words, and he could hear the defensive edge in her voice. He didn't want her to jump into that mode—she was so prone to doing that where he was concerned.

"I believe you," he said.

"I just wasn't sure it was going to stick. I've had so many false starts up until now, and it's so embarrassing not to be able to do what I left here to do, what I trained to do, that— Wait. You're not mad?"

"No." He shifted his head a little, side to side. "I'm not going to pretend I wouldn't have liked to know you were trying again, but I also can't imagine how scary it was to think you'd never paint again. What I do is hard, but it isn't like this. I can work without having to flip some creative switch. You can't. So no, I'm not mad. I trust you would have told me when you were ready. Of course, now you don't have to, because I'm smart and I figure out everything."

That got him a smile. "Uh-huh."

"Is it okay that I'm here?"

She chewed her lip, then nodded slowly. "Yeah. I want you here. Just . . . don't tell anybody else, okay? I'm not there with it yet. I'm not ready."

I want you here. She might as well have told him he'd won the lottery. The rush he got was the same.

Still, she was scared. It was the first time she'd really let him see it, and that aching pull he felt in his chest intensified. He'd seen her anger, her hurt. But not the fear. He was struck all over again by the depth of the wounds she'd incurred here. Which made it even more remarkable that he was standing here with Sam in his arms.

Maybe I'm pushing too hard with this weekend. The thought came out of the blue with a surprising amount of strength. But Jake just as quickly brushed it aside. They both needed this—Sam so she could see that he wanted to show her off to his friends, not hide her, and him so he could find out whether his suspicions about the relative shallowness of his most important friendships were correct. He needed to know. And if there was one surefire way of finding out all at once, this was it.

He and Sam would be accepted as a couple, or he'd be starting over again in some ways just as surely as Sam was. Strangely, the thought didn't cause him as much pain as he might have expected. He'd never really left the Cove—even through college he'd come back more often than most—but in some ways, he felt as though he was only just starting to see it.

And the things that resonated most deeply with him weren't at all the things he might have expected.

"You should want people to see these," Jake said softly. "They're *you*, Sam."

"That's exactly why I'm not sure about showing them here," she replied with a nervous laugh. "I'm not sure that the Cove is ready for all this *me*."

"You'll be great," he said. "Whenever you're ready."

She looked up at him curiously. "Well. Thanks." She moved her fingers against his back absently while she thought, the play of them sending pleasant little frissons of sensation over his skin.

"So . . . did you just come in to say hi? I thought you were working today."

"I am." He remembered all at once and pulled away, catching her hand in his to tug her toward the door. "I'm on my lunch break. Did you eat? Zoe said I could steal you for a few."

Sam put on the brakes, though her smile was all pleasure. "I didn't eat, and, yeah, I'd like to, but I'm not going outside like this!"

"Why not? You look cute."

Her eyebrow arched. "I look like a mess. Let me switch shirts and I'll be right with you."

He thought of the creamy skin beneath the sweatshirt and forgot about lunch. "Can I help?"

She shoved him out the door, tipped her chin down to give him an exasperated look, and then shut it. "No, because I really am hungry and I know you. Go downstairs. I'll be right there."

Grinning, Jake turned and headed down.

*   *   *

This wasn't how she'd planned to tell Jake she was painting again, but since she hadn't actually come up with a real plan anyway, Sam guessed this had worked out as well as anything else.

His easy acceptance was a relief, though the more she thought about it, she shouldn't have been surprised. Against all odds, Jake genuinely seemed to want her for her. Whatever trust deficit she still had, he was on a mission to make up for himself. But then, even as teens, barely knowing her, he'd been able to share himself in a way that she'd been incapable of. She had so many memories of it.

"I'm going to have my own animal hospital here someday," Jake had said, hands tucked behind his head as they lay talking beneath the branches of their tree, hidden from the world. It was where they always met—his friends weren't interested in sitting in parks, and hers . . . well, she didn't have any friends to speak of, so it worked out fine. Sam watched him, tanned and beautiful and for the moment, hers. She loved to listen to him talk. He chattered easily about all sorts of things. Sometimes she forgot who they were, where they were, and managed to talk just as much as he did. And he always listened, those gold eyes bright with interest, like she was the only girl in the entire world to him.

It was a pretty fantasy, and she knew it . . . but she figured that knowing it was a sort of protection.

"You'll have to do a bunch of art for me, Sam," he said. "I don't care how big you make it in New York. I want a bunch of your stuff on the walls. People will come in just to see it, and I'll have the coolest practice in the state."

She laughed, and his grin deepened so that his dimples

showed. *"You want me to do a bunch of fluffy puppy and kitty pictures?"*

"No. Well, I mean . . . you can draw them with swords and armor or something. That would be pertinent but still badass." He poked her with a toe. *"Help me out, here. A combo gallery-and-vet-clinic. It could work."*

"You're really weird, Jake. But you get points for enthusiasm."

"That's a yes, right? I know that's a yes."

She rolled her eyes. *"Yes. Battle-ready fluffies just for you. We'll make a fortune."*

"Yesss." They laughed together. And then he looked at her so long she thought, not for the first time, that he might actually think about kissing her. Instead, though, he pulled one hand from beneath his head, reached between them, and threaded his fingers through hers. Then he lay back, staring into the branches. And all she could do was feel the beat of his heart through his skin, slow and steady in comparison to the rapid fluttering of her own.

Sam shook her head, pushing the memory away as she threw her sweatshirt over the back of the chair and headed downstairs.

He was waiting there for her, a small cooler in one hand, talking easily to Zoe. Her heart constricted painfully, just for an instant. He was still the boy she'd loved with all her stupid, teenage heart. And he was so much more.

It made him so wonderfully, terrifyingly easy to love all over again.

"Hey," he said, eyes lighting up when he caught sight of her. "You're going to want to get your coat. It's nice out, but it's not warm."

"Okay." She got it quickly, already suspecting what he had in mind. By the time she headed outside with him, her heart was fluttering just the way it used to. He caught her hand in his, and they walked down toward the square, then crossed over into the park.

"I forgot a blanket," he apologized as he led her toward the Witch Tree. "But the ground should be dry."

"We managed just fine without one before," Sam replied, and earned a wink of his dimples in return.

They settled themselves in one of their old spots, where the branches draped low enough to form a canopy for them, giving them a small hideaway from the rest of the world. Sam laughed when he opened the cooler and pulled out a pair of subs he must have picked up from the deli on his way to work.

"Outsourcing, I see."

"I know my limits. My sandwich skills don't go any farther than two slices of bread and some prepackaged turkey. For you, I went fancy."

He handed her one of the subs and some napkins, then went to work unwrapping his own. Sam hesitated for only an instant, then did what she'd never been able to get up the courage to do the last time they'd been here together. She scooted over to sit pressed against him, pausing to drop her chin affectionately on his shoulder before digging into her sandwich.

They ate and talked, peering through the branches and laughing together when Jason's truck pulled in front of the gallery, Jake listening to Sam's stories about his cousin's in-store antics with his eyes crinkled in amusement. He told her about his day. And she began to open up about her ideas for future paintings. They might have grown up, Sam thought, but it was still a revelation to discover how quickly it could feel as though they'd never been apart.

"You should paint the tree," Jake told her, taking her crumpled sub wrapper and stuffing it into a plastic bag he'd brought along for trash. "It always made me think of you."

"Yeah?" Sam smiled, quietly delighted. "I'd love to. I just need to decide how I want to approach it. I want to do it right."

"You will," he said. "In the meantime, you should paint something that reminds you of, oh, say . . . me." He bumped her with his shoulder, eyes full of mischief.

"That's easy," she replied. "I'll just paint a giant pudding cup. You can hang it in your office."

"Hey." He made a wounded face as Sam reached in to draw out the desserts he'd brought. "Those belong to one of the food groups, you know. I'm not sure which one, but they're totally in there."

"You can have both," Sam said. "Whatever food group those belong to, I'm okay operating with a deficiency. It's like eating the slime you used to be able to get out of the quarter machines down at the supermarket. Except brown."

Jake looked at the pudding, looked at her, and then put them back in the cooler. "And there goes my appetite."

"Sorry."

"Yeah, that's why you're laughing." He grinned at her, put the top of the cooler back on, and then rested his arms on his knees. "So when do I get to find out about your supersecret party costume?"

The mention of the Halloween party was the first sour note of the afternoon, but Sam tried to brush it off. It was happening. She'd get through it.

"You get to find out when you see it," she said. "Since you won't tell me what yours is."

"Because it's that cool. Besides, I want you to have *one* thing to look forward to about Saturday." He tilted his head at her when she pursed her lips. "It's going to be fine, Sam. We'll have fun—I promise. I want to be able to go out and do things together."

"*Things* is kind of a broad category. We could do lots of things in places where Cici and company aren't."

He sighed. "Sam."

"I know," she said, tilting her head back to look up into the blazing orange leaves. "I know. It's a package deal. Not all of your friends are complete jerks. Give it a chance. I know."

"I don't actually care what they think," Jake said. Startled, Sam turned her head to look at him.

"Then we're going why?"

"Because the Cove is home, and people might as well get used to seeing us out together. Plus, I mean it . . . I love the Halloween party. It's fun. I want to share the stuff I like with you. Just give it a chance, okay?"

She heard what he said, but she knew what was beneath it. *I want you to like them. I want them to like you. Please give it one more chance.* He hadn't quite given up. And she didn't have the heart to tell him exactly how impossible his hopes were. Maybe, when this worked out about as well as she feared, she'd tell him why. And then he really was going to have to choose. Most of those people were never going to accept her. And she'd matured enough to know that she deserved better than to live on the periphery of somebody else's life.

She wanted to build something new with Jake. But no matter what he said, she was still afraid that when it came right down to it, he wouldn't be able to let go enough to really try.

As though he sensed her thoughts, Sam felt the brush of Jake's hand, then the warmth as he threaded his fingers through hers. The echo from the past shook her to her core.

Don't let go of me, she thought. *Please don't let go.*

Chapter Twenty-Two

"Does this look stupid?"

Andi looked up from the book she was reading. Peaches was attacking her sneaker, batting wildly at the laces, tangling herself in them, and then dashing off behind the chair only to emerge again moments later to repeat the whole thing. Loki was weaving in and out of Sam's feet. She wasn't sure whether that was love or impending homicide.

"No, you don't look stupid!" Andi smiled. "I like it. Literary and so . . . not black!"

"Yeah, well, I figured that the lack of black alone would make it hard to recognize me, but I felt like I should pick an actual character, too," Sam said. She'd actually branched out a little on an impromptu shopping trip yesterday, going with the "little goes a long way" theory of color management. She'd bought a pretty blue scarf, and a pair of indigo earrings that would go perfectly with this shirt she'd seen . . . not that she was quite there with buying it yet. Everything else was making her head spin, but fortunately, she didn't have the money to go at any speed but slow with changing up her wardrobe.

The costume she'd bought was another matter. That had been a splurge, and she was still questioning her sanity, but the desire to surprise everyone had overridden common sense. It had been tough to find much, digging through the available options—slutty pirate, slutty princess, slutty superheroine. She'd considered modifying a semi-slutty Bride of Frankenstein costume, but a bout of Internet wandering after she'd put away her brushes for the night had brought her to what she was wearing.

"You should have dressed Loki up as a dragon," Andi said. "He's on your shoulder often enough."

"He'd probably breathe fire on people if he could, too," Sam said. "No, he can stay home. I'd rather carry a sparkly dragon egg purse. Fans of the series will get it."

"Yeah, and the rest of them will just gawk at you," Andi said, then winked. "In a good way. Does Jake know what you're going as?"

"No, I decided to surprise him," Sam replied. "I didn't want him to feel like he had to dress up as a Dothraki warlord. I'm . . . not even sure he knows what a Dothraki is."

"Bet he'll want to find out," Andi said, quirking an eyebrow before looking back down at her book.

Sam smirked as she swished out of the room, the long layers of pale blue and gold material moving with her. The material gathered at the tops of her shoulders, baring her arms, and draped down behind her to flow in her wake. She'd crimped her hair and then pulled the sides away from her face with thin braids, letting the rest cascade down past her shoulders. There was an intricate gold belt, like lacework, and of course the bejeweled egg she carried that doubled as a purse.

She wouldn't admit it to anyone else, but even though baring this much skin and wearing this much color was completely out of character for her, she felt amazing. Almost like the woman she was dressed as. Which was good, because considering the gauntlet she suspected she was about to run, what better thing to be than the Mother of Dragons?

Of course, she had no actual dragons, only a cat that was now threatening to put a hole in her new dress.

"Damn it, Loki! Go try to conquer something else. Go play with your sister. Come on."

He didn't even bother to look at her, gamboling merrily along as he tried to catch the folds of her dress. She had a feeling that if this went on much longer, he was going to step on one of her gold-sandaled feet and draw blood while he was at it. This was what she got for saving his furry butt.

She expected the Tavern would be packed, which was probably a good thing. If things went poorly, she'd have more places to hide. She still wasn't sure if Zoe was coming. Getting dressed up and dancing in a cramped space while people spilled beer on you was apparently not her idea of a good time. Still, Sam thought there was a chance she'd see her, if only because Zoe needed to blow off steam. The most recent encounter with Jason, who Sam had nearly called Treebeard to his face, thanks to Zoe, had not gone well. He'd brought more of the woods to grace the gallery's floors, and more of his particular flavor of sarcasm. The usual tangle had ensued.

She was on Zoe's side . . . mostly. But Jason had a twisted sense of humor that she couldn't help but appreciate. Sam still hadn't figured out where on the lust/hate spectrum the two of them fell. Some things were safer ignored.

The doorbell rang, and Loki bounded off to take up a strategic position beneath the nearest piece of furniture.

Relieved, Sam headed for the door, nerves tangling in the pit of her stomach. What would Jake think? He was into her hair, so she'd gone with something that really played it up. After all, it was Daenerys Targaryen's defining feature. It was weird that she'd be nervous, she thought, considering the various states of undress he'd seen her in this week. But then, this wasn't about just the two of them alone together. That worked. This? This was more like a coming-out party. From hell.

She took a deep breath, straightened her shoulders, and opened the door. Immediately, she burst out laughing.

"Hey, Cap!"

Jake had managed to find a very good—and appealingly tight—Captain America costume. Had she mentioned her thing for this particular Avenger, or was he just psychic? Either way, his boyish good looks fit the part perfectly. She wondered if it would be rude to ask him to turn around so she could stare at his butt. Then she wondered if maybe she could convince him to keep this on for a while after the party.

"Jake? What is it?"

His mouth was slightly open, and he seemed to be taking a long time to take in her costume.

"I, um . . . what did you say?" he asked.

She tilted her head. "I am the blood of the dragon," she said.

When his eyes met hers, they were endearingly earnest. "Can I just take you home?" he asked.

"Yes. Now?" she asked hopefully.

"Soon. Definitely soon," he said, then held out his hand. With a resigned sigh, she took it, and they headed to the truck.

*   *   *

The Harvest Cove Tavern was a squat white building just off the square that had been built and rebuilt several times since the town's founding. It was famously haunted, since it had always been an inn of some sort, and always crowded on the weekend and nights when there was a big game on TV. Jake parked up the street, and the music was loud enough to hear outside. Sam got out, shivered because she hadn't bothered to bring a jacket, and tried to bolster herself.

Okay. I can do this. Okay.

"I think everybody's here," Jake said with a grin. "Come on, your highness." He caught her hand in his, which made her feel immeasurably better, and they headed for the door. Jake paid the cover, and they walked into a crush of people and throbbing music. There was a bar along the left side of the room, and a smallish dance floor in the back that was already overflowing. With the low ceiling and wooden pillars, Sam had always found the place a little claustrophobic, but she guessed it had its charm. When it was empty.

She had to hang on to Jake so they could go get a beer, which took some time, considering the crowd. When he finally handed it to her, she'd actually started to hope that Cici and company just hadn't shown up. She saw faces in the crowd that she recognized, some from working at the gallery, others from long ago. Most, to her relief, were friendly. All were surprised, which she got a kick out of. She had several wild urges to clamber on top of the bar and yell, "I will take what is mine with fire and blood!"

Maybe later. For now, she sipped her beer and watched the parade of male pirates, slutty pirates, slutty vampires, half-naked punk rockers of both genders, and the obligatory pregnant nuns. A Bo-Peep whose breasts were only barely hanging on in the costume came running up to them. It took a minute, but Sam finally identified her as Jake's receptionist, Angie.

"Oh my God, you guys look great!" she yelled. "Come on, everybody's over here!"

It was friendlier than Sam had seen her. But then, Angie was drunker than she'd seen her. Maybe tonight wouldn't be so bad after all if that was going to be the case all over. Jake gave her an encouraging smile and pulled her in the direction of the dance floor, where she was presented, after all these years, with the sight of a fully constituted high school clique that she'd never wanted to see again. There was Max and Thea, who she knew had gotten married after college, dressed as the Flintstones. Shane was Monty Python's Black Knight, looming over everyone and minus one arm, which Fitz was swinging over his head while he danced. Fitz was wearing a fake mustache, which seemed to be the entirety of his costume. Kallie Monroe was a cheerleader in pigtails, while Ryan was barely recognizable as a slightly terrifying Oompa Loompa. Dave Garrity, who they all called Stump for reasons she didn't want to know, was a lumberjack. And of course, there was Cici in a skintight leotard as Catwoman. She looked fantastic. Sam wanted to scream, but she settled for leaning into Jake's side and chugging the rest of her beer. He looped his arm around her as all of them turned their heads and stared.

She had a flashback to the cafeteria, and the endless walk to and from her lunch table from the line. On a good day, no one noticed her. On a bad one, she'd get a few mocking whistles and jokes. On a really bad one, she'd trip or something and there would be applause. Much of it coming from this crew.

Somehow, she'd felt better about running into them in bits and pieces. But this way, all of them at once, felt like facing a firing squad. Complete with the sense of impending doom. She swallowed hard, wondering why she'd ever agreed to this. Only her pride, tattered but healing, kept her from bolting out the door.

"Yay!" cried Cici, bouncing over and grabbing Jake's arm. "You're here!"

Apparently she'd decided to forgive him for their spat the other night. Wonderful. Sam dug her nails into Jake's other arm, in case he'd forgotten his promise to her. He winced, but she needn't have worried.

"Hey," he said coolly, and didn't let Cici tug him anywhere. "We're here." He offered a casual smile, extracted his arm from her claws, and guided Sam into what she thought of as the lion's den. There were a bunch of good-natured greetings for him, and a bunch of uncomfortable looks for her. Fitz, at least, was friendly.

"You look amazing, khaleesi!" he said, shouting into her ear so she could hear. That he knew the Dothraki title for her character marked him as a fellow *Game of Thrones* geek, and she smiled at him, happy to have found at least one person to talk to.

"Thanks! Nice moustache!"

"I decided to be dashing for Halloween. How much more of a costume do you need?" he asked, then winked at her.

"It works on you," she said.

When she turned her head, she caught Thea staring at her, who then jerked her head away rapidly without saying anything. That didn't exactly surprise her, though she still didn't feel sorry for punching her. Thea was the only person she'd ever punched. Others might have deserved it, but the only one who'd pushed her past the point of no return was Wilma here.

Kallie tried to be friendly, ooh-ing over her costume, and Sam appreciated that. The rest of them were operating under various degrees of discomfort, and she found herself bopping silently to the music and looking around while Jake traded joking barbs with Max and Shane. Fitz reappeared at her side, pressing a fresh beer into her hand.

"Here. You look like you need this," he said.

"You think?" she asked, widening her eyes. "Thanks." She took a long pull from it and watched Big Al Piche, who was wearing a pair of booty shorts, a THIS IS MY HAL-LOWEEN COSTUME! shirt, and a clown wig, trying to climb up on one of the speakers. Fitz followed her gaze.

"That's not gonna end well," he said.

"Never does," she replied.

A popular song with a heavy beat started up, and the crowd started moving. Jake pulled her into his arms, and she had to laugh as she imagined the visual they must present. He smiled down at her.

"What is it?"

"Superhero meets high fantasy. We're very high concept," she said.

"I'm glad you came," he said into her ear.

"I'm glad, too. It would have been really awkward to ask you to dress up as Captain America for me in any other context," she said. He laughed, and she slithered up against him and into the song, forgetting about everything else as she danced with him. He was a good dancer, she discovered. He'd had plenty of grace on the athletic field. She'd watched him practice a few times from afar. And sketched him. A lot.

Jake spun her around to dance behind her, and she giggled until she caught sight of Thea and Cici whispering. About her, naturally. The smirk in her direction was hard to miss. The fun she'd been having evaporated instantly. Her smile faded as she turned back around. Jake, to his credit, picked up on it right away.

"What's wrong?" he asked.

"Nothing," she said. It might make her sick to her stomach, but she'd be damned if she'd go running off just because some people had nothing better to do than gossip about her. *Still.* It was going to be a long night, though. Fitz boogied up behind her, smashing her against Jake before laughing and dancing—very badly—off in another direction.

Sam steadied herself with her hands at his waist and looked up at him.

"You look sad all of a sudden," he said, tracing his thumb down her cheek and frowning. "Why?"

She thought about it, and then lifted up on her toes to speak in his ear. "I . . . I just don't really think I belong here, Jake."

"Sure you do. Just as much as everyone else." He smiled. "You're a townie now."

"Ha. Really, though. This isn't—oh my God, she came!" Jake looked confused, then turned his head to follow her gaze to where a stunning woman with long braids, wearing a headband, a leather vest, black jeans, boots, and carrying a long plastic Katana blade was making her way through the crowd to enthusiastic hoots. She carried two chains as leashes for a pair of "armless" zombies who shuffled along behind her. One of them had a voluminous beard, which had been covered in a lot of fake blood. The other had a pink streak in his hair. Both grinned at her.

Jake's brows lifted. "Can I take both of you home?"

Sam smacked him.

Zoe looked awfully pleased with herself by the time she reached Sam.

"I can't believe you told me you were just going to throw something together if you came," Sam said. "You sit on a throne of lies."

Zoe threw her head back and laughed. "Surprise. I like to make an entrance, you know. But I wasn't going to do it unless I could corral a couple of zombie minions. Zeke and Aaron were available. And look at *you*. I almost didn't recognize you. You're all *vibrant*."

"Well, the point is to not look like ourselves, right?"

Zoe rolled her eyes. "Uh-huh. Nice outfit, Cap. You didn't happen to bring Thor with you, did you?"

"Nope. No superheroes, only pets."

She feigned disappointment. "Damn. Guess I'll stick to zombies." She jerked her thumb behind her. "The bearded one is Zeke Majors, who makes amazing things out of wood when he isn't growing facial hair, and the dude with the pink streak is Aaron Maclean, who I believe you met the other night, Jake. He's pretty mouthy for a member of the hungry undead."

"I like the pink," Sam told him.

"Thanks. I have hair ADD. Do you want a zombie minion for the night?" he asked Sam. "I love your dress. And she's mean." He glanced behind her, and Sam knew from the look on his face he'd spotted Ryan. It was a little like watching a bird of prey zero in on its target.

"I didn't know you were into Oompa Loompas," Sam murmured to him. His smirk was wicked.

"When they're blushing through their makeup and trying not to stare at me I am."

"What are you whispering about, minion? Don't make me hit you again," Zoe said, brandishing her sword at him. Aaron stuck his tongue out at her and rattled his chain.

They were so reassuringly here, so reassuringly *hers*. Sam threw her arms around Zoe, who jumped a little before hugging her back.

"I am really, really, really glad you're here," Sam said.

"Yes, I am," said Zoe. "So let's party, because the chances of me doing this again before next year are slim to none."

A speaker crashed to the ground behind them, followed by raucous cheers. Zoe's eyes closed. "It's him, isn't it?"

"Just be happy it's not at the gallery," Sam said, as Big Al was helped up by the idiots who'd helped him get onto the speaker to begin with. "Let's go get you a drink." She looked up at Jake, pressed a quick kiss to his lips.

"Be right back," she said, and with her three friends in tow, vanished into the crowd.

Jake watched them go, struck by the immediate change in Sam when Zoe showed up. Even barely knowing her, he liked Zoe. Anyone who would wear that costume and find zombie minions to match kind of had to be likable. Still, their appearance had pretty much killed any efforts to bridge the gap between her and his friends. Not that it had been going very well anyway.

Small wonder why. Cici's hand was on his arm as soon as Sam was out of sight. He sighed.

"You're free for a few minutes," she said, "so dance with me."

"Cici," he said as she began to wiggle up against him, "what are you doing?"

She looked up at him with an expression he knew very well. It was feigned innocence, and he wasn't in the mood. She seemed to realize that, and the mask dropped quickly.

"Okay, so I'm apologizing."

He leaned closer, unsure whether he'd heard her right. "You can elaborate on that."

Cici rolled her eyes. "Apologizing. I came on too strong the other night and I pissed you off. I don't blame you. Or her." Her smile was thin and humorless. "She might be weird, but she's not stupid. You're worth hanging on to."

It was flattering and discomfiting all at the same time. They hadn't really talked since she'd been back . . . not beyond just scratching the surface of things. This seemed like an odd place to want to have this discussion, but Cici had always done things on her own timetable.

"That was a long time ago, Cici. I don't even know where all this is coming from. You left."

"I made a mistake," she said. "A big one. It was good here. *We* were good here."

"We were kids," he said. They'd stopped dancing, standing close to hear each other as the party continued around them. This close, he could see the changes in her—the hard edge to her smile, the bitterness in her dark eyes. Whatever had happened with her marriage, it had hurt her, even if she would never say so. She'd never wanted to admit to any imperfection. But he knew, even now, that there were plenty of feelings underneath.

It was what made it so hard to accept the willful cruelty that she'd always been capable of.

"I was happy here. I had friends here," she said. "Look at you. All of you. It's like stepping back in time to the better days. The *best* days. Nothing is different except the one thing I really want." Her eyes were huge, pleading, and he did feel sympathy for her, even if he couldn't give what she was asking. "Give me another chance, Jake. We were perfect. We can be again. I know what I walked away from now."

He shook his head, exasperated despite the grudging affection he still felt for her. She'd always been dramatic. But he knew she believed what she was saying. She wasn't looking for him, though. She was after something that was long gone.

"We were never perfect, Cici. What are you remembering? We fought all the damn time. And by the time we broke up we were both sick of the ups and downs. I know you miss how it was. You can have some of that. We're all still here, and I'm happy to try to be your friend. But we're not going to work any other way. Maybe it all looks the same to you, but it isn't. We all grew up."

There was a flash of pain before her eyes hardened. "So that's it. You're more interested in hooking up with the school freak than coming back to something you *know* could be just as good as it was."

He clenched his jaw. He'd said no to her. Now would come the lashing out. It was an old pattern, and one he watched with an old weariness. "Yes, I'm with Sam now. You won't want to hear exactly how good it is, and that's fine, but you're going to have to respect my choice."

Cici snorted. "Some choice. She's still the same old Sam underneath. Everybody seems to see that but you."

"I don't think I'm the one who can't see what she is," Jake said. "You could at least try to be nice to her. You and Thea."

"Nice? Seriously? That little bitch punched her," Cici snapped. "You don't forget things like that."

The disdain that dripped from her voice was an ugly surprise. "No. There are things you don't forget, even if you want to."

She seemed to have realized she'd overstepped, panic flickering across her face. "Sorry. I shouldn't have called her that." But she wasn't sorry, and he knew it. Jake looked around at the group of them, the people he had depended on since grade school, and for the first time didn't much like what he saw. It was unsettling, to have his foundations shaken that way. They were the same people they'd always been. But there had been pieces he hadn't wanted to see, thrown into sharp relief now, of all times. They'd been good to him because he was one of them—popular, athletic, easygoing, attractive. He'd loved being a part of something when his home life felt so broken, feeling important when he'd never been quite good enough for his father. But he wasn't a kid anymore. And standing here, he could see that most of them were still completely invested in breaking the Cove into two groups: us and them.

Thea and Kallie were busy making fun of someone's costume, Max was complaining to Shane about whatever Max's latest complaint was, Ryan and Stump were getting obliterated . . . and Cici wanted him back in her bed, with no interest in how that might affect things outside her little universe. Fitz had vanished, but that was Fitz. He was the only one who'd maintained a life outside of the rest of them. And wouldn't you know it, he was the only one Sam seemed to like.

This was the first time he'd really stood on the outside looking in.

Maybe they were his friends. But they sure as hell weren't anybody else's. And that didn't say much for any of them.

It made him wonder what the hell he'd been doing all this time. And he was certain, as Sam had insinuated more than once, that he'd missed things—and people—he might have enjoyed if he'd just bothered to wake up and have a look around.

"I'm done. I'm going to go find Sam and get out of here. I hope you find what you're looking for, Cici. But it isn't me." Frowning, he turned away and started to walk. The music was suddenly too loud, the crowd too thick. It was the same damn thing as every other year—they'd all drink too much, and then Max and Thea would want everyone to go back to their place and have a bonfire, which they'd do even though the only sober person would inevitably be someone who wasn't much good at making a fire. Which meant they were always in danger of burning the yard down. And this time . . . he tried to imagine Sam enjoying herself while they all talked about the same old people and most of them pretended she wasn't there. He'd expected better.

He wasn't going to get it.

Cici came around the front of him so fast she stumbled a little, leaning against his chest with her hands. He jerked to a halt.

"Jesus, Jake, don't just walk away like that. Wait," she said, wide-eyed. She seemed genuinely shocked that he would simply leave.

"There's nothing left to say," he told her.

She studied him, her lips pressed together into the distressed little line that meant he'd actually managed to score a hit through one of the tiny cracks in her armor. Once, it had given him an ugly sort of satisfaction. Now, it just made him tired.

"There's one thing," she said. "One thing left."

He'd been crazy about her once. Now, he felt sorry for her. The sentiment surprised him, mingling with old affection that he knew Sam wouldn't understand, not that he blamed her. People were complicated things. And because he had seen the best in her once, because they shared a lot of great memories and he understood why she wanted to relive them instead of moving forward, he leaned in to listen to whatever she wanted to tell him. He hoped it was "good-bye."

It happened so fast that he couldn't stop it. One moment she was looking up at him, lips parting to speak. The next, she'd wrapped herself around him, pressing her mouth and body to his. For a brief instant, his arms came around her, more instinct to steady himself than anything. Her lips tried to move, to draw him in, and he pushed her away. She didn't go easily, but she did let go. Shock quickly gave way to anger as he stared at her, her eyes glittering with triumph. She seemed to think that would do it. But the contrast to what he felt with Sam couldn't have been more stark. There was nothing left here for him.

Not that he'd needed this kind of proof.

"Damn it, Cici," he said. "I told you, I'm done!"

She stared at him as though she'd never seen him before, eyes wide and glistening with a thin sheen of unshed tears. Then she smiled, laughing a little, even though it was a bitter, desolate sound. She looked past him, just for an instant.

"Yes," she said, "you are."

And he knew what she'd done, even before she turned on one bootheel to walk stiffly back to their friends. Her friends. He didn't know what they were to him anymore. He guessed they'd each make their own decisions about that. Sam had never asked him to make a choice. But he had. He'd finally made the right one.

Just in time for the choice to be taken from him.

He spun around, and his heart sank. He saw a flash of pale hair as Sam pushed through the crowd, and a look from Zoe that was nothing short of murderous as she went after her. He clenched his jaw and went after them, hoping he could get out the door before she got away. But the Tavern was packed, and it seemed like people were throwing themselves into his path on purpose. It was infuriatingly slow going, and by the time he made it to the door, he was afraid she'd be gone.

The night air was cold and crisp, the sky clear and scattered with stars. He could hear Sam's voice, rapid, sharp words bumping up against Zoe's cooler ones. And he could see them by the road, Sam's agitated gestures, Zoe's hands on her arms.

"Sam!" He jogged to her, even as he saw her backing up, her hands in front of her.

Zoe looked between them. "I'll go get the guys, honey. You just hang on." Another venomous look at him, and she walked away. He gave her credit for not getting involved, though he almost wished she'd stick around to hear what he had to say.

"Don't," Sam said, and he could see the way her eyes glittered in the dark. Tears. Jesus. He had some talent.

"It wasn't what you think. I was trying to say good-bye to her, Sam," he said. "She—"

"It's always something like that, right?" she interjected, her voice wavering. "Hanging out here, a kiss there, and all of a sudden, one of these days I'll get a call from her to tell me that once again, she wins. Or maybe she shows up with your thug friend again to scare me off. Either way, maybe she's right. Maybe sad little Goth girls like me don't get guys like you. So whatever it is this time, I'm going to make it easy for both of you. I quit."

He stared at her. "What?"

"I quit. She's not going to, not until she gets what she wants. Your friends hate me but they love her, and you're just so damn attached to them, so what do you think is going to happen? I've lived it already. I know."

"Sam—"

"I honestly thought it was different this time," she said.

He looked at her, at the vindication writ large across her face, and knew the truth. "No, you didn't," he said. "Not really."

Her eyes flashed. "What's that supposed to mean? If you think that, then explain why I agreed to go out with you in the first place."

"Same reason I asked. You couldn't forget me. And I couldn't forget you. That's different than believing it'll work. You've been waiting for me to walk away since day one."

"Bull," she said. "You want me to turn into something I can't be, Jake. You've got this life here you want me to fit into, and I don't. I never did."

"That's bull, too," Jake shot back, his own temper flickering to life beneath the hurt. "You fit in your own way. This, the Cove, all of it, is your place too, Sam. You use the misfit stuff as a handy excuse for when you want to run away, just like you're doing now."

She narrowed her eyes. "Yes, it's just an excuse. All those people in there who are so important to you were really just waiting to be my friends. I just misinterpreted the words 'freak' and 'bitch' and 'psycho.' I'm sure we'll all sit down and have coffee together really soon. Which we could, if things were different, because I'm *not* running. Where do you think I'm running to, Jake? I'm stuck here." She threw out her arms with a bitter laugh. "I. Am. Stuck!"

"You're running away from me."

Her face tightened. "I can't do this. You kiss your ex and I'm the bad guy. You won't make a clean break but I'm the one hanging on to the past. Whatever." She jerked her head. "You should go back to your friends. I'm sure they'll be thrilled I finally took off."

He heard the frustration creep into his voice. "I don't give a damn what they think, Sam. I give a damn what you think."

Sam's pain was clear in her expression, in the way she held herself. "And I don't know what to think. The way you looked at her . . ."

"I cared about her once, Sam. She's looking for something that isn't there anymore," he said, silently willing her to give in, just a little, and let him in. "But I don't think this is all about her, is it?"

She just shook her head. "It's so easy for you to stand there and tell me how I feel. You have no idea."

He raked a hand through his hair. "I would if you'd tell me! You always listened, Sam. I'd listen too, if you'd give me a chance. But we're going nowhere if you can't let me in. You've got to forgive me if we're going to get anywhere together. Because it's pretty obvious you haven't."

"Forgive you? I *loved* you," she said, her voice breaking. Simple words that arrowed straight through his heart.

"Sam, I . . . I . . ."

"I loved you," she said again. "You weren't just some guy I liked who hurt me. You were my first love, and you broke my heart. So while I get what you're saying, you're the one who doesn't understand. That stupid picture I did for you forever ago . . . You know, when you pretended you didn't know me in front of your friends? That was my stupid, clumsy way of telling you how I felt. You made me think I mattered. Instead, when it came right down to it, you treated me like a stranger. Worse than a stranger. So you left, and I left, and I stayed gone. There were other guys. I cared about them. A couple I cared about quite a bit. But there was never another you. Then I came back. . . ."

Her voice wobbled a little, and she wiped angrily at the corner of her eye with her fist. "I came back, and there you were. Looking at me differently because I changed up the packaging, I guess, and I knew that, but"—she looked at him helplessly—"I'm still the girl you walked away from without a second thought. And it's so hard, because underneath it all, I *am* the same. And the way I feel about you hasn't changed at all. I still love you."

"You love me," he echoed, amazed. He'd never known. And looking back, he had no idea how he hadn't. But he finally understood just how deeply his rejection had cut. And he wished like hell he could go back and change it, because there were some things she didn't understand, either.

"Yeah," she said, sniffling a little before she straightened and gave a small, humorless smile. "I do. So. I'm going to go home now. Because you're right. I haven't managed to forgive you, not really. I definitely haven't forgiven them," she said, jerking her head back toward the Tavern. "And you're all bound up in one package, even now. It's impossible to reconcile."

"I didn't know," he said softly. The emotion in her voice was staggering. There had been more, he realized. More he didn't know about, more cruel barbs thrown at her because of what he'd done.

How could he begin to explain why?

"At the time, I figured you must. People thought I'd . . . that we'd . . ." She shook her head, her smile bitter. "Well, why else would you have been sneaking around with a girl like me, right? It was all a big joke. But you know what? It doesn't matter anymore. We don't get do-overs. All we can do is lug our baggage around with us and do the best we can. And I'm lugging mine home."

"Sam," he said. "I don't even know where to start. But I need you to listen to me. I didn't know, but I should have. I should have paid attention instead of burying my head in the sand. My life was so wrapped up in other people, my friends, teammates, in who I thought I was around here. I thought if I broke away, if I made myself forget about you, I'd still have enough. I was so damn afraid of losing myself, not to mention the only people I thought I could depend on."

"You could have depended on me," she said, and in the darkness she was sixteen again, the heart he'd broken in her hands for him to see.

"I wasn't expecting you," he said. What else could he say? "You were perfect, and the way I wanted you scared the hell out of me. I didn't know what to do."

"And now?"

He shook his head, still reeling from everything she'd said. "I just want to figure it out together, Sam. Together."

She stared at him, then shook her head slowly. "If you haven't figured it out by now," she said, "then it's better for both of us to just . . . stop. Otherwise it's just going to keep hurting, and I can't . . . I just *can't*." Her anger was gone, replaced by a sadness that seemed to envelop her completely. And he knew she meant to start again by finally letting him go.

"Good-bye, Jake."

Zoe reappeared with her friends, moving like the phantoms they'd appeared to be. None of them spared him a glance as they encircled Sam and ushered her away from him. All he could do was watch as she walked away.

Chapter Twenty-Three

Over the next week, Sam threw herself into work. It was what she had, and what she knew, so she hung on tight and waited for the hurt to go away.

He didn't call. She hadn't really expected it, because crying in your costume in the parking lot of a bar while you told a guy you'd been in love with him for over ten years wasn't usually the way to start a lifetime of happiness. Still, she'd needed him to know, before things went any further, before Cici got her hooks in any deeper. And before she completely lost her footing and let herself imagine a future that just wasn't in the cards.

They were too different. Eventually, he'd figure out that beneath the swan there was still an ugly duckling, same as she ever was. And she needed to be with people who she was sure liked the person she was, who weren't going to eventually be disappointed by an illusion.

This was best. Even if it hurt like hell.

She painted. That, at least, had returned, along with all sorts of emotions that she tried to appreciate being able to tap into. She went to the gallery and let Zoe tease her out of her unhappiness for brief periods of time. She let her mother coddle her, and her sister give her instructions on how to move on even though she had no idea what Emma's qualifications to be any kind of a relationship counselor were. It was probably better not to ask.

She didn't know what Jake did. She had no idea where he was, or what he thought, or what he was doing, apart from working. She knew because she'd passed his truck sitting in the parking lot of the animal hospital all week. Seeing it had prompted some car crying—like, ugly, sloppy crying—so she now took pains to go a different, albeit longer, way to the gallery.

It was better for both of them to move on, she told herself.

It would just be nice if she could quit feeling like some important part of herself had died.

By Friday, Sam had gone from devastation to just feeling hollowed out inside. She guessed that was an improvement, even though it didn't seem like one. She was quietly dusting everything, which was an excellent cover for brooding. Zoe had gone out to get them lunch. When the little silver bell rang above the door, her heart clutched like it always did.

Knock it off, she thought furiously. You have to stop waiting for something that isn't going to happen. You said good-bye; he took it seriously. Move on.

Plastering a smile on her face that she hoped was at least semi-convincing, Sam turned. The smile froze.

"Shane," she said. "What can I help you with?"

He seemed to take up an inordinate amount of space, like he always did. It was a shame he was such a jerk, Sam thought, because he was actually handsome. Not that she'd wish him on anyone. Shane shifted uncomfortably in his expensive suit, looking as out of place as she'd ever seen him. He lingered just inside the doorway.

"He didn't know," Shane said.

Her eyebrows lifted. "Excuse me?"

"Jake. He didn't know that Cici went after you the way she did. He never knew what Thea said to you, either." He paused, frowning at a painting. "I think, if he had, things might have been a little different."

She didn't know why he was telling her this, why he'd bothered to come. Sam carefully set the polish and dust rag aside and walked slowly toward him. He looked as though he thought she might hit him too, even if she'd have to stand on her tiptoes to do it. She didn't feel anger, though. That seemed to have been exhausted last weekend. All she felt was weary.

"I know that already. But it wouldn't have been much different if he had," Sam said. "We were a bad fit, Shane, when it comes down to it. I appreciate you telling me, though, even if you don't like me much."

"It's not that."

"No?" She arched an eyebrow. "Did I miss something?"

Shane exhaled loudly and tipped his head back, shifting his weight from one foot to the other. He seemed to be struggling with something. She didn't feel too bad about letting him, curious though she was. Finally, he looked at her, his blue eyes serious.

"I don't dislike you. I don't even really know you. I do know that whatever's going on with you and Jake right now is partly my fault, which means I need to do what I can to try and fix it."

Sam frowned. "It's not your fault, Shane."

"Some of it is, yeah. I know I gave you a rough time back in school. I'm sorry for that. You didn't deserve it."

She shrugged. "No. I didn't."

"I liked how things were. I would have liked it even

better if Cici had given up on Jake and taken a look at me, too, but kids are stupid. She was upset; I got upset on her behalf. It wasn't justified. But that was what happened."

"Ah," she said, remembering the way Shane had been so focused on Cici the day she'd gotten her warning. That explained his presence—puppy dog syndrome. But it still didn't change anything. "I appreciate the apology, Shane. I'm okay. It was a long time ago." And right now, it felt like about a million years.

"It was and it wasn't," Shane said. "I didn't expect you to like me, Sam. After all that, I figured it wasn't worth putting any effort in. Why bother? I was a complete dick to you. And I figured this was some kind of weird closure thing with him, so I tried to ignore it. But he's different with you," he continued. "He's happier. Well, he was." He looked away. "Don't walk away from him just because he has shitty taste in friends."

Sam chewed at her lip for a moment, considering him. Then she said, "The fact that you came here to tell me all this is kind of a testament to your non-shittiness as a friend, Shane."

He breathed out a soft, rueful laugh. "Yeah, well, he's not really feeling that way right now. I told him what happened back then. He didn't know we all knew he was seeing you. Or whatever you two were doing. He had no idea how we all tried to get in the way. Things always got messy when he and Cici broke up, and everybody just wanted a kickass summer. She wanted him back, so we put them back together. You didn't matter." He looked pained. "I mean, you did. You know what I mean. You being so different made you easy to hurt. I told you I'm kind of a dick."

Sam sighed. "Kind of. But I can see why he likes you."

"Really?"

"Yeah," she said, crossing her arms. "There's an honesty to your assholery that is almost endearing."

"I get that sometimes," he said. "Anyway, he's my best friend. He's a good guy. And he's crazy about you. I don't think he ever got over you. I thought it was weird, but I don't actually have relationships. So."

Sam watched him, unsure of how to react. He didn't seem to have much of a filter. But he also didn't seem to be quite the irredeemable jerk that she remembered. Close, but not quite.

"Well. Like I said before, Shane, I appreciate all this, but it's not just one issue. Jake and I—"

"He pretty much told all of us to fuck off," Shane interrupted. "If that makes you feel any better."

She almost said no, then decided not to bother lying about it. "Kind of."

"Sad thing is, the only ones who bothered to hunt him down afterward were Fitz and me. So he's stuck with a couple of us." He shrugged. "He's still pissed at me, but I'll just wear him down until he gets over it. He's miserable, though," he continued, "and I can't fix that. You can."

She remembered what he'd said to her: *I wish you'd have a little faith in me.*

But she hadn't. She'd been so determined that history would repeat itself that she'd made sure it did. Only this time, she'd been the one to walk away. He hadn't told her he loved her . . . but he'd been standing there in shock, too. And even if he wasn't there with it yet, the fact that Shane was here pleading on his behalf meant something.

Maybe more than something.

I'm an idiot. She'd brought this past week of misery on herself. But maybe she'd needed it to figure out that it wasn't the past holding her back any longer. It was just her. And if she was going to move forward from here, the path her life would take was entirely her choice. She knew she could make it here in the Cove on her own.

But she didn't want to. This place was home . . . but not without him.

"Damn it," she muttered, then looked at her watch. Jake would be eating lunch. His sad little brown bag lunch with his pudding cup. The man really did need a keeper. It might as well be her.

Zoe walked in the front door carrying their lunch and looked between Sam and Shane. "Did I miss something?" she asked.

"I need to do something," Sam said. "Can I . . . Do you mind . . . ?"

She seemed to understand immediately, and under other circumstances, Sam might have laughed at Zoe's obvious relief. "Go get him, Sam."

She dashed to the back and got her purse. On her way out, she grabbed Shane's arm, lifted up on her toes, and planted an impulsive kiss on his cheek. He looked down at her, stunned. "I seriously did something right?" he asked.

"Yes. And thank you."

Shane grinned. "Awesome. He so owes me."

Sam shook her head and hurried out the door.

The office was fairly quiet when she walked in. The only sound was the pounding of her heart in her ears. She hadn't been this nervous since the first time she'd come in, though this was still different. Then, she hadn't wanted him to get too close. This time she was afraid he wouldn't want to.

But whatever happened, she owed him this.

"Sam," Cass said, smiling at her. "Love the coat."

"Oh, thanks," she said, flustered. Coat? What coat? She looked down and remembered the new plum-colored coat she'd bought a few days ago during some retail therapy.

"You want to see Jake? You can head on back, he was just eating his lunch."

"Yes. Thanks," Sam replied, feeling a little silly at how breathless she sounded. She almost missed the encouraging little smile Cass gave her as she headed past her. She knew. Of course she knew. This was the Cove and everyone knew everything that was going on. But suddenly, that didn't bother her at all.

The door to his office was open. She took a deep breath, turned the corner . . .

"Jake, I—"

But he wasn't there. His desk was empty, a crumpled brown bag sitting on the top of it. Sam let out a shaky breath as the adrenaline rushed through her system unchecked. She stepped inside, unsure of whether to wait or leave a note. Then her eyes went to where his Iron Man poster had been, and she went completely still. It was something framed and matted. Something new.

No, she realized. Not new. It was her picture.

She moved forward, barely feeling it as her feet hit the ground, until she was right in front of it. He'd smoothed out the wrinkles, though she could still see the faint creases beneath the glass. And as she looked at it, the memory of making it came rushing back. She'd used oil pastels, the bright, young green of the Witch Tree in late spring leaping off the paper. Beneath the tree were two figures. A girl with long purple hair, leaning against the tree holding a book. And a boy with spiky brown hair, resting his head in her lap as they watched the day go by. On his shoulder, their hands were joined.

It was everything she'd wanted. And the memory of her feelings as she'd worked on it was so strong that she ached.

"I told you I never forgot you." Jake's voice, soft and sweet and right behind her. She turned to see him standing there, close enough to touch, his hands stuffed in the pockets of his lab coat. The look in his eyes told her everything.

"The truth is, Sam, I love you, too. I've loved you for the longest time. I just wasn't smart enough to realize it until you came back home. Don't make me lose you all over again."

She tried to speak, but nothing would come. There was too much to say. So she simply walked into his waiting arms and kissed him until he could have no doubt that she was done running. Done running from home, and done running from him. After a time, she pulled back just enough to touch her forehead to his, looking into eyes that were full of everything she'd ever wanted, if she were brave enough to reach out and take it.

"I'm not going anywhere," she said. "I'm home."

Epilogue

The snow fell in fat flakes, drifting past the windows of Two Roads as the women hurried to make last-minute adjustments.

"Sam, get out of the cookies! Do you seriously think I can't see you?" Emma gave her arm a smack as she walked by carrying yet another pot of poinsettias. She'd rearranged them a dozen times in the last hour, Sam thought. Why not one more?

Sam polished off the rest of the cookie, brushed off her hands, and looked around. "You know," she said, "this is pretty classy for the first annual Harvest Cove Misfits Christmas Party. Maybe we should have gone more low-key. Plastic tablecloths. Staple up some of those Christmas lights that you can set to 'seizure.'"

"You want that, you and Jake can do this in your garage next year," Zoe said, making an adjustment to a painting that was already perfectly straight. "This isn't just a Christmas party. It's your coming-out party, and it's going to be special whether you like it or not."

"Mean," Aaron sang, gliding by. He'd changed the streak in his hair from pink to red for the occasion and was wearing the most god-awful Christmas sweater Sam had ever seen. He seemed to think it was hilarious. He was also spending a lot of time looking out the window, since Ryan had accepted his invitation to come. She supposed this finally counted as a first date, though mentioning it to Aaron was just going to make him impossible. Well, more impossible.

"Sammy," her mother called, waving her over to the largest of the paintings she'd done for the show. Sam obliged, spike heels clicking on the wood floor. She walked over to stand beside her mother, who slid an arm around her.

"This one," she said. "This one is my favorite."

"Mine too," Sam said.

"Mine too," said a warm voice at her ear. She turned her head to look at Jake, who gave her a lingering kiss. His hair was still a little mussed from when he'd caught her in the back room and tried to convince her to defile the sanctity of Zoe's desk. He hadn't convinced her . . . yet. But he'd had a good time trying.

He rested his hand on her shoulder, and her hand came up to cover his. The ring he'd presented her at Thanksgiving glittered and flashed in the light, a reminder of just how much she had to be thankful for this year. Some mornings she still had to remind herself that this was her life now—Jake warm in bed beside her, a cat on her head, a dog knocking over things on the dresser with his tail trying to wake everyone up.

It was perfect. She didn't just have her life back . . . she'd gotten her family back.

Even better, she'd gotten to add to it. And she was keeping them all.

"Here come the cars," Emma called. "Looks like Shane and Fitz. And Jason."

There was a distinct groan from Zoe's direction.

"Mom, Jo and Cathy are here, too. Oh my God, I hope we have enough food. And . . . Jake, did you tell Shane he could bring Big Al?"

Sam widened her eyes as she looked at him. The mischief in his eyes was unmistakable.

"I thought this was a Misfit Christmas Party. Do you want to hurt Big Al's feelings by leaving him out of that? He works really hard at being one."

Sam shook her head as Zoe stalked by, making a decidedly un-Christmas-y gesture at her fiancé. "It's on now, Dr. Smith," she said. "I know where you sleep."

He chuckled. Andi gave her a kiss and hurried off to greet her friends. Sam leaned into Jake as he slipped his arm around her waist, pulling her close. She leaned her head on his shoulder and looked at the painting she'd done just after she and Jake had gotten together for good. It was the Witch Tree, but as it had never been, the branches elongated and graceful, all curving to one side in some invisible wind. The leaves shimmered in shades of orange and copper and gold, brilliant against a sky that was aglow with dusk. And beneath it, nearly hidden in the tall grass, was an unmistakable figure, two tiny black ears and eyes like candles peering at them from his hiding place.

"What do you call this one again?" he asked. "*Bad Moon Rising*?"

She bumped his hip. "*New Moon*," she said. "And he's not that bad. He deserves to be in there," she said. "Loki started it all."

"Hmm," Jake said, turning her in his arms so that she was pressed against his heart, touching his nose to hers. "He continues to start things, too."

"And yet you keep us."

"I do, and I will," Jake said, as their friends and family began to arrive and the sounds of their conversation mingled with the carols playing softly in the background. "You can be a misfit all you want, Sam Henry, as long as you stay mine."

"Deal," she said, and pulled him close for a kiss.

Continue reading for a special preview of the next book in the Harvest Cove series,

EVERY LITTLE KISS!

Available from Signet Eclipse in March 2015.

Breaking up a wild party in his own neighborhood wasn't Seth Andersen's idea of a fun Saturday night, but he found himself trudging up the walk toward the door of 121 Juniper a little after midnight anyway. It wasn't a big deal—he'd nearly been home when the call had come in, technically off-duty but still in uniform, and Jess, the dispatcher, knew he'd take it. Harvest Cove was a small place. He could manage what would probably amount to nothing more than a "knock it off" conversation with the guy who lived three houses down. Hell, the sight of a uniformed officer at the door was usually enough to drive the point home, and he'd had an impromptu cookout with Aaron Maclean only a week ago. This shouldn't be a problem.

The little saltbox, not too different from his own, sounded like it contained several hundred more people than it ought to. Seth was halfway to the door when it opened on its own. At first, he thought Aaron had seen him and was coming out to save some time, but there was nothing masculine about the figure that stumbled through the door and nearly toppled into the bushes. Nothing masculine, Seth realized, but everything familiar.

It was just a little sad that he had the curves of a woman he'd never spoken to so thoroughly memorized.

"Emma?"

He blurted her name before he could think better of it, and the blank look she gave him as she shoved her hair out of her face only confirmed what he'd suspected: He'd been in Harvest Cove for six months, and Emma Henry still had no clue who he was. Maybe it was the time he'd spent in the Army. . . . He'd gotten good at blending in with the scenery when he had to. But Seth thought it was more likely that Emma just didn't notice anything that wasn't already on her to-do list. She sure seemed that type, and nothing he'd heard about her had ever changed the impression. Everything from her tailored suits to the way she clipped around in those sexy heels screamed *all business, all the time.*

Not tonight, though. Turned out, she owned a pair of jeans after all . . . and from the smell, he thought she might have been wearing as much beer as she'd imbibed.

"Something wrong, Officer?" Emma straightened, shoved her long dark hair out of her face again and put on what he expected she thought was an innocent expression. Not a bad effort, really. But her inability to stay still while maintaining her balance was kind of ruining the effect.

"Nothing too bad, Miss Henry," Seth replied, remembering his manners this time as he ambled forward. He was just some random cop to her. Probably just as well. "We've had a few complaints about the noise from the neighbors. I came by to let Mr. Maclean know that he needs to either calm things down or break it up."

"Oh. Are we that loud?"

"Yes. Yes, you are."

"Wow. I'm sorry."

Her eyes rounded. The light out here was dim, but Seth knew from his previous almost-encounters with her that they were a startling forget-me-not blue made even more striking by her fair skin and dark hair. Usually, she had all that hair pulled back, but he liked it this way, with the thick waves down past her shoulders. Some of the ends were damp, though, and Emma was having a hard time keeping it out of her face. She shoved at it again, frowning, her already full lower lip plumping further when she stuck it out to concentrate.

She was cute. And really, really drunk. It seemed so utterly out of character for her that he had to work at suppressing his amusement. As he got closer, he could see that her shirt was even damper than her hair, the dark fabric clinging to her breasts. He couldn't help but notice—her curves were impossible not to notice, even at his most distracted. Still, her bedraggled, slightly bewildered appearance left him feeling more protective than turned-on. She needed to be home, tucked in and sleeping this off, not wandering outside at this hour. Bad things happened everywhere, even in the Cove.

Seth sighed inwardly. His bed was looking farther away than he'd hoped.

"Do we know each other?" Emma asked, wrinkling her nose and looking utterly confused.

"No."

"How'd you know my name, then?"

"The Cove's not that big, Miss Henry," he said. "You run the party-planning business down on the square. I've only been here for six months, but knowing who's who is part of my job."

That seemed to satisfy her, at least well enough to change the subject. "Oh. Well, Officer . . ."

"Andersen."

She blinked and appeared to mull that over for a moment. "Okay," she finally said, and Seth knew she had tried—and failed—to place what should have been a familiar last name. "You're not going to arrest anybody, are you? It'll ruin my sister's party if you do."

"Your sister's party?"

One dark brow arched. "She's getting *married*."

He had to swallow a laugh. Not everyone could be wasted and beer-stained and still pull off "haughty" this well.

"Ah," Seth replied. Now her presence—not to mention her condition—made sense. "Bachelorette party, then."

"Yeah."

Seth's eyes went to the door, considering it. "Please tell me there aren't any strippers in there."

She snorted. "If there were naked people in there, I would know. I mean, I think. I *hope* there aren't any naked people in there."

Her small smile hinted at the promise of an absolutely gorgeous full one. He'd never seen her smiling. But he'd certainly like to.

Jesus, Andersen, just get this over with and go home.

He cleared his throat. "Well, whatever the stripper situation is, I need to speak to Mr. Maclean, Miss Henry. Are you heading back in?"

She hesitated, then turned her head to look at the house. "I guess."

His eyes narrowed. "You weren't planning to drive home, were you?"

"No! Why would you think I'd do something that stupid? I don't even have my keys!" The words were slightly slurred, but they were loaded with real offense. He wanted to believe her. He didn't want her to be the kind of person who did the sorts of things that so often left behind devastating messes for people like him.

Seth didn't know why it mattered. It just did.

"It's not an unreasonable question, Miss Henry. You wouldn't be the first person to make that mistake."

Emma glared at him a moment, then closed the distance between them, weaving a little but maintaining her bearing until she was glaring up at him, close enough to reach out and touch.

"Listen, Officer Ab . . . Alf . . . Amster . . . Whatever," she said, waving her hands dismissively before settling them on her hips.

Seth tried not to let his eyes linger, but it was tough. He was a sucker for an hourglass figure, and hers was just about perfect.

"*I* am a *respectable businesswoman* in this community," she informed him, the picture of angry, wounded pride. "I don't know who the hell you are, but just because you get to carry a gun and handcuffs and whatever doesn't give you the right to . . . to impugn my integrity."

He found himself caught between wonder and gut-busting laughter. It took everything he had not to give in to the latter.

"I'm not impugning anything, Miss Henry," he answered while struggling to keep a straight face. He wondered what other fifty-cent words she liked to throw around when she was mad. The woman was probably a veritable dictionary when pissed off and sober. He found the idea ridiculously sexy. "I'm just concerned for your safety. I don't want you to get hurt."

The change in Emma's expression was instant. Her eyes widened, anger vanishing to become innocent surprise. Her lips parted, just a bit, as she looked up at him and became the picture of vulnerability.

"Really?" she asked.

Seth blinked. He'd dealt with plenty of drunks in his line of work, but he was having a hell of a time finding his footing with this one. She'd been surly and sweet in equal amounts, shifting between the two fast enough to give him whiplash. Right now, though, there was something winsome about the way she looked up at him — something that pushed a few buttons he hadn't expected to have pushed tonight or anytime soon. Those buttons had gotten pretty rusty, but it seemed like they were still there.

He guessed he should have been glad he could still feel attraction like this, like a hot punch straight through his chest. Maybe he would have been, if the sensation had ever foretold anything but trouble.

Since she appeared to be waiting for an answer, Seth nodded his head. "Really," he said.

She swayed for a moment, her gaze inscrutable. Then she smiled, that big smile he'd been waiting for that crinkled her nose. For a few long seconds, all Seth could do was stare. Whatever he might have imagined, this was better. As beautiful as she was, that smile was like someone had turned a light on inside of her.

"You should smile more often," he said softly, realizing too late that the words hadn't stayed in his head where they belonged. At least they didn't seem to faze Emma, who simply shrugged, nearly losing her footing in the process. Seth moved by instinct, reaching out to catch her beneath the arms before she went down on the walk. Her hands gripped the front of his shirt as she regained her balance. When she looked up at him this time, her face was only inches from his. He caught the faint smell of her perfume, something light and musky, a whiff of exotic smoke. Its sensuality was a startling contrast to Emma's normally buttoned-up image. A hint, maybe, of the woman beneath.

Do. Your. Job. Andersen.

"You have pretty eyes," she sighed, fingertips running down the front of his shirt to his hips. His stomach muscles flexed in reaction, and his breath caught in his throat. Parts of him that had no business stirring when he was working stirred. And that's what this was—part of his job. This would be a good time to remember that.

"Thanks," Seth replied, forcing out the word while removing his hands and stepping back. "I need to—"

"Will you take me home?"

It took him a few seconds to close his mouth. "What?" His voice sounded hoarse to his own ears. She couldn't possibly have said that. If she had, she couldn't possibly have meant it. And if she had, there was no way he could say yes, because that would require a level of awfulness he was nowhere near achieving.

Emma looked up at him with those big luminous eyes, and he wondered whether he'd somehow taken a wrong turn and landed in Hell.

"I want to go home. I can't drive. Can you take me?"

"Uh . . . why don't you just . . . hang on a sec?" he said. "Stay here." This was not his problem. This was Aaron's problem, because it was Aaron's party. He walked away quickly, trying not to run, thinking of every unappealing thing he could to erase the wildly erotic images trying to cascade through his brain. He blamed his fatigue. The last few nights hadn't been good ones, sleepwise, and it seemed like that had caught up to him all at once. How else to explain his reaction to her? She was a beautiful woman, sure. But while he might not be Channing Tatum, he hadn't exactly had a hard time finding a date when he'd wanted one.

The front door opened again just as he reached it, and Seth was relieved to see his neighbor emerge, purple-streaked hair and all. It was a wonder they got along as well as they did. The only art Seth had ever spent much time looking at was World War II pinup girls, and Aaron had been very up-front about the fact that the feminine form, outside of a basic aesthetic appreciation, was not his thing.

As long as Aaron kept his lawn mowed and wasn't a complete jerk, Seth didn't much care who the man brought home.

"Emma?" Aaron looked past him at first, to where Emma had just been standing. "Are you okay? Zoe said that somebody told her you didn't feel good and— Oh. Hey, Seth." He watched Aaron take in the uniform, then wince. "Oh. I guess it's Officer Seth tonight. This is about the noise, isn't it? Sorry."

"Yeah." Seth shifted his weight from one foot to the other and thought again of his bed. His body was telling him it would actually stay asleep for a solid block of time tonight. That was, if he could ever get to his bedroom. "We've had a few complaints. I said I'd stop by on my way home to let you know, since I didn't think you'd have a problem taking care of it."

Aaron shook his head with a sigh. "No, of course not. This got to be a little bigger than I was expecting." He swept an arm toward the cars parked up and down the street. "Guess it's what happens when you throw a big party in a small town. The whole world shows up. It was supposed to be ladies only, but we've gotten a few infiltrators."

Seth snorted. "Uh, you might want to look in a mirror."

"I do. Frequently," Aaron replied with a flash of a grin. Then he shrugged. "I'm the host. I get a free pass."

Lucky bastard.

"You want me to help clear everyone out?" Seth asked, relieved when Aaron immediately shook his head no.

"Nah, I can handle it. Sam and her friends are staying over. Everyone else can leave the same way they got here. I was starting to worry about what was going to get broken first anyway. House parties are a lot more fun when they're not at *your* house, you know?"

"I can imagine."

Aaron arched an eyebrow, a smile playing at the corners of his mouth. "Not a partyer, Officer?"

"Very funny. And, no, not so much. Used to be, but I guess I kind of outgrew the appeal."

"Hmm. You're kind of young to sound like such an old fart." Aaron tilted his head, regarded him with a fair amount of curiosity, but then returned his attention to the woman farther down the walk. "Emma, why don't you come back in?" Aaron called. "I don't think sleeping on the concrete is a great idea."

Aaron pursed his lips and exhaled loudly through his nose. "Look I hate to ask, but can you watch her while I kick everyone out? Even if you can just get her into the grass so no one steps on her . . ."

"He's taking me home."

Her voice was so clear, it took Seth a moment to register the fact that it had come from Emma. He looked sharply at her, seeing Aaron's startled look out of the corner of his eye as he turned his head.

"Miss Henry—"

"Emma," she interrupted him, just as clear. Her head lifted ever so slightly, though her hair covered most of her face. "An' you said you would."

"I didn't say that! I just told you not to go anywhere!" He knew he sounded defensive, but the last thing he needed was for his neighbor to think he'd been hitting on his drunken friend on his way to telling him to shut down his party. He looked beseechingly at Aaron. "I didn't say that."

Aaron simply waved him off. "I'm sure you didn't. She's just channeling Jose Cuervo right now. It's kind of like speaking in tongues, but with a lot more sexual innuendo."

Relieved, Seth laughed and shook his head. "Been there. Do you have a way to get her home? She seems stubborn enough to try and walk there if she manages to get up again."

"Oh, she'll be fine here."

"No, I won't," she insisted. "I don't feel good. He said he'd take me home. He's a—a policeman." She gave a woeful-sounding hiccup. "I have beer on me. I want my bed. I hate the ground."

Seth arched a brow when he returned his attention to his neighbor. "You sure about that?"

Aaron frowned and sighed. "No. If she really wants to go, I'm sure there's somebody who can . . . well . . ." His brow furrowed, and Seth knew he was mentally going through the list of people trustworthy enough to deliver

Emma home. Finally, Aaron sighed. "Shit. I'm not putting her in some random person's car and hoping for the best. And not to sound like an ass, but she doesn't have a lot of friends anyway. Emma's kind of . . ." He trailed off, seeming to consider his options, and finally chose a word. "Independent."

The simple statement struck an unexpected chord with Seth. "Independent" could mean a lot of things, but he was pretty sure that Aaron didn't mean it as an insult. He understood not being close to a lot of people, whether by choice or simply by temperament. Maybe he and Emma had some things in common after all. Didn't seem likely, but neither did finding her drunk as a skunk and hanging on to the earth to keep from falling off of it. Anything was possible. And the solution to this particular problem was inevitable.

"I'll take her."